THE CHRONICLE OF BENJAMIN KNIGHT

BOOK 3

NEW LIGHT

Cover designed 2014 by Spiffing Covers
(www.spiffingcovers.com)

Edited 2014 by Hercules Editing and Consulting Services
(www.bzhercules.com)

ISBN 978-1-910256-15-2

For Karen, Jessica and Jacob.
Thank you for believing in me.

And to my author friend Thomas Manning.
Your input has proved invaluable as always.

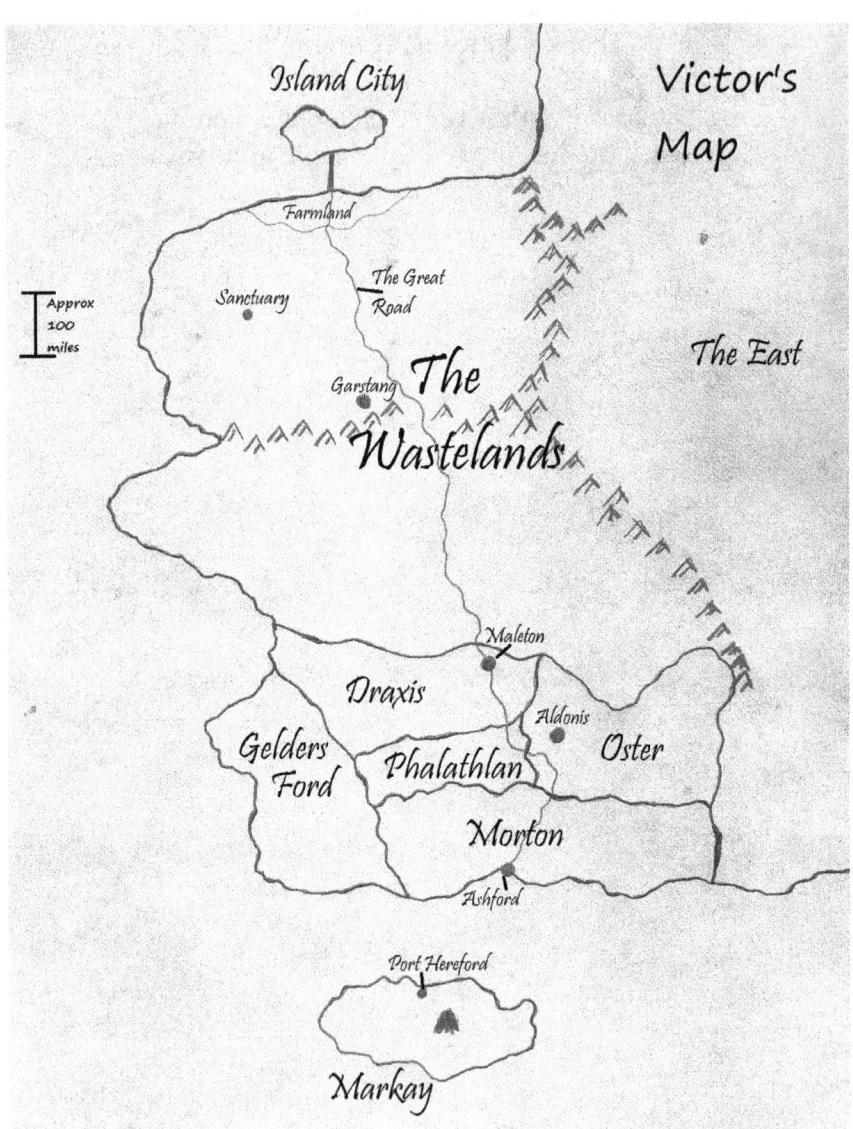

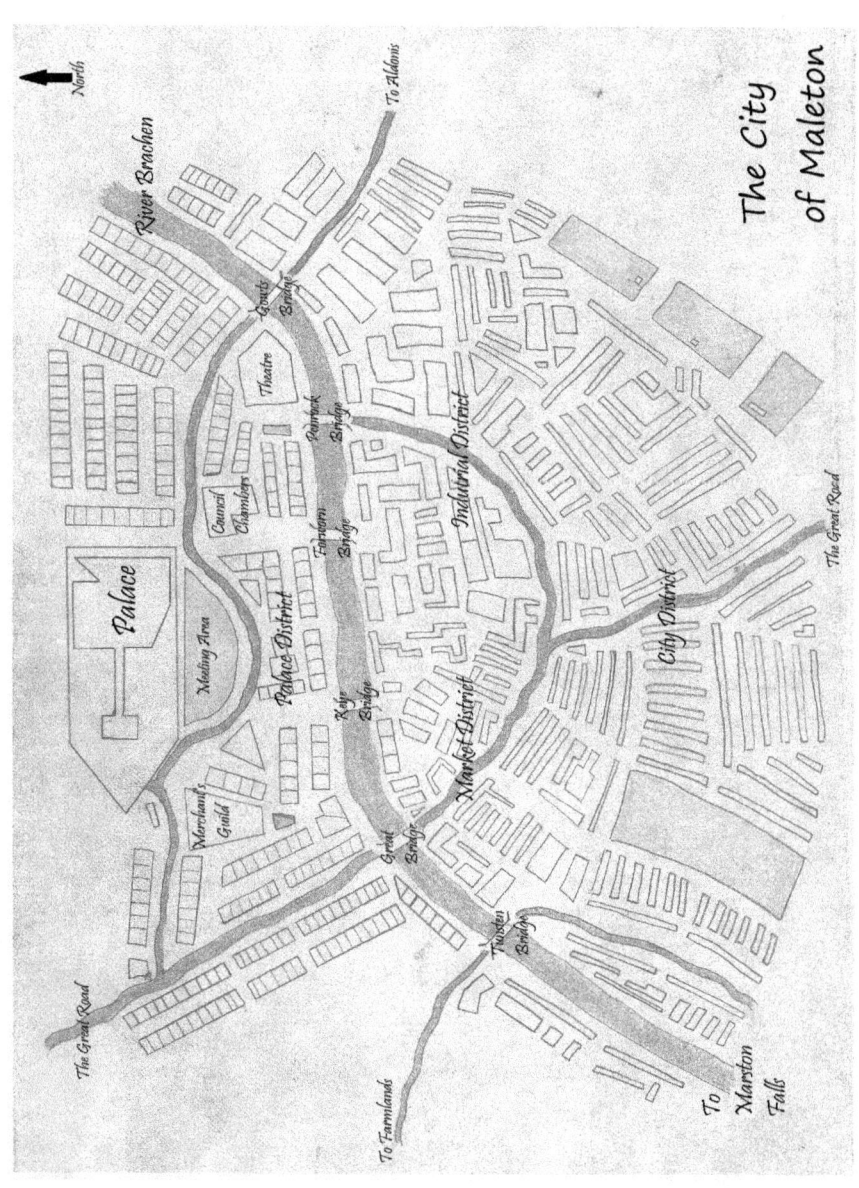

PROLOGUE

Forty seven years before, Anwin and Darwin of the Thackary tribe were playing outside of their home as they waited for their mother to finish the evening meal. Anwin was eight and Darwin just three, and Anwin adored his little brother. They had different fathers, Anwin's father having been killed four years before defending their home from a neighbouring tribe, but Darwin's father loved them both equally and raised Anwin as if he were his own.

They grew quickly, learning to hunt and forage as well as how to tend to the crops and animals. Life was good, days filled with joy and laughter and nights spent in the rejuvenating sleep following a hard day's work.

Anwin was fifteen summers when he first heard his mother's thoughts. They were sat at dinner and he was confident that she hadn't spoken. *It hurts so much*, she had thought, and as Anwin concentrated he felt the pain that she was experiencing. Every mouthful of the food seemed to stick in her gullet, a tearing sensation as it went down, and Anwin felt it all as though his own body was suffering.

His mother deteriorated rapidly, losing weight and going first pale and then yellow. He tried to look into her mind and use his power to push away her illness, but his wishes did not help. She quickly succumbed and died less than two months later, a mere shell of her former self, writhing in agony for hours before she passed.

Their father was inconsolable, turning to drink to try and hold his sorrow at bay. Anwin and Darwin tended to farm, maintaining the crops and caring for the livestock. Their father sold more and more of their harvest, leaving the boys to go hungry as he drowned himself in drink.

When the drink would no longer take away his pain, he turned to Droca, a herb with the power to dull the senses and disorientate the mind. It was during one of his Droca fuelled rages that he turned on the two boys, blaming them for the death of his beloved. He lashed out at Darwin, knocking him to the floor, and in a fit of rage Anwin screamed at his father, "Stop."

Stop he did, standing as still as a statue, staring at his step-son with empty eyes. "I wish you were dead," Anwin said next and instantly regretted his statement, but unfortunately his regret was too late. His father took the pistol from his belt and placed it firmly against his temple, pulling the trigger. The two boys held each other as their father lay dead before them.

The tribal leaders supported the boys as best they could, offering guidance and support. At fifteen, Anwin was already a man and he maintained the farm with his brother's help, both of them growing strong. Anwin refused to use his ability again. They lived off the land, Anwin hunting with his bow and rifle, and teaching his brother how best to use a blade. They struggled through and prospered, and a year on, the farm was again flourishing from their dedication.

It was three years later, when Anwin was eighteen and Darwin thirteen, when the Sutton tribe marched through their part of the Wastelands. They moved like a plague, taking or destroying everything in their path. The men were cut down as they defended their homes, the women and children murdered or taken to be added to the Sutton tribe.

As their farm burned to the ground, Darwin was dragged away as Anwin fought bravely against the attackers. He was a skilled fighter, but no match for the five men that assaulted him. As he was driven to the ground, the killing blow about to be dealt, he instinctively lashed out with his mind, demanding his attacker turn on the other men. The attacker did as he was commanded, cutting his friends down before they had realised what was happening. After freeing Darwin, Anwin gave the final order, that the attacker should take his own life.

Anwin and Darwin fought their way to the village, Darwin slicing his way though as Anwin lashed out with his mind. Enemies became allies as Anwin turned more and more of the Sutton tribe against their brothers and sisters, killing each other as he made his way to the central meeting hall.

As he neared the remains of the meeting hall, he realised that he was too late. The Tribal Leaders, the same men and women who had supported him and his brother after their father's death, were dead. Their bodies were displayed before the meeting hall, the brutality of their slaughter plain for everyone to see.

Once the members of the Sutton tribe fell to the remaining members of the Thackary tribe, Anwin strode through the remains of the settlement. Almost all of the men and many of the women were dead or dying, children weeping as they huddled around fallen loved ones. Anwin walked amongst them, offering kind words and a promise of support.

The day became night as family members were buried and the bodies of the invaders were burnt, great pyres that illuminated the sky. Once the work was done, many of the survivors looked to Anwin for guidance. He stood upon the steps to the meeting hall and said, "Friends and neighbours of the Thackary tribe, I feel your pain and share in your loss. Our homes are gone, the crops destroyed and the animals slaughtered. We cannot stay or we will not survive the winter. Gather whatever is most precious to you and follow me. We will find a new home, together."

They hesitated at first, searching the remains of their homes, trying to construct shelters from the burnt and damaged wood and stone, but after a while they realised that he was right. Anwin led them south through the dense forest, following the same narrow path that he had taken only months before when he had sold meat to the Frakes tribe. The Frakes tribe were reluctant, but once they heard of the defeat of the Sutton tribe and the safety which that afforded, they welcomed the remaining members of the Thackary tribe into their number. The Thackary tribe was no more. They were now Frakes until the end of their days.

The winter was harsh and took many of the survivors, who had to fight to find a place within the Frakes tribe. There was little food, even less for the newcomers, and they looked to Anwin for support. Anwin went to the Tribal Leaders, asking for their aid. The remains of the Thackary tribe would work for food he promised, they expected noting for free. In return he was mocked and dismissed. "You should be grateful for what we have given you," they told him. "Accept it or be banished to die out in the snow."

Anwin was angry. He and his tribe had lost everything and all they wanted was a chance to work and rebuild their lives. He turned on them, yelling at them. "I would be better for this tribe than you," he said.

"You would be better for this tribe than us," the tribal leader agreed.

The other leaders laughed, thinking it a joke, until Anwin said, "Agree with him," and turned to look at each of them in turn. One by one they agreed, and at only eighteen summers, Anwin was declared leader of the Frakes tribe.

Other members of the tribe resisted at first, but with a word or thought they soon rallied behind Anwin, ready to follow his lead. By spring their food supplies were scarce and their livestock gone. They were unable to support themselves, and looked again to Anwin for instruction.

Anwin thought about his past, and what he wanted for his future. The more he used his ability, the more he grew to enjoy it, and began to think of himself unstoppable. He looked upon the tribe, now his tribe, and came to a decision. They would suffer no more. He would lead them west through the Wastelands and they would take what they needed. None would stand against him.

He did just that, leading his people from tribe to tribe. The tribes that agreed to join him, he accepted under his rule. Those who resisted, he forced to fight amongst themselves, killing each other for his entertainment. If he saw a woman he liked, he would order her to his bed. Should she have a husband or father to object, he would make him walk away, or on occasion watch, as he relished in the abuse of his power in every way imaginable.

When Darwin turned eighteen summers, Anwin placed him in charge of the tribe's soldiers. Along with James, Darwin's childhood friend, they led the forces of the Frakes tribe from settlement to settlement, taking whatever they needed, and soon whatever they wanted. With Anwin and Darwin at the head, they truly were unstoppable.

By the time Anwin was twenty-five and Darwin just twenty, much of the south-western region of the Wastelands was either controlled by, or in fear of, the Frakes tribe. The brothers celebrated their victories and did whatever they pleased, living each day to the full.

It was spring of the following year when everything changed. Darwin met Selene and, at just nineteen, she was the most beautiful woman he had ever seen. He fell for her instantly, and she with him, seeing the good man beneath his warrior exterior. They spent their days together whenever they could, and their nights in each other's arms as they slept beneath the stars.

Soon after, Anwin set his sights on anther tribe and sent his brother to learn all that he could. Selene wished to go with him, but Darwin told her of the danger, insisting she stay with the tribe. Unfortunately, once his brother had left, Anwin took Selene for the night, casting her from his tent the next morning as she wept at the realisation of what she had done. Darwin found her a while later, still crying and begging him for forgiveness. She had not wanted Anwin, had never wanted him, but was powerless to resist.

His anger all consuming, Darwin drew his knives and ran towards his brother's tent. He knew of his brother's power, but had never imagined that he would use it against him in such a way. "Darwin," Anwin said, smiling, as he burst into the tent, "I have been expecting you. Forgive Selene and forget this, believe that it never happened."

"No," Darwin replied, and slowly stepped towards him.

Anwin was shocked. He had never known anyone be able to resist him before. He tried again, thinking at Darwin to stop, to turn around and leave, but on he came, knives glistening in the light of the torches.

Anwin retrieved a machete from the table, and the two men fought, dodging and weaving as each fought to gain the upper hand. Both men were physically strong, but Darwin was faster and soon gained the advantage, pinning his brother to the floor. "Why?" Darwin asked. "Why did it have to be her?"

"I have tried to teach you so much," Anwin replied, "but in the end, the answer is simple. I took her because I wanted her, because I could."

Darwin screamed, a cry of pain and anguish, as he drove his knife into his brother, burying it hilt deep in his gut. Anwin looked up at him, a smile on his face as a trickle of blood ran from the corner of his mouth. "What man will you become?" he asked. "Will you do what you do because you can, or because it is right?"

Darwin stood, leaving the knife where it was, and returned to Selene, though she was not where he had left her. He ran through the forest, calling her name, but she was nowhere to be found. James helped him look, but their search was fruitless, and by nightfall they returned to the tribe empty handed.

Much of the tribe had already left, wandering off through the Wastelands. Those that remained seemed lost, confused, as though waking from a dream and wondering if they were yet truly awake. Darwin told them to go, to leave and find a new home, to forget what they had done and start again.

James stuck with him, searching the surrounding forest for any sign of Selene. Spring became summer and there was still no sign of her. By autumn, they found themselves in Feldinger, a large settlement in the southern Wastelands. They were tired and hungry and wished to put their past behind them. Darwin accepted that Selene was gone, and together with James set out for the Southern Baronies, that they may both start over and begin life anew.

Darwin took a new name in an attempt to escape his past, that he could truly begin his life anew. He took the name of his father, hoping to someday honour his memory, and was henceforth known as Deacon.

As for Anwin, everyone believed him dead. His body was left where it lay, the knife protruding from his abdomen. It was mere chance that brought the lady through that part of the Wastelands, taking a detour from her chosen path upon seeing a large group of people heading her way.

At first, she too believed him dead, and set to scouring the tent for anything that may be of use to her. It was only when he breathed, just once, that she paid him more attention. When she placed her fingers against his neck to check for a pulse, he opened his eyes and looked at her.

She whispered to him, "Who are you?"

He focussed upon her, trying to smile as he spoke. She had to lean in close to understand the breathy whisper that escaped his lips. "I am free," he said.

NEW LIGHT

CHAPTER 1

They threw a new man in here with us this morning and he's huge, bigger than Carl even! He hasn't said anything, but he keeps looking at Carl and smiling. The locals seemed to have sided with him, and it looks like it's only a matter of time before they try and kill each other.

I hope Carl can take him. I've seen enough TV to know that if he can't, my time in here will get a lot worse.

Thinking about it, I really miss TV. I never even got to find out how Fringe ended.

I

"Mom!" Safran cried, ignoring the Baron and running past the throne towards her voice. Tears ran down her face as she threw herself into her mother's waiting arms.

"Safran," Karan replied, weeping herself as she squeezed her daughter tightly. "I thought, they told me, oh Safran, I thought I'd lost you."

They held each other that way for what seemed like hours, crying into each other's shoulders. Neither of them noticed Baron George step from the throne and walk slowly towards them. "My Ladies," Baron George said quietly, and with much more kindness in his voice than when he addressed Safran just minutes before. "Please, let's retire to one of the state rooms. I'm sure you have a lot to discuss."

Karan looked up and nodded to him, though she refused to let go of her daughter as they shuffled towards one of the small state rooms. Baron George ordered for drinks and fruit to be brought to them as they took seats around the dark wooden table, Karan and Safran still gripping each other's hands.

"Mom," Safran asked once the lump in her throat had passed. "How long have you been here? What happened? What about Justin?"

"Your brother is fine," Karan said with a smile. "He's playing out in the gardens. We've been here for almost a month now and he loves it out there.

"When the soldiers attacked our home, your father sent us through the tunnels beneath the palace. The guards who escorted us used a boat from the docks to take us to Marston Falls, and we walked from there. Baron George here was so kind to take us in." Karan looked towards George and smiled.

"There's been little news from Draxis," Karan continued, "but I was told that you were dead." Upon speaking it aloud, Karan began to cry again.

"It was a lie, mom," Safran told her. "They're all lies. It all started in Island City, when one of Cotran's advisers killed him and took the post of Regent for himself. They made it look like I was responsible and used it as an excuse to attack our home.

Alexander, the new Regent, he's there now, sat in father's throne."

"And Stephen?" Karan asked. Safran looked down towards the table, saying more with her face than her words ever could. Karan only nodded, fighting to keep her emotions under control. She had suspected that her husband was dead, but having it confirmed seemed only to magnify the pain that she felt.

They were silent for a moment, lost in their memories, until Baron George brought them back to the present. "How did you know your mother was here?" he asked.

"I, I didn't," Safran told him. "We tried to catch a boat to Markay. Oh Ben, Carl! They're still locked in the prison. Please, you have to help them!"

"I'll send word," Baron George promised, calling over one of the servants by the door to relay his instructions.

"What's in Markay?" Karan asked.

"Matthew wanted Ben and me somewhere safe," Safran continued. "Matthew was going to Oster to find allies, to help retake our home."

"I'm just so pleased that you're safe," Karan said. "This Ben, is he from Island City too?"

"No," Safran said coyly. "He's from somewhere else. The new Regent, he wanted Ben, wanted something he knew. Mom, so much has happened and I want to tell you all of it. It's just, I'm so tired."

Karan smiled at her, leaning forward to stroke her hair, just as she did when Safran was tiny. "Come on," Karan told her. "You'll sleep with me tonight, Justin too. I can't bear to let you out of my sight."

Safran smiled back before allowing herself to be led to her mother's chambers, where she would have the first untroubled night's sleep in months.

II

"He just keeps smiling at you," Ben whispered to Carl as they ate.

"Yes, he does," Carl said, returning the smile.

"Can you beat him?" Ben persisted.

"We'll find out soon enough," Carl replied solemnly. "I'm more worried about what we do afterwards."

"Afterwards?" Ben asked.

"If he doesn't kill me, I mean," Carl said with a mocking smile. "If I'm dead, well, afterwards is your problem."

"Thanks," Ben said, unsure as to how serious Carl was being.

"We've been in here, what, three days?" Carl continued. Ben nodded in agreement. "It won't be long until we go before the Elders or whoever deals with the laws here. Then, if they don't execute us, we either get brought back here or somewhere else even more secure."

"More secure than this?" Ben asked, shocked.

"Keep your voice down," Carl hissed. "I've seen the inside of a few of these places in my time, and trust me, the security could be a lot worse."

"So you think we can get out?" Ben persisted, much quieter than before.

"It won't be easy," Carl replied, "but, yes, I think we can."

"What about Safran?" Ben asked. "We can't just leave her here."

"No, I won't do that," Carl promised him. "Look, when it starts, just keep your head down and follow my lead, okay?"

"How will I know?" Ben wondered.

"You'll know," Carl said with a grin.

They ate the remainder of their meal in silence. Carl was surprised at how good the food was, several of the items were easily identifiable as pieces of fruit and meat chunks in some sort of stew. The water looked relatively clean too.

They had just finished when the cellmate stood and stepped towards them, still smiling. Carl gripped the tray tightly in his hands as he stood to meet him. Ben would never have believed it possible if he hadn't seen it with his own eyes, but the man had a good three or four inches on Carl, taller even than Nathan. He looked down at Carl, cracking his knuckles as he balled his hands into fists.

"I don't suppose you want to talk about it?" Carl asked, looking up towards the man. The man shook his head slowly in return, his smile growing wider with each rotation of his head.

They were interrupted by the sound of heavy bolts being

moved on the cell door. The man took a step back as two guards entered. "You two," one of the guards said, pointing first towards Ben and then at Carl.

Carl took a step towards them, and with a speed that surprised everyone, he slammed the edge of the tray into the first guard's throat and had the second guard in his grip before anyone knew what was happening. Ben scurried along behind them as Carl forced the guard back into the hallway.

By now the other prisoners in the cell had realised what was happening, and had started towards the door. Ben was quick to get it closed and bolted before anyone else was able to escape.

"Now he's definitely going to kill us if we get caught," Carl said as the other prisoners in the cell began to bang loudly against the door. "Let's go and find Safran."

III

"Ah, Larson," Alexander asked as he relaxed upon his throne, "any news on the prisoners?"

"Sadly not, my Liege," Samuel replied. "They're still unconscious and defy all of the physician's techniques to wake them."

"Perhaps it's time I tried?" Alexander suggested, a wicked smile upon his lips.

"As you wish, Regent," Samuel continued. "But I must say, the men have been particularly rough with both of them and have yet to see any response."

"Perhaps you're right," Alexander agreed. "I'll be patient. Have you managed to identify them?"

"The man," Samuel told him. "He's a smith from the Industrial District. My men suspected him some weeks ago of working with Safran, but he disappeared after the assault on Deacon's warehouse. The woman, I don't know."

"She looks familiar somehow," Alexander said, more to himself than to Samuel. "Is there any possibility that she could be Deacon?"

Samuel thought about it for a moment before answering. "I think not, my Liege," he said. "All of the witness reports point to Deacon being male, though the descriptions of him differ considerably."

"I suspect you're right," Alexander agreed. "We'll just have to wait until they wake. Do you have anything else to report?"

"We're still questioning others from the theatre," Samuel continued. "But so far we've learned nothing new. As far as we can tell, the two of them were acting alone."

"Maybe," Alexander mused. "But I doubt it. Anything else?"

"Yes, my Liege," Samuel said with a wry smile. "Unfortunately, Elder Mathis was shot and killed at the theatre. A stray bullet from one of the two assailants would appear to be the cause."

"Most tragic," Alexander replied. "I'll report it to the Elders in the morning."

"Of course," Samuel said. "Will there be anything else?"

"Not for now, Larson," Alexander told him. "Be sure to inform me as soon as they wake."

"Without delay," Samuel replied before returning to his duties.

IV

Stan and Gavin stuck to the shadows as best they could as they made their way through the Industrial District to the City District beyond. They had been amongst some of the first to get out of the theatre, carried along by the crowd as first shots were fired and the smoke and debris began to fall.

Stan had tried desperately to get back inside but it was impossible to fight against the tide. Then the large doors at the entrance to the theatre had been shut tight, and no one was able to get in or out. They were left with no option but to return to Deacon and let him know what happened.

They descended the steps to the cellar two at a time, running past the crates and barrels and activating the hidden switch. Deacon and Bran were waiting for them, the eagerness on their faces plain for anyone to see. The sudden activity woke Sanjay and Dean, who hurried to join them all at the table.

"Well?" Deacon asked as the boys took their seats.

"I think it worked," Stan told him. "The fireworks, the smoke. Catrina definitely got a shot off. I think he's dead."

"That is not the same as knowing," Deacon said bluntly. "Where are Catrina and Nathan? Did they get away?"

"I don't know," Stan admitted. "We were forced outside as everyone tried to run."

"Then the doors were closed and bolted," Gavin added.

"We tried to get back inside," Stan continued, "but there was no way that we could. The Watch were shooting up into the catwalks, I hope they got away."

"You did good," Bran said. "Both of you."

"Yes," Deacon agreed. "You did, but now we have another problem. If the Watch have them, it is only a matter of time before they learn where we are and come for us. If they did not survive, well, we shall see."

"Nathan and Catrina, they're strong," Stan insisted. "They won't talk."

"Everybody talks," Deacon informed him. "It is only a matter of time and how much they can endure."

"You're wrong," Stan persisted. "They won't."

Bran interrupted before Stan said anything that may inflame Deacon. Deacon was not accustomed to being told that he was wrong, and everyone could already feel the tension building at the news that Nathan and Catrina could be in the hands of the Watch. "He's right," Bran said, looking directly at Stan. "Everyone talks eventually. A skilled torturer can keep someone alive for days, weeks even, just alive enough to keep feeling the pain."

"Then we get them out," Stan suggested. "We break them out before that happens."

"We are getting ahead of ourselves," Deacon said, rising from his chair and beginning to pace about the room. "We do not know where they are, or even if they are still alive."

Stan was about to interrupt when Deacon silenced him with a look. "We will wait until morning," Deacon continued. "They may already have returned by then. If not, we will learn of their fate and act accordingly."

"You can't just leave them to be tortured and killed," Stan persisted, tears in his eyes.

Deacon looked at him, the pain evident upon his face. They had all lost so much, and Deacon had already resolved with himself that he would lose no more. "I give you my word," Deacon affirmed. "If they are alive, and can be rescued, we will do everything in our power to make that happen."

Stan nodded and tried to smile as Gavin placed a comforting arm around his shoulders.

V

Safran woke early but was reluctant to move, sandwiched as she was between her mother and brother. She placed an arm around her mother, pulling her closer as she imagined that the previous few months had been nothing but a dream. She knew deep down that wasn't the case, and soon she'd have to move from her mother's side and return to the real world, but she was determined to prolong that reality for as long as she could.

Safran turned her head to examine the room, illuminated as it was by the early morning sun shining through the tall windows that occupied one wall. The room was spacious, with colourful tapestries and portraits showing scenes and important figures from Morton's past. One door lead out to a long corridor, whilst another led to a large bathroom with a huge gilded bath. Furnaces in the palace cellar maintained hot water that was available day and night.

Safran moved to watch Justin lying beside her, sucking his thumb as he slept. Justin was eight years old and had been so excited to see his sister that he had leapt into her arms, hugging her so tightly that she struggled to breathe. He talked to her non-stop about the journey from Maleton and the new friends that he had made in Ashford.

He asked several times about their father, but Safran couldn't bear to break his heart so soon. She told him that he wasn't with her, which wasn't really a lie, but it wasn't the truth either. Their father was dead, and there was nothing that anyone could do to change that, but that didn't mean her brother had to find out right there and then.

"Safran?" Karan asked sleepily as she stirred.

"I'm here, mom," Safran replied with a smile. "I'm not going anywhere."

"No, you're not," Karan said.

They stayed like that for another half hour, enjoying each other's closeness until a knock at the door drew them back to the present. Karan slid quietly to the door, hoping not to wake Justin.

"My Lady," the young serving maid said once Karan had opened the door. "The Baron requests that you join him for breakfast. He asked that you take the time to freshen yourself and your children before joining him in the grand dining hall. Lady Safran's companions will be there too."

Safran leapt from the bed upon hearing that Ben and Carl were already in the palace, waking her brother in the process. "Are they okay?" she asked, running towards the door.

"I haven't been told otherwise, my Lady," the serving maid replied, bowing slightly as Safran approached.

"Come along Safran," Karan told her. "Let's get washed and find you some clean clothes. We'll find out soon enough." The serving maid bowed again as Karan closed the door.

They washed quickly and Safran chose one of Karan's fine dresses to replace the road weary clothes. It was too big for her, she still hadn't put back on all of the weight that she had lost since fleeing Island City, but a wide belt managed to hide most of it. The pain as she brushed her hair reminded her of how long it had been since it had seen a proper brush, but in just over thirty minutes they made their way to the dining hall.

Carl and Ben were still wearing the same weather beaten clothes that they had been wearing when they left Maleton, worse now for their stay in the prison, but Safran ran up to them anyway. "Carl!" she exclaimed, wrapping her arms around his wide chest.

"Safran," Carl replied. "I'm glad, ow, just, take it easy there."

"Oh no," Safran said, taking a step back and taking in the bruises to Carl's face. "What happened?"

"Ben and I," Carl said sheepishly. "We didn't know that you were meeting with the Baron. We tried to make a break for it, and find you too of course. When the guards caught up to us, they didn't take too kindly to us being outside our cell. We were lucky the warden intervened when he did."

"Are you going to be okay?" Safran asked.

"A day or two, I'll be fine," Carl assured her. "I've had worse, believe me."

Safran turned to Ben, noticing that he was sporting a dark bruise around his right eye. "That looks painful," she said sympathetically, touching it gingerly.

"It's fine," Ben replied. "Like Carl said, I've had worse." His mind flashed back to the beatings that he had received in the dungeons in Island City, before Alexander resorted to drugs to learn what he wanted to know.

"Well, come here," Safran said, pulling Ben in for a hug that seemed to last just a second or two too long, a hug Ben returned once he remembered how to move his arms.

They all turned as a servant announced the Baron's entrance, Ben following Carl's lead as he dropped to one knee, though Safran, Karan and Justin remained standing. The dining hall lived up to its name, larger than the throne room with a long, dark wooden table that could easily seat forty or fifty guests. The Baron took the seat at the head of the table, and the others sat to either side of him, Safran to his right and Karan to his left. Fresh meats and fruit were placed on silver trays before them, and once the Baron had helped himself to a selection, the others took turns doing the same.

"Thank you again, Baron," Carl said, "for your timely intervention at the prison, and for your gracious hospitality."

"No need," Baron George replied. "You kept Karan's daughter safe, that's thanks enough."

"I'm still hopeful Safran and I can return home some-day," Carl proposed.

"Mind your manners," Karan interrupted. "She is My Lady or Baron to you."

"I meant no disrespect," Carl insisted.

"Mother!" Safran exclaimed. "Carl's saved me more times than I care to remember, Ben too. If anyone's earned the right to call me by name, it's them."

"We'll see," Karan replied, giving her daughter a fearsome look.

They continued their breakfast in silence, polite smiles the only exchange between mouthfuls of food. Once the meat and fruit was all gone, the servants removed the silver trays and returned with two pots of what smelled to Ben like strong coffee. Everyone, including Justin, was poured a cup of the steaming dark liquid.

"To your health," Baron George said, raising his cup and taking a sip.

"And to yours," Karan replied. She waited until everyone had raised their cups and they sipped in unison. Ben was right in his assessment, the beverage tasted like a strong, bitter coffee. He looked around for any sugar, but found none.

"Now," Baron George said, breaking the uncomfortable silence. "I understand from Safran that times are difficult in Draxis?"

"They are," Carl agreed. "The army from Island city has already taken Draxis and Phalathlan. They looked to be marching east towards Oster. It's only a matter of time before they turn south."

"And you saw this army with your own eyes?" Baron George asked.

"We did," Carl assured him. "There looked to be tens of thousands of troops."

"Safran mentioned that your employer," Baron George began.

"Matthew," Safran added.

"Yes, Matthew," Baron George continued. "He travelled to Oster to warn them about the army and seek their aid in taking back Draxis?"

"That was the plan," Carl told him, "but we don't know how successful they were."

"There have been rumours of fighting in the north," Baron George told them, "but details are still awaited. Perhaps the forces of Oster have been engaged in a counter attack?"

"I hope that's the case," Carl stated. "But if not, any help that you could offer, please, it could make all the difference."

"I have already made arrangements to put your case before the council," Baron George said with a grin. "For now, how about we find you a bath and some fresh clothes, yes?"

Carl returned the grin and thanked the Baron for his generosity, though he knew full well that Baron George had purposefully changed the topic of conversation. Carl was under no illusion about the likelihood of aid from Morton.

They had packed up quickly, discarding what they could do without and marching through the night. Small trenches had been dug and the soldiers had taken position around the fields to obtain the best cover and lines of sight. Then they waited, watching, for the first sign of the invading force.

Marcus stood with Richard and Lucy, surveying the battlefield before them. They knew that there were almost four thousand men and women out there, hidden as best they could, and they were hard pressed to see more than a handful of them.

"We were lucky to have a little time to prepare," Lord Richard said, passing the binoculars to Marcus. The three of them looked exhausted. They had spent all night and most of the morning organising their forces into smaller units, moving the small number of cannons that they had to the best firing positions. They had tried to raise morale as best they could, but the news from the scout had spread like wildfire through the camp. The enemy forces were vast, at least five times the number currently waiting to repel them, maybe more. Once the element of surprise had passed, they had very little chance of success.

"Marcus," Matthew said, a little breathless from his long run. "Arian and Juliet are safe, or at least as safe as they can be."

"On the boat?" Marcus asked.

"They are," Matthew agreed, "and they know to leave if there's any sign of trouble heading their way. That's not to say they'll do it though."

"But they're out of harm's way," Marcus said sombrely. "At least for now."

Arian and Juliet had been reluctant to leave their men, and had argued into the night about why they should be allowed to fight. Juliet was no soldier, but Arian was well versed in the use of firearms and insisted that her father let her fight. In the end, it was Matthew who had been able to convince them to leave.

Following his fight with Marcus, many of the soldiers had looked to Matthew to lead, and he had earned more respect with that one act than he could have done with years of military service. Richard had instructed him to oversee the deployment of several of the smaller fighting forces, to direct them into the fray when he felt the time was right. Both men now had the lives of so many under their command, and second guessing their decisions because of the proximity of their loved ones may lead to more unnecessary deaths.

Richard unrolled a map of the local area, the others crouching down to get a better look at it. "We have eyes and rifles covering these positions," he said, indicating several of the hastily dug trenches, "and cannons are here, here and here, though we don't have a lot of ammunition for them."

"Then we wait until we have we have an optimal firing position," Lucy suggested, tracing her finger from position to position across the map. "Each time I look at this map, it seems our odds get worse."

"This will be but one battle, not the war," Marcus reassured her, placing a hand on her shoulder. "We need only to hold them back, make them hesitate. Once Aldonis sees the threat they'll send reinforcements and supplies, recall the armies from the east. We only need to hold them off long enough to make that happen."

"I hope you're right, Marcus," Lucy replied.

"Me too," Richard agreed. "Aldonis and Baron Anita aren't looking too friendly right now."

"They'll come," Marcus insisted. "They have to."

By early afternoon, they had caught sight of the invading forces, marching confidently from the west. Marcus and Richard surveyed the advancing troops through the binoculars, describing what they saw. As Boshtok had insisted, the Phalathlan forces marched at the head, though they bore no banner to declare their past allegiance. Behind them came the siege engines, long lines of cannons and catapults pushed or pulled on oversize carts. Before long, the binoculars were no longer needed as the enemy seemed to span the entire western horizon, and still they advanced.

"There's at least twice what the scout reported," Marcus said, bewildered. "More than ten times our forces."

"We slow them down," Richard insisted. "Remember, a battle, not the war. When the time comes we sound the retreat, fall back to the city. You were right, Marcus. The others should have seen it, and now they will. I'm sure that scouts and runners for the Elders and the Baron are already describing this scene to them."

"Now we do our job," Lucy added, raising her hand in salute. "My Lords, if we don't make it through this day, know that it's been an honour to serve with you, to know you and call you friends."

"Truly an honour," Richard said, returning the salute.

"That it has," Marcus said, saluting his comrades.

With an unspoken agreement, they each lowered their hands and set off to oversee their troops, minds focused on the task at hand. This is what they had trained for, lived for throughout their military career, and if they were to die, it would be with honour.

Richard and Lucy moved north, to direct the cannons and riflemen as they engaged the enemy. Marcus and Matthew moved south, where many small groups of gunmen and skirmishers were hoping to move around the enemy and attack their flanks. That they underestimated the size of the enemy would make their task more difficult, but not impossible.

The advancing forces drew to a halt approximately two miles from them, outside the range of the rifles and the cannons. They spilled out to the sides, forming ranks and lines, as intimidating a sight as any of the Aldonis soldiers had ever seen. The Phalathlan forces were at the fore, six large battalions to lead the assault. Behind them, several smaller groups readied themselves to attack.

The world seemed to hold its breath as each sided waited for an order or for the other side to make a move. Matthew was crouched beside forty skilled riflemen, each of them already picking their targets, knuckles white as they gripped their rifles to their chests. The overwhelming sense of fear was palpable as each of them looked to each other for support.

"Just hold until the cannons start firing," Matthew said to the man on his right, startling him as he placed a hand on his shoulder. "Choose your targets and don't hesitate to fall back."

His words were interrupted by the sound of horns from the enemy troops, a call that spread from one side of the army and back again. Upon hearing the call, the Phalathlan troops let loose a yell as they surged forwards, pistols and rifles firing either into the air or randomly ahead of them.

"Get ready," Matthew said, as he removed the assault rifle from his back and checked that it was ready to fire. He tucked it tight against his shoulder and prepared the shot, lining up his target as the first of the cannonballs struck the group ahead of him.

VII

General Boshtok surveyed the battlefield ahead of him. His officers had the troops lining up nicely, ready to begin the assault. His scouts had brought word of the Aldonis forces gathering to stand against him, and even though he didn't know exactly where they were positioned, it wouldn't take him long to flush them out.

His plans were going perfectly. The Phalathlan forces were ready to go, to charge ahead and flush out the enemy. His instructions had been simple; advance when ordered, or be cut down by the Island City forces behind. He didn't expect many of them to survive, but they would have served their purpose and that was all that mattered.

Standing tall, he saluted the soldiers in their ranks before ordering the trumpets to sound. The noise echoed back and forth across the ranks as the Phalathlan forces surged forwards, screaming a battle cry of their own. Within seconds the first of the cannonballs tore through their ranks, throwing dirt and body parts in all directions. When the second ball hit, he was able to pinpoint the location of the cannon and ordered his troops to aim the siege weapons at it.

It took three attempts, but the cannons that stood atop the small hill were destroyed. From the numbers reported by his scouts, the enemy would have to split the cannons into three or four smaller units to make the most of the geography, and a short while later he had already identified a second enemy cannon placement and ordered its destruction.

The horns sounded a second time and the next wave of troops advanced upon the enemy. These marched more slowly, watching for signs of combat amongst the Phalathlan and enemy forces, taking well aimed shots that cut through the enemy units. Raising his binoculars, he could see that the Phalathlan troops had torn through the underbrush like a plague, disturbing the enemy soldiers as they fought to stay hidden with their trenches. Close quarters combat became the norm as they sliced at each other with knives and swords, the blood of the dead and dying painting a path for his second wave to follow.

It was a massacre. The forces of Oster fought with honour, Boshtok noted, but were hopelessly outnumbered and out gunned. As his third wave of troops moved around their flanks, ready to cut off the retreating soldiers, he knew that victory was his, and there were still two hours to sunset.

VIII

The first wave of enemy soldiers had come running at them, screaming as they fired in all directions. The cannons had cut them down, but still they came, overrunning the trenches and camouflaged encampments. Matthews forces thinned them out further, but more seemed to follow, an endless tide of anger and fury bearing down upon them.

Matthew ordered those around him to retreat as their position was overrun, though many chose to stay and fight enemy forces that descended upon them. Rifles were cast aside as the soldiers drew daggers and swords from their belts, slicing left and right as they fought for their very lives.

A deafening explosion to the north let Matthew know that the third and final cannon emplacement had been destroyed, and their gamble had been lost. They were fools to think they had a chance, any chance against such an overwhelming force. He had led hundreds of men and women to their deaths, and in the end it would count for nothing. His arrogance had killed them all.

All around him they were running, away from the hordes that wanted only to consume them. A young woman to his left pushed him to the floor as bullets tore through her chest, painting him with her blood. She was dead before she hit the ground, but Matthew checked anyway, feeling for a pulse in her neck.

He lay there on his belly, the dead and dying all around him, the feet of his comrades moving past him in a blur. He looked to the east where he saw Marcus had gathered troops to his side, perhaps two hundred men and women forming an irregular line.

Rising to a crouch, Matthew fired his rifle blindly over his shoulder as he set off at a sprint, bullets whistling past him with every step.

He crossed the battlefield in seconds, diving at Marcus and driving him to the floor as bullets whizzed past their heads. "Sound the retreat!" Matthew screamed into his face.

"We just need to hold the line," Marcus insisted, struggling to stand. "Just a little while longer."

"It's lost," Matthew persisted. "We've lost. Let them run, give them a chance to survive this!" Their eyes locked as Matthew pinned the older man to the ground, willing him to see sense. The sound of one of the surrounding soldiers screaming as he was gunned down called them back to their senses.

"Retreat!" Marcus yelled. "Retreat! Fall back to the city! To Aldonis!"

The remaining men and women didn't need to be told twice, and were soon sprinting towards the buildings only a short few miles away. How many would make it would be impossible to calculate, but if only one of them could survive the slaughter, Matthew hoped the day would not yet be lost.

Matthew helped Marcus to his feet and dragged him along behind him, heading towards the south of the city where Arian and Juliet would be waiting for them. The enemy forces seemed to be pushing towards the city itself, and soon the sounds of gunfire and explosions were a way behind them. Red faced and breathless, Marcus pulled Matthew to a stop and slumped to his knees.

"What have we done?" Marcus said, looking at the blood that stained his hands and clothes.

"We did what we thought was right," Matthew replied, though there was no conviction in his words.

"This morning, there were nearly four thousand men and women under my command," Marcus continued, his voice barely above a whisper. "Now, how many remain? How many people have I sent to their deaths today?"

"We don't have time for this," Matthew told him. "They were soldiers, soldiers who knew the risks. They made a choice to stand with you, with us."

"History will judge us on that," Marcus said quietly, striking the ground with his fist in frustration.

"We fought and we lost," Matthew said defiantly. "Now it's up to the Baron, the Elders, to negotiate with them, to surrender. If history remembers us at all, I hope it will remember that we tried. We'll return, Marcus, both of us. We'll free our homes and defeat this enemy, but today the battle is lost. It's time to go."

Marcus shook his head as he stood, his face racked with pain as he turned to look upon Aldonis one last time. It had always been his home. It had cared for his family in his absence, and he had always returned there regardless of where his military career had taken him. It was with a heavy heart that he turned and followed Matthew as he made his way towards the River Talon.

IX

Alexander paced around the throne room, debating what he was going to tell the people who had gathered outside. There had been no announcement that he would speak, but after the events at the theatre the previous night the people were expecting him to explain what had happened, to reassure them that everything was going to be okay. He was a victim of his own success.

"My Liege," Samuel said as he entered. "The meeting area is full to capacity and the people are becoming restless. What are your orders?"

"They are eager today, aren't they?" Alexander said mockingly. "I suppose there's no time like the present." Preparing himself, he stepped out onto the balcony and silenced the crowd with a gesture.

"Citizens of Maleton," he began, relaxing into his comfortable stance and tone. "I apologise for keeping you waiting, but it has been a most difficult day. As you are no doubt aware, Safran and her supporters used the night of celebration as a cover to stage another brazen attack against this city and its people.

"This morning I learned that the rebels used his appearance at the theatre to kill Elder Mathis, and I have reason to believe that other members of the Elder Council were also targeted. It was only through prompt action by the City Watch that the assassins were captured, and are imprisoned in the palace dungeon as we speak.

"Fear not, good people, it will only be a matter of time before they share their secrets and we can finally end this pointless slaughter!" There were cheers and shouts for the prisoners to be brought forward, for their heads to roll just as the Baron's had done. Alexander let them continue for a moment before raising his hands for silence, casting out his will as he brought the crowd back under his control.

"I hear you," he continued, "and once we have learned all that we can from them, they will be tried and they will be sentenced for their crimes.

"For now though, I bring news from the remaining Elders whom I met with just this morning. It is our understanding that Elder Mathis was targeted, just like Elder Janis before him, because of the council's search for a suitable heir for the throne. The Baron's son and his wife are still unaccounted for, and we suspect Safran is targeting the Elders to prevent anyone claiming the throne but her."

There were further shouts of anger and disgust from the crowd. They would see her dead before she was allowed near the throne. It was to be hers no longer.

"I understand your anger," he told them, "but remember, she is not in her right mind. She has been twisted, manipulated by her father and the people from the Road Trains. Though her actions are deplorable, and she will be made to answer for her crimes, remember that she does not act alone.

"With this in mind, and with the support of the Elder Council, I am here to inform you that I will remain in your city until this crisis has passed. I don't wish to outstay my welcome, but until Safran and her conspirators are apprehended, anyone who takes their place upon the throne will become a target. She has already tried, and failed, to kill me, and I do not fear her!

"For Maleton! For Draxis!"

The crowd erupted into a cacophony of cheers and applause as Alexander bathed in their admiration. They already wanted him to stay, to lead and to rule them until the end of his days. He would resist a little longer, maintain the council and the Merchants Guild until they were no longer of use to him. But one day soon, when Safran and the other rebels lay dead at his feet, he would graciously accept their offer, to no longer be a caretaker ruler but to take his rightful place upon the throne.

It should have been his after all, why would he refuse?

X

"What do you think?" Carl asked as he stepped from the bathroom, wearing the fresh clothes that the Baron had provided. He was dressed in black trousers with a light blue shirt, the sleeves rolled up to his elbows.

"Looks good," Ben replied with a grin. "Very cool."

"It's not cold," Carl told him. "Actually the shirt's quite thick. Here, have a feel."

"No, it's, I meant," Ben replied, struggling to suppress a laugh. "I meant you look really good, Carl."

"Thanks, Ben," Carl replied. "You're not looking too bad yourself."

Ben stood and examined himself in the long mirror. He was dressed similarly to Carl, though his trousers were a little lighter and his shirt darker. The Baron's tailor had measured them only that morning, and they had both been supplied with ample changes of clothes for the journey ahead. They had also taken turns to have a long soak in the bath, letting the mud and grime of a month on the road wash away, making them feel almost human again.

Ben really wanted to see about a haircut, it was almost long enough to tie in a ponytail at the back, but didn't want to push his luck after everything that the Baron had done for them already. Carl's hair was sticking up in a variety of directions after his bath, and seemed to insist on doing so regardless of what he tried to do with it. Ben resigned himself to putting up with it for a while longer, and besides, Justin's hair was long, maybe Safran liked it that way?

"So, what next?" Ben asked to the empty silence that had gripped the room.

"I suspect you're not talking about dinner with the Baron?" Carl asked wryly.

"I mean tomorrow, the day after," Ben continued. "How long do we stay here for? Do we stay for good? Safran's mom and the

Baron seem to be getting along okay."

"You heard him this morning," Carl replied, "when I asked about aid. He made some excuse about the council and changed the subject. I doubt we'll see any help here."

"Maybe Matthew had more luck in Aldonis?" Ben suggested.

"I hope so," Carl told him, "but there's no guarantee, and we might not find out until the northern armies cross the border and attack this palace."

"So what are you saying?" Ben asked, though he felt that he already knew the answer.

"We stick to the plan," Carl said. "It's still my job to make sure you and Safran are safe and as far away from Alexander as possible. We asked for help, but I don't think we'll get any, so I say Markay is still our safest option."

"Do you think Safran will see it that way?" Ben said with a smile.

Carl laughed out loud at the thought of talking to Safran about leaving. "I never said it'd be easy," he replied, "but hey, I can always carry her out of here!"

"Now that's something I'd like to see," Ben said, and soon both of them were laughing loud enough to be heard as far away as the docks.

XI

Sanjay took the stairs two at a time as he hurriedly made his way to the secret room beneath the brewery. He'd taken a winding route back from the meeting area at the palace just as Bran had told him to, hoping to lose anyone who might be following him. They'd be eager to hear the news though, and he didn't want to keep them waiting any longer than he had to. Flicking the switch behind the shelving, he slipped through the hidden door while it was still only a crack to find everyone staring at him in anticipation.

"Sanjay," Deacon said, sliding his hand back from the pistol that lay on the table before him. "I am pleased you made it back safely. You have news, I trust?"

"They didn't shoot the Regent," Sanjay replied breathlessly. "They killed someone called Mathis instead. They're alive though, in the palace dungeons he said, and they haven't said anything."

"Then we may yet have time," Deacon announced. "Bran, do you know anything about the tunnel entrance to the palace?"

"Only what I've heard in rumours," Bran said. "Same as you I suspect. Supposed to be near the Gowts or Penrock bridges I think."

"How do we find out?" Stan asked, the overwhelming sense of hope rushing throughout his body impossible to ignore.

"The answer is simple," Deacon said with a malevolent smile. "We ask."

XII

General Boshtok's forces made short work of the survivors as they regrouped and continued their determined march towards Aldonis. The dying were slaughtered, left to rot beside their fallen comrades, as the seemingly endless tide of Island City soldiers stepped around or upon their enemy. A mile out from the city they stopped, allowing General Boshtok and his officers to March ahead. A small delegation from Aldonis were already heading towards them, furiously waving a white flag of surrender, while civilians and soldiers alike hovered on the outskirts of the city, watching events unfold.

"General? It is General, isn't it?" the elderly man at the forefront of the group stammered. "I am Elder Seely, and I'm here representing Aldonis and the Barony of Oster."

"I demand to speak to your Baron," Boshtok replied, staring intently at the older man.

"She is, well, she's not available," Elder Seely told him. Boshtok laughed, turning to face his officers, slowly shaking his head.

"The soldiers you fought," Elder Seely continued, "they were acting against the will of the city and its people. We have no conflict with you. I am authorised to discuss terms."

"Terms?" Boshtok said loudly, turning on the man. "What terms?"

"Why," Elder Seely said hesitantly, seeming to shrink before the imposing General. "The, the terms of, of our surrender?"

Genera Boshtok stepped forward, his face a hair's breadth away from Elder Seely's. "Present Baron Anita to me by dawn," Boshtok told him, "and I may consider, terms."

"But, but, General," Elder Seely responded, taking an involuntary step back.

Boshtok slid the pistol from its holster and shot Elder Seely between the eyes, killing the old man instantly. The remainder of the Aldonis delegation screamed and cowered as Boshtok levelled his pistol at each of them in turn. "Bring me your Baron!" he demanded, screaming as loudly as he could, before returning to his forces without another word.

CHAPTER 2

I'm really pleased that Safran found her mom again, her brother too. They're all so happy. They've been inseparable since, sleeping together in Karan's room every night.

It makes me think about my own mom and dad, I hope they're okay. I know that I didn't see them very often before I came here, but I still miss them. Mom, Dad, if somehow you ever get to see this journal, and I can't tell you myself, know that I love you. I love both of you so much, and I'm sorry for what happened, for what Excelsior did to you, to all of us.

If I could do it all again, I would never have left home, I promise.

I

"My Liege," the guard said hurriedly once Alexander had opened his bedroom door. "The suspect, he's awake."

Alexander smiled and closed the door, dressing quickly in the relative darkness of his room. A brief look through his window showed a faint glow on the horizon, telling him that it was somewhere around five in the morning. He still felt the effects of casting his will out into so many people the night before, but his weariness would pass once he started with the prisoners.

The guard led him down narrow corridors and slippery stone steps, descending further into the depths of the palace and the dungeons below. The dungeons were rarely used, crime and punishment having been taken over by the Watch and the cells within the seven Watch Houses throughout the city. However, with such prisoners as the Baron and the would-be assassins, Alexander wouldn't allow them to be detained anywhere else.

Alexander turned into a gloomy corridor, lit by two dull oil lanterns along one wall. Two guards stood outside a door at the far end of the corridor, watching the cell that the young woman currently occupied. The guard who had interrupted Alexander's slumber had informed him that she was still unconscious, though the man who had been with her was now awake. They were kept at opposite ends of the corridor. There was to be no communication between them unless Alexander wanted it, and turning right from the stairs led him directly to the male prisoner's door.

"My Liege," the two door guards said, bowing slightly as Alexander approached. Alexander waved them away and unfastened the three thick bolts himself, opening the heavy wooden door with a groan. The large, dark skinned man turned his head to watch the door open as Alexander entered, the three guards slipping in quietly behind him. Nathan was sat upright in a metal chair, hands bound tightly behind his back whilst chains around his waist and ankles held him securely. The chair itself was bolted to the floor, so there really was no way for him to move.

Alexander paced around him once, never taking his eyes off

the man before him, smiling as Nathan struggled to follow his progress as he stepped outside of his field of vision. "Nathan son-of-Daniel," Alexander said slowly as he walked, emphasising each word. Sometimes this was the part of the proceedings that he enjoyed most, the anticipation as he built up the levels of fear and anxiety in his prisoner. He enjoyed the actual torture too of course, but there was always something to be said for watching the realisation dawn in a man's eyes, knowing that whatever they had been through, the worst was still yet to come.

"You and your companions have been a veritable thorn in my side," Alexander continued, standing directly in front of Nathan. "I had planned to just kill you at the theatre and have done with it, but then you go and surprise me, healing like that. How did you do it? Was it you, or did the woman have something to do with it?"

"Where is she?" Nathan demanded, though his mouth and throat were so dry that the words were difficult to make out. "What have you done with her?"

"All in good time," Alexander replied. "When you begin to answer my questions, perhaps I'll consider answering one of yours, yes?"

Nathan flexed his huge shoulders, straining at the chains and restraints about his person. The guards had done a good job and he was barely able to move at all. Alexander watched it all with interest, admiring Nathan's strength but confident that it would do him no good in the days to follow.

"Guard, give me your knife," Alexander said suddenly, stepping around towards Nathan's back. "And bring me the lantern."

Nathan tensed as he felt the cold steel against the back of his neck, though the pain he imagined never materialised. Alexander pulled tightly back on the back of Nathan's shirt and cut it down the middle, tearing it apart to expose his flesh. Handing the knife back to the guard, Alexander traced his fingers across Nathan's skin, searching for the wounds that he had watch heal before his very eyes only two nights before. There were still patches of dried blood, but no sign of any wound or injury. The skin was entirely free of marks or blemishes.

"How did you do it?" Alexander asked again. "How did you heal like that? Just tell me, and this can go a lot easier."

Nathan was taken aback. He was expecting to be questioned about the theatre, about Deacon and Catrina and what they had planned. Was Alexander just trying to confuse him? It didn't make sense.

Alexander saw the confusion as it crossed Nathan's face. "You really don't know, do you?" Alexander asked with a grin.

"Let me out of here," Nathan began, finding his voice. "You can't keep me like this. I'm a citizen of Draxis and I demand to be tried by the Elder Council!"

"Oh dear, demands already is it?" Alexander said sarcastically. "This isn't how I wanted our first meeting to go. It's quite simple really. I ask you questions and you answer them. If you don't answer me, honestly and promptly I may add, then I have to make you answer.

"Now, I'm not saying that I won't enjoy making you talk, but trust me when I say that you won't enjoy it one little bit. And the council, really? Where have you been for the last few months? This city, this Barony, is mine, and I will do as I please. You have no rights in here, there are no laws. There is only how much you can endure before you talk, and you will talk, believe me.

"So, I'm going to go and have some breakfast and leave you to think about what I've said. When I come back, we'll try again and pretend this little unpleasantness never happened. Good day to you, Nathan son-of-Daniel. I'll see you soon."

II

General Boshtok stood and observed the small group as they approached from Aldonis. The sun was just rising to the east, casting long shadows that slid towards him from the city, hiding their details.

He wasn't worried though. If they were planning on attacking him, his men would cut them down before they began, and if they somehow managed to get close to him, he would be happy to end them himself. He wasn't a young man anymore, and he'd filled out around the middle as men of his age tended to do, but that wasn't the same as being old, or slow, or soft. He'd known other military leaders travel on carts or raised chairs during their campaigns, but not him. He would march at their head or by their side, day in day out, and he didn't need a Road Train like the Regent.

Thinking about the Regent sullied his mood a little as the small group came closer. He knew full well what his orders were towards Aldonis, and today he was going to make a conscious decision to ignore them. The further he was away from Alexander, the more he remembered how much he hated him. Alexander, with his sarcastic comments and manipulative words. Alexander, who had convinced him of the reasons to kill Regent Cotran. So much had happened since, but when lying awake at night, struggling to sleep, Boshtok had a hard time remembering exactly what those reasons were.

"General," the young officer said quietly, pulling Boshtok back to the present. "The City Elders have returned with the Baron."

Boshtok made a point of looking them over as they crossed the final few meters to stand before him. The Elders were the same as yesterday he noted, minus the man he had shot, and there were no guards escorting them. Instead there was a plump, middle-aged woman with her hands bound in chains before her.

"Ah, Baron," Boshtok said. "At last. I can see why the Elders were so reluctant to present you."

"I am still Baron," Baron Anita said defiantly, "and I will be treated with courtesy and respect."

"Is that right?" Boshtok replied with a smile.

"I am here to discuss terms," Baron Anita continued, as though Boshtok hadn't spoken. Even chained and muddy, her clothes bearing none of their former glory, she still managed to present an air of authority.

"You wish to offer your complete and unconditional surrender?" Boshtok suggested.

"I, what, no!" Baron Anita replied. "I have an agreement with your Regent. I wish to discuss the terms of our unification."

Boshtok laughed out loud, looking to his senior officers who quickly joined in. "I suspected something like that," Boshtok said at last, once he had the laughter under control.

"Send for Stuart, my adviser," Baron Anita persisted. "He

speaks for your Regent. He has all of the official documents." The Elders stared at her, shocked at the news. They had suspected that something was going on, but hadn't realised the magnitude of what she had been doing.

"Of course, Stuart," Boshtok replied. "He visited me only last night to discuss the orders from the Regent. Major Hamlyn, please bring Stuart here that we might listen to what he has to say."

Major Hamlyn nodded and left the small conclave, returning a minute later with a blood stained sack. Standing before Baron Anita, he upturned the sac, dropping the decapitated head of Stuart at her feet. She screamed as the sight of it, the ragged looking skin at the neck and the empty eyes that looked back at her.

"As you can see, Baron," Boshtok continued. "Stuart no longer has anything to say on the matter. Whatever arrangement you had with Regent Alexander, you do not have with me."

"You serve the Regent," Baron Anita persisted, her voice tinged with hate.

"I serve Island City and its people," Boshtok retorted. "Regent's come and go, but the Treaty of Aldonis decimated my people, neutered them, denying us the right to build up our army in return for what? Trade with you southern skeets? You and your city are a living embodiment of that deception, one I intend to remove from the map."

Baron Anita was silent, shocked at the realisation that her entire world was about to be destroyed. "Major Hamlyn," Boshtok said, turning towards him. "Sound the horns and ready the catapults. I want this city torn down to its foundations. I want to see fires so large they turn night into day, and anyone who stands against us, man, woman or child, is to be cut down and cast to the flames."

III

Deacon and Bran made their way through the Industrial District to The Baron's Retreat, a run down tavern on the waterfront near Gowts Bridge. The inside was as dirty and dilapidated as the outside, and they wouldn't have been within spitting distance of the building if they hadn't needed to see the Walkers, three brothers who ran the smuggling operation from one of the tavern's back rooms.

The Walkers had always been one of the small time gangs in the city and one Deacon that was happy to allow to exist, as long as they paid him his share. Their father had been a smuggler before them, and they already had a network of contacts up and down the River Brachen, contacts Deacon was happy to exploit when he needed to.

"I am here to see Saul," Deacon announced as he made his way past the tables and into the back room. The barmaid and the few patrons that were drinking at that time of the morning looked on in awe.

Saul was the eldest of the three brothers, and by default the leader of the Walkers after their father had died. He was sat at a small round table playing a card game with his brothers, Terry and Charlie, when Deacon burst in unannounced. They were caught off guard, casting their cards aside as they each struggled to get to their feet and draw weapons from their belts, knocking the table over in the process. Deacon and Bran looked on, amused, Bran quietly closing the door behind him.

"You did not have to stand, Saul," Deacon said with a smile, "but I do appreciate the respect."

"You aren't supposed to be here, Deacon," Saul replied, relaxing slightly, though his hand remained resting upon the pistol at his belt. "The Watch are turning this city upside down for you."

"So I hear," Deacon replied, stepping forward to right the table and sitting himself down. Bran remained standing behind him, shoulders wide enough to obscure the door and anyone who might enter. The room was long and narrow with crates and barrels stacked everywhere, no doubt recently appropriated from one boat or another and waiting to be moved.

"Do sit back down," Deacon continued. "I see that you were enjoying a game of cards. There is no need to stop on my account." Though his smile remained, his tone suggested that it was not a simple request that he was giving them.

All three men looked very similar, in height and build as well as mannerisms. Saul was larger around the middle than his brothers, and Terry was balding more quickly than the other two, but their similarity was striking in such close proximity. Both Terry and Charlie looked to their brother, before reclaiming their chairs and joining Deacon at the table.

"What do you want?" Saul asked gruffly, his right hand still resting on the pistol now hidden beneath the table.

"We have had a good working relationship, have we not?" Deacon asked. "We have both profited from our endeavours? I ask only that we continue to work together."

"From where I'm sitting," Saul said scornfully, "you haven't got anything left to offer."

Deacon nodded. "It may look like that from over there," he said, "so let me put it another way. We will continue to work together, and in return I will allow you to live."

Saul looked to his brothers and laughed, Terry and Charlie quickly joining in. "You're done, Deacon," Saul exclaimed. "Your boys are either dead or locked up, your businesses are all shut down. You've got nothing! We're done!"

"Here, we should just turn him over to the Watch ourselves," Terry suggested. "I bet there's a nice big bounty for him."

Terry stood and drew the knife from his belt, pointing it towards Deacon. Faster than his eye could follow, Bran gripped the wrist holding the knife and squeezed it tightly until Terry let go. With one swift movement Bran picked up the knife and brought Terry's hand down, driving the blade through the flesh and into the wood below, pinning Terry in place. Terry screamed, his eyes wide with fear and pain as he fought to free his hand from the table.

Deacon hadn't moved at all. "I had hoped to avoid this unpleasantness," he said with a sigh before standing slowly and dusting himself off. "Bran, kill them please. I will be waiting outside."

Bran smiled, teeth showing, as Saul and Charlie got to their feet, jostling the table as they did so and causing Terry to scream once more in pain. Bran quickly disarmed both of them, taking the guns from their shaking hands as they brought them up to fire, before gripping each by the neck and beginning to squeeze.

"Deacon!" Saul mouthed breathlessly, a squeak the only sound escaping his lips. "Wait! Deacon!"

"Deacon," Bran said, still squeezing. "I think this one's trying to speak."

"Really?" Deacon asked. "I distinctly heard him say that we were done."

"No, please," Saul mouthed.

"I think I heard something that time too," Deacon stated. "Let them go for a minute, Bran, you can always kill them later." Bran did as he was told, releasing both men and letting them drop to the floor where they held their throats and sucked in whistling gulps of air.

"So, Saul," Deacon said, leaning against the table. "What was it you wanted to say?"

"I'm sorry, Deacon, we're sorry," Saul said hoarsely. "Terry, he was just messing with you, that's all. We didn't mean anything by it."

"Ah, now I see," Deacon said, an unsettling smile upon his face. "A joke. Most amusing. Good one, Terry." Terry fought to stand completely still as he tried in vain to remove the dagger with his other hand. Bran slapped him hard on the shoulder, almost knocking him to the floor and making him scream as the dagger tugged and twisted in his flesh.

"Please, Deacon," Saul continued. "What is it you need? Anything, just name it?"

"I need to get into the palace," Deacon replied. "Discreetly. I had heard that you may know a way in."

Saul looked to his brothers, who were still suffering from the treatment that they had received. The tunnel entrance had been a family secret, something known to his father's father. Everyone wanted things that they couldn't get through regular channels, including palace staff and Barons. He had rarely given up its location, unless the Deniras were too many to resist. One such deal had presented itself only months before and look how that ended for them, executed with their heads outside the Council Chambers for all to see.

"If you cannot help me," Deacon persisted, "I am sure that Bran here would be happy to continue where he left off." Bran took a step forwards, reaching for Saul.

"No, no need," Saul said hurriedly. "I know it, we know where it is. It's on the other side of the river, between the Penrock and Gowts bridges. There's a small jetty across from here, by the theatre. It's mostly rotted away now, but the hook there, for a lantern, it opens the passage. You need to turn it right all the way round, left the same, and then a right half turn. The door will open right up, I promise."

"I am sure it will," Deacon said with a grin. "Thank you, Saul, you have been most helpful. And do not worry about this week's cut for now, I will send someone to collect it in a day or two."

"You might want to help Terry there, though," Bran suggested. "He's gone a bit pale and his hand's still bleeding."

Saul nodded and turned to his brother as Deacon and Bran left the back room and returned to the main room of the Baron's Retreat. There was a loud scream from behind them, from Terry as Saul or Charlie trying to remove the dagger they assumed, and everyone stared at them, wide eyed and fearful.

"I do hope that we are not going to have a problem?" Deacon asked as he made his way slowly towards the door.

IV

Alexander sat in the palace infirmary waiting for the prisoner to be brought to him. The beds had been removed and replaced with a single metal chair bolted securely to the floor, along with a selection of chains and restraints situated on the floor and around the room. He had kept most of the medical equipment though, his imagination going wild as he had turned each piece over and over in his hands.

His own selection of knives and clamps lay wrapped in their leather pouch on the small table before him, still hidden from view. He didn't expect the prisoner to talk, not for one minute, but he enjoyed the performance of unrolling it in front of them, showing him each piece of equipment before he decided which one to employ first.

"My Liege," the guard said, standing in the doorway with the bound and beaten body of Nathan in front of him.

"Ah, Nathan son-of-Daniel," Alexander said with a smile. "Please, do take a seat." The guards dragged him to the chair where he was forcibly seated and his hands and feet bound tightly. Finally, one of the lengths of chain was wrapped around his chest and securely fastened to one of the many hooks now to be found in the floor.

Once he was happy that the prisoner was securely bound, Alexander dismissed the guards and sat watching Nathan as he fought against his restraints. "No need to tire yourself out, Nathan," Alexander told him. "I made sure that the restraints would be strong enough for any man, even one as strong as you. Now, when last we spoke, well, I say we, I seem to remember that I did most of the talking. Well, last time we were together shall we say, I explained the rules to you, and left you time to consider them.

"They were simple really, but I'll remind you just in case. I'd hate for there to be any confusion between us. Now, what I am going to do is ask you some questions, and all that you need do is answer them, honestly and promptly, and this can all end. That's not to say that you'll be going free of course, you'll die in here one way or another, but only you have the power to determine if that death will be quick and painless, or slow and agonising.

"I asked you before about your wounds, and how you healed them so quickly. You looked as confused as I did, and I'm prepared to believe that you have no idea how it happened, but I should ask again just to be sure. How did you heal the two gunshot wounds in your back?"

Nathan listened to what Alexander said, though it made as much sense as it had done earlier. If he'd been shot, he'd be dead, or in a lot more pain than he was. He thought back to the theatre and found a nagging fragment of memory that wouldn't come to the surface. He remembered the stairwell and the soldier who opened fire. He remembered stepping in front of Catrina and the burning sensation across his back, but there was nothing more he could recall, just waking in the cell that morning.

He noticed Alexander scrutinising him as the thoughts ran through his mind. "You certainly like the sound of your own voice," Nathan said at last.

Alexander smiled. "Yes, that's been said before," he replied. "Okay, I'm prepared to believe that you have no idea what happened to you and why you're still here, so I'll let the question go, for now. Tell me who the woman is who was with you at the theatre? No one seems to recognise her, but she's familiar to me all the same. Who is she?" Nathan said nothing, staring at Alexander as he waited for the inevitable.

"No?" Alexander asked. "It's a simple question really, and it won't be long until I find out who she is, so you might as well tell me. If you tell me who she is, we can stop for today and I'll arrange for the guards to bring you some food and water?" Again Nathan remained silent, watching Alexander as he spoke.

"As you wish," Alexander sighed, beginning to unroll the leather pouch upon the table. "Remember, I did promise you that I'd make you talk, and that you wouldn't enjoy it. Last chance, Nathan?"

Nathan fought once more against his restraints, trying to move the chair or loosen his bonds but all to no avail. Alexander made a show of examining his tools, holding them in turn to the light to assess the sharpness of the blade before finally selecting a long serrated knife. He stepped slowly towards Nathan, placing he tip of the knife against his cheek and tracing a thin line of crimson towards his jaw.

Nathan struggled once more, pulling against his restraints with all of his strength, but the more he moved the tighter they felt. The pain grew in intensity as the blade cut deeper, the first warm trickle of blood dripping from his chin. It took all of his will power not to cry out.

Alexander walked slowly around him, making shallow slices casually as he did so. "Choices, choices," he said. "Where to begin."

V

Baron George called them to the throne room early that afternoon. He had requested only Safran and Karan to attend, but Safran had been quick to inform Carl about the meeting, suspecting that it related to the Baron's meeting with the City Elders that morning. Ben followed along for good measure.

"What do you think he'll say?" Safran asked Carl as they were escorted along the corridor to the throne room.

"You heard him yesterday," Carl replied. "Maybe I'm wrong, but he didn't seem too keen on the idea."

"He just needs the council's permission, that's all," Safran said hopefully.

"I hope you're right, *Baron*," Carl said with a wry smile.

"Stop that!" Safran demanded, punching him playfully on the arm. "I don't know what my mom was thinking, speaking to you like that."

"She was just looking out for you," Carl assured her. "Come on, let's see what our host has to say."

The guards opened the door to the throne room, allowing them entrance. Baron George was sat upon his throne with Karan to his right, already engaged in conversation. Upon seeing Safran and her friends enter, the conversation stopped and he greeted the trio with a warm smile. Ben followed Carl's lead, dropping to one knee before the throne whilst Safran remained standing.

"Safran, a pleasure to see you looking so well," Baron George said, "and your friends too. I hadn't realised that they'd be joining us?"

"My apologies, Baron," Safran replied, "but they're as invested in this as I am, and their information may prove invaluable to your military leaders."

"Straight to the point," Baron George said with a nod of his head. "Your father taught you well."

"Safran," Karan interrupted, seeing the petulant look forming upon her face. "Baron George is our host. Please listen to what he has to say."

Safran nodded for George to continue. "Thank you," he said with a smile. "I met with the council this morning and relayed your concerns, as promised. I'm here to report that the council think as I do in this matter. Ashford and the Barony of Morton have never succumbed to an enemy force, and we see no need to panic our good citizens at this time."

"So you're going to do nothing?" Safran exclaimed, her voice louder than she intended.

"Not at all," Baron George said sternly. "I have recalled the armies to garrison outside of Ashford, that they may defend the city and its people. There are over forty thousand troops at my command, more than enough to repel the army you described."

"Were you even listening to what Carl described?" Safran yelled. "Forty thousand may sound like a lot now, but you haven't seen this army. They may number twice that for all you know!"

Baron George stood, his face red with anger. "You are a guest in my home," he announced. "Do not forget your place, my Lady."

Carl stepped forward and placed a comforting arm on Safran's shoulder. "Please, Baron George," he said. "Baron Safran meant no disrespect. She's passionate about her people and the threat this army poses to the Baronies as a whole, that's all. If I may speak plainly, though, her description of the armies was valid. Forty thousand troops may not be enough."

"I appreciate you candour," Baron George replied, "but you'll forgive me if I don't take military advice from a trader's assistant. The army you described will have already gone on to battle with the forces of Phalathlan and Oster. If by some chance they have defeated both of those Barony's soldiers, forty thousand will be more than enough to deal with the stragglers if they choose to push on Ashford."

"And what about Draxis?" Safran asked, overwhelmed.

"Once the threat has been neutralised," Baron George announced, returning to his seat, "I have pledged to aid you in reclaiming your homeland. I suspect, though, that once their army has been defeated, the remaining northern forces in Maleton will scurry back to Island City."

Safran looked to her mother, who was still standing beside Baron George, watching events unfold. Safran didn't know what had happened between them in the weeks that Karan had been hiding in Ashford, but she was surprised that her mother had remained so quiet during the meeting.

After a moment, Karan noticed her scrutiny and stepped towards her daughter. "Listen to him, Safran," she said. "Morton is a large Barony, and Baron George has ruled them well for many years. I trust in his word that he'll help, as soon as he can."

"Mom, please" Safran said with tears in her eyes. " The longer we wait, the longer another man sits on father's throne, spreading lies about him, about me. We can't just stand by and watch."

"We're not," Karan assured her. "Morton will come to our aid, just as Baron George has promised."

"This is the best I can offer," Baron George said.

"Thank you, Baron George," Safran replied, standing tall and holding back tears, "and I understand your position. My companions and I will resume our journey to Markay as soon as we're able, and petition the Baron there for further aid in our cause."

Karan looked horrified at the news that her daughter would be leaving again so soon, though Baron George only chuckled to himself. "As you wish, my Lady," he said with a smile. "I wish you luck on your travels."

"Safran, no," Karan demanded. "You can't leave, not now. I won't let you."

"I have to, mom," Safran told her. "I'll understand if you won't come with me, but I won't stand by and do nothing while our people suffer. I've seen this army for myself, and whatever Baron George says, I don't believe his forces will be enough to stop them."

"Please, Safran, don't leave me, not again," Karan pleaded.

"Then come with me?" Safran suggested.

"I can't," Karan replied. "I need to think of Justin, of his safety. Ashford's the best place for him, it's too big to fall."

Safran nodded, a single tear running down her cheek as she realised that she would be leaving her mother and brother behind. She knew arguing with her mother would be pointless, so instead she slipped her arms around her and squeezed her tight. "I love you, mom," Safran whispered through her mother's sweet smelling hair.

"I love you too, my sweet," Karan replied, returning the embrace.

Carl and Ben tried to look anywhere but at the two women, feeling uncomfortable at the intensity of emotion on display. As the silence grew heavier Baron George coughed politely, drawing the room's attention back to him. "Baron Safran," he said, his voice holding far more compassion than it had done previously. "I understand your desire to travel to Markay. If you'll permit me, I'll arrange for my fastest ship to take you there." Safran nodded and smiled, lacking the confidence in her ability to speak.

"Then allow me to make the arrangements," Baron George

continued. "I'll let you know as soon as the ship's ready to sail."

VI

Once the guard had informed him that the woman was awake, Alexander ordered the mutilated Nathan to be returned to his cell and the woman be brought to him. He opted not to clean any part of the room before her arrival, hoping that the smudged pools of blood on and around the chair she was to sit in would incite more fear than his words would alone.

Two guards brought Catrina to the door, her hands bound in front of her and her feet chained together with just enough chain to let her shuffle along. Alexander only smiled at her before nodding to the guards to place her in the chair. If Catrina was distressed by the room's appearance, she didn't show it. Instead she glared constantly at Alexander, her features full of anger and resentment.

"You're so familiar somehow," Alexander said once she was securely restrained in the chair. "Would you care to tell me how?"

"You murdered my family," Catrina spat scornfully, her hatred of the man palpable.

Alexander chuckled to himself. "Unfortunately, that doesn't really narrow it down," he replied. "No matter, you'll tell me eventually, they always do. I really should be asking you about Safran and Deacon and you're ongoing plans, but that was before your friend, Nathan, survived two fatal gunshots without a mark on him."

Catrina stared at him, unblinking, determined that she would tell Alexander nothing. He would slip up, somehow, sometime, and that was all she'd need. Just a second, an instant, to end his life and have her revenge.

"You do know something, don't you," Alexander said, scrutinising the minute expressions that crossed her face. "Nathan didn't seem to have any idea what happened in that stairwell, but you do. Are you going to tell me now or later?"

Catrina gritted her teeth and tried to hold herself as still as a statue, wary that her thoughts and feelings betrayed her as they showed plainly upon her face. Her eyes remained locked on

Alexander's, hoping to convey her lack of fear for what he was about to do.

"Later it is then," Alexander continued. "Truth be told, I'm pleased that you made that choice. Nathan held his tongue for almost an hour before I made him cry out, so let's see how you do, shall we?"

Catrina tried her best to hold her face expressionless as Alexander went to the small table and began examining his tools, though the sound of her heart beating in her chest and the overwhelming lump in her throat reminded her of exactly how scared she was. She would tell him nothing, she was confident of that, but whether she could hold in her cries of pain was another matter entirely.

"Now, you see," Alexander said as he strolled casually towards her. "Nathan managed quite well to resist simple cuts and slices. I had to get, creative, shall we say. What do you think? Will you manage a full hour before I hear you scream?"

Catrina braced herself as Alexander walked slowly around her chair, tracing the tip of of a fine blade against her shoulder and then her upper back, barely breaking the skin. Before long, he'd come full circle and was staring at her again, his face only inches from her own.

"Last chance," he said with a grin. "If you'll just tell me who you are, we can put a stop to this for today?"

Catrina nodded slightly, causing Alexander to edge closer, though not close enough that she could reach him. Instead, she gathered what little saliva that she was able to make and spat in his face, the sticky glob of phlegm striking his right cheek.

Alexander stood, wiping his face with the sleeve of his shirt, his look of revulsion turning to one of glee. "I did warn you," he said, smiling as drove his blade deep into her left shoulder and dragging it down slowly towards her chest. The wound bled profusely as Catrina struggled to hold her tongue, teeth gritted and eyes tightly closed. Nausea overwhelmed her as the pain intensified, making her feel lightheaded.

Alexander stepped back, admiring his work, reaching for a cloth to help stem the bleeding. The momentary flash of anger had made him cut too deeply, and having her pass out or die from blood loss was something he had hoped to avoid. As he reached forward to apply pressure to the wound, he saw tiny blue lights shoot from one side of the incision to the other. Then the whole area seemed to glow as wound began to knit together itself. He dropped the cloth and edged closer in amazement, mouth hanging open as he watched the wound disappear completely.

Catrina felt the wound heal, a burning, tugging sensation that was almost as painful as the cut of the knife. She opened her eyes slowly, struggling to look down as the last of the light faded and her skin was whole again.

"How?" Alexander asked, confused and bewildered. "How did you?" He cast the knife casually upon the table and began to pace around the small infirmary, muttering to himself as he struggled to understand what he had just seen. Catrina smiled to herself as she brought her breathing back under control, the pain fading as quickly as it had come.

"That's, I've never seen anything like that," Alexander said to himself as he came full circle and stood in front of her again. "How do you do it? You healed Nathan too, didn't you?" Catrina smiled back at him, her confidence building as she watched him struggle for answers.

"How much can you heal?" Alexander persisted. "Is it just your skin? What about bones?" Without warning, Alexander stepped forwards and bent the little and ring fingers of her left hand backwards, snapping both digits. Catrina had been unprepared for the assault and cried out as he cruelly manipulated the broken bones.

Seconds after he stepped back, her left hand began to glow as if a light shone from directly inside it, followed by grinding and cracking noises from the bones themselves. Catrina cried out again as she felt the bones knit back together, twisting beneath her skin.

"This is fascinating," Alexander exclaimed, stepping forwards again to examine the now healed fingers. "Do you know your limits? How much damage can you take before it's too much? What happens if-."

Alexander moved quickly to the table, rummaging through his equipment until he found what he was looking for. Kneeling down in front of Catrina, he forcibly removed the boot from her right foot and the sock along with. Gripping her foot tightly with his left hand, he placed the broad scissors against her toes and squeezed, removing the two smallest toes from her right foot.

Catrina screamed again, struggling to release her foot from his grasp, but the chains that held her to the chair limited any such movement. Alexander watched as the blood slowed and the light glowed from the wounds that he had made, though he was disappointed to note that the two severed toes didn't grow back. Instead, coarse scar tissue grew over the stumps, covering the jagged bone where the scissors had done their work.

Catrina felt lightheaded again, exhausted and unable to stay awake. Alexander reached up and slapped her about the face, but try as she might to resist it, her head slumped forwards and the world around her faded from her senses.

Alexander stood and examined her, trying again to wake her but without success. "Don't worry," he said quietly. "Next time you wake, we'll find out exactly what your limits are."

VII

Matthew placed a comforting arm around Arian's waist as the boat moved southward from Aldonis. They had relied on the oars initially, urging the small vessel to move faster and away from the invading army that would surely follow. When no such pursuit occurred, Marcus opted to raise the small sail whereupon a gentle wind carried them along with the current.

The smoke had seemed insignificant at first, small streaks rising into the air, but despite getting further away from Aldonis, the smoke had increased over the last hour, merging into a broad column of sooty blackness that drifted southeast with the wind. The four of them had been unable to take their eyes off of it.

"Did we do this?" Marcus asked, more to himself than anyone around him.

"No," Matthew said defiantly. "We tried to stop it." Marcus looked at him and nodded once before returning to his own thoughts.

"What do we do now?" Arian asked a short while later.

"I hadn't really thought that far ahead," Matthew admitted. "Maybe we should try to get to Segway or Midbrook, warn Oster's remaining forces about the attack?"

"I sent runners yesterday," Marcus told them, "as soon as we got word that the enemy had been sighted. I don't know what good it'll do them. Even if all of Oster's military had rallied in defence of Aldonis, Island City would still have us outnumbered two to one. I don't understand how their forces are so large."

"The way Carl and Catrina described it," Matthew told him, "most of them are civilians, driven into a frenzy by the new Regent, promised blood and glory over their enemies."

"Was there ever any hope?" Marcus said bitterly.

"Don't think like that," Arian interrupted. "There's always hope, there has to be."

"Your daughter's right, Marcus," Matthew added. "Once you think you're defeated, the enemy has already won. There'll be more battles to fight before this war's over."

"I know," Marcus said sombrely. "But how many more people will have to die?"

Matthew left Marcus and Juliet alone, escorting Arian to the front of the boat that they may have as much privacy as the small vessel would allow. "He'll be okay," Arian assured them both. "He just needs time. The men and women who, who died today, he's served with them a long time. He's never known defeat, not like that."

"I wish I could tell him it gets better," Matthew confided, "but whether you lose five people or five thousand, he'll still see their faces every night when he sleeps."

Arian placed her hand upon his cheek and kissed him gently on his lips. "You're a good man, Matthew," she told him. "Anyone who follows you does it because they believe in you, because they trust you. Believe in yourself."

Matthew smiled at her and returned the delicate kiss. "What would I do without you?" he said tenderly. "Let's tell your father I've made a decision. We're taking this boat into Morton, all the way to Ashford if we can. This fight's not over yet."

VIII

Ben and Carl were watching Safran play with Justin, the two of them chasing each other around the extensive palace gardens or taking it in turns to play hide and seek. She looked like she didn't have a care in the world, though Ben and Carl knew that that was far from the case.

"I'm proud of her," Carl said quietly, more to himself than to Ben.

"Sorry?" Ben replied, roused from thoughts of his own as he watched Safran run and wrestle with her brother, smiling constantly.

"Standing up to the Baron like she did," Carl continued. "And her mother. I think she'll make a great leader when this is all over."

"You're right," Ben agreed with a smile. "These last few weeks, on the road, she seems like a different person, more confident and self-assured."

"It's just a shame she's losing her mother again so quickly," Carl mused. "She's only just found her again, you know, after not knowing if she was alive or dead. That's got to be tough."

"And it's not like she can just pick up the phone and check how she's doing," Ben replied.

"Phone?" Carl asked, a little confused.

"Sorry, Carl," Ben said. "It's something that lets you talk to people over a long distance. They're everywhere at home, even mobile ones you can carry in your pocket."

"That would be something," Carl agreed. "Could we speak to Matthew, Catrina, anyone?"

"If they had their own phone," Ben said, "then sure, why not."

"It's a shame you didn't have any of those at your laboratory," Carl considered.

"Even if there were," Ben agreed, "they'd need a network, towers to transmit the signal, batteries and ways of charging them."

"I don't have any idea what those things are, so I doubt we have them," Carl said with a grin. "More of that electricity stuff, is it?"

"I told you before, Carl," Ben replied, smiling. "Electricity runs everything at home. Without it, the whole world would fall apart in a matter of days."

"Certainly would make things easier though," Carl suggested. "It'd be nice to hear from Matthew about now and have him tell us the Oster forces wiped out Alexander's army."

Ben sat back and thought about what Carl had said. True, even if he still had his iPhone, it wouldn't do them any good. But what if he could allow Safran to speak to her mother, no matter how far away they were? People all over the world used short wave radios to talk to each other, why couldn't it work the same in this new world?

"Carl," Ben said at last, an inquisitive look on his face. "Do you think we could find some of the old tech here in Ashford?"

"I guess," Carl replied. "We should be able to find something in the Market District. Why?"

"I think I might be about to make Safran's day," Ben said with a smile.

Carl looked surprised and then laughed out loud. "I'll go and find us some Deniras," he suggested, shaking his head in disbelief as he strolled back into the palace.

IX

"Are you sure this is how you want to do it?" Bran asked as he added some extra ammunition and two explosive charges to a backpack.

"No, I am not sure," Deacon told him. "But we are running out of time and options. They have already been in the palace dungeons for almost two full days, how much longer do you think they can hold out?"

"I know," Bran agreed, checking his rifle for the fourth time, "but it's just not like us, pulling a job like this without checking the place over first. We don't know the layout, the number of guards, exit routes. We could be handing ourselves straight over to the Watch."

Deacon smiled to himself as he listened to Bran speak. Bran was already in the right frame of mind for what they were about to do, treating it as a job, just like any of the others that they had done together in the past. "We will not be taken by the Watch," Deacon assured him. "No matter what happens."

"Deacon, you know I'm with you, no matter what," Bran said. "I just wanted to make sure you'd thought it through, that's all."

"I appreciate your counsel, Bran," Deacon said. "I always have. I agree that this is not ideal, and under any other circumstances I would not consider it, but I gave my word. If you take a look around, it might be all I have left that is worth anything."

Bran stopped what he was doing and turned to look at his employer. Considering what they'd been through in the preceding weeks, they were both holding together very well. Bran knew how much the boys had meant to Deacon, more a like family than anything else. Inside, he'd be grieving for each and every one of them.

"You're saying these two are worth the risk?" Bran asked at last.

"They are," Deacon replied, slipping the backpack over his shoulder. "Time to go to work."

Bran followed him to the doorway, where Stan and Gavin were standing, a bow over Stan's back and a pistol tucked into his belt. "We ready?" Stan asked.

"Bran and I are ready," Deacon told him, a look of confusion upon his face. "You will not be accompanying us tonight."

"No way," Stan exclaimed. "You promised, Deacon, you said we'd get them out."

"I did, and I will," Deacon agreed. "But I did not promise that you would join us." Stan opened his mouth to speak until a look from Deacon silenced him.

"You have proven yourself many times over, Stan," Deacon began. "Gavin too. This is not a matter of your skill or your conviction. This is a matter of what is best for the task at hand."

Stan opened his mouth again and Deacon continued speaking over him. "We have two pairs of the night time spectacles that young Ben provided for us," he continued. "This will be our only advantage in the tunnels beneath the palace. I assure you, if it is still possible, we will bring Nathan and Catrina home."

"But we could help," Stan insisted, a tear in his eye. "Please?"

"Your time will come," Deacon promised, placing a comforting hand upon his shoulder. "Tonight though, remain here and take care of Sanjay and Dean. If for some reason Bran and I have not returned by morning, take whatever is of use to you here and leave the city. Do not look back, and do not try to come for us. If we have not returned, there will be no one left to rescue. Are we clear?"

Stan nodded, eager to turn his face away before the tears began to fall. He felt responsible for Nathan and Catrina, for their capture at the theatre, though he knew deep down that there was nothing that he could have done. If he'd tried to intervene, he'd just be sharing a cell with them, or worse. Unfortunately, that knowledge didn't alleviate his guilt.

Gavin placed an arm around him, turning him towards the bunks on the far side of the room. "Thank you, Deacon," Gavin said, relieved that Stan would not be put in harm's way again so soon. "We'll be waiting for you to get back."

Deacon nodded and, after a final check of their weapons, led Bran out into the night.

X

When Catrina came to, she was still firmly secured to the metal chair in the palace infirmary. There were no windows, and she had no idea how long she had been out. As her bleary eyes opened, she looked up to find Alexander watching her, the same wicked grin upon his face as when he had cut off her toes.

"Finally!" Alexander announced as he rose to his feet. "We'd almost given up hope that you'd be back with us this evening. Isn't that right, Nathan?"

Catrina followed Alexander's gaze to find Nathan chained to the wall, bound at his wrists and ankles. His head was slumped forward, his torso and limbs covered in lacerations and dried blood. The sight of him shocked her, forcing her to wakefulness as she locked her malevolent gaze on Alexander.

"From the look on your face," Alexander said with a fearsome smile, "I can see this was the right way to go. He's important to you, is he?" Catrina said nothing as she continued to glare at him.

"Still not talking?" Alexander continued. "No matter, I'm confident I can change your mind. I had a thought you see, whilst you were sleeping. I know there's no point hurting you, you just heal. And Nathan, well, he's stubborn, but what if you had the power to stop Nathan's pain? How much will you let him suffer?"

Catrina fought against her restraints, trying in vain to stand, to get closer to Alexander and tear him apart. A scream of rage escaped her lips as she struggled, growing louder as her struggle proved to be fruitless.

"Now that's what I was after," Alexander said before chuckling to himself, his face full of glee like a child in a toyshop. "Are you prepared to answer my questions?"

Catrina looked to Nathan, who had raised his head slightly at the sounds of Alexander's voice. Their eyes met, and a faint shake of his head told her to hold her tongue. His face was as bad as the rest of him, deep cuts that ran down his cheeks, and seeing what he had endured brought a tear to her eyes. If Nathan had suffered that much and kept his silence, it was her duty to try and do the same.

Catrina looked back to Alexander and smiled, though it was more forced than during their last encounter. Alexander gave her an inquisitive look before shrugging his shoulders and reaching behind him for one of his blades. "Last chance?" he offered, taking a step towards Nathan. "Tell me who you are, and I'll see that Nathan's wounds are tended to."

Catrina said nothing, though her tears betrayed her as Alexander slid the tip of the knife slowly into Nathan's flesh. Nathan raised his head, teeth gritted and eyes firmly closed as he held back the scream that was fighting to get out. Blood trickled down his chest and onto his abdomen, dripping to form a shallow pool at his feet.

"I'll ask you once before I cut him," Alexander continued. "Every time you refuse to answer, you'll cause Nathan to suffer. Who are you?"

Catrina's tears flowed freely now as she watched Alexander cut Nathan a second time, and then a third. Before each slice, Alexander asked her name, just once as he had promised. By the seventh cut, Nathan could no longer hold his tongue and cried out as the knife cut deep into his flesh.

"Stop, please," Catrina said quietly. "That's enough."

"Tell me your name?" Alexander replied, holding the knife poised against Nathan's right upper arm.

"Catrina," she told him. "Daughter-of-Ellabelle."

Alexander returned the knife to the table and stepped closer to Catrina, smiling down at her as he spoke. "You see?" he asked. "You see how easy that was, Catrina daughter-of-Ellabelle? You've done as I've asked, and now I shall do as I promised. I'll make sure Nathan's wounds are tended to, and tomorrow we can start again. Unless there's anything else you'd like to share this evening? Safran's whereabouts? Deacon's?"

Catrina shook her head, sobbing and unable to wipe away the tears than ran down her cheeks. She felt lost and alone, so vulnerable at that moment, as though she had betrayed everything that she believed in by surrendering her name. If she'd had to watch Alexander cut Nathan one more time, she would have told him anything.

"No?" Alexander continued, returning to the table where he used a dirty rag to wipe some of the blood from his hands. "Then don't worry, Catrina daughter-of-Ellabelle, we'll be back here tomorrow, and the day after that, until you tell me everything I want to know."

Alexander walked towards the door where, as he was about to summon the guards, he turned back to face her, a look of realisation upon his face. "You were at the dinner, in Island City," he said, looking very pleased with himself. "You were with the Road Train people, weren't you? I knew we'd met before."

Catrina said nothing, willing Alexander to leave, to get help for Nathan's wounds that continued to bleed as she watched. "You know where the boy is, don't you?" Alexander asked. "Benjamin Knight and his electricity?"

Catrina said nothing, staring at Alexander as he scrutinised the minute changes crossing her face.

"No matter, you'll tell me one way or another," Alexander said to himself, and with a self-satisfied smile he returned to his rooms to wash and change before dinner.

XI

It was almost midnight when Deacon and Bran edged along the rotten jetty situated below the theatre. Several of the planks were missing, forcing them to take cautious steps as they approached the far end where the rusted iron bracket protruded from the wall. There was no lantern hanging from it, but Deacon assumed it to be the switch that Saul had described.

After checking his footing, Deacon moved the bracket first to the right and then to the left, just as Saul had instructed. It moved much more easily than he had expected it to, as though it had been used recently, a thought that instantly put him on edge. He cast a wary glance towards Bran, who was having similar thoughts, before making the final half turn which rewarded him with the faintest of clicks and a hiss. As they watched, a section of the mould covered stone swung gently inwards, the only sound a faint squeak from the hidden hinges.

Bran went in first, the silenced pistol held before him, gripped in both hands. He moved it up to shoulder height as he edged around the partially opened door, ready to fire at the slightest movement. The faint glow from the moon illuminated little in the tunnel, but as far as Bran could see, he was alone. Deacon came in behind him, crouched low, ready to return fire or drag Bran backwards if needed.

Bran took two small, hesitant footsteps into the tunnel and stood still, eyes closed and listening. A faint wind moved towards them, carrying the smell of damp and mildew, but no sound travelled upon the breeze. Bran stood there for a minute or more, focussing upon all of his senses, but as far as he could tell, they were alone. With a nod of his head, more to himself than Deacon, he opened his eyes and took a one last step into the tunnel. Deacon stood to his full height and joined him, the door swinging shut behind them, a click as it locked them in.

The seal around the door was perfect, a testament to whoever had built it, and not a single shaft of light made its way through the door. They stood and waited for their eyes to adjust, but with no light from the opposite end of the tunnel, they were in total darkness. Bran reached for Deacon and turned him around, reaching into the pack upon his back. He removed the strange devices that Catrina had retrieved from Matthew's warehouse, handing one to Deacon and strapping the second onto his own head. They had experimented with them a little, though not as much as Bran would have liked, especially after Catrina had warned them that they worked by electricity, news that carried awe, fear and disbelief in equal measure.

Reluctantly, Bran reached up and flicked the switch. There was a flash in his vision and suddenly the tunnel was visible, painted in shades of green as the goggles turned night into day. He slid the goggles up on his forehead, convinced that the tunnel must have been lit by a torch or lantern, but without the goggles before his eyes, it remained as black as pitch. Sliding the goggles back down, he turned towards Deacon, whose teeth positively glowed as his smile widened.

"Let us be off," Deacon whispered, taking a further cautious step into the tunnel.

They made slow but steady progress, the goggles allowing them to make out any imperfections on the tunnel floor that may cause them to trip and fall. The tunnel looked to be man-made, hewn from the rock and earth beneath the city streets. It was approximately seven feet high, with wooden supports along its length, many showing signs of age. In other sections the roof had started to collapse, and they had to drop to all fours to make it through. He had ever been particularly claustrophobic, but without the benefit of the night vision goggles, Bran imagined that he would have had a hard time making it through.

Slowly the tunnel began to change, the rough floor lined with cobbles, the walls constructed of several beams or cemented blocks of stone. As they turned a sharp corner, their path was suddenly blocked by a large wooden door.

Bran tucked the pistol back into his waistband and knelt down in front of the door. He tried it gently, but it was securely locked. After listening for any sound from the opposite side, he set to work with his picks, making short work of the simple mechanism. Both men were skilled with locks, but Bran was perhaps a little faster, and as he depressed the final tumbler the door moved inwards slightly, allowing them access to the palace dungeons beyond.

The corridors in the palace dungeons were just like those of any other prison. Harsh stone walls that seemed to wind in and around themselves, the constant stench of death and decay, a sense of cramped spaces and foreboding that burrowed its way into the very bones of those entombed there. There were still no lanterns or torches as they made their way from one similar looking corridor to the next, the small slits in the numerous heavy doors showing only barren and decaying cells beyond. Nothing moved around them, as though even the rats had long since left the dungeons behind.

Both men were startled by a noise, a voice echoing along the corridor before them. They stopped dead in their tracks, pistols raised in a shooting stance as they strained to determine what the man was saying.

"...patch him up..." they heard one man say.

"...woman....bleeding...last the night...." another voice replied.

The sounds became quieter again, the words too difficult to make out as Deacon and Bran moved slowly along the corridor, almost silently on the balls of their feet. Deacon reached the corner first, his back pressed tightly against the wall as he edged his head around. The goggles made spotting them easy; two man-shaped blocks of green surrounded by a flickering halo, the light from the lantern one held before him. Seeing no one else in the distance, Deacon and Bran raised their pistols and steadied their breathing, aiming carefully for the back of each man's head. Upon squeezing the trigger, there was the softest of sounds before the guards slumped forwards onto the ground, dead before they realised that anything had happened to them.

Moving as quickly as they dared, Deacon and Bran checked that the guards were truly dead before dragging them back along the corridor and hiding their bodies in the nearest cell. Bran took a moment to extinguish the guard's lantern, its flame excessively bright through the goggles, before placing it beside the body and bolting the cell door.

After a wordless agreement between the two men, they set off again along the path that the guards had been taking. They had been talking about a man and a woman, Nathan and Catrina, Bran hoped, it had to be. He started walking a little faster, anxious that the guards had mentioned 'bleeding' and 'last the night', until a hand on his shoulder drew him to a stop.

Deacon had heard the faint cough, as if someone cleared their throat, though it appeared that Bran had somehow missed it. Deacon mimed for Bran to stay put while he edged forwards to get a better idea of what they faced. The corridor ended in nine stone steps, slippery beneath Deacon's feet as he cautiously ascended. Three from the top, he strained to listen as he leant forwards onto his stomach, looking first left and then right. The corridor atop the stairs ran in two directions, ending quickly in tight corners that led further into the dungeons. Deacon found it impossible to determine from which direction the sound had originated, and he lingered there for a while longer, waiting for something, anything, that may tell him which way to go next. Unfortunately, the man who had had cleared his throat was happy with the outcome and remained silent.

Deacon waved for Bran to follow him and directed him left at the top of the stairs whilst he went right, creeping slowly along until he neared the corner. Peering around, he was stunned to see three guards heading his way, a lantern held out before them, almost blinding him. He could run, but they would be on him within seconds, and he wouldn't have had time to warn Bran and to get away himself.

Sliding the goggles up onto his forehead, Deacon slowed his breathing and and checked his pistol. With a wicked smile, he stepped confidently around the corner and raised his pistol in one clean movement, shooting the lantern. The oil exploded over the foremost guard, engulfing him in flames. He screamed as he staggered back, waving his arms wildly as he fought to extinguish the fire that was consuming him, his two companions rushing forward to try and help. The fire illuminated them perfectly, and Deacon was able to shoot one and then the other with ease before ending the final guards misery with a perfectly placed bullet through his forehead.

Bran was suddenly there, gun raised, pushing Deacon to one side as he fought to get between his employer and the threat. The guards body was still burning brightly, and he too had to remove the goggles before he could fully inspect the scene.

"No more sneaking," Deacon whispered, a hand on Bran's shoulder. "Anyone that does not look like Nathan or Catrina, we put them down. Are we clear?"

"Sure, Deacon," Bran acknowledged. "You okay?"

"Never better," Deacon replied, and set off at a jog along the corridor, leaping nimbly over the flames.

Sounds of commotion echoed from somewhere ahead of them, shouts and calls to action, heavy footfalls upon the stone floor. Deacon slipped into one narrow doorway as Bran did the same on the wall opposite, both men once again relying on their night vision goggles. Four guards turned the corner in formation and focussed immediately upon the burning remains of their comrades, ignoring the shadows crouched only a short distance ahead of them. Deacon and Bran dispatched them quickly before stepping over their remains and moving deeper into the palace dungeons.

Sounds seem to come from all directions as they advanced, echoing back and forth along the narrow walls. The two men moved more slowly, Bran keeping an eye on the rear as Deacon continued the search. Every cell they passed was still empty, and looked as though it had been for some time. It wasn't until they turned into a more brightly lit corridor that the smell of death became overwhelming and the cells held the rotting remains of what looked to be palace servants and guards. Deacon quickly closed the narrow hatch he had opened in one of the cell doors, hoping to drive the odour back behind its rusted metal bolt.

Two more guards appeared before them, more cautious than the last, weapons raised. Deacon was able to kill the first, but the second managed to get off two shots before Bran ended his life. The bullet ricocheted off the wall to their right, and the sudden burning sensation in Deacon's right upper arm let him know that he had been hit. Transferring the pistol to his left hand, he quickly inspected the wound; a graze, nothing more. Bran was already moving ahead, swiftly replacing the clip in his gun as he did so.

There were more shouts and banging somewhere ahead of them. Bran was sure that the voice was higher, a woman's maybe, Catrina's. Deacon was close on his heels as they broke into a sprint, each step bringing them closer and closer to the source.

"Help me!" Catrina screamed, kicking her cell door. "In here! Help! In here!" Bran was there first, sliding back the latch and opening the viewing window. Catrina's face was suddenly in front of him, pressed tightly against the bars as though trying to squeeze between them.

"Step back," Bran insisted as he crouched down beside the

lock and set to work, Deacon trying to cover every direction at once.

"Where is Nathan?" Deacon asked her.

"Far end of the corridor," Catrina replied. "He's hurt, Deacon, he's hurt bad."

"We will get him out," Deacon assured her. "Just be ready."

Bran worked the tumblers until the door clicked open, Catrina throwing it wide as she burst into the corridor. "This way!" she yelled over her shoulder as she sprinted down the corridor ahead of her, Deacon only a step or two behind.

They found Nathan behind the third viewing window they opened, lying on the wooden cot and covered in blood stained bandages. Catrina fought with the handle before Bran moved her to one side and set to work on the lock. The sound of running footsteps was getting closer, and Bran passed Catrina his pistol as he worked to open the door. Deacon fired at something Catrina couldn't see, pushing her to the ground as bullets peppered the wall to his left.

"Bran," Deacon said quietly, the single word both a question and an instruction.

"Done," Bran replied as he opened the cell door and hurried inside, Catrina at his heels.

There was no light in the small cell, and only Bran's goggles allowed him to take in the full extent of Nathan's injuries. The bandages that wrapped his limbs and flesh looked a pale green in places, with dark patches of green in others, blood that had soaked through from the deep wounds below. Nathan barely responded to their presence in his cell.

"Nathan," Catrina said breathlessly, falling to her knees beside his cot. "I'm so sorry, I should have, just for my name-"

"Any time, people," Deacon called from the corridor as further bullets struck the wall beside him.

"Please, help me move him," Catrina begged, looking to Bran through tear stained eyes. He looked so strange, the goggles obscuring half of his face, but he nodded once and leant down to help Nathan to his feet. Nathan groaned as Bran slipped his arms beneath his shoulders, but he was just able to bear his own weight with Bran's support.

Deacon fired twice more into the gloom before moving

cautiously back along the corridor. Bran followed next, almost carrying Nathan as they made their way towards the tunnels, with Catrina at the rear, pistol raised and ready to fire. They took one turn and then another, the sound of footsteps still some way behind before Deacon stopped.

"What is it?" Catrina whispered, moving closer to him. "What do you see?"

"Follow Bran," Deacon replied. "He will lead you out of here."

"Deacon, wait," she continued. "What do you mean? What about you?"

"Alexander, the Regent," Deacon told her. "This is the closest that we have ever been to him. The palace is right above us and I will find him."

"No, you can't" Catrina pleaded. "There are too many guards, you won't make it on your own."

"Perhaps," Deacon agreed, "but for my boys, for your boys, for Nathan and his father, I must."

"No, Deacon, you don't understand," Catrina persisted, gripping tightly onto his sleeve. "Things have changed, with me, with everything. It's Nathan, I can help him, save him. You have to listen to me."

"I am sorry, Catrina," Deacon replied, "but nothing has changed. The Regent will die, or I will die. There is no other way."

Catrina slapped him, hard across his cheek. "Watch," she said, tearing at the bandages across Nathan's chest. Slamming her palm against one of the open wounds, she closed her eyes and willed for him to heal, to recover. The warmth washed over her again as her hand glowed blue, illuminating the corridor around them. Both Bran and Deacon slid their goggles up as the light intensified and the wound closed before their very eyes.

"You see," Catrina said breathlessly, slumping against the wall. "No one else has to die, not anymore, only him."

Deacon helped her to her feet, supporting her as the exhaustion that had consumed her slowly dissipated. He could think of nothing to say, unsure of what he had just witnessed and what it could mean. He knew that the chances of getting to the Regent were slim, but would they really have another chance to make him pay for what he had done? Catrina seemed to think so, and she was right, something was certainly different, but could he risk it?

The decision was made for him as further noise announced the approach of several more guards. "We have to leave, sir," Bran insisted, slipping the goggles back over his eyes and carrying Nathan towards the exit. Deacon looked to Bran and then to Catrina before nodding his head and joining them.

Light grew behind them as the guards neared the junction. Carrying Nathan, Deacon realised that they couldn't outrun their pursuers and dropped to a crouch with Catrina at his side, ready to take them on. "Keep moving," Deacon called behind him. "We will be right behind you." Bran grunted in agreement and moved as quickly as he could towards the exit.

"Distract them," Deacon ordered as he crouched down and slipped the backpack from his shoulders. Catrina readied her pistol and fired twice into the first man who came around the corner, knocking him back into his comrades as they scurried for cover. She fired again as another guard popped his head around, though this time failed to hit her target.

"Whatever you're doing," Catrina hissed as one of the guards fired blindly around the corner, "make it quick."

Deacon chuckled to himself as he slid the backpack along the floor and dragged Catrina to her feet. "Run," he said, turning and sprinting in the same direction that Bran had taken. Catrina didn't need telling twice and she was inches from his heels when the shock wave threw them both off their feet.

New Light

CHAPTER 3

We leave for Markay tomorrow or the day after, depending on when I can get the radios working. I was amazed at some of the bits and pieces they had for sale in the market, not that any of the stall holders knew what they were selling. Capacitors, diodes, copper wire, speakers, they had everything I needed, some of it already assembled into components I could use. It reminded me of some of the bits and pieces Matthew had for sale on the Road Trains, but the merchants here could give him a run for his money.

I can't say I'm looking forward to the boat ride though, I feel sick just thinking about it. I've only been on the cross channel ferry once, and it was the worst experience of my life. I bet they don't have travel sickness tablets either.

Where's Boots the Chemist when you need it?

I

Alexander felt the explosion before he heard it, a deep rumbling beneath his feet that shook the walls of the throne room around him. As he watched, a deep crack opened up in the south wall, a fine mist of plaster dust drifting down on the night air.

Everything had been going so well. He had remembered the woman from the Road Trains, and already she was opening up to him. True, she had only told him her name, but that was just the beginning. He knew how to manipulate her, to control her, and a few more cuts to Nathan would have had her telling him everything. Everyone had their weakness, and he had found hers so easily.

If only he knew how she was able to heal like she did. It had to be a power, like his he supposed, but different too. He could change how people felt, how they thought, but it was nothing like the power that she demonstrated, knitting together lacerated flesh and broken bones.

Once he had learned everything that he could from her, he had planned to experiment on her, to discover what made her so different to him and all of the other people out there. What else could she do? What were her limits? He had already seen that she couldn't grow back a severed toe, but what if it was a hand? An arm? Her head?

No, there would be no more fun to be had, no more secrets to be learned. Something had happened, someone had made a monumental mistake, and once he discovered who he would make them pay.

Alexander walked purposefully from the throne room, not running but with a stride that told anyone who saw it to get out of his way. He was met in the long corridor by several of his personal guard, their pristine uniforms marked with dust and dirt.

"Explain," Alexander demanded of the man closest to him, a wide eyed officer who seemed dazed and disorientated. Alexander grabbed him by the shoulders and turned him until their eyes met, shaking him until he seemed to focus again on the world around them.

"My, my Liege," the guard stammered, as though recognising

the Regent for the first time. Alexander pushed him aside, searching instead for someone who could tell him what he needed to know.

The guard at the rear of the group appeared to be directing the remaining guards away from the dust filled stairwell and up into the long corridor and out of the palace. Alexander placed a hand on his shoulder, drawing his attention. He was as filthy as the other guards in the corridor, but held a determined gaze and commanding demeanour.

"Regent," the guard said as he turned to see who had interrupted him. "I implore you to leave, this area isn't safe."

"Tell me what happened," Alexander demanded.

"Safran or her conspirators, they managed to get into the dungeons somehow," the guard began. "They freed the prisoners and detonated an explosive. Much of the dungeon has collapsed and the lower floors too, the palace may come down around us. My Liege, please, get to safety."

"Were the prisoners caught in the explosion?" Alexander asked.

"We have no way of knowing," the guard replied. "Several of my, I mean your men, sir, were down there when blast hit them. How many were trapped, how many survived, I, I don't know."

Alexander sighed. "Escort your men to the courtyard," he commanded, "and send for the physicians and any stone masons within the city. I want the Elders and the Merchants brought here too, and somebody bring me Larson!"

II

Catrina's head was ringing, a droning buzz that seemed to echo within her skull as she struggled to her feet, feeling her way in the absolute darkness that surrounded her. She staggered forwards two steps, her hands finding a coarse stony surface, though if it was part of the wall or the remains of the collapsed tunnel she was unable to tell.

The dark had never scared her before, but it was different somehow, terrifying in a way she had never imagined. Her mind was screaming that she was trapped, buried alive beneath the streets of her home city, lost and alone to await her fate.

A hand on her shoulder made her catch her breath as she felt herself being spun around on the spot, her arms flailing in front of her as she attempted to fight off the invisible attacker.

"Calm yourself," Deacon said to her. "It is me. I still have Ben's night time spectacles, and I can see a way out."

"Deacon?" Catrina asked, the lump in her throat starting to subside. "What about Nathan, and Bran? Are they okay?"

"They were ahead of us when the explosives detonated," Deacon replied. "We will go and find them."

Deacon led the way, Catrina's hands on his shoulders, turning when he turned, ducking when he ducked. She could see nothing at all, not even the faintest flicker or glimmer of light. Time seemed impossible to measure as they made their way through the tunnels. At one point, Deacon took her hands in his and directed her to lie on the floor, scurrying along on her stomach beneath an unseen obstacle. A short while later, he caught her as she tripped over a chunk of stone that now lay in her path. They could have been going around in circles for all she knew.

"I see them," Deacon said as they turned a corner, hurrying ahead as Catrina struggled to keep up. What she couldn't know, but what Deacon could see clearly in shades of green, was that Bran was standing beneath a wooden beam, bracing it against his back as he fought to stay upright.

"About time," Bran mumbled breathlessly as he adjusted his footing, keeping the ceiling from falling and blocking their path. Deacon said nothing, pausing only to tap his friend comfortingly on the shoulder as he directed Catrina through the small gap. Deacon followed as quickly as he could before wrapping his arms around Bran's waist, ready to pull him as far from the falling stone as he could. Bran counted down, three, two, one, and on the last count, Deacon pulled for all he was worth, dragging his closest companion away from the falling rubble. They fell in a heap, laughing at yet again cheating death.

"What is it?" Catrina asked nervously, the unexpected laughter echoing all around her.

"I am sorry, Catrina," Deacon said. "Everything is fine. It is something of a tradition to laugh in the face of danger. Come, the exit is nearby."

Deacon helped Nathan to his feet, supporting him as Bran led the way to the exit. From that side, there was only a simple lever to open the door, not the combination mechanism Deacon had used only a few hours before.

Outside it was still night time, but travelling as they did from absolute darkness, Catrina still had to shield her eyes a little from the brightness of the moon and stars above. Bran returned the night vision goggles to his backpack, tying it securely, while Deacon supported Nathan as the two men made their unsteady progress along the dilapidated gantry.

"Thanks for coming," Nathan managed to mutter as he winced with every stumbling step.

"We may not have always been on the same side," Deacon said quietly, "but you have always been honourable and true to your word. I hope you now see that we are not so different." Nathan nodded once as he began the painful climb up the stairs.

The streets south of the river were almost deserted, a light rain their only company as they took back roads and alleyways towards the brewery. Progress was slow as Nathan struggled to maintain even the slowest of speeds without needing to rest and recover from the agony that racked his entire body. Deacon knew that the Watch would be out in force, but hoped that following the explosion they would focus on the palace and associated district before searching wider afield. Bran and Catrina kept a careful eye for any sign of pursuit, as well as checking corners and darkened passages before Nathan braved them, and just as the sun began to brighten the horizon, they were descending the metal stairs that led deeper into the brewery.

Stan, Gavin, Sanjay and Dean all leapt as one as the door to the hidden room opened. The questions that hung on their lips stopped abruptly as they saw Nathan, their mouths hanging agape as Deacon helped him onto one of the cots at the rear of the room.

"What happened...is he?" Stan asked as he took an involuntary step towards the cot.

"I can help him," Catrina announced as she hurried past Stan, dropping her weapons and backpack onto the table as she passed.

"What do you need?" Stan asked, desperate to help the man who had been there for him for most of his life.

"Just give me some space," Catrina replied. "Deacon?"

Deacon remained standing beside the cot, the only remaining obstacle to Catrina and her desire to help the man who had suffered so much for her. "There is a lot we need to discuss," Deacon reminded her.

"And we will, I'll tell you everything," Catrina promised. "Please, just let me help him first, let me save him."

Deacon looked towards Nathan, and then back to Catrina, nodding once before stepping aside. Catrina dropped to her knees beside the cot, pushing more bandages out of the way. She placed one hand on Nathan's upper chest and the other on his abdomen, closing her eyes as she focussed upon the man before her. Each time she used her power, she found it a little easier to call forward, coaxing forth the heat that seemed to nestle within her chest. It washed down her arms and into Nathan, spreading out from her palms to find every injury.

The others watched as Catrina's hands began to glow, a deep blue that grew in intensity before enveloping Nathan, sparking around the many lacerations that covered his body. If Nathan's injuries had shocked them, it was nothing to watching them close impossibly before their eyes, broken skin knitting together as the light grew brighter and brighter. They each found themselves shielding their eyes but reluctant to look away, and as quickly as the light had appeared it was suddenly gone, leaving behind only an after image.

As they lowered their hands from their eyes, they watched as Catrina slumped forwards, her head resting on Nathan's naked torso. Deacon hurried towards them and, after checking her neck for a pulse, picked Catrina up and laid her gently on the adjacent cot.

"What happens now?" Stan asked.

"Now?" Deacon replied. "We wait."

III

"You there," Alexander demanded. "What's your name?"

"Malcolm, my Liege," the stunned looking stonemason replied. "Son-of-Thomas."

"So tell me, Malcolm son-of-Thomas," Alexander continued, "what do you have to report?"

"The damage is extensive, Regent," Malcolm told him. "Many of the lower levels have already collapsed, or will do so shortly. The kitchens, I wouldn't recommend using them until my men and I can add some additional supports to the floor."

"Yes, yes," Alexander interrupted. "And what of the throne room and my chambers?"

"The south side of the palace fared better," Malcolm said quickly, "but the crack along the throne room worries me. We'll put up some additional supports until they can more fully examine the roof and outer walls."

"Get to it," Alexander told him. "Your men will work around the clock, do you hear me?"

"Yes, yes, my Liege," Malcolm stammered before bowing and returning to his colleagues.

Alexander returned to Samuel Larson, who was stood beneath the large crack in the throne room's ceiling. "Are you safe here?" Samuel asked.

"For now," Alexander replied. "What do you have to tell me?"

Samuel hesitated, the anger on Alexander's face already plain to see. "My men have been unable to find any signs of how they accessed the dungeons," he said, unable to look Alexander in the eye. "Some of the local Watchmen tell of rumours of a tunnel, a secret way in and out of the palace, but no one seems to know anything more than that. The information we have so far seems to suggest that, whoever got into the dungeons, perished in the subsequent explosion."

"And what information is that?" Alexander said, his voice rising as he turned on Samuel.

"It's just," Samuel began, but Alexander cut him off before he could say any more.

"Facts, Larson," Alexander said, poking him in the chest. "No theories, no suggestions, just facts. I want to know how they got in. I want to know what they did whilst they were in here. I want to know if they got out again, and I want to know where they are now. Am I making myself clear?"

"I, just, my Liege," Samuel tried, but Alexander cut him off again.

"It was a simple yes or no question," he yelled. "Am. I.

CLEAR!"

"Yes, yes my Liege," Samuel said quietly. "Most clear."

Alexander took a deep breath, closing his eyes as he composed himself. The surrounding Watchmen, guards and stonemasons were all trying their best not to watch as Alexander tore strips from the Commander of the City Watch, but it was theatre too intrusive to ignore.

"So, Larson," Alexander continued, his voice measured and controlled. "The information you have that leads you to believe that the terrorists were killed in the explosion?"

Samuel stayed silent, the sound of his heart beating in his ears drowning out his thoughts. "No, you know nothing, do you," Alexander said scornfully.

Samuel was growing a darkening shade of red the more Alexander spoke, holding his fists clenched at his sides. "I will return to my enquiries," he said at last, turning towards the long corridor, eyes fixed firmly upon the marble at his feet.

"See that you do," Alexander said bitterly. "And I do not expect to see you again until you can bring me facts. Or better still, heads. Yours or theirs, I no longer care."

Samuel strode from the throne room without another word.

IV

Shortly after lunch, Matthew spotted the hamlet in the distance. As they drew closer, it became clear that the river passed through the eastern region of the small town, a few houses and a mill to either side.

"Mooring fee is ten Deniras a night," the young man on the jetty called out.

"We'll only be here a little while," Marcus called back. "We just need a few supplies and we'll be on our way."

"Still cost you ten," the young man replied, arms crossed as though he could wait there all day.

Marcus nodded and tossed him the mooring rope as Matthew steered from the back of the boat. Once the boat was secured, Marcus stepped from the boat and handed the young man his money.

"I'm here every day," the young man informed him, "just in

case you need anything. If I'm not about, ask at the tavern for Scratch."

"Scratch?" Marcus asked, a little taken aback by the unusual name.

"Don't ask," Scratch said with a grin. "Some things, people never forget." Marcus nodded in agreement and stepped back onto the boat.

"We need to warn them," Arian was saying to Matthew as she checked the supplies. "The northern army, they could be here in a matter of days."

"We will," Matthew assured her, "but let's just make sure we get enough food for the rest of the journey first. I've never travelled this far south before, and I don't know how long it'll take to get to Ashford."

"At least another four days," Marcus informed them. "If the wind stays at our back."

"We could make this last four days," Arian said, holding the food up to Matthew's face.

"You're right," Matthew replied, placing a comforting hand on her shoulder. "I'm sorry. Let's speak to the town and get on our way. We'll make do with what we have."

Arian took his hand in hers and brought it to her lips, kissing it gently. "Thank you," she said, smiling up at him.

Marcus and Juliet remained on board whilst Matthew and Arian made the short journey from the jetty to the middle of town. A single tavern, flanked to either side by a butcher's and a general store, was surrounded by perhaps thirty or forty houses arranged in a loose circle. They were a way east of the Great Road, and it looked as though the locals used the river to transport the flour that they ground at the mill, as well as bring in any supplies that they couldn't make themselves or harvest from the farms.

The tavern, The Watership Down according to the sign hanging over the door, was warm and welcoming. The barman gave them both a friendly wave as they entered. "Afternoon," he bellowed with a grin. "What'll it be?"

"Good afternoon," Matthew replied. "Two pints and perhaps a minute of your time?"

"Grab a seat," the barman told them. "I'll bring the drinks

over."

Matthew and Arian sat at a small table to the left of the door. The two other patrons ignored them for the most part, nursing their own drinks as they pondered whatever troubles had brought them to the tavern in the middle of the day. A moment later, the barman sat himself down beside them, splashing the table with ale as he placed the two full mugs before them.

"That'll be four Deniras," he announced, holding his hand out.

"Thank you," Matthew said, handing him the money. "And for your time?"

"My time's free, as long as you're drinking," the barman said with a knowing smile. "You come down by river?"

"We have," Matthew told him.

"We've fled the fighting to the north," Arian added. "Near Aldonis."

"Fighting you say?" the barman replied. "There's been rumours these last few weeks, mutterings from the traders, but that was Draxis and Phalathlan at it again. They didn't say nothing about Oster getting involved."

"It's not Draxis, or Phalathlan," Matthew insisted. "It's an army from Island City, and they're coming this way."

"What?" the barman exclaimed. "Like in the old stories? You're having a laugh, surely?"

"It's true, I promise you," Arian said, placing a hand upon the Barman's arm. "Is there a local Elder, or a Magistrate? Someone we can talk to, please?"

"I don't know what sort of game you're playing," the barman said, rising to his feet, "but I'll thank you to finish your drinks and be on your way."

"No games," Matthew said, standing. "We're heading south, as far as we can. You should think about doing the same, you and the people here-"

"The people here," the barman interrupted, "are decent, hard working folk. We don't have time for nonsense, so I'd appreciate it if you you'd just leave us out of it. Whatever grudge Draxis and Phalathlan have with each other, it's got nothing to do with us.

"Here," he said, tossing the four Deniras onto the table. "Find somewhere else to tell your stories."

By then the other patrons were watching the proceedings, waiting to see if it would descend into violence. Arian began to protest until Matthew placed a hand on her shoulder. "Thank you for your time," he said. "We'll be on our way." The barman glared at them as they made their way into the afternoon sunshine.

"There has to be someone else that we can talk to," Arian insisted once they were outside.

"Perhaps," Matthew agreed, "but do you really think they'll listen? We're strangers, and a small town like this, they'll only trust what they know."

"It's just," Arian said, searching for an answer.

"I know," Matthew said comfortingly, kissing her forehead. "At least we tried, and you never know, once the barman starts telling his customers about us, maybe they'll reconsider. Go and help Marcus ready the boat, please. I'll get what we need from the store."

Arian nodded dejectedly and returned to the boat.

V

Ben was leant over the collection of components, a pair of tweezers in his hand as he fixed the capacitor into the circuit. He had managed to find most of what he needed, and a spool of copper wire and an old clock radio had allowed him to build the rest. He didn't notice Safran enter the makeshift workshop, and almost jumped out of his skin when she tapped him on the shoulder.

"Ben, it's just me," she said, laughing as Ben almost fell from his seat, his face a mask of terror and confusion. The resistors and capacitors were scattered as he scrambled to stay upright.

"Safran," Ben exclaimed. "I just, it's, are you okay?"

"I just thought I should come and check on you," Safran said coyly. "You've hardly left this room all day."

"It's easier to work without any distractions," Ben told her.

"Oh, so I distract you, do I?" Safran said quietly, leaning closer to him as she spoke.

"No, it's not that," Ben said quickly, feeling his face flush as Safran leaned in.

"So I don't distract you?" Safran replied, taking a step back. "Do you even notice if I'm around or not?"

"I didn't say that," Ben stammered, his face almost glowing as it went from pink to red.

"So what are you saying," Safran demanded, fighting to hold back the smile as she pretended to pout. Ben opened and closed his mouth, struggling for the right thing to say. She stared at him for as long as she could until the giggles overwhelmed her.

"You're just too easy," Safran said at last. "Come on, it's time to eat, and the Baron won't be kept waiting." Ben nodded and followed her wordlessly to the door.

"You know what," Safran said as they entered the corridor. "I'm really pleased that you're coming with me to Markay. It wouldn't be the same without you." Ben smiled and blushed even more as she led him by the hand towards the dining hall.

VI

Alexander stepped confidently onto the balcony, taking a moment to examine the crack running through the outside wall of the throne room as the crowd below watched. With a theatrical shake of his head, he turned and leant over the stone railing, looking down at those below him.

He didn't extend his will, he didn't need to. He wasn't trying to convince the people of anything, he wasn't hoping to sway their opinion. It was time for the gloves to come off, and for the people below him to be punished.

"People of Maleton," he announced. "This is a grim day for the alliance between us. As you will no doubt have heard, last night Safran and her rebels staged a cowardly attack on this very building, detonating a bomb in the cellars beneath the palace. If they were hoping to harm me, they failed, yet again, but sadly they succeeded in killing many of the staff and servants inside. They also managed to kill the prisoners that were to be questioned here, which I suspect was their plan all along. It would have been only a matter of time before they were convinced of the error of their actions and told us all that they knew.

"This is the second terrorist attack in less than a week, and there can only be one conclusion. They are being aided and supported by citizens of this city."

There was a cacophony of noise as the people below looked to their friends and neighbours, searching for those Alexander that was speaking of. Alexander raised his hands, and the crowd was quickly silenced.

"I have been kind," he continued, "and I have been patient, understanding even, but that stops now. Every day, I am informed of more dead Watchmen, more cowardly attacks, and still we're no closer to apprehending Safran and her conspirators. This ends today.

"I am implementing measures to safeguard the security of this city and its people. The curfew will be enforced by any means necessary. Anyone found out after dark will be detained and questioned until I am satisfied with the answers they give. Anyone who resists will be shot.

"Anyone with known ties to Safran and her supporters will be detained and questioned. Anyone suspected of being involved with the rebels will be questioned. If you have acted against this city in the past, you will be questioned. And anyone who my officers believe may be involved in some way, will be questioned. Any and all resistance will be dealt with most harshly.

"Now, if you have done nothing wrong you have nothing to hide, but I will end this. If you disagree with me, blame me, don't. Blame the terrorists who threaten our safety. Blame your friends and neighbours who support their abominable acts. Look to yourself, and ask what more you can do.

"If you bring me the rebels, life will go back to normal, but until then, I will do everything in my power to stop them.

"Return to your homes," Alexander said as he turned towards his throne room. "You have an hour until curfew."

VII

It was well after midnight when Samuel Larson returned home, and he was surprised to find Marie waiting up for him. "I thought you'd be in bed," he said as he hung up his jacket.

"I missed you," Marie said, flashing a most flirtatious smile.

"This morning seems like a lifetime ago."

Samuel paused to lean down and kiss her before removing his boots. "Just one more awful day in a week, no, a month of awful days. I'm sick of it, his outbursts and his rants. I've had enough."

"Sit yourself down," Marie suggested. "Let me get you a drink."

She left for the kitchen and returned a moment later, a bottle of liquor and a full glass in her hands. Samuel downed the glass in one before holding it out for Marie to refill. She did so with a smile before sitting down next to him, resting her hand on his.

"I heard about the speech," she said. "Stephanie came by before curfew. I'm surprised the council agreed to it, but I suppose it was the palace that was attacked."

"And that's all my fault too, apparently," Samuel replied, finishing his second glass which Marie promptly refilled. "I just don't get it," he continued. "I follow his orders to the letter, and still I'm wrong.

"And now this, rounding people up just because someone thinks they might be involved. No evidence, nothing. The Regent spent all that time convincing the Elders and the people about his intentions, I mean, he even organised that whole mock trial just to-"

Samuel knew he'd made a mistake as soon as the words left his mouth. He looked down at the glass in his hand, noticing for the first time that he was already a little woozy from the two large drinks in quick succession.

Marie was staring at him, her mouth agape. "What do you mean?" she asked. "Baron Stephen's trial?"

"I'm sorry, I," Samuel began. "No, not that, I didn't mean, no, not that trial."

"Sam, please," Marie said soothingly. "You can tell me. I know you, I love you. Whatever happened, whatever you did, I know you didn't have a choice. You were just following orders."

Samuel considered it, the secrets he knew, the things he'd done in the Regent's name. How many people had died at his hand, just because Alexander had told him to? And then to speak to him like that, in front of everybody? Blaming him for everything that had gone wrong with the grand plan.

No, he'd done everything that the Regent had ever asked of him, and that was how he was treated. And now, sat with the woman he loves, a woman who loved him back, was he really going to choose Alexander over her?

"Samuel?" Marie asked again.

"The Baron's trial," Samuel began, speaking quietly. "I don't know everything that happened back in Island City, but I know that some of the evidence was manufactured to convince the Elder Council. The Regent, Alexander, he's got all these plans, secrets within secrets.

"Safran's escape from the dungeons. Phalathlan. Oster. It's all part of something bigger, something to do with a boy and a laboratory with electricity."

"Electricity?" Marie interrupted, clearly confused. "What have children's stories got to do with all of this?"

"That's it," Samuel replied. "I don't know. Honestly, I think he's losing it, losing his mind. I hear him sometimes, talking to himself about it. And then, with Janis. Elder Janis. He asked the wrong questions, asked about electricity. He had to be silenced."

"So, the rebels?" Marie asked once she had let it sink in.

"No," Samuel continued, "they didn't. It wasn't them. Nor Elder Mathis. Alexander's responsible, for everything."

Marie took the drink from his hand and downed it in one. She felt as though she didn't really know the man that she had shared so much of herself with. "What now?" she asked, anxious of what he may do now that she knew the truth.

"Now, I try to get some sleep," he told her, "before it starts all over again." He looked at her and noticed how pale she had become.

"That's not what you meant though, is it?" he asked. Marie shook her head nervously. "I won't let him hurt you," he assured her. "I promise. Me and you, that's what's important, not him and his plans. I'm here for you, always."

Marie smiled and kissed him, chaste at first and then more passionately, before allowing him to lead her to the bedroom.

VIII

The battle had lasted two days, the siege weapons making

short work of the town defences. The fighting rapidly spread to the streets, young and old, rich and poor, all standing together in defence of their homes. Boshtok had been relentless, driving his soldiers forward, cutting down any and all resistance without hesitation.

He marvelled at the level of destruction as he strolled casually through the streets. All around him, buildings still smouldered and smoked as the fires spread rapidly. The smell of burnt wood, with a second aroma of charred flesh, filled his nostrils.

He felt pride as he marvelled at his success. He had achieved something that no other officer in the Island City army had ever managed before him, the complete destruction of a Barony stronghold, and a capital at that. Those that fled the city had been allowed to do so, and those that stood against him had fought with honour. Now nothing remained but his victory.

"General," the young officer said, drawing Boshtok back to the present. "Your Senior Officers have gathered as requested and await your orders."

"Good job, Hastings," Boshtok replied. "Let them know I'll be along shortly." Hastings saluted and sprinted towards the centre of the city, leaving Boshtok to continue his leisurely stroll.

His route brought him back to The Fosseway, the tarmac now strewn with rubble. The palace in the distance still burned, the dark smoke rising high into the air. It became his beacon, his marker as he made his way towards his soldiers. Before long, he was crossing the Justice Bridge, smiling at the name and its history.

His troops had successfully destroyed the Overlook, Beggars and Copsway bridges, but left the route to the palace open. The enemy had been funnelled there, backs against the River Talon, with nowhere to run or hide. From that point on it had been easy.

Many of his troops had gathered upon Hangman's Bluff, drinking and singing as they celebrated their victory. Those he passed cheered his name, offering drunken salutes and mugs of ale. Boshtok returned the salutes and declined the ale, wishing to keep a clear head for his meeting.

Boshtok stepped into the palace courtyard, where his tent had already been assembled, illuminated by the flames that still licked from the palace windows. His officers waited for him inside, standing to salute him as he entered. Boshtok smiled and returned the salute before taking his seat at the head of the table.

"General," Major Bravil said. "Your victory here is unprecedented. If you would allow me, I would propose a toast." He paused while glasses were raised aloft. "To General Boshtok, honourable in battle, noble in victory, and forever stout of heart. We salute you!"

There was a shout from the others of 'we salute you' as the glasses of wine and mugs of ale were clashed together before their contents consumed. Boshtok smiled and returned to his feet.

"Men and women of this great nation," Boshtok began. "This is not a victory for me. This day is a victory for all, for every man, woman and child who swears allegiance to Island City.

"No more will we be dictated to by our enemies. No longer will we cower and hide, fearful of what our southern oppressors might say. Today we have taken back our freedom. Today we have torn up the treaty of Aldonis and cast it to the flames. Today we have honoured both our ancestors and our children!

"To Island City, free at last!"

"Free at last!" they cried out in unison, draining what remained in their glasses before reaching to refill them. Boshtok returned to his seat and met them with a measured look.

"Take this night and celebrate," he told them. "Join in with those you command and take pleasure in your victory, but know that this war is far from over.

"Bravil, tomorrow you will take half of our forces and march east, just as you did in Phalathlan. Let any and all know that they are now citizens of Island City. I suspect that you will encounter forces from the Oster Military, so give them the chance to surrender and join you. Cut down any that refuse, and leave them as a marker to those who would stand against us.

"The remainder of our forces will rejoin the Great Road and march south towards Morton. Bravil, once you are happy that Oster is secure, join us at the border. Ashford shall be ours before the end of the month!"

"Thank you, General," Bravil replied, momentarily lost for words, "for granting me this responsibility. I will not fail you."

Boshtok smiled. "Go, all of you," he said, "and enjoy."

IX

Catrina woke in the middle of the afternoon, groggy at fist and ravenously hungry. Nathan had surfaced an hour or two before with little memory of what had happened in the dungeons, but he was quick to fill Deacon and Bran in on the night at the theatre. Deacon had heard most of the details from Stan and Gavin, and the pieces that he had put together himself tied in perfectly with what Nathan told him.

"How do you feel now?" Deacon asked.

"Better thanks," Catrina replied between mouthfuls of bread and jam.

"I am pleased," Deacon replied, "though I am still not clear on what happened. Nathan was near to death when we found him."

"You know," Nathan interrupted, "you think I'd stop feeling so sick each time you say that out loud."

"We were all really worried," Stan added. "We tried to wake you, to get you to eat something, but nothing worked."

"It was the same after the theatre," Catrina told them. "I think, when I use the, power or whatever it is, it takes it out of me, drains me somehow."

"This, power as you put it," Deacon continued. "Where did you find it? Is it like the night time spectacles Ben gave to you?"

"No, it's," Catrina began, searching for words. "It's not tech, like the glasses. It's something else, I, I don't know how to explain it."

"It's okay, take your time," Stan offered.

"Nathan," Catrina said. "Do you remember when Matthew and Carl left, when we were in Deacon's warehouse? I told you about Victor?"

"You weren't really yourself," Nathan said honestly. "A lot of what you said didn't make much sense."

Catrina smiled. Nathan was right, she had let her grief overwhelm her and was lost in a world of pain. Discovering that Alexander was still alive had brought her back, restored her purpose and determination.

"No," she agreed. "I wasn't. Well Victor, he was someone I met in the Wastelands, in a town called Sanctuary. He told me I was a healer, that I could heal myself and others. I didn't believe him, I mean, it sounds crazy, doesn't it? But he could do things too, strange things. He proved it to me, made me burn my hand in a fire. I couldn't resist."

Deacon sat forwards, visibly disturbed by what she had said. "His name?" he asked, gripping her arm tighter than he intended. "You said his name was Victor?"

"That's what he told me," Catrina replied, the pain from Deacon's grip visible upon her face.

"You are sure he said Victor?" Deacon demanded.

"Deacon," Bran said quietly, placing a hand on his employer's shoulder. "I think you're hurting her."

Deacon looked down at his fist, the knuckles white as he squeezed Catrina's arm. He released his grip slowly. "I apologise," he said. "My mind, it was elsewhere."

"What is it?" Nathan asked.

"A story for another time," Deacon replied sombrely. "The man you described, he reminded me of someone I used to know. He is dead now. Please, Catrina, do continue."

Nathan, Bran and Catrina exchanged confused looks, but Deacon remained silent, waiting for Catrina to continue her tale. "Victor told me that he thought I'd inherited my ability from my mother," she continued. "Just as he had inherited his from his father. If I would just accept it, try to use it, I could eventually learn to control it. He was right. Every time I heal, it gets easier."

"And what of the dungeons?" Deacon asked, his voice returning to normal. "You were clearly tortured, what did they learn?"

"Nothing, Deacon," Nathan said quickly. "Just like I said when I woke up. They don't know where you are, I swear it."

"Catrina?" Deacon prompted.

"I told him my name," she admitted. "He remembered me, from Island City. Nathan's right though, we told him nothing else." Deacon nodded, accepting them at their word.

"So what now?" Stan asked.

"Now we continue the fight," Deacon replied. "While you were sleeping, Alexander began rounding up anyone he thinks may be involved with us. Our true allies are safe, but his actions are becoming more reckless. He is finally scared."

"Then this is our chance!" Nathan announced. "People won't stand for that, surely? They'll finally see Alexander for the liar he is."

"That's a good point," Bran said. "Maybe it's time to start increasing our numbers?"

"Perhaps," Deacon agreed. "But I doubt it will be so easy. True, there may be some who finally see that what he is doing is wrong, but so many others will stand by and watch, believing that it is for the greater good, or that he is right in his actions. Even those who know that his actions are wrong will say nothing, not daring to step away from the crowd and bring attention upon themselves."

"So what?" Nathan asked. "We just do nothing? Or carry on the same as before? We won't get another chance against the Regent, not like we had in the theatre."

"You are right," Deacon agreed. "We will not have another such chance against Alexander. We alone will not finish this fight, but we must be wary of who we allow to learn of our intentions. Should the Watch learn of this place, everything could be lost.

"Bran, I would like you to visit Jimmy, see if we may make use of his rooms. Do not pressure him, and if he declines, there are to be no repercussions. Make sure that he is aware of that before he decides. Stan, perhaps you will accompany him?"

"Of course," Stan agreed.

"If we can make use of suitable rooms," Deacon continued, "we can try and make contact with others like us, those who see the Regent for what he really is."

"I'll go tomorrow, before he opens," Bran said with grin.

"Nathan, Catrina," Deacon continued. "Your faces are too well known. You will need to remain here for the time being."

"I could do with the rest," Nathan said. "I should probably take a couple of days before I'm *near death* again."

Gavin chuckled, though the others at the table failed to see the humour.

X

Marie paced around the kitchen, the food on the table long

since gone cold. Samuel was late, as usual, and every minute that ticked by was another minute she had convinced herself that he wasn't coming home at all.

She still hadn't gotten over what happened just a few weeks before, the explosion that had killed two Watchmen and nearly taken Samuel from her. Now that she knew the details of what Alexander had done, and how deep Samuel was involved in it all, she didn't think she'd ever get a restful night's sleep again.

"Marie," Samuel called out as he pushed open the front door. "I'm sorry I'm late. I bet dinner's ruined?"

Marie rushed from the kitchen at the sound of his voice, wrapping her arms around him before he had even had chance to remove his coat. "What was that for?" he asked, leaning down to kiss her.

"Do I need a reason?" Marie asked, smiling up at him. "The food's cold, but it wouldn't be the first time you ate it that way."

Samuel slipped of his coat and boots before joining Marie at the table, tucking in to the cold meat and vegetables as Marie looked on. After three large forkfuls, Samuel paused. "It won't always be like this," he promised her.

"Like what?" Marie asked. "Late nights and early mornings? Being dragged out of bed at all hours when The Regent wants to yell at you about something? It's been like this since the first day I met you."

Samuel put his fork down and gave her his full attention. "I know," he said. "It's just, these last few weeks, everything seems to be going wrong. And now, with all these tips about possible supporters we're getting. It's non-stop."

"You need to learn to say no," Marie said. "Make the Regent find someone else to do his dirty work."

"With what I know?" Samuel exclaimed. "With, with what I've done? Do you really think he'd let me walk away?"

"So if Safran and her supporters don't kill you," Marie cried, "Alexander will? Is that what you're saying?"

Samuel left his seat and placed an arm around Marie, pulling her close as the tears began to flow. "No one's going to hurt me," he told her. "Not again. I'll be fine. We'll be fine."

"How can you say that?" Marie sobbed. "You're dragging people from their homes, questioning them, and who knows what else. Any one of them could be involved with Safran and he followers."

"I might not agree with the orders," Samuel replied, "but I still have to follow them. You know that. Besides, I'm never on my own out there. I've always got someone covering my back."

"It's just," Marie told him. "I can't lose you. Every time you go out that door, I'm scared you won't come back."

"We're getting closer," Samuel said. "I know it. It won't be long before Safran and Deacon are in the dungeons or dead. Without someone at the head, their supporters will fade back into the background, you wait and see."

Marie wiped her eyes with the back of her hands. "You really think that?" she asked.

"I think Deacon or members of his gang were killed in the explosion at the palace," Samuel told her.

"And Safran?" Marie continued.

"I don't think she's even in the city anymore," Samuel replied. "There's been no reported sightings of her for weeks now. Come on, let's leave the dishes until tomorrow."

"Maybe it should be you up there in the palace," Marie suggested. "The things you tell me make a lot more sense than what the Regent announces from his balcony."

"That's kind of you to say," Samuel said, wiping away the last of her tears with his thumb. "Just don't ever say it outside of these walls, he's got spies everywhere."

The ice cold shiver that ran down her spine froze her to the spot.

XI

Matthew caught sight of the torches shortly after midnight. The others were sleeping in the cabin, and Matthew waited until he was confident in his assessments before he woke them.

"What is it?" Marcus asked as he peered into the dark, his eyes still half closed with sleep.

"It's either a town or a fort of some kind," Matthew told him, "but looking at the way the torches flow upwards, I'd wager my last Deniras on it being military."

"Underbrook Lodge," Marcus said. "One of the three main

garrisons outside of Ashford, and the only one on the banks of the river as far as I remember. Have they spotted us?"

"I haven't seen anything," Matthew replied, "but I'd be surprised if they haven't."

"Do you think they'll stop us?" Arian asked, her voiced tinged with concern.

"The river's used for trade in and out of Ashford," Marcus told her. "They'll likely have someone inspecting the goods as they pass downriver."

Marcus was right in his assessment. As they neared Underbrook Lodge, Matthew was able to spot a wooden barrier across the river, guards with torches posted to either side. As he lowered the sail, several of the guards raised their weapons towards the boat.

"Bit late to be out on the river?" one of the guards shouted. He lowered his weapon and held a hand out towards the boat. "Toss me the mooring rope." Matthew didn't think it wise to argue.

The guard pulled the boat towards the small jetty and tied it securely before stepping aboard, looking each of them up and down in turn. "And who might you be?" he asked, extending a hand towards Matthew.

"Matthew, son-of-Astor," Matthew replied, returning the handshake. "This is Arian, and her parents, Marcus and Juliet."

"A pleasure," the guard said. "Now, it's a bit late to be out on the river with the family, wouldn't you think?"

"We need to get to Ashford," Matthew said. "War's coming."

CHAPTER 4

I hate boats. There, I said it. Or is it a ship? I don't know, but either way, I hate it. The way they sway from side to side, it's not natural. I've got this constant acid taste in the back of my throat that just won't go away.

Everyone else seems fine too. Carl's been spending a lot of time with the sailors, learning about the sails and the wheel. He said it's his first time on a boat like this, first time at sea, and he's taken to it like a 'duck to water' as my nan would've said. He's already been talking about getting himself a boat if Matthew doesn't get the Road Trains up and running again.

Safran's being really nice to me, all smiles and support. I might consider making my move, if only I could be sure I wasn't going to vomit all over her. I might be wrong, but I'm fairly sure that's something that girls don't like.

I

"This'll really let Safran talk to her mother all the way from Markay?" Carl asked as he inspected the device before him. It looked nothing like the usual pieces that he had found with Matthew on the Road Trains. Instead of the sleek moulded sides of manufactured technology, this was a collection of wires and components, held together with clips and solder, screwed down into a wooden box. A handle, similar to a bicycle pedal, stuck out from the side.

"It should do," Ben assured him, "but that's why we're going to test it first."

"So what do you need me to do?" Carl asked.

"The other radio is in our room at the end of the corridor," Ben replied. "It's far enough away that we won't be able to hear each other speaking. Turn the handle for two or three minutes to charge the battery, and then talk through the microphone here." Ben held it up for Carl to see.

"Easy as that?" Carl said, both impressed and a little confused.

"I hope so," Ben said with a grin. "You stay here and start turning this handle, I'll go to our room and do the same. Baron George will be waiting for me."

Ben left Carl slowly turning the handle, the droning of the wind up generator seeming to follow him as he made his way down the corridor. He would have preferred to be alone as he tested his invention, but Baron George had insisted. As Carl had reminded him, it wasn't the right thing to do to refuse a Baron, especially one who was currently giving them a roof over their head. There was always space back at the prison.

"Finally!" Safran announced as he opened the door to his chambers. "It seems like we've been waiting here for ages."

"I thought..?" Ben replied, clearly confused by the presence of Safran, Karan and Justin standing beside the Baron.

"Thought what?" Safran said with a wry grin. "Thought I'd miss seeing your talking boxes? No way, silly."

"Oh. Okay." Ben stammered. He tried to put them out of his mind as he made a final check of the connections and began to turn the handle.

"So," Safran continued, leaning over the box and inspecting its contents. "Is this like the, what did you call it, televisuals you told me about?"

"No," Ben said distractedly. "Well sort of, but no, not really. This is, well, it's a radio. There's no pictures with this, just sound."

"And we'll be able to hear what Carl says?" Safran asked, placing a hand inside the box which Ben quickly grasped and removed.

"That's the plan," Ben replied. "And he should be able to hear us in return."

"Fascinating," Baron George muttered. "And where did you say you come from, Ben?"

"He's from the east," Safran said for him, staring intently at Ben as she did so.

"Yes, of course, that's what you said," Baron George continued. "Most remarkable though, wouldn't you agree?"

"Er, I suppose," Ben said hesitantly, looking to Safran for support. "If it works."

The Baron chuckled, a deep sound that seemed infectious, Karan and Justin soon joining in. "Then shall we find out?" Baron George said at last.

Ben nodded and stopped turning the handle, giving the internal components one last look over before picking up the microphone. "Carl? Carl?" Ben said through the microphone. "Can you hear me?" They waited and listened, the low hum of static the only sound in the room.

"Carl?" Ben persisted. "Are you there?" Again, nothing.

Ben checked the connections again before a thought came to him. "Carl," he said, "you need to press the button on the microphone to speak."

"...utton is he talking about?" Carl's voice said from the speaker. "This black thing? Hello? Hello? Ben, can you hear me now?" Safran let out a delighted giggle as Baron George slapped Ben on the shoulder. Ben couldn't help but smile at himself.

"That's great Carl," Ben replied. "I can hear you. We can all hear you."

"Hello?" Carl continued shouting through the speaker.

"Hello!"

"You need to take your finger off the button to hear me," Ben said.

"Hello!" Carl bellowed. "Hello! So much for the talking box-"

"Carl, take your finger off the button," Ben said again.

"...smart for his own good that one," Carl continued. "Thinks he's the first lad to ever fall for a girl. He can barely speak to her without going red in-"

"Carl, let go of the button!" Ben said, his face going from red to crimson the more Carl spoke.

"*Oh, Safran,*" Carl imitated. "*I know my talking box didn't work, but please kiss-*"

"Okay," Ben said quickly, flicking a switch on the front of the box and turning the radio off. His face was so red with embarrassment it positively glowed. Safran was blushing too, and both Karan and Baron George didn't know where to look. Only Justin still seemed to be in awe of the radio before him.

"That was," Baron George began, searching for the appropriate words. "Remarkable. Truly remarkable. It can really send a voice all the way to Markay?"

"Not yet," Ben replied. "I mean, it will, I just need to connect it to the bigger aerial. And put it outside somewhere, high up."

"Remarkable," Baron George said again.

"Well, I think I've had enough excitement for now," Safran said quietly. "Mom, didn't you say you wanted to talk to me?"

"Did, I did!" Karan said with a smile. "You're right, we should go and talk about it now."

Karan led Safran and Justin away, turning to offer Ben one last smile before closing the door behind her. Ben tried to look busy inspecting the radio as Baron George paced around the room.

"So, this radio" Baron George said at last. "Quite common are they, in the *east*?"

"I, er, I don't know," Ben replied sheepishly. "I guess."

"And only one of many marvels?" Baron George continued, staring at him intently.

"I suppose so," Ben said as he felt the world close in around him.

"So name your price?" Baron George said with a reptilian smile.

"I don't," Ben began.

"Don't be foolish," Baron George said, his voice suddenly tinged with anger. "I want what you know, so name your price."

"What, money?" Ben asked.

"Deniras. Jewels. Just name it and it's yours," Baron George persisted, puffing his chest out as he spoke.

"No," Ben replied. "They're, no, I'm not for sale."

"Ah," Baron George said, leaning towards him with a knowing smile. "She has grown into quite the beautiful young woman, hasn't she. You'll need lands, status, if you want her as your bride."

"No!" Ben exclaimed. "I didn't, I mean-"

"Your talking box isn't working," Carl announced as he barged into the room. "Ah, Baron, my apologies."

"No need," Baron George replied. "I believe young Ben here and I had just finished. Thank you, again, both of you. It really was most enlightening."

Carl bowed as Baron George left. "What was all that about?" Carl asked once they were alone.

"I'll tell you later," Ben replied, letting out the breath that he had been holding. "And the radio worked just fine. You should be on the stage, you know, impressions like that. Thanks for ruining my life all over again."

Carl stood, open mouthed, utterly lost for words.

II

Samuel Larson led the group of twenty Watchmen through the Industrial District to the City District beyond. He stopped them at a large crossroads, dividing them into teams of four and handing each team a list.

The names had come from a variety of sources; tips from the public, individuals known to be questionable or suspicious to the old Watch, and from reports of public disorder or vandalism against the city. So far, the City Watch had over a thousand names to work through, and Samuel had the unenviable task of assessing each and every one.

"I'll stick with you," Samuel said to the second of the five teams. "I hear this Kieran is a nasty piece of work, and he's seldom alone, according to the reports."

"Thank you, Commander," Sergeant Blake, one of the Watchmen, replied.

Kieran's residence was run down and dirty, the front yard overgrown and an upstairs window cracked. Even at such an early hour, they could hear the sounds of an argument from inside.

"Shut your hole, woman," a male voice yelled. "I'll do what I like In my own house."

"This ain't your house," a female voice screamed back, followed by the sound of something breaking.

"Leave him be," a different male voice bellowed. "He's my kin, so my house is his house, you hear?"

"And you can get out too," the female voice screamed back. "Shouting and drinking all night, I'm fed up of it. Get out and don't come back till you've both sobered up!"

Samuel knocked loudly upon the front door, his officers standing behind him, hands on their weapons. There was a pause before a very large woman opened the door, brandishing a wooden broom.

"What do you want," she said, eyeing them suspiciously.

"We're here for Kieran," Samuel announced, holding up the piece of paper for her to inspect, though he doubted that she could read.

"He ain't here," she said, moving to close the door.

"Do you want to check again?" Samuel asked, placing a hand on the door to hold it open. "Or should we come in and look for ourselves?"

"Skeets, the lot of you," she said under her breath before turning back towards the house and yelling. "Kieran! Kieran! What you done now? City Watch is here!"

"I ain't done nothing, woman," the second male voice, Kieran, announced, as he tried to squeeze past his wife. "Who said I has?"

"I've come to escort you to the Watch House," Samuel told him. "I'd like to ask you a few questions."

"About what?" Kieran persisted. "Like I said, I ain't done

nothing."

They were interrupted by the sounds of commotion at the end of the street. As Samuel turned, he saw a young woman running towards him followed by four Watchmen who were shouting as they chased after her. As Samuel stood and watched, one of his officers raised his rifle, taking careful aim before firing. The woman stumbled and fell, lying unmoving on the street.

Samuel felt a sudden tightness in his chest as he realised what had happened. They'd shot her, most likely killed her, and for what? Having her name on a list?

"All right, all right," Kieran said, raising his hands. "I'll come and answer your questions, and I won't give you no trouble, promise."

"Blake," Samuel said, turning to one of the officers with him. "Take him down to the Watch House, I'll join you there shortly."

"Yes, Commander," Sergeant Blake replied, pulling Kieran out onto the street.

Samuel jogged towards the fallen woman as Kieran's wife behind him screamed, "Skeets! Filthy skeets the lot of you! You leave my husband alone. He said he ain't done nothing!"

The young woman was clearly dead, the growing pool of blood trickling towards the drain. The four Watchmen stood around her body, unsure how to proceed. "Who was she?" Samuel asked, checking for a pulse anyway.

"Don't know, Commander," one of the officers replied. "We went asking for Derwood, and she answered the door. Turned and ran as soon as she saw us, she did. We called for her to stop, but she just kept running."

"And so you shot her?" Samuel asked, perplexed. They had been tasked with bringing people in for questioning, people who may or may not be guilty of any crime. They had no idea who the woman was, and what, if anything, she had done. She was scared, and they had gunned her down for it.

What was he doing, really, dragging people from their homes on nothing more than rumour and suspicion? Was it really necessary, or was it another manifestation on Alexander's growing paranoia? Would it really bring them any closer to finding Deacon and the rebels?

"She ran, sir," the Watchman said again, as if that was answer enough. "By any means necessary, weren't they the Regent's orders?"

"You're right," Samuel replied, closing his eyes to avoid seeing the dead woman at his feet. "By any means necessary, that's what he said." Samuel hated himself, Alexander, hated the world for what he had become. Every day another suspect order came down the line, another questionable action that he had to obey or find himself its victim. Where would it end?

"Go and speak to Derwood," Samuel continued. "See if you can find out who this woman was. I'll expect your report on my desk later this afternoon."

"Yes, Commander," the Watchman replied, leaving Samuel alone on the street to mourn the last of his humanity.

III

Bran hammered away at the back door of The Skeever's Claw, his knocks becoming louder with each strike. Stan fidgeted nervously, anxious that he may be recognised at any minute.

"I'm coming," Jimmy called out from somewhere inside. "This had better be important."

Bran stepped back and paced slowly around the small yard as he waited for Jimmy to finally let him inside. "Hello, Jimmy," he said as the door opened just a crack.

"Bran?" Jimmy replied, opening the door fully and taking a careful look outside. "Deacon not with you?"

"Not today," Bran told him. "I'd like a word?"

"Oh, yes, of course," Jimmy said nervously. "Come in, come in."

Bran followed Jimmy inside, where he took his usual place behind the bar. Stan lingered for a moment outside before deciding to join them, closing the door firmly behind him.

"First of all," Bran said, taking a seat, "Deacon told me to tell you that you can refuse. There wouldn't be any repercussions."

"Refuse what?" Jimmy asked, surprised by Bran's words.

"Deacon sent me to ask for your help," Bran continued, pausing to let the words sink in.

"Deacon and I," Jimmy said hurriedly. "We spoke about this already. I'm done with all that."

"It's not fighting or information," Bran informed him. "Nothing like that. He was hoping to make use of a room, here at the Claw."

"What for?" Jimmy asked, reaching below the counter for a glass. "You want a drink?"

"Not for me," Bran said, whilst Stan shook his head.

"Well I hope you'll excuse me if I do," Jimmy said, pouring himself a glass of liquor and downing it in one.

"Deacon's looking for somewhere to meet some people," Bran continued. "Like-minded people, if you get my meaning?"

"He's recruiting?" Jimmy exclaimed. "That's suicide."

"Why?" Stan interrupted.

"You attacked the palace," Jimmy continued. "The Regent's lost it, rounding people up, torturing them. He told everyone that it wouldn't stop until Deacon and Safran were dead or in chains. Have you any idea what it's like in this city at the moment?"

"Tell us," Bran said, resting his hands upon the bar.

"People are scared, Bran," Jimmy began. "I mean really scared, especially around here. Anyone who's ever heard of Deacon and his boys are likely to be picked up and questioned. People are just disappearing off the streets, or being dragged from their homes in the early hours. Not all of them come back, either."

"That's why it's time to act," Stan suggested. "People won't stand for that."

Jimmy shook his head. "Oh the naivete of youth," he muttered. "Look at it this way. After every one of your attacks, against the soldiers or the Watch or whatever, it's been the people who've suffered. Curfews, rationing, arrests. Now people are offering up their friends and families in the hopes that they won't be questioned themselves.

"If they hand Deacon over, life goes back to normal. Think about it, he never had many supporters before all of this. Do you think any of them will think twice about telling the Watch where he could be found if they knew?"

"I understand," Bran said, rising slowly to his feet. "I'll let Deacon know."

"Just, just wait a minute," Jimmy said, placing a hand on Bran's arm. "This isn't about me protecting my own skin. This is about protecting Deacon, from himself if needs be. He's my friend, as strange as it is to say that out loud. I don't want to see his head on display outside the Council Chambers."

"Thanks, Jimmy," Bran said with a smile. "I'll talk to him. I know you've got his back."

"Try and make him see sense," Jimmy conceded.

Bran stepped out into the mid-morning sunshine, Stan at his heels as they made their way stealthily back to the brewery. "Was he right, in what he said?" Stan asked.

"Every word," Bran replied sombrely.

IV

Alexander decided that he had kept them waiting long enough and stepped into the meeting room, flanked by four guards. The room had seen minor damage from the explosion below the palace but had fared better than many of the rooms around it. The Merchants and Elders, who had been speaking amongst themselves, quieted instantly upon his entrance.

"Gentlemen," Alexander said, taking his seat. "I understand that you demanded to speak to me?"

"You've gone too far this time," Elder Paul stated. "The threats, the arrests, it has to stop."

"Does it?" Alexander said questioningly. "And you all feel the same?"

"We are unanimous," the head of the Merchant's Guild announced.

"Well then, your objections have been noted," Alexander replied.

"So what are you going to do about it?" Elder Paul demanded.

"Do?" Alexander said. "I'm going to continue to do exactly as I please."

"What?" Elder Paul exclaimed.

"Come now," Alexander continued. "I thought you understood. None of you are in a position to object. Your roles are token at best, and I've endured you for as long as I can stand."

"You can't do this!" the head of the Merchant's Guild cried.

"Haven't you been listening?" Alexander yelled, rising to his feet. "I can do exactly as I choose! I will do whatever it takes to secure the safety and prosperity of this city and its people. Under your watch, gangs have run rampant, and now they support the rebels?

"Get out of my sight, all of you. Maleton does not need nor want you. You are unfit to speak for its citizens."

"You'll regret this!" Elder Paul insisted.

"I find that highly unlikely," Alexander replied with a sneer. "Leave, now, or you might find yourself enjoying the hospitality of my cells. Are we clear?" The guards with him raised their rifles, emphasising his point.

"You've not heard the last of this," the head of the Merchant's Guild said as he followed his comrades through the door.

"We'll see," Alexander replied, ignoring the ongoing objections as the guards forcibly removed them from the palace.

V

Matthew pulled again at the chains that bound his wrists to the chair, finding them as secure as the last hundred or more times that he had strained against them. He had been sat there for twelve hours he estimated, and had long since given up screaming and shouting for his jailers to return to him.

He was worried about Arian and her parents. They had all been marched through the winding corridors of Underbrook Lodge, arms secured tightly behind their backs, before being split up and locked away in separate rooms. The walls of his room were a thick, dark stone, and no sound seemed to pass through them. The only noise he had heard since his incarceration was the occasional footfalls passing by the heavy iron door.

He knew how strong Arian was, but he still worried about her. He was sure that she would be equally worried about him, and he wanted to tell her more than anything that he was okay, that everything was going to be okay.

The single torch adjacent to the door flickered as the door swung open, Lord Howard's shoes sounding incredibly loud against the stone floor. He was the senior officer of Underbrook Lodge and had introduced himself to Matthew shortly after their arrival. He held a pitcher and a wooden cup and stopped before Matthew to offer him a drink of water.

"I'm sorry to have kept you waiting," Lord Howard said, holding the cup to Matthew's lips and allowing him to drink.

"Where are the people who were with me?" Matthew demanded. "What have you done to them?"

"They're fine," Lord Howard replied. "They've been most helpful."

"What do you want?" Matthew asked.

"Only to talk," Lord Howard said.

"Then let me out of these chains?" Matthew suggested, rattling them against the chair.

"Of course," Lord Howard agreed. "As soon as you give me the answers I'm looking for."

Matthew sighed and settled back down into the chair. "What do you want to know?" he asked.

Lord Howard stepped out into the corridor and retrieved a chair, placing it directly opposite Matthew. After placing the pitcher and wooden cup on the floor at his feet, he rested his hands in his lap and stared at Matthew for a full minute before speaking again.

"Tell me why you were travelling in the middle of the night?" Lord Howard began.

"We were trying to get to Ashford," Matthew replied. "To warn the Baron about the army that's coming. I told them all this when you dragged us in here."

"And you're going to tell me again," Lord Howard remarked. "How did you come by this information?"

"I fought them!" Matthew exclaimed. "There's thousands of them, and they're probably already on their way."

"You look remarkably well for someone who's been fighting a war?" Lord Howard suggested.

"I was lucky," Matthew muttered. "We were lucky, Marcus and I. Many of those who fought by our side weren't."

Lord Howard examined Matthew, watched the pain as it crossed his face, a mask that was soon replaced by anger and frustration. It was a look he'd seen too many times before, and more than once in his own reflection. "My condolences," he said. "Losing men and women under your command, it never gets any easier."

"Then let me out of here," Matthew begged. "Help me gather Morton's forces and put an end to this?"

"Perhaps," Lord Howard replied. "Tell me why you think these forces are from Island City? All the rumours coming this way suggest Draxis and Phalathlan are responsible for the hostilities."

"I was in Island City when this all started," Matthew insisted. "I've been trying to stop it ever since."

"What would a citizen of Oster be doing in Island City?" Lord Howard asked.

"I'm Draxian," Matthew replied. "A trader, from Maleton."

"And yet you fight for the Oster military?" Lord Howard continued. "You see why I'm confused? The more you and your companions tell me, the more outlandish it seems. It's far more likely that you're a spy, sent to disrupt Morton's forces or gather information for your leaders. If the Draxian military really is on the march-"

"The Draxian soldiers are dead!" Matthew yelled. "Phalathlan and Oster's too by now! If you don't let me out of here, warn your leaders, you'll be overrun before you even know what's happening."

"Morton has never fallen to an enemy force," Lord Howard insisted.

"There's never been a force like this before," Matthew muttered under his breath.

"Yes," Lord Howard said sarcastically. "Tens of thousands, soldiers and civilians marching as one. Odd, then, that my latest intelligence reports mention Draxian troops pushing on the borders of Oster and Phalathlan."

"He made it look that way," Matthew replied. "He tricked everyone into thinking he was allying with Draxis, and then he killed them all. He's been planning this for years."

"And he is?" Lord Howard prompted.

"Alexander," Matthew told him, his tone and posture betraying the weariness he felt. "Regent of Island City."

"Someone in none of our records," Lord Howard replied. "How convenient. I'll give you a little time to think over what you've told me, see if you can remember anything else that may give weight to the claims that you're making."

"What about Arian?" Matthew pleaded. "Her parents?"

"They're well, as I told you." Lord Howard told him, walking towards the door. "Perhaps if you all start telling me the truth, they'll get to stay that way."

Matthew stopped himself before the curse words left his lips. It wouldn't help his case, and angering Lord Howard further may make him take it out on Arian or her family. There wasn't any more truth to tell, but that didn't mean that Lord Howard would believe him. There wasn't any evidence to present, only what he had seen and experienced himself. He made one last futile struggle against his restraints and resigned himself to waiting for Lord Howard to return.

VI

Ben marvelled at the three-masted vessel before him, lingering before the gangplank for as long as he could. "It's like something out of a film," he muttered to himself as he took it all in.

The schooner rocked back and forth against the jetty, the early afternoon waves lapping against the wooden supports. Ben took a tentative step onto the swaying gangplank before stepping back quickly onto the sturdier support of the dock.

"Get a move on," Carl said from behind him. "What's the point of the Baron giving us his fastest ship if you take forever to get aboard?"

"After you then," Ben suggested, stepping back and allowing Carl access. Carl was hesitant at first, but once accustomed to the gentle rocking motion of the gangplank, he strolled towards the ship without looking back. Sliding easily over the railing, he turned and smiled towards Ben, waving.

"Thank you," Safran said to the Baron as he escorted her towards the ship.

"Think nothing of it, my Lady," Baron George replied. "And rest assured, your mother and brother will be perfectly fine with me."

"I know," Safran said, smiling back. "You've been so kind, taking them in as you did after, after my father-"Her voice broke as a lump lodged in her throat.

"It has been my pleasure," Baron George assured her, taking her small hands into his large ones. "You are a brave young woman, Safran. Your father would have been proud."

Safran looked towards her hands and then back towards the Baron, a single tear running down her left cheek. "Besides, thanks to young Ben here," Baron George continued, "you'll be able to speak to your mother whenever you wish."

"You'll need to wind the handle for at least five minutes every day," Ben interrupted. "And then whenever the radio's used."

"I have arranged for someone to sit beside it, day and night," Baron George assured him. "They will follow your instructions to the letter."

Baron George extended a hand which Ben reluctantly took. Ben winced as the Baron squeezed a little too tightly, looking intently towards Ben as he spoke. "Now be gone, both of you," Baron George told them. "My fastest ship and my finest crew are at your disposal."

"Thank you, again," Safran replied, casting a confused look in Ben's direction.

"Oh, come here, my sweet," Karan said, pulling Safran into a tight embrace and interrupting her train of thought. "I'll miss you so much."

"I'll miss you too, mom," Safran replied, hugging her in return. "I'll be back soon, I promise."

"I know you will," Karan told her. "The Baron's right you know, your father would've been so proud."

Safran kissed her mother's cheek before releasing the embrace and stepping up onto the gangplank. After Ben's further hesitation, she gripped him by the hand and dragged him towards the ship and a moment later they were both aboard. The crew quickly began preparing the Aero for sail, stowing the gangplank and weighing the anchor before unfurling the main sail. Safran turned and waved to her mother and brother as the ship slowly edged from the harbour.

"Please tell me she'll return safely," Karan said to Baron George as the ship sped quickly away.

"She'll be back before you know it," Baron George replied

with a smile.

"Do you think Markay will grant her request and send soldiers to fight?" Karan asked.

Baron George chuckled to himself. "Markay has no standing army," he said jubilantly.

"Then why did you let her go?" Karan demanded, turning on him.

"She would've gone anyway," Baron George informed her. "At least this way she'll be safe. I promise you, Karan, Baron Eliza will take good care of her. Markay has an impressive flotilla, perhaps fifty vessels or more and almost a thousand men between them, but no standing army. If the island were ever attacked, a people's army would take up arms to defend it, but Baron Eliza would never agree to mobilise them, not unless enemy troops had already set foot upon the island.

"No, this way Safran gets to petition the Baron for help, just as she wanted, and my men will ensure her safe return. By the time she gets back, this will all be over. Morton's forces are more than a match for any stragglers from Island City."

"Thank you, George," Karan replied sweetly. "I should never have doubted you."

Baron George smiled down at her. What he hadn't mentioned was that his men would also bring Ben back to Ashford, and then his work could really begin.

VII

"I suppose that I should have expected that response," Deacon said, taking a seat in the kitchen area of the hideout beneath the brewery. "He could not be convinced otherwise?"

"No way," Bran replied. "He made a lot of valid points, too."

"I am sure he did," Deacon said. "I suppose that you wish to discuss them?"

"This is suicide, Deacon," Bran stated, "going public like this. If the Watch don't kill you, someone else will."

"If everything goes according to plan," Deacon replied, "the Watch will never know. Did you think I intended to announce a meeting by use of the criers?"

"I don't know what you're thinking Deacon, not anymore,"

Bran said dejectedly. "Ever since we got back from rescuing Nathan and Catrina, you've hardly said a word. You really would've gotten yourself killed, wouldn't you, going after the Regent?"

"What would you have me do," Deacon exclaimed, striking the table with his fist. "Hide down here, scurrying like a rat. They were my boys he slaughtered, mine! I will make him pay!"

The others in the room who had been trying hard to ignore the conversation looked to each other before looking to Bran, hoping for an indication of what they should do. Deacon slowly relaxed, resting back into his chair before continuing.

"I am sorry, Bran," he said. "You are right. I have always valued your counsel, and I should not have left you out of these decisions. Come, all of you. You should hear this." Nathan and Catrina joined Deacon at the table, whilst Stan, Gavin, Dean and Sanjay stood a little further back.

"Eight of us alone are not going to win this fight," Deacon continued. "That is not to say that I question your skill or your conviction, it is merely a fact. Though we have had some successes, we will need numbers if we are to truly take this fight to the enemy.

"As you will have heard, I asked Bran here to find suitable rooms, that I may meet with like minded people and obtain their support. Bran, it seems, assumed that I would be announcing the location and my presence to any that would listen. I assure you, that is not my plan.

"By now, news of our visit to the Walkers will have spread throughout my former associates. They will know that I am very much alive, and that they should still fear me. I intend to meet with them, convince them that together we can achieve so much more, and give them the opportunity to do what they love. Fighting and killing Watchmen. I will only insist that they do it at a time and place of my choosing."

"But what if the Watch do find out?" Nathan asked, voicing the question that was on everyone's lips.

"Then I hope they come in force," Deacon replied. "If not, I suspect that between us and the other gangs in attendance, we will make short work of a few Watchmen."

"I still don't like it," Bran insisted.

"I understand," Deacon told him, "but ask yourself this. If we continue as we are, what can we hope to accomplish? True, we may inconvenience the Regent and his supporters, but in time the Watch will pick us off, either one at a time or all at once. We cannot hope to succeed in this alone.

"With sufficient numbers, acting in a coordinated manner, we can cripple the soldiers on our streets and finally take on the palace itself. While most of his soldiers are off fighting his war, Alexander has left us an opportunity to end this once and for all."

"But Jimmy said no to us using The Skeever's Claw," Stan reminded them all.

"True," Deacon replied, "but there are many buildings that would suit our purposes. I was only hoping that Jimmy's presence would have helped our cause. No matter, I will think on other suitable establishments.

"In the meantime, we need something big, something spectacular to remind the Regent, and the people, that we are still here. That we are still fighting and will we resist him, to the end."

VIII

"Where are you taking me?" Matthew demanded as the two guards escorted him from his cell. They had unshackled him from his chair and bound his hands before him, all without a single word. "What's going on?" Matthew persisted, and still the guards would not respond.

Matthew drew to a sudden stop, catching the guards off balance. He could have taken them there and then, even with his hands bound, but he restrained himself as the guards tried to drag him along. "I'm not moving until you tell me what's going on," Matthew said sternly. The two guards exchanged an uneasy glance, hands resting on the butts of their pistols as they considered their options.

"Lord Howard sent us to get you," one of the guards said at last. "Something's happened that's got him spooked."

"You don't know what?" Matthew asked.

"No," the other guard replied. "But whatever's going on we've been given an hour to make ready to march."

"So why are we waiting around here?" Matthew said sarcastically. "Show me the way."

The dim corridors and tunnels that made up the bulk of Underbrook Lodge were a veritable maze, and Matthew had the distinct impression that he was being led around in circles. The guards seemed to know there way around though, never hesitating at the many junctions they passed.

"Matthew!" Arian exclaimed as he entered a large storage room.

"Arian," Matthew replied, shaking off his guards and running over to her. With their hands bound an embrace was impossible, so he gripped her hands in his and kissed her passionately. "Are you okay? Have they harmed you in any way?"

"No, no," Arian assured him. "They've treated me well, mother and father too."

Matthew noticed Marcus and Juliet for the first time, stood together beside the large crate set in the middle of the room. Matthew led Arian over to them.

"Do you know any more than I do?" Matthew asked Marcus. "The guards mentioned an order to march, but that's all they were told."

"That's news to me," Marcus replied. "We were dragged here only moments before you were. I tried to tell them about the northern army, but they wouldn't listen."

"Me too," Matthew told him. "Let's just hope it's not too late."

"My apologies," Lord Howard announced as he strode purposefully into the room. "It appears that it may have been a mistake to ignore your warnings. I've been recalled to Ashford to make ready for the advance of an enemy army. Whether they're from Island City as you claim or another Barony remains to be seen, but I'll bring you before Baron George to make your case."

"Finally," Matthew exclaimed. "When do we leave?"

"Within the hour," Lord Howard informed him. "It pains me to leave Underbrook Lodge undefended, but those are my orders."

"And what of our shackles?" Marcus asked. "It's a two day march to Ashford, surely we no longer need to be tied up?"

Lord Howard thought it over, pacing around the enclosed

space as he did so. "Very well," he said at last. "Untie them. I'll have your belongings returned to you, but I'm sure you'll understand if I hold onto your weapons for now."

"Of course," Matthew agreed, flexing his wrists as the guard released them. "Let's be off, we've wasted enough time already."

IX

Nathan finally managed to catch Catrina alone, interrupting her as she scrutinised a map of the city.

"What is it?" she asked, keeping her gaze fixed upon the map. "Deacon asked me to look for something to remind the people that we're still here."

"It's just," Nathan began. "After the theatre, we've not had chance to talk."

"I already told you," Catrina replied angrily, "same as I told them. I don't know how it works, it just does."

"That wasn't," Nathan said, struggling to find the words. "That wasn't what I wanted to say. The night before the performance, what I said to you. I'm sorry, I shouldn't have."

"I don't remember," Catrina lied, maintaining her gaze upon the map.

"That's good then, I suppose," Nathan mumbled, turning to leave. "I'll leave you alone."

Catrina hesitated, biting her lip as she fought against her desire to stop him, to say something. She remembered what he had said and how she had pushed him away. Was she really going to do it again?

"Nathan, wait," she said, unsure for a moment if she had actually spoken the words aloud. Nathan stopped and turned to face her, their eyes meeting. "You don't love me," she continued. "You might think you do, but you don't, not really. You can't."

"I know my own heart, Catrina," Nathan replied. "I've loved you since we were children, always have and I always will. I'm not asking for anything in return, I just wanted you to know that you aren't alone. I'm here for you."

"Don't say that," Catrina demanded. "No one's here for me, or you, or anyone."

"You don't really believe that do you?" Nathan asked,

surprised.

"I have to!" Catrina exclaimed, her voice louder than she intended. "When you're gone, Stan, Deacon, it'll be just me again, all alone."

"We're not going anywhere," Nathan said, his voice tinged with confusion.

"Neither was Edward," Catrina replied quietly, her eyes glistening with tears.

Nathan didn't know what to say. So much had happened, it was hard for him to believe that it had only been a few months since Catrina had lost her husband and children to Alexander's villainy. He placed his large hand on her shoulder and she allowed herself to be pulled into him, crying on his chest.

"Everyone close to me dies," Catrina mumbled through the tears.

"That's not your fault," Nathan said soothingly. "None of it."

Catrina didn't respond, only succumbed to the pain that was always just below the surface. She knew it was all her fault, that Nathan was wrong. Anyone close to her, or that she became close to, died. Edward and her children, Nathan's father Daniel, Peter and the others who had tried to help her stop the northern armies. It didn't matter who pulled the trigger, she had come to realise that she was responsible for their deaths, all of them. It was all her fault.

She couldn't allow herself to become close to Nathan, even if she did care for him. It would be like giving him a death sentence, one more victim to add to her list. Perhaps when this was all over, when Alexander was finally dead, she would die and the others would finally be free. If she even could die anymore. Was that her burden now, to keep living without ever allowing anyone to get close to her? Even so, she had a responsibility to protect those around her, and that meant keeping them at arm's length.

She forced herself to stop crying and suppress the deep sadness that lived within her. The pain fought back, trying to be free, but ultimately she managed to hold it at bay, to bury it behind the mental wall that she had created long ago. Nathan looked surprised as she pushed herself away, wiping forcibly at the tears that lingered upon her cheeks.

"It's okay to cry," Nathan told her, trying in vain to pull her towards him. Catrina fought back, twisting away from his embrace and stumbling to her feet.

"We don't have time for tears," she said bitterly, turning away from him and scrutinising the map before her. "And I'm sorry, but I don't share your feelings. Forget about me, Nathan, I'll never be the person you want me to be."

"I told you," Nathan replied. "I don't want anything from you."

"You say that," Catrina replied harshly, "but it won't always be that way. You'll always think there's a chance, a possibility that we could be together. I'm telling you now, that'll never happen. I could never think of you like that.

"We hadn't seen each other for so many years, Nathan, and that was how I liked it. When this is done, and the Regent is dead, I'll be happy to never see you again."

She hated herself for saying it, but she knew that she had to stub out any embers of hope he may hold for a future with her. Pushing him away was the only way she knew to keep him safe.

"We'll see," Nathan replied, his voice tinged with anger, and perhaps the barest hint of regret.

X

The winds had been favourable and they made good time, coming within sight of the island Barony of Markay a little over forty eight hours after leaving Ashford. Ben had felt nauseous within five minutes of leaving port, but had only vomited twice, and both times out of sight of Safran.

Ben's first view of the island was the rim of the large volcano near its centre, Mount Canis, Safran informed him. Below the volcano was lush forest, green as far as the eye could see, and then the first blurred views of Port Hereford. It reminded Ben a little of Hawaii, where one of his favourite television shows 'Lost' had been filmed, or perhaps pictures of Mauritius where his parents had been on honeymoon.

Safran explained that Baron Eliza lived inland, in the sprawling city of Lorton, and after docking at Port Hereford they would make the journey by road. Ben was already complaining before the Aero had docked, but Safran just waved his objections away.

"You've had two days to rest and relax," she told him. "The sailors have been doing all the work. It shouldn't take more than three or four days to get there."

"All I've done is walk from place to place since I got here," Ben exclaimed. "I bet I've even shrunk a few inches."

"Well that's good, isn't it?" Safran asked with a smile. "It'll stop you being so high and mighty all the time." She tried to hide it with her hand, but was soon laughing too loudly to conceal it.

"Hey," Ben remarked, smiling himself. "Since when do you get to steal my expressions?"

"I'm sorry," Safran continued, "but I couldn't resist. Besides, I think all the walking and the sunshine has done you some good. Your tan really brings out the green of your eyes."

Ben blushed instantly as Safran looked away in embarrassment, unsure why her mouth had blurted out what she had been thinking. Fortunately, they were both spared further discomfort by Carl's timely arrival.

"You got everything you need from the hold?" Carl asked, a quizzical look on his face as he examined Ben's bright red cheeks.

"I, I think so," Ben stammered in reply.

"And you, my Lady," Carl said with a low bow and a wide grin.

"What? Yes," Safran replied distractedly, not even realising that Carl had been baiting her. He shook his head and returned to the guard rail, ready to watch the small group of sailors as they began to dock.

Before long, the ship was secured and a gangplank arranged to allow them access to the long wooden jetty. Carl and Safran went first, followed by a nervous Ben who was convinced that he would fall in at any minute.

"My men will remain aboard the Aero," Captain Reid informed them, "but I've been ordered to escort you to Lorton to meet with Baron Eliza."

"That won't be necessary," Safran replied.

"Perhaps, but those are my orders," Captain Reid said defiantly. "I bear a letter from Baron George confirming your identity." Safran made a disgruntled sound before turning and walking purposefully towards the city.

"He's just doing what he's told," Ben said as he hurried to catch up with her.

"It's just another way for Baron George and my mother to treat me like a child," Safran replied bitterly.

"They worry, that's all," Ben suggested. "They could've stopped you coming altogether."

"They could've tried," Safran said sternly.

Ben smiled. "I know that," he told her, "and so did they. This way, they get to feel like someone's looking out for you and let you go off on your own at the same time."

Safran stopped abruptly. "When did you get so wise?" she asked.

"I've always been wise," Ben replied with a smirk. "You just haven't noticed. It's just that I hardly saw my parents the last three or four years, so I had to learn to live without them. One of my best friends at the lab, Susan, she had a daughter a bit younger than me. She was always talking about her, how much she missed her and how long it was until she got to see her again. I guess it kind of rubbed off on me a bit."

"That's nice," Safran replied. "I don't think I've heard you mention her before?"

"No she, she died," Ben said sombrely, averting his gaze.

"I'm sorry," Safran said, placing a hand on his arm. "I didn't realise."

"I know," Ben told her, trying to smile. "It's okay."

Ben tried hard not to think about what had happened at the laboratory. When he first arrived in his strange new world he had almost convinced himself that it was all a dream, at least until Alexander started torturing him for information and he didn't wake up. His memories had taken on more of a surreal quality since then, abstract images of gunmen and explosions as the laboratory around him was destroyed.

Unfortunately though, he could still remember Susan's death in perfect clarity. He could feel her hands as she pushed him out of the soldier's path, see the blood as it burst from her chest, smell the gunpowder as it filled the air around him, and hear her lifeless body as it struck the ground at his feet. It had become one of his most frequent nightmares, the feeling of helplessness upon waking leaving him voicing a silent scream. Where the faces of his other colleagues had become blurred and indistinct, the detail in Susan's death persisted, despite his best attempts to forget.

"We should find somewhere to spend the night," Captain Reid interrupted. "And a hot meal."

"There's still a few hours of daylight?" Safran replied.

"That's true, my Lady," Captain Reid continued, "but we may struggle to find a tavern along the road. I believe it's best to sleep here in the city, and start out fresh early tomorrow."

"He's right," Carl added. "Ben here didn't rest too well on the ship, and we could all do with a decent meal before we set off."

Ben nodded in agreement, but doubted that he would have a better night's sleep on dry land, not with the images of Susan's death running so graphically through his mind.

XI

"Baron George will meet with us shortly," Lord Howard informed them as he entered to the small antechamber.

"Thanks," Matthew replied, shuffling back and forth in anticipation.

They had walked almost without break from Underbrook Lodge, pausing only to heat up rations before moving on. They were all exhausted but it had been worth it, the regiments of soldiers were already taking up positions outside of Ashford. Lord Howard had escorted them directly to the palace where they were awaiting an audience with the Baron.

Within minutes, two guards were escorting them along the brightly lit corridors and into the throne room. Baron George was sat atop his throne, looking down at them as they entered with a wry smile upon his face. As he rose to his feet, the small group before him dropped to their knees.

"Be upstanding," Baron George instructed them with a wave of his hand. "I believe you have important news for me?"

"Yes, Baron," Matthew replied. "We bring word from the neighbouring Baronies of an impending attack by the forces of Island City."

"As you will have no doubt seen," Baron George announced,

"that is not news to me. Morton's forces are already taking up positions around Ashford, ready to repel any such attack. I believe it was you yourself who sent Lady Safran here for protection?"

"She's safe?" Arian interrupted, momentarily forgetting where she was. "My apologies, Baron, I didn't mean to speak out of turn."

"No need," Baron George told her. "She arrived last week in the company of two of your men. They set sail for Markay the day before yesterday."

"Thank you, Baron," Matthew replied. "I'm glad they're safe, though I must admit I would've liked to have spoken to them before they left."

"Then that is something I may be able to help you with," Baron George said cryptically. "But first, please tell me of the forces set to invade my lands?"

"If I may?" Marcus said.

Marcus spoke at length about the troops both he and Matthew had faced in the defence of Aldonis. He detailed the tactics that the enemy had used, and the strategies that he had employed to halt their advance. Baron George listened intently to it all, nodding where appropriate but not saying a word.

"As you can see," Marcus concluded, "the situation's dire. I believe it will take everything you have to stop them."

"An interesting assessment," Baron George replied. "I've already recalled the forces from Underbrook Lodge, and I'll put your concerns to my military advisors."

"What of the garrisons at Fort Solitude and Fort Danzig?" Marcus asked.

"My my, your spies have been busy," Baron George said, smiling devilishly. "I appreciate the concern, but the threat of an incursion from Gelders Ford or the Kurns to the east is too much to ignore."

"Baron," Lord Howard added. "Please forgive me, but I have spoken with these men at length. I believe their assessment of the threat to be accurate."

"Do you now?" Baron George replied. "I'm sure your superiors will speak with you if they require your tactical analysis of the situation. For now, I'm confident that the superior forces of Morton are more than a match for any remaining stragglers from Island City.

"I appreciate you bringing this to my attention, and I thank you for being instrumental in the defence of Morton and its people. Rooms will be made available for you tonight, here at the palace."

Marcus was about to object until Juliet placed a cautioning hand on his arm. The Baron had made his decision, and the more that they objected, the greater the chance that they would be prevented from speaking up at another time. Marcus had also informed her of Baron Anita's betrayal and her plans to ally with Island City. Could they be sure that the other Baron's hadn't also made similar deals?

"Now, if you will excuse me," Baron George continued, "there are still further preparations to be made before I retire. Matthew, if you will stay behind a moment, there is something I wish to discuss with you in private."

Matthew exchanged uneasy looks with his companions, but did as he was told. Once the others had left, Baron George led him further into the palace, promising to explain more when they arrived at their destination. When Matthew was shown into one of the bedrooms, the wooden box that he was presented with was the last thing he expected to see.

"What is it?" Matthew asked, peering at the wires and components inside.

"I believe Ben called it a 'radio'," Baron George replied.

"And what does it do?" Matthew continued.

"He explained it would allow someone to talk to him in Markay," Baron George informed him. "He built it to allow Safran and her mother to speak, as I understand it."

"And it works?" Matthew said, his voice full of amazement.

"That's why I brought you up here," Baron George said with a grin. "I thought perhaps we could try it out, allow you to speak to your man Carl as you requested."

"Thank you, Baron," Matthew replied.

"Not at all," Baron George said, resting a hand on Matthew's shoulder. "You're a trader, yes? From Draxis? Carl spoke most fondly of you, and Safran and young Ben hold you in very high regard."

"Thank you, again," Matthew said, listening to the faint hum from the machine as the young soldier turned the handle that was attached to its side.

"So I'm sure you'll appreciate what I can offer you?" Baron George continued. "This 'radio' is but one of many marvels, according to Ben, although he seemed reluctant to speak with me further. He is most loyal to you and your companions though, Matthew, to a fault some might say."

"I really don't," Matthew began, until Baron George stopped him.

"He's young," Baron George said quietly, his reptilian smile shining through. "He doesn't understand the importance of money, influence, power. We're men of the world, though, aren't we? I'm sure you realise how much easier I could make your life in the Baronies, or how difficult. Perhaps if you could see your way to discharging Ben from your employ, encouraging him to work with me and construct more of these remarkable things, it could be beneficial for both of us. What do you say?"

"Yes, of course, Baron," Matthew replied, fully realising the implications of what the Baron was saying. They were all at his mercy, staying as they were within the palace, and the Baron could just as easily place them in the dungeons instead of the guest rooms, or worse.

"Good," Baron George said. "So let's see if this radio works, shall we?"

XII

Carl was just drifting off to sleep when a loud hammering on the door brought him back to the present. He was stretched out on the floor and got quickly to his feet, checking his pistol as the door was struck again. He edged to the side of the door and directed Ben and Safran to get down low, the three of them reluctant to be parted in the strange city.

"Lady Safran?" Captain Reid bellowed through the door. "Carl? Open up, please, I have important news."

Carl eased the door open slowly, his pistol aimed through the gap. He allowed Captain Reid in and checked the corridor behind him before closing the door. The corridor was otherwise empty, but he kept the pistol in his hand, just in case.

"What is it?" he asked. "You scared us half to death."

"My apologies," Captain Reid replied, bowing in Safran's direction. "I bring word from the Aero. Baron George is talking through the box in the hold, he demands to speak to you at once."

"Then lead the way," Carl said hesitantly, casting a wary glance to both Ben and Safran.

They gathered their backpacks and made their way quickly through the streets and alleyways of Port Hereford. Ben noticed for the first time how dark the city looked, especially in comparison to Maleton or Ashford. Where most of the stone in Maleton was cream in colour, many of the buildings in Port Hereford were constructed of a much darker stone, almost black in places, with a slightly pitted surface. In the more affluent parts of the city, the buildings were brightly painted, but around the docks it was difficult to see more than a few metres ahead.

They arrived at the ship without incident and were directed immediately to the hold, where one of the sailors was carefully turning the handle attached to the radio. Ben was instantly reminded of the swaying of the ship as the warm meal he had eaten only an hour or two before fought to escape the confines of his stomach. Carl reached for the microphone, but Ben was quick to remove it from his fingers, remembering with embarrassment the last time he had spoken through the radio.

"Baron George, it's Ben here," Ben said, unsure if he should finish with the word *over*.

"Hello? Can you hear me?" the Baron's voice replied. "I have someone here who wishes to speak to you."

"We can hear you," Ben continued.

"Hi, Ben," Matthew said. Ben, Carl and Safran exchanged surprised looks.

"Matthew!" Safran exclaimed, leaning into the microphone.

"It's good to hear your voice, boss," Carl replied with a grin.

"You too, Carl," Matthew replied. "Are you all okay?"

"We're good," Carl continued. "What about you? And Arian?"

"We're safe, here in the palace," Matthew told them, though the tone of his voice suggested that there was more to say.

"You don't sound like the bearer of good news?" Carl said,

the temperature of the hold becoming noticeably cooler.

"I'm afraid not," Matthew continued. "Aldonis has fallen to the northern forces and soon they march upon Ashford." Matthew wanted to say more, to explain the dire predicament that he and all of the Southern Baronies were potentially facing, but with the Baron listening to his every word he had to hold his tongue.

"We saw them in Phalathlan," Carl continued. "Has Baron George changed his mind?"

"He's been most supportive of our cause," Matthew replied quickly, "and organised most of Morton's forces in defence of the city. I'm grateful for everything he's done."

Carl knew not to press the issue, recognising the change in Matthew's speech as he mentioned the Baron. "I'm glad to hear it," Carl replied. "He was really good to us, even provided us with one of his ships to get us to Markay. We leave tomorrow for Lorton, Safran hopes to speak to the Baron there and request soldiers to help defend the other Baronies."

"But Markay has no standing army?" Matthew replied, the confusion evident in his voice. Carl and Ben looked to Safran, silently requesting an explanation. She too looked confused for a minute, before the memories of her studies came flooding back to her.

"Oh, how could I have been so stupid," Safran said to herself. "Markay has a people's army, my father taught me that."

"What does that mean?" Ben asked. "A people's army?"

"If Markay is attacked, then the people take up arms in its defence," Safran replied. "As an island, they've no need to patrol their borders, and the Baron's fleet of ships defend against pirates from the south." They were all silent for a minute as they took in what Safran had said.

"Do you think the Baron will agree to calling up her army?" Carl asked, though he suspected that he already knew the answer. They'd experienced enough rejection from those with an army ready and waiting to march. Calling people from their day to day lives to fight in a war that didn't concern them, at least not yet, was even less likely to be successful.

Safran looked back and forth between Ben and Carl, biting her lower lip as she tried to hold back tears. "I'm sorry," she said at last. "I've wasted everyone's time."

"No, you haven't," Carl said sympathetically. "The whole reason of coming to Markay was to get you somewhere safe, not to raise an army. We did what we set out to do."

"He's right," Ben agreed. "Don't worry, we'll work something out, we always do. It's a shame we haven't got Victor here, that man from Sanctuary. From what Catrina said, he could have convinced the Baron to do anything he asked."

"Are you still there?" Matthew asked through the radio.

"Sorry, Matthew," Ben replied with a press of a button. "We're still here. What do you want us to do? Shall we stay here or head back to Ashford?"

"I think you're still safest-" Matthew began before Carl cut him off, taking the microphone from Ben's grip.

"I've got a better idea," Carl said. "Matthew, do you remember what I said to you back in Maleton? About the enemy of my enemy?"

"I do," Matthew said cautiously. "And I also remember how that turned out. What are you thinking?"

"Something Ben just said gave me an idea," Carl replied. "Trust me, boss, I think I might be onto something."

"I don't think I'm going to like it, am I?" Matthew asked.

"I suppose that depends on how it all works out," Carl said with a grin. "I'll keep them safe, though, no matter what."

"I know you will, Carl," Matthew said honestly. "Just don't keep me in the dark for too long."

"I won't," Carl assured him. "Next time we speak, I just might have some good news."

"Okay, and good luck," Matthew replied. "I'll see you all soon?"

"Count on it," Carl told him, as the sound of static erupted from the speaker.

"What was all that about?" Ben asked as he switched the radio off.

"We're taking another trip," Carl said happily. "Captain, I'll need to see your maps. You're taking us to the Wastelands."

CHAPTER 5

We've been back at sea for two days now and I think the crew are finally warming up to us again. Captain Reid wasn't too happy about taking us to the Wastelands, at least until Safran pointed out that Baron George had put him and the Aero at our disposal. She reminded him that, as a Baron herself, she could have him removed if he disobeyed a direct order.

Either way, we should be making landfall in another five or six days, as long as the weather holds. That's something I'm not looking forward to, my first storm at sea.

Oh, and pirates.

Ever since Safran mentioned them I've been convinced that every ship we see wants to sink us. I'm sure they're not really like television pirates either, all witty one liners and unnecessary swagger. No, these will be the stab everyone and take the gold types, all black teeth and scars.

Anyway, at least I seem to have gotten my sea legs, isn't that what it's called? I've not been sick again once, and I even managed to eat something this morning. It was some sort of dried meat in water.

Haven't they ever heard of scurvy?

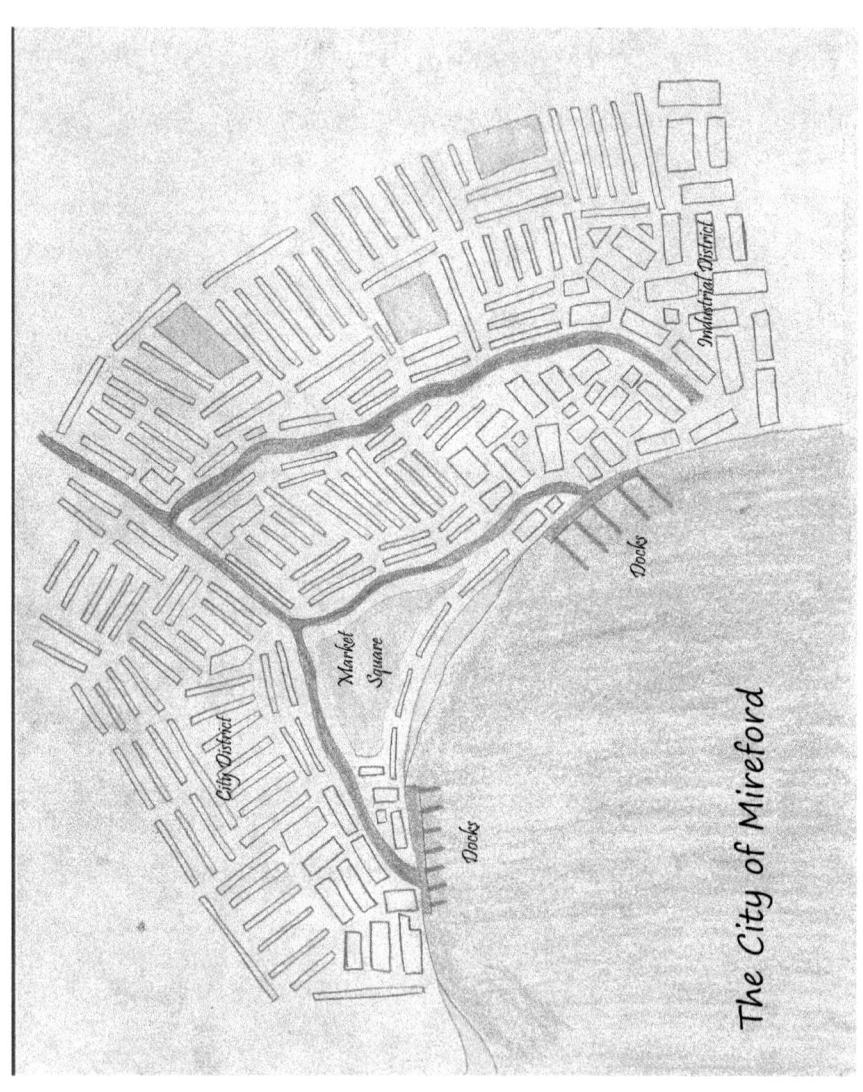

I

Bran checked the fuses for the third time, removing the kinks and running them along the dock. Footsteps on the bridge above him made him pause, but soon they were lost amongst the sounds of water lapping against the stone at his feet. When he was happy that the fuses would burn equally, he whistled once into the cool night air.

Stan rose from his hiding place, lying as he was upon the roof of the butcher's shop that looked out onto the bridge. He had ducked when he heard the two soldiers, chatting quietly amongst themselves as they walked their route through the streets and alleyways of the Market District. They had stepped out onto the Keye Bridge before becoming lost in the darkness and fading from sight. As far as he could see, the streets around him were otherwise empty.

Stan whistled the response and swung nimbly down onto the iron gutters and then the roof of the porch below. This was the moment when Bran would light the fuses before racing towards the meeting point. Stan arrived before him, carefully painting 'Safran Lives' in red paint upon the white stone wall.

"Is everything set?" Stan asked as Bran sprinted around the corner, almost knocking him from his feet. As it turned out, Bran didn't need to answer, the sound of the explosion and a flash of light answering Stan's question as soon as he'd asked it. A second bang, and then an enormous splash, let them both know that their mission had been successful.

"He said he wanted something big," Bran said to himself as he peered around the corner. "There's no way anyone will be able to ignore that."

Stan chanced a look himself and was momentarily taken aback at the sight before him. The Keye Bridge was no more, reduced to nothing but a pile of rubble partly damming the River Brachen.

II

Samuel Larson was woken from sleep for the second time

that week. The first had been following a tip that Safran and Deacon had been spotted entering a warehouse in the Industrial District. When the soldiers had forced their way in, they had found only a skeet fighting ring and the criminals behind it. Suffice to say, their heads were soon displayed on pikes for everyone to see. He really was beginning to believe that the threat of Deacon and his gang was over.

"Tell them to deal with it themselves," Marie grumbled as Samuel eased himself onto the edge of the bed and struggled to clear the fog from his mind.

"I will," Samuel lied, leaning down to kiss her forehead. "I'll be back to bed in a minute."

He was pulling on his boots when the officers below hammered against the door for a third time. Samuel almost tore it from its hinges when he finally made it downstairs. "This better be good?" he hissed.

"It's Safran, sir," the sergeant replied. "She's blown up the Keye Bridge."

"Son of a skeet!" Samuel exclaimed, pulling his jacket from the hook and following them out into the night.

III

"How did it go?" Gavin asked as Stan and Bran hurried into the hidden room beneath the brewery.

"Oh, you should've seen it!" Stan exclaimed. "Boom, and then the bridge was just rubble in the water!"

"And no problems?" Deacon asked, looking up from the selection of pistols that he was cleaning.

"No, Deacon," Bran replied. "Everything went perfectly. We didn't hang around for the Watch, but Stan got the message out as to who was responsible."

"Yes," Stan continued, still bubbling over with excitement. "Safran Lives!"

"And how are the preparations for the meeting coming along?" Deacon asked Bran, trying to ignore Stan's enthusiasm.

"I've paid the market waifs to spread the word to a select few," Bran told him, "and then the news should spread to those who need to know. I'm still worried about the Watch getting word of it though."

"I understand your concern," Deacon said, "but I have made my decision. We will meet with them tomorrow night as planned. What is the word on Ray's unwanted enterprise?"

"The Watch shut it down," Bran said. "Word is, Ray's head is currently displayed on a pike outside the Council Chambers."

"That is good news," Deacon replied with a smile. "If two people choose to fight each other, that is one thing, but forcing two wild animals to kill each other for entertainment is quite another. I do hope that this will serve to remind our colleagues that I am still here, and that my rules still apply."

"Between the bridge and shutting down the skeet fights," Bran agreed, "there won't be any doubts."

"Just the way I like it," Deacon said, returning to his work.

IV

"My Liege," Samuel said, keeping his eyes low. It was the first time he had met with the Regent since the explosion beneath the palace, and Alexander had made it clear that he blamed Samuel for everything that was going wrong with his plans. Now Samuel had to report yet another act of terror by Safran and her supporters.

"I called for you an hour ago," Alexander replied, not looking up from the papers before him. "Where have you been?"

"There's been another attack, Regent," Samuel told him.

"Yes, yes, the Keye Bridge," Alexander said dismissively with a wave of his hand. "Unless something else has exploded since I last looked out of my window?"

"No, Regent," Samuel replied, keeping his eyes fixed upon the floor. He really didn't expect to be leaving the palace again, and was trying desperately to remember what he had said to Marie before he left to examine the destruction. Had he told her that he loved her?

"Well, that's something I suppose," Alexander said. "What have you learned?"

"The explosives look like they were placed along the length of the bridge," Samuel reported, "and focussed around the supports. Whoever planted them meant for the bridge to fall, and make sure a repair was out of the question. It'll need to be rebuilt from scratch."

"There are five other bridges, I think the people can make do for now," Alexander replied mockingly. "Have you been able to determine who was behind it?"

"I believe it was Safran and her supporters, my Liege," Samuel said with a sigh. "The graffiti we found looked to have been painted by the same person who defaced the Watch House in the City District."

"So, you wish me to believe that today's attack was carried out by the same people you *assured* me were dead beneath the palace?" Alexander said with a sneer.

"Yes, Regent," Samuel replied, waiting for Alexander to make his move.

Alexander got to his feet and began to pace around the throne room, stopping to examine the large crack that still ran the length of the south wall. "So," he asked. "What's your next step?"

Samuel looked up, surprised that Alexander wasn't poised ready to drive a blade into his heart. "I intend to double the patrols along the remaining bridges," he began. "Safran and her supporters will see this as a success, and will likely plan to attack another bridge in the near future. If we lie in wait, I think-"

Alexander cut him off with a wave of his hand. "Do stop thinking, Larson," he said sarcastically. "It's not something you excel at. If you increase the guards on the bridges, you'll need to take them from elsewhere. That'll just give these terrorists chance to blow up the Council Chambers or, even better, set another charge beneath the palace.

"No, leave the bridges be, they can destroy them all for all I care. Leave them trapped on the other side of the river with all the other miscreants who insist on hiding them.

"I called for you on another matter. What have you heard about a meeting that Deacon is planning to attend?"

"I, I've heard nothing," Samuel said.

"I suppose I shouldn't be surprised," Alexander replied, beginning to pace again around his throne. "My agents in the city got word to me of a meeting tomorrow night, at a warehouse near the Tunsten Bridge."

"What would you have me do?" Samuel asked, remembering

his earlier mistake.

"I want you to have someone infiltrate the meeting and find out what they're planning," Alexander told him. "Pick someone whose face isn't well known, someone who can blend in. They'll need to get close to Deacon and his supporters, work with them if necessary. Once we know where they're all hiding, we can move in a put a stop to this once and for all."

"Of course, Regent," Samuel said. "I'll get right on it."

"And keep me updated," Alexander reminded him. "I want to know the minute something develops."

Samuel hurried from the palace, thankful for the chance to live a little longer.

V

"That's it," Carl said, raising his hands. "You want to put your whole body into the punch."

Ben lashed out wildly with his fist, missing Carl's hand completely and almost falling flat on his face. If Carl hadn't caught him, he was sure that the deck would have won that fight.

It had been Ben's idea, something to help pass the time as they followed the coastline north. He was tired of always having to be looked after and protected so he asked Carl to teach him how to fight.

"Okay, not bad," Carl said through gritted teeth, "but you need to keep your eyes open when you punch." It was turning into a very long day.

"Sure, yes, makes sense," Ben agreed, bobbing and weaving on the spot like someone out of a Rocky movie.

"And stand still!" Carl demanded, gripping him by the shoulders. "Is all that dancing around supposed to frighten me or something?"

"I don't know," Ben said, pausing. "It's what they do in films."

"Well, whatever a film is," Carl suggested, "this isn't. Come on, let's try again."

A small group of sailors had gathered along the rail to watch the afternoon's entertainment, and had been quietly betting amongst themselves as to how long it would take before the young boy knocked himself out. The odds were currently in favour of Ben falling overboard in the process.

"Okay, you ready?" Carl began, raising his hands as before. "Just stand still, right foot back, lean into the punch. Got it?"

"Got it!" Ben replied with a grin

"Now, when you're ready, eyes open," Carl continued. "I want you to hit me as hard as you can."

"Ow!" Ben exclaimed as his fist made contact with Carl's outstretched hand. Carl sighed as he watched Ben cradle it against his chest, blowing on the knuckles.

"Are you quite finished?" Carl asked, exasperated.

"That really hurt," Ben complained. "I think I've broken something."

"What, something other than your pride?" Carl said with a grin. "Let's try something different, shall we? See how you get on with defending yourself?"

"So, what, you get to hit me this time?" Ben asked. "No thanks. I think I'll just go and hide somewhere until we reach land."

"I'm not going to hit you," Carl promised. "Stand up straight and let me show you something."

Ben stood, fists raised as Carl had showed him. As Carl leant back, arm ready to swing, Ben covered his head with his arms and dropped to his knees. His reaction was met with laughter and applause from the onlooking sailors, who had decided that nothing was going to get them back to work.

"What are you doing?" Carl asked, dragging Ben to his feet.

"You said you wouldn't hit me," Ben complained.

"I haven't hit you," Carl reminded him.

"Well, I just thought," Ben trailed off, looking at his feet.

"Just sit down for a minute," Carl sighed, "we'll try something else." Carl turned towards the onlooking sailors and asked, "Any of you want to take his place?" The sailors looked to each other until the largest of the group stood and rolled his shoulders before coming to stand in front of Carl.

"Right," Carl said, having to look up a little to meet the sailor in the eye. "Swing at me so I can show the lad here how to block it."

The sailor smiled, flashing a row of black and yellow teeth as he raised his fists. Carl raised his in return and watched as the sailor adjusted his posture to be able to get his full weight behind the punch.

"Whenever you're ready," Carl said, smiling back as he relaxed into his stance. The sailor shrugged, hoping to catch Carl off guard before swinging. As the sailor drove his fist forwards, Carl leant back slightly, deflecting the sailors arm to swing uselessly past his jaw, knocking the sailor off balance.

"You see," Carl said, taking a step back, "this man here almost screams what he's going to do moments before he does it. Watch his shoulders."

The other sailors were cheering now, shouting for their comrade to 'show him how to really fight' and to 'put the old guy on the deck'. Carl gave them a mock bow before turning to face his opponent.

This time the sailor lashed out with a flurry of blows, left, right, left, right, that Carl took on his forearms. As the sailor paused for only a fraction of a second, Carl lashed out with a single sharp jab that bloodied the sailor's nose. He staggered back, hand trying in vain to stop the bleeding.

"Sorry, my mistake," Carl said, offering the sailor a hand. The sailor lashed out, pushing Carl away before spitting blood over the side of the boat.

"You're mine," the sailor said menacingly, striding purposefully towards Carl. Carl smiled and raised his arms.

The sailor went for jabs at first, quick and random. Carl managed to deflect some, but others landed on his ribs and abdomen. The sailor relished in his successes, becoming more confident as Carl continued to deflect only every other blow. As the sailor leant back to land a heavy strike, Carl sidestepped and caught the sailors arm as he swung. Pulling him close, Carl managed to lock his arms around the sailor's throat, forcing him into a choke hold. The sailor kicked and swung his arms wildly, but within seconds he was already going limp. Carl lowered him to the floor as his face went from red to purple.

"I thank that's enough for today," Carl suggested to Ben. "I hope you learnt something?"

"Yes," said Ben. "If we run into any more trouble, I'll just stay behind you."

Carl shook his head, watching as the other sailors helped their fallen comrade to his feet.

VI

"Good day, gentlemen," Lord Jonathan said. The leader of Morton's forces had begrudgingly agreed to meet with Matthew and Marcus, though he had made it very clear that he had no interest in anything that they had to say. "Lord Howard was quite insistent that I meet with you."

"Thank you," Matthew replied. "We need to tell you first-hand about what you'll be facing."

"Indeed," Lord Jonathan said matter-of-factly.

"The forces of Island City cut through our defences in a matter of hours," Marcus informed him. "Their siege weapons were able to target out cannons most easily."

"I've fought against siege weapons before," Lord Jonathan replied. "I suspect your tactics were deficient for such an encounter, *Marcus*."

Marcus tried to ignore the slight, that Lord Jonathan had purposefully refused to call him by his title, but between that and the man's stupidity he was struggling to hold his tongue. Even though Lord Jonathan was shorter by several inches, his broad shoulders and strength of character made him an imposing figure. The tent on the outskirts of Ashford, where he had agreed to meet them, suddenly seemed much smaller.

"We did the best with what we had," Matthew said, trying to diffuse the tension that was developing between the two older men.

"Considering what our agents tell me of the Oster Military," Lord Jonathan said sarcastically, "I am not at all surprised."

"How dare you!" Marcus cried, rising to his full height.

Lord Jonathan took it in his stride. "Just look at the two of you," he said. "The rising star of the Oster forces trusting his decisions to a foreign trader. You are not worthy or my respect.

"Whilst you busy yourself with pointless field exercises and petty border squabbles, my men fight real battles with the Kurns to the east. I was stationed at Fort Danzig for eleven years, and trust me when I say this, whatever you faced from Island City, it's nothing compared to what those barbarians would send our way."

"I've fought my fair share of Kurns over the years," Marcus retorted, "so trust me when I say this; you've never fought an army like this. Not in size, and not in tactics. They seemed to know our every move before we did."

"So you allowed spies into your ranks as well as traders," Lord Jonathan spat. "Come, *gentlemen*, see what a real army looks like."

Without another word, Lord Jonathan barged past them out through the tent flap and onto the field beyond. His dark red tunic, adorned with medals, ruffled slightly as the wind blew through the gap. Matthew and Marcus exchanged an uneasy look before following him.

Lord Jonathan was already several steps ahead, flaked to either side by two of his senior officers. Matthew and Marcus hurried to catch up with him, but he didn't speak again. Instead, he led them along a winding path and up a small hillock where they had a good view of the Great Road and the plains and farmland that surrounded Ashford.

"Behold," Lord Jonathan announced, "the true might of the Oster military."

Stretched out before them were hundreds upon hundreds of tents of various colours, battalions of soldiers engaged in training exercises, enormous cooking pots, and wagons containing an assortment of live cattle, food, and armaments. At the northern end of the camp, giant catapults and rows upon rows of cannons spread out towards the horizon.

Lord Jonathan turned to address Matthew and Marcus, looking at them with undeniable scorn. "Now do you see?" he asked. "Why should I fear this army from the north when they would do better to fear me?"

VII

"They really blew up a bridge?" Marie asked as Samuel wearily entered their home a little after ten.

"You didn't go and look?" Samuel said, hanging his coat on the hook beside the door. "I think everyone else did." He had spent the day organising the Watch, as it seemed half of the city wanted to get a first-hand look at the devastation. He was surprised there were so few injuries, despite several of the onlookers falling into the river as those at the back pushed forward for a better view.

Five guards at either side of the bridge, with orders to fire into the air to disperse crowds, had managed to slowly get the situation under control.

"I had a busy day at the market," Marie said. "Come on and tell me about your day."

Samuel followed her through to the kitchen where the oven was keeping his meal warm. It was the first thing he had eaten all day and he tucked into it heartily. He was thankful that cooking was one of Marie's many talents.

"You don't want to know," he said between mouthfuls.

"Tell me," she said, smiling sweetly. "You had to meet with the Regent again, didn't you?"

"That wasn't the worst of it," Samuel said cryptically.

Marie waited for him to continue, but when it looked like he wouldn't she asked, "Why?"

"It, it doesn't matter," Samuel told her, though the haunted look upon his face was hard for her to ignore. She waited a moment longer, resting her hand on his, looking longingly into his eyes.

"I'm here for you," she said at last, "and nothing you say could ever change that."

Samuel paused, resting his fork beside his plate and grasping her hands in his. "I think I sent one of my men to his death today," he told her, waiting for her to recoil. When she didn't, he relaxed a little, thankful again that she was in his life.

"That's tough," Marie replied. "You had no choice?"

"I don't know anymore," Samuel said honestly. "I could say no, but really, he'd just do it anyway. At least if I, maybe, I don't know. Maybe if I choose, they have a chance? Anyway, it's done now, it's done."

"You did the right thing," Marie consoled.

"Did I?" Samuel asked.

His appetite lost, he sat back in the chair and considered the woman before him. He had never met anyone like her before;

strong, passionate, driven, but with a caring side so deep he could fall into it and never reach the bottom. She was the first thing he thought of upon waking, and his final thought before falling asleep. She already knew all of his secrets, Regent be damned, so why should this one be any different.

"The Regent's spies got word of a meeting," he began, "with Deacon and his supporters. He wanted me to send someone to infiltrate it."

"Shouldn't you go in force?" she asked, the confusion evident upon her face. "Kill him and end this once and for all?"

"Alexander believes that, if we attack Deacon," Samuel continued, "Safran and the other rebels will go into hiding for good."

"And what do you think?" Marie prompted.

"I think we should storm the warehouse while we can," Samuel said defiantly. "If the others get away, so be it. At least we'd be better off than we are now."

"So why don't you?" Marie asked.

Samuel paused, running it over in his head. He already knew the answer though, deep down all the answers were the same. "He'd kill me for disobeying him," he said at last. "Or worse, he'll kill you just to get at me. Every time I see him, his paranoia, it's getting worse. I didn't know if I'd even be allowed to leave the palace today, the way things are."

"Then don't go back," Marie said. "Not ever. We could leave, tonight, just you and me."

"And go where?" Samuel asked. "He has spies everywhere. He'd find us wherever we went. I'm stuck with him, I know that. I'd understand if you wanted, needed to-"

"No," Marie stated. "You and me, Sam, that's how it is now. I'm not going anywhere."

"You're sure?" Samuel asked.

"I am," Marie said, leaning in to kiss him. He pulled her close and kissed her back.

"Where is this meeting anyway?" Marie asked matter-of-factly. "I want to make sure I'm nowhere near."

"Oh, tomorrow night, a warehouse near the Tunsten bridge," Samuel replied.

VIII

Carl was surprised to see how close they were to land as he climbed up onto the deck to stretch his legs. The hammocks in the hold were comfortable, and the rocking motion of the Aero had given him some of the best night's sleep he had had for a while. "There a problem, Captain?" he asked as he joined Captain Reid at the wheel.

"A problem?" Captain Reid replied. "What makes you think that?"

"I could pick the fruit from the trees if we were any closer," Carl said with a grin. He stepped aside as one of the crew needed to pull upon a thick rope to keep the sail into the wind. Carl was constantly amazed at the hustle and bustle on deck at all hours of the day as the crew worked tirelessly adjusting the sails and rigging.

"No, no problem," Captain Reid assured Carl. "We're just running low of fresh water, so I'm going to dock at Mireford and resupply. The crew weren't expecting such a long trip."

Carl didn't know how to respond to that. The crew had come to accept that they were travelling north to the Wastelands, and that their unusual passengers were in charge for the time being. They'd even shared a bottle of rum with them after the evening meal the night before.

"Mireford?" Carl said, more to himself than anyone else. "Can't say I've heard of it."

"It's one of the largest of the cities in Gelders Ford," Captain Reid informed him. "Second only to Dunston, the capital, really."

"Gelders Ford?" Carl asked, the worry evident upon his face. He'd been hearing the stories for years, about people disappearing once they crossed the border into the Barony, never to be seen again. No one had been in or out of Gelders Ford for over forty years, as far as he knew.

"I see you've heard the stories," Captain Reid said, laughing. "Hearsay and rumour, the lot of it. My crew and I have docked once or twice along the coast and been greeted with nothing but hot food and friendship."

Carl rubbed at his coarse beard as he considered what the Captain had said. If there really was nothing to worry about, why were the Baronies so concerned? He looked up to see Captain Reid scrutinising him as the thoughts ran through his mind.

"Stay aboard the Aero if it bothers you that much," Captain Reid continued. "I was going to give the men a few hours shore leave, but you don't have to join them."

"Maybe," Carl said absent-mindedly as he watched the cliffs turn into beach as the city of Mireford appeared through the haze ahead.

From what he could tell, Mireford looked to be as big as Port Hereford, maybe even Maleton. Long wooden jetties stretched out to sea with ships of all sizes docked along their length. As they pulled into the slip, the crew tossed roped to middle aged men who helped pull the ship in and secure it tightly. Captain Reid turned the wheel carefully until he was sure that the Aero was safe and secure.

Carl watched with Ben and Safran as the crew disembarked. Two men stayed behind for security, but Captain Reid had pointed out that sea trade was so important to Mireford that the Aero was probably safer there than back in Ashford.

"Last chance?" Captain Reid said as he stepped up onto the gangplank. "We've about six hours until high tide if you want join me?"

Carl looked questioningly at his two companions. "What do you think?" he asked.

"When will we ever get another chance to visit such a beautiful city?" Safran suggested, her eyes lingering on the golden beach that stretched away from the docks to her left.

"Ben?" Carl said.

"Erm, I, well," Ben stammered, as his brain tried to stop his mouth from saying yes. Safran had that dreamy look in her eyes that made his heart beat faster and his stomach turn somersaults. "I suppose it'll be okay." Safran clapped her hands together and ran towards the gangplank, smiling from ear to ear.

Captain Reid led them along the docks and into the city, following the low coast wall that stopped them from falling to the beach below. Stairs allowed people to descend at regular intervals, and many people were relaxing on the golden sand or swimming in the sea. They cut between a row of terraced houses and found themselves walking out onto a large field that Captain

Reid informed them was the city's market square.

"I'm going to organise the fresh water and supplies," Captain Reid informed them. "Feel free to explore the city and get a hot meal."

"Thanks," Carl said, increasingly nervous for reasons he couldn't explain. He was about to suggest that they make their way back to the Aero when he noticed Safran pulling Ben forcibly back towards the beach.

"Come on," Safran said excitedly. "A bit of sunshine will do you good."

Carl followed closely behind, his nerves on edge as Safran and Ben descended the steps to the beach below. Safran removed her shoes and ran around on the sand, experiencing the feel of it between her toes for the first time.

"It's even better than the stories my father told me," she exclaimed. "Why didn't he tell me it was so beautiful?" She picked up handfuls of sand and watched it fall from between her fingers.

"Just stay where I can see you," Carl told her, resigning himself to the inevitable and taking a seat on the lowest of the stone steps. Ben shrugged and joined her, dragging her towards the sea where she ran squealing into the cold water, kicking it before her. Before long, Ben had removed his shoes and rolled up his trousers, and the two of them were splashing each other and having the time of their lives.

As Safran and Ben ran around some more, Carl began to notice the other people on the beach watching, some with looks of sorrow and regret, others weeping openly, comforted by those around them. Some looked at him, pity in their eyes, before looking again at the two teenagers frolicking in the sun.

Carl stood, the prickling sensation from the hairs on the back of his neck putting him on edge. "Time to go," he called out, his deep voice carrying. Ben and Safran turned to object but the look on his face let them know that it wasn't open to discussion. Begrudgingly they returned to Carl and followed him back towards the docks.

"Carl, what's wrong?" Safran complained. "We were only having a little fun."

"We're going back to the ship, now," Carl explained.

"Carl," Ben said, pulling him to a stop. "What happened back there? You look, well, scared?"

"There's something wrong here," Carl continued. "Can't you feel it? Either of you?"

Ben and Safran exchanged a confused look, before turning their gaze back towards Carl. They'd been having so much fun on the beach that they hadn't noticed the looks that everyone else had been giving them.

What they hadn't noticed, but what Carl had just then realised, was that there weren't any other children or young people, not anywhere. He thought back to the docks, the market, the beach. He Hadn't seen any signs of children at play or grumpily being dragged along behind a parent. Something was terribly wrong in Gelders Ford, just as the rumours had suggested.

"Just get back on the ship," Carl said at last. "You're getting below deck and you're not coming out again until this place is far behind us."

IX

Deacon sat on the edge of the desk, arms folded, watching as members of the various gangs stood around the room eyeing each other warily. A wry smile crossed his lips as he took it all in.

They had come as he knew they would, either out of fear or because they believed that they could take him. The price on his head had risen considerably since the attack on the bridge, and he wondered how many of the men and women in the room were hoping to claim it.

It didn't matter, though. They were still beholden to him, operating only because he allowed them to. If some of them had chosen to forget that, it was about time to remind them.

He stood and walked casually behind the desk, taking his seat. The warehouse was a little darker and smaller than the one he used to operate out of, but it was more than adequate for the night's proceedings. Bran stood at his right shoulder, watching everything.

"Ladies and gentlemen," Deacon began, the room quickly falling silent. "I am so pleased that you decided to heed my invitation. There is a lot that we need to discuss, as I am sure you will agree."

"What's this about, Deacon?" one of the younger men at the front demanded.

"I am sorry," Deacon replied with a smile. "When I said discuss, I meant that I will speak and you will listen. That may not have been clear before so I will let it go, this time."

The young man's face turned red, his shoulders tight as he debated with himself about what to do next. Deacon stared him down, his smile never wavering, his hands resting comfortably upon the desk before him. Finally the young man nodded and relaxed, ever so slightly.

"Now," Deacon continued. "I believe there have been rumours of my demise? I have come here tonight to alleviate those fears. As you can see, I am very much alive and in control of the situation. Business has been badly affected by the arrival of the Regent, yes?" There was a general murmuring amongst the small crowd.

"Then allow me to tell you how we will put that right," Deacon said. "But first, let me remind you that my rules still apply. By now, you will have heard about Ray and his skeet fights? As you may or may not have suspected, that was my doing."

"So you working with the Watch now?" a woman shouted from the back of the room. Deacon recognised her as Ray's mistress.

"No, Esme," Deacon replied, "but that is not to say I do not use them for my own ends. We may not be able to buy this new Watch, but that does not mean that we cannot make use of them.

"My rules are simple. No Droca. No skeet fights. No slave trafficking. No killing civilians. Have you forgotten so soon?"

"No, Deacon," a brash, middle aged man with Esme stated. "We haven't forgotten. We just decided that we don't care anymore. You've had it easy for far too long, taking your cuts from our businesses and going on about your rules. Have you any idea how much the Droca trade could be worth in this city?

"We're done with your rules, Deacon. We're done with you."

"My my, Gareth," Deacon said. "When did you grow that backbone? Are we going to have a problem?"

"Oh yes, we've got a problem," Gareth continued. "You haven't got your boys no more, Deacon. You haven't got the numbers to boss us around like that anymore."

"Foolish little man," Deacon said sarcastically. "I did not need my boys, they needed me."

Deacon rose to his feet as Gareth and Esme pushed forward, four loyal lieutenants in their wake. "We can take him now," Esme cried, looking to the gangs who stepped out of their way.

"You don't have to follow his rules no more," Gareth added. The other gangs looked to each other, waiting for someone else to side with them, but ultimately Gareth and Esme stood alone.

"It is not too late to end this," Deacon told them.

"I came here to end you," Esme spat, removing a small pistol from her overcoat.

Deacon feigned right and darted left, driving a blade hilt deep into the first lieutenant's chest. Esme fired, but Deacon had already positioned the now dead body of the lieutenant to take the shot. As Gareth and the other lieutenants reached for their weapons, Deacon moved forwards, slicing one throat and then another before taking the pistol from the third. Esme continued to fire, hitting her own men and the wall behind them, Deacon was a blur that never stood still long enough to get a clear shot.

The other gangs held back, waiting to see who would come out on top. Though some of them may have agreed with Gareth and Esme, that wasn't the same as taking their side in a fight against Deacon.

Deacon raised the pistol and fired, taking Gareth cleanly through the forehead before turning and levelling it straight at Esme's face. Esme froze, her weapon hanging uselessly to her side.

"I am sorry," Deacon told her and fired, killing her instantly. The fourth lieutenant, from whom Deacon had taken the weapon, cowered against the wall, trying in vain to hide. Deacon adjusted his jacket and refastened the button, returning to his seat behind the desk. The entire fight had taken less than a minute.

"If there are no other objections?" he asked as the crowd tried to step around the slowly growing pools of blood. "No? Good. Let me continue."

"As I was saying, business has been badly affected by the

arrival of the Regent. I see the course of action as simple; we remove him. My blows to the city and the Watch have been substantial, but not enough to end his reign. What Gareth said was right; I no longer have the numbers for such an endeavour.

"Which, of course, brings me to why I called this meeting. Working together we have the numbers to end this new Watch and drive the Regent from his palace. We alone have the power to put things back the way they were."

The crowd spoke quietly amongst themselves as they considered what Deacon had said. He could see that they had questions, but after his reaction to Esme and Gareth, they were reluctant to speak up. "Speak your mind," he said.

There was a pause before one of the men to the left of the room spoke up. "What proof do you have that things will go back to the way they were?" he asked. "What deal have you made with Safran?"

"Do not believe the lies that the Regent spouts from his balcony," Deacon said. "I do not work with Safran, and she has been gone from this city for many weeks as far as I know. I can make no promises, but I would suggest to you that it could not be worse than it is now.

"I am no politician, but I suspect that the Elder Council would restore the City Watch to what it was; men and women like you, who would rather return home to their families with a few extra Deniras in their pocket than risk a bullet. We had rules before, an arrangement, and it served us all well for many years."

"So what about that army the Regent arrived with?" a woman called from the crowd. "What's going to happen when they get back from Phalathlan and we've killed their boss?"

"The situation is in hand," Deacon informed them cryptically. This was met with further exasperated mumblings from the group.

"This is where we find ourselves," Deacon said, "and I am offering you all the chance to make a stand, to do what is right for yourselves and this city. Stand with me or stand aside, but I will remove the Regent from his throne!"

The crowd fell into silence as Deacon raised his voice. He slowly composed himself as the onlooking groups shuffled nervously. "I will return here, one week today," he told them. "If you will stand with me, be here. If not, so be it, but I am committed to this fight, with or without you."

There were further mumblings as the people slowly dispersed, leaving in their small groups one after another. Though they barely spoke above a whisper, both Bran and Deacon could tell that none of them left happy.

"Help me clean up this mess," Deacon said to Bran, indicating the blood-stained bodies on the floor.

"Sure," Bran replied, grabbing the feet of the nearest victim. They both pretended not to notice the young woman lingering near the door, but both men kept her in their peripheral vision just in case.

"Excuse me, Deacon?" the small voice said, drawing their attention. They both turned to see the young woman stepping cautiously towards them.

"Meeting's over," Bran replied.

"Please," the young woman continued. "I came to speak with you."

"I do not know you," Deacon pointed out. "You do not look like you run with any of the gangs around here."

"I'm Marie, daughter-of-Cilest," Marie said hurriedly. "Please, let me have a minute to speak to you." Deacon nodded and returned to his seat.

"You're right, you don't know me," Marie continued. "I run one of the fruit stands in the Market District."

"I do not need any fruit," Deacon said sarcastically.

"No, it's," Marie said, blushing. "I've come to offer you, offer a deal."

"Now I am intrigued," Deacon replied, scrutinising the petite woman before him. She was clearly nervous, terrified even, but she had a strength of resolve that shone through.

"Commander Samuel Larson and I," Marie continued, "we're, we're together."

"An interesting choice of spy," Deacon suggested.

"He doesn't know I'm here, I promise," Marie said quickly. "Please, you tried to kill him before. I couldn't bear it if I lost him. That's the deal."

Deacon looked surprised. "What is the deal?" he asked.

"Don't hurt him, please," Marie demanded. "I can help you,

he talks to me, but you can't hurt him, not again."

"He is in a dangerous line of work," Deacon reminded her. "What makes you think I have tried to harm him before?"

Marie became angry, her face getting redder as she took an involuntary step towards the desk. "Don't you dare," she yelled. "I know what you are and I know what you do. I paid what you asked of me to keep my stall and I saw what you did to those that didn't, so don't you dare lie to me. I despise you and what you do, but still I'm here, and I'm not leaving until you agree to what I say."

"Oh my, you are feisty," Deacon said with a smile. "Does Commander Larson know this side of you?"

Marie floundered. "That's nothing to do with you," she replied.

"As you wish," Deacon continued. "So what exactly are you offering?"

"Sam talks to me," Marie told him, "about his day, the orders he gets. I can pass that onto you."

"And what would you suppose I would do with that information?" Deacon asked.

"I heard you before," Marie replied. "You want to kill the Regent, put things back the way they were. What I hear, it can help you."

"That is true," Deacon agreed, "but I will leave behind a trail of blood. If what you say is true, the secrets that you tell me will get people killed. Will you be able to live with that?"

Marie paused, considering the full ramifications of what she was doing. Was she really prepared to get other men killed, men like Sam, just to keep him safe? When she thought of it like that, the answer came easily. "I will," she said defiantly, her gaze unwavering.

"Then go ahead," Deacon said. "What do you have to offer?"

That stumped her. Marie hadn't considered that he would ask her straight out for proof that she could deliver what she promised. She racked her brain for some snippet of what Samuel had said. "He sent someone to spy on the meeting," she blurted out. "Tonight, one of his men was here."

"Not really surprising," Deacon replied. "Do you have a name? A description?"

"No," Marie acquiesced.

Deacon nodded and rose to his feet, extending his hand. "Thank you, Marie," he said, "this has been most interesting. Bran, please escort the young lady home, the streets are rife with criminals and gangs tonight. Show her one of the drops, somewhere safe that she can leave messages for us.

"Perhaps if you can give me something I can work with," he said, turning back to face her, "I may consider this deal of yours."

Marie nodded and retrieved her hand, the impending sense of doom growing stronger with every step towards the door.

X

As night fell and Ben and Safran retired below deck, Carl lingered by the wheel, waiting to catch Captain Reid alone.

"You look troubled?" Captain Reid said, smiling towards the older man. "We're making good time, I assure you."

"It's not," Carl began, casting an uneasy glance towards the first mate. Captain Reid saw the gesture and ordered the first mate to leave them.

"I wanted to speak to you about something," Carl continued. "Back in Mireford, didn't you feel it? Something was wrong there."

Captain Reid offered Carl a confused look. "Everything seemed fine," he said. "We got what we needed and I paid a fair price. What's bothering you?"

"When we were on the beach," Carl replied, trying to find the words what wouldn't make him seem crazy. "The looks people were giving Ben and Safran. Where were all the other children? Did you see any?"

"Have you been listening to the stories?" Captain Reid asked with a chuckle. "About the piper who steals away the children? It's just a story, Carl, a common tale in these parts. The children were in school, it was the middle of the day."

"All of them?" Carl persisted.

"They really got to you, didn't they?" Captain Reid asked sympathetically. "Honestly, I've sailed these waters for years and I've heard all the stories. No one's stealing children, but if it'll make you feel any better we'll dock at Mireford on the way back, have a proper look around."

Carl thought it over. He still couldn't shake the uneasy feeling that something was wrong, but what else could he do? At least Captain Reid was prepared to listen to him and try to allay his fears.

"Tell me the story?" Carl asked. "About the piper?"

Captain Reid laughed aloud. "Now here's a story that's worth telling," he began. "The tale's been told for centuries, of a man who would appear in a long coat and hat, taking children from their beds in the middle of the night. Some say he played a flute or a whistle, enticing the children to follow him, while others claim he had an army of children who wanted only to swell their ranks.

"Parents in these parts tell their children to be good and do as they're told, or the piper would come for them and steal them away."

Carl laughed to himself, thinking about what Captain Reid had said. "Thanks," he said. "You're right, it's crazy. If something like that had really happened, you'd know about it."

XI

Alexander strolled confidently down the corridor towards the throne room. Outside, the city burned, the beacons of flame illuminating his every step. His enemies screamed for mercy on the streets below, though there was no more mercy and they were cut down where they stood, their bodies quickly cast to the flames.

Alexander smiled, enjoying the sounds of his victory. He knew that, once he had taken his seat upon the throne, it would be done, and the Southern Baronies would be his forever. He fought the urge to speed up, relishing in the sounds of carnage that bombarded him.

He tripped, stumbled, slipped, the stone at his feet becoming stickier with every step. He looked down to see the floor slick with bright red blood, flowing from behind him to form a path on which he walked. Each step became more difficult and he started to move faster, to run as best he could towards the throne.

He tripped again, falling forwards, arms outstretched to break his fall. He hit the growing river of blood, going deeper than should have been possible, soaking himself as he turned and struggled to come up for air. He managed to stand and saw that he was waist deep in the crimson fluid. He began wading through it, focussing upon the throne as it grew ever closer with every step.

One hand and then another, blood stained and strong, pulled at his clothes, pulled at his flesh, trying to drag him under. He fought against them, pushing them away, twisting himself free, eyes always ahead, the throne almost within his grasp.

Then they stood, for the hands had arms, and the arms, bodies. Two men barred his path, dripping with blood as they wrapped their strong arms around him. As the blood dripped from their faces, Alexander made out their features and knew that he was lost. To his right stood Elder Janis, and to his left, Baron Stephen. Alexander fought against them, but his strength had gone.

He suddenly felt helpless as his body was carried backwards, the throne getting smaller and smaller with every step the two men took. Alexander made one last effort, one last push to break free, but the men gripped him tighter, lifting him from his feet. All he could do was turn his head, to see where the two men were dragging him.

As he turned, he saw the faces, the bodies, dripping with blood, the blood that he had spilt. The drips became a river, became a flood, roaring its way down the corridor towards him, the walls cracking in its wake. He opened his mouth to scream as the wave hit him-

Alexander woke, his skin slick with sweat, arms flailing against the tidal wave of blood. The scream caught in his throat as he slowly became aware of his surroundings. He felt sick, scared, lost and alone, desperate for a light to chase the shadows away. His hands were shaking as he struck the match and it took him three attempts to light the candle beside his bed.

Slowly his breathing settled and the nausea subsided as the candle grew brighter and drove away the night. Once he felt sure that his legs would support him, Alexander hesitantly stepped towards his sink. After washing and drying the sweat from his skin, he dressed and gathered up the papers that lay strewn upon his desk. He sat and tried to read them, though his mind was on other matters.

This wasn't the first time that he had had the dream, far from it, but each time it bothered him more, stealing away his sleep and leaving him weary. He had the dream every night of late, or a variant of it, and the tiredness was really beginning to takes its toll. Alexander had felt his mind slowing, his memory slipping. Every day it became more difficult to concentrate on the matters at hand.

It was just a matter of time, he reasoned, until the dream passed and his sleep became peaceful again. He knew what he needed to do, the dream had given him the answer. While he still had enemies, those who would keep him from his goal, he was vulnerable. But once he was victorious, with the Southern Baronies under his control, he would finally be able to sleep.

He would be happy to spill a tidal wave of blood if that's what it took to complete his goal.

XII

Captain Reid called the order to trim sails as he manoeuvred the Aero along the coast. He didn't have any detailed maps of the Wastelands, and he was looking for a suitable place to drop anchor and disembark.

From the crude maps that he did have, and the tattered map that Carl still carried around with him, the closest that they could get was still around two hundred miles from Sanctuary, assuming that the map was accurate.

As the Aero edged slowly past a rocky outcrop, Captain Reid spied a beach that led to dense forest beyond. "All stop and drop anchor," he cried, driving the crew into a flurry of activity.

"You think this is it?" Carl asked, handing Captain Reid the telescope.

"Let's take a look," Captain Reid replied, scanning the beach and forest with the aid of the spyglass. He scanned the beach for footprints, animal or human, and the forest for paths or plumes of smoke. Wherever he looked, there were no obvious signs of recent activity.

"I think this'll be fine," Captain Reid continued, "but let's get ashore and have a proper look around."

Carl watched as the crew lowered a small row boat over the side of the ship, winching it down to the sea below. Captain Reid descended the rope ladder shortly after, securing the boat to allow the others to climb down.

"Have I mentioned how much I hate boats?" Ben whispered as he watched the rope ladder sway beneath him.

"Boats or ships?" Carl asked mockingly, holding Ben's arm as he began his descent.

"I don't know, both," Ben replied as he made his way slowly down the ladder. "Aren't they the same, anyway?"

"Not at all," Captain Reid said gruffly as he gripped Ben's waist and helped him onto the boat. "In simplest terms, you can fit a boat on a ship, but not a ship on a boat."

"Okay," Ben said, "I think I've heard that before. So, if I got a really big ship, and put the Aero on it, would it become a boat?"

"No," Captain Reid replied sternly, looking at Ben as though he was simple.

"But-" Ben began, rocking the boat as he stood up excitedly.

"Ben," Carl interrupted, "why don't you leave the good Captain to help Safran onto the boat, eh?"

Ben was about to object when, as he looked up towards Carl, he caught sight of Safran descending the ladder. The view was enough to make him blush, so he sat down quickly, trying to make it look as though he was looking anywhere but at Safran's bottom. Within seconds she was aboard the boat and Carl began his descent.

"What's the matter?" Safran asked as she sat on the small seat next to Ben.

"What, me?" Ben said incredulously. "Nothing, nothings the matter with me. Why? What's the matter with you?"

"Nothing, silly," Safran said, flashing her perfect smile and making Ben blush even more.

Before long, Carl had taken his seat and Captain Reid had called for the rope ladder to be pulled up. Using one of the oars, Captain Reid pushed them away from the Aero and began rowing them towards shore. Ben willed for his cheeks to cool down, but the more he thought about it, the redder they became.

"Here, hand me one of those," Carl said to Captain Reid, taking an oar from him. Working together they made short work of the trip to the beach. As the boat scratched its way up the sand, Carl and Captain Reid leapt from it, pulling it ashore.

The beach wasn't as nice as the one they had left behind in Mireford, but Safran couldn't help herself, running and skipping barefoot along the shore. "Time to leave," Carl called after her, much to her disappointment.

"Really?" Safran asked.

"I'm afraid so, my Lady," Carl replied with a mock bow. "Time for another trek through the Wastelands."

CHAPTER 6

I finally got around to asking Carl why this area is called the Wastelands, but unfortunately he didn't know. Apparently it's always been called the Wastelands, and that's that. I tried pointing out the lack of 'waste' amongst the lush forest, and he just shrugged his shoulders. He didn't know why Draxis was called Draxis either, it just was, so why should the Wastelands be any different.

Captain Reid is a lot more fun off the ship than on it. He's got hundreds of stories of his adventures, and he insists that they're all true. Safran's not convinced, but the stories pass the time between eating and sleeping.

I wonder if anyone would believe this story if I ever get home?

I

General Dowager Boshtok emerged from his tent to watch the rising sun to the east. The warm summer air blew gently against his face as he surveyed the thousands of tents that surrounded him and his army.

Major Bravil had returned from the eastern regions of Oster on the previous night, his men weary but triumphant. The remnants of the Oster forces stationed at Midbrook and Highbrook had succumbed easily, many surrendering to the overwhelming forces, and the Major had gathered almost four thousand male and female conscripts from the surrounding towns and villages.

"General," Hastings said quickly as he emerged from the neighbouring tent, still in a state of undress. "I hadn't anticipated you waking so early. Please forgive me."

"Don't worry yourself, Hastings," Boshtok replied. "I'm happy to enjoy this beautiful morning while you attire yourself. My breakfast can wait."

"Thank you, General," Hastings replied with a salute. "I won't make this mistake again."

Officer Hastings had become General Boshtok's aide shortly after the army left Garet, preparing his meals, cleaning his uniforms, and running errands and messages as the General demanded. Boshtok was hard on him at times, but the young man had potential and Boshtok didn't want to see it go to waste.

He had already shown himself to have quite the keen tactical mind, understanding Boshtok's plans and processes when other, more senior officers, looked on in confusion. Whilst he may not be General material, Boshtok could see a bright future for the man.

Hastings emerged from his tent only minutes later, his uniform pristine and his face cleanly shaven. His rapidity, while still paying attention to detail, was another mark of a promising soldier, Boshtok thought to himself.

Hastings busied himself with breakfast, salted meat and eggs with a large mug of hot tea freshly prepared on the small iron stove. Meanwhile, Boshtok reviewed the handful of reports that had accrued overnight. There were the usual scuffles between soldiers, but only one man was currently in chains, charged with the murder of his senior officer. Deserters had become something of the past, the men and women jubilant after their victory in Aldonis.

Boshtok made short work of his breakfast before taking his usual stroll through the camp. He was a man of routines, of order and structure, and he enjoyed his daily walk amongst his troops. As his commanding officer had once told him, the best way to determine the readiness of your forces was to spend time amongst them and ask.

"You there, what's your name?" General Boshtok demanded, scaring a young soldier to attention.

"Miller, General," Miller replied, standing awkwardly as his blood stained right arm struggled to salute. "Corporal Miller."

"And what happened there?" General Boshtok continued, pointing to the soldiers wounded arm.

"My apologies, General," Miller replied, struggling again to hold his arm in the proper salute. "Bullet to the shoulder, in Highbrook."

"So why aren't you in the infirmary, man?" Boshtok asked.

"Full, sir," Miller told him. "They're dealing with the more seriously injured, sir, told me I'd be okay in a week or two."

General Boshtok shook his head and marched determinedly towards the infirmary tents on the northern side of the camp. He entered without preamble and inspected the interior.

It was the smell that struck him first, rotting meat, blood and faeces. He held his hand to his nose as he walked the length of the tent, the dead and dying all around him. Some would scream as he passed them by, reaching out for him, while others laid still, their faces pale and their eyes half closed.

Several were missing limbs, while others were wrapped in blood stained bandages, the cause of their suffering more difficult to ascertain. Boshtok almost didn't see the nurse as she walked towards him.

"General!" she exclaimed, dropping the metal bowl as she stood up straight. "Are you hurt?"

"No," he said sternly, looking her up and down. He imagined that she could be quite pretty normally, but her untidy hair and deep rings beneath her eyes, as well as the blood and other stains that decorated her clothes, did little for her appearance. "Are the other infirmary tents equally stretched?"

"I, yes, I believe so, General," the nurse replied. "The number of wounded who arrived over the last two days, they've pushed us to our limits."

"How many wounded?" Boshtok continued.

"You'd need to speak to the doctor, sir," the nurse said meekly. "She's operating at the moment, but I can get her if you wish?"

"No, no," Boshtok said more sympathetically. "Leave her to her work. I'll arrange some help for you and your staff, and when they arrive you make sure to get some rest. You look dead on your feet."

"Yes, General," the nurse said with a hint of surprise. "Thank you, General"

General Boshtok turned on his heels and stormed out into the camp, Major Bravil the target of his growing rage.

II

"Good morning, Marcus," Matthew said with a tired smile.

"Matthew, Arian," Marcus replied as he pulled the seat out for Juliet to sit. "How did you sleep?"

"About as well as you, by the looks of it," Matthew remarked.

After they had met with Lord Jonathan, they had been made to feel very uncomfortable staying in the palace. They had found rooms in a tavern in the Waterways, but between the dock workers and the sailors, the revelry below them often went on late into the night. No one had had a decent night's sleep in days.

They ordered breakfast and drank deeply from the cups of hot bean coffee that the serving maid brought to them. As the beverage worked its way into their system, they slowly began to feel more energised and alive.

"They should be well on their way to the border by now," Marcus commented between mouthfuls of warm buttered bread.

"You still think we should have gone with them?" Matthew asked.

"They made it very clear how unwelcome you were," Juliet reminded them.

"You're right," Marcus agreed. "It was just, the arrogance of that man. From the look of his forces, I doubt many of them had seen any real combat outside of their training exercises."

"You could probably say the same for the Island City forces," Matthew remarked, "but I know what you mean. Morton's forces didn't have the benefit of someone whipping them into a frenzy of blood lust and hatred."

"I hope Lord Jonathan's right," Marcus continued, "and they do make short work of Island City's forces, but I doubt it."

"We tried," Matthew said. "I don't know what else we could've done." They were quiet for a minute as they reflected upon what Matthew had said.

"So what do we do now?" Arian asked, breaking the silence. "How long do we stay in Ashford?"

"I don't know," Matthew admitted. "I've been wondering the same myself."

"We've still heard nothing from Oster," Marcus remarked. "The smoke we saw over Aldonis, we'll need to go and see what's left at some point."

"Our home," Juliet said sombrely. Marcus wrapped his arm around her and pulled her close.

"I'll admit," Matthew said, "I'm nervous about heading back that way. We could find ourselves in the middle of a battle, or get captured by the Island City forces. We might be fine, but I'm not sure we should risk it. Just like you, I wish I knew more about what was happening at home."

"Catrina, and Stan," Arian said quietly. "I hope they're safe."

"They're tough," Matthew reminded her. "If anyone can make it, they will."

"I know," Arian replied. "I just worry, that's, oh, please excuse me."

"Are you okay?" Matthew asked, his voice full of concern. Arian had suddenly gone pale and leapt from her seat, running towards the toilet with her hand clamped over her mouth, almost knocking over the serving maid in the process.

"Leave it to me," Juliet suggested, following Arian into the rest room.

III

General Boshtok sat behind his desk, his back straight and his face expressionless. Officer Hastings sat to his right, taking notes, while Major Ellis sat to his left, enjoying watching Major Bravil squirm.

"General, please, allow me to explain," Major Bravil said, his face red and glistening with sweat. "It was never my intention to deceive you."

"And yet here we are," Boshtok replied. "Tell me again how the Oster forces, how did you put it, *succumbed easily.*"

"Casualties were to be expected," Major Bravil protested. "We were victorious, surely that was all that matters?"

"You lost over two thousand men and women under your command," Boshtok retorted, raising his voice, "and a similar amount were seriously injured. Those are the details that are important to me."

"They were infantry, nothing more," Major Bravil continued. "No one of consequence."

"They were soldiers, man!" Boshtok yelled. "Men and women, just like you and me. What gives you the right to ignore that which they have sacrificed for the greater good?"

"I, I didn't," Major Bravil stammered.

"Enough!" Boshtok screamed. "You are to be stripped of all rank, effective immediately. I think your time is best spent fighting alongside those men and women you hold in so little regard."

"Please, you can't," Major Bravil begged.

"Take it like a man," Boshtok remarked bitterly, signalling to the guards to take Major Bravil away.

"You won't get away with this!" Major Bravil screamed as he was dragged forcibly from the tent. "You won't!"

General Boshtok shook his head in disappointment. "Ellis," he said. "I want a full report on the numbers and combat readiness of the troops."

"Yes General," Major Ellis replied, standing to attention and snapping a salute. "You'll have it first thing tomorrow."

"Make sure I do," Boshtok said coldly. "Or I'll be sure to find a spot on the front lines for you alongside Bravil."

"Yes, General," Major Ellis said, though with far less enthusiasm than before.

IV

Bran looked on as Gavin, Sanjay and Dean circled each other, each of the boys looking for a weakness in their opponents defence. It had been Stan's idea, asking Bran to show them how to better handle themselves. Stan was the best with a bow, and wasn't too bad hand to hand, but he had nothing on Bran when it came to an actual fight. Stan had momentarily considered asking Deacon, but had very quickly thought better of it. He didn't think the boys would be as keen to practice if there was a real possibility of one of them ending up dead.

"Keep your guards up, both arms," Bran instructed. "Keep an eye out for movement. You'll rarely have the luxury of just fighting one opponent."

Dean faked a blow towards Gavin, who ducked instinctively, whilst simultaneously lashing out with his left leg towards Sanjay, who yelped in surprise.

"That really stung," Sanjay complained, rubbing his bruised shin.

"So what're going to do about it?" Dean mocked, his voice awash with bravado.

Sanjay lashed out with a quick left-right, which Dean managed to deflect, allowing Gavin to grab him around the waist and drag him to the floor.

"That's not fair," Dean complained. "That was two against one."

"Whoever said anything about it being fair?" Bran said, laughing.

Dean shook himself off and got to his feet, while Sanjay hobbled towards Bran, ready for a rest. "Just you and me then," Dean said to Gavin, rolling his shoulders.

"Fine by me," Gavin said with a grin, raising his fists.

Dean led with a fake left, which Gavin recognised and managed to easily sidestep the subsequent kick. This left Dean off balance, allowing Gavin to throw a swift jab to his ribs, winding him. Dean couldn't help but drop his guard, holding his side as Gavin followed up with a left hook that caught Dean on the chin, knocking him to the floor.

"Outstanding!" Bran exclaimed, rushing forwards.

"Ow!" Dean complained, rubbing his painful jaw. Gavin was staring down at his fists in disbelief.

"You okay?" Bran asked, offering Dean a hand up.

"He got me good," Dean replied, "but yes, I'll be fine. Nice one, Gav."

"Thanks," Gavin said, still a little bewildered. "I didn't mean to, I mean, are you sure you're okay?"

"Don't worry, it's all good," Dean told him, wincing as he tried to smile. "You're going to have to show me how you did that. I never saw it coming."

"Me either, I think," Gavin said honestly.

Bran laughed again, a hand on each of the boy's shoulders. "Go take a break," he said. "We'll pick up again this afternoon, take things a little slower. Now I've seen you all rough housing, I know what we need to work on."

"That's more like it," Dean said. "You show us a few moves, and we can take it to the streets. Teach those Watchmen a few things."

"That's the spirit," Bran agreed. "I'll see you here after lunch."

Dean and Gavin joined Sanjay who was lying on his bunk, the three of them talking excitedly about the punches that they had dealt out and received. Bran smiled mournfully before joining Deacon on the other side of the room.

"Well?" Deacon asked, though he had been watching the sparring intermittently.

"It went about as well as we expected," Bran replied. "They're good boys, spirited, but they're nowhere near ready, not for the real thing."

"They are young," Deacon reminded him. "These things take time."

"I know," Bran agreed. "Before, when we had the older lads, they'd take the younger ones along, show them a thing or two. Over the years they'd learn to look out for themselves, handle themselves. If we took any of them out on a job now, ran into a patrol, no, it just wouldn't be worth it."

"I trust your judgement, Bran," Deacon said. "How do you think Stan will take it?"

"Honestly?" Bran asked. "I think this was what he was after. Him and Gavin, they really seem to care for each other, and he's been finding it more difficult to keep saying no when Gavin wants to come along on one of our attacks. This way, we're the ones saying no, but at the same time as trying to make him ready."

"He is a smart one," Deacon said with a wry smile.

"Capable too," Bran said. "With the hunting and climbing he learned on the Road Trains, and that fancy fighting Matthew taught him, he's a real asset."

"But we are still only five," Deacon remarked.

"I got the feeling in the meeting that some of the gangs would stand with us?" Bran suggested.

"Maybe," Deacon agreed. "What of the drop point?"

"Nothing so far," Bran replied. "If the Commander's lady really was telling the truth, she's not left any notes yet. She could've had a change of heart, once she realised the consequences."

"Perhaps," Deacon said. "Whatever the reason, we still require the identity of the informant. Check the drop again tomorrow, but I would like you to pay close attention to those who join us at the warehouse tomorrow night."

"You got it, Deacon." Bran told him. "Anyone I don't recognise, I'll be sure to ask them to stay behind and have a nice chat."

V

"Marie?" Samuel exclaimed as she entered his office at the Watch House. "What are you doing here? Is everything all right?"

"Everything's fine," Marie replied, her warm smile alleviating his anxiety. "Now that we don't have to keep our relationship a secret, I thought I'd come and surprise you."

"That's, great," Samuel said, momentarily lost for words.

"Don't worry, I won't stay long," Marie assured him. "I brought you some lunch. Do you have to eat it in here?"

Samuel looked at the pile of paperwork on his desk, duty rotas that needed his approval, crime reports that he had to decide whether to investigate, and anonymous tips that usually led nowhere. "Not today," he said assertively. "Can you wait here a minute, though, I just need to make sure things don't fall apart without me."

Marie nodded and smiled, waving him away. As soon as Samuel was out the door, she edged over to the desk and began carefully inspecting the piles of papers. Several of the reports that she leafed through detailed ongoing operations designed to locate and apprehend the rebels, but none of them seemed to mention Deacon's meeting or his warehouse. She was desperate to find something, anything, and kept looking through even when the rational part of her brain was screaming at her to stop, that Samuel would return at any minute. She almost jumped out of her skin when he burst through the door.

"Sorry," she said quickly, trying to push the papers back into a reasonable pile. "I couldn't help myself. Is this the sort of stuff you have to go through every day?"

"Sadly," Samuel replied, but Marie thought that she noticed a hint of suspicion in his voice. "If anyone ever suggests that the life of a Watch Commander is exciting, be sure to set them straight."

There was an uncomfortable silence as Samuel watched her, holding the door open for her to leave. "Sam," Marie said at last, "I really am sorry. I never meant to read anything, it was just, there, and, well, and I really didn't think it would be so dull!"

That made Samuel laugh as he beckoned her out to the corridor. "Nothing juicy for the next time you meet Sandra for a few drinks then?" he remarked.

Marie punched him playfully on the arm before following him out of the building. Outside, it was a warm summer afternoon, full of promise and expectation, as people wondered about lazily from one errand to the next. It was far too hot to do anything quickly, and Marie enjoyed the sensation of meandering hand in hand with Samuel through the streets of the Palace District.

A short walk brought them to one of the small green parks dotted throughout the more affluent part of the city. No bigger than most of the gardens that surrounded it, the park had two public benches placed beneath leafy trees, the shade a welcoming respite from the glaring sun.

The basket Marie carried contained cheese and bread, as well as two bottles of beer. Samuel popped the tops and drank deeply from his, relishing in the taste as it slid easily down his throat. "You should bring me lunch more often," he said with a smile, handing Marie the other bottle.

"Maybe I will," Marie said coyly.

They sat together in comfortable silence as they ate, watching the world go buy. Neither of them knew how long they had been sat there when a breathless officer from the Watch House ran up to them.

"Commander," he said between large gulps of air. "I'm sorry but, I was sent to fetch you sir. He said it can't wait, and he'll only speak to you."

"What is it, Manson," Samuel barked, clearly annoyed at the interruption. "What can't wait?"

"Sergeant Blake, sir," Manson replied. "He said he needs to speak to you, and only you."

"Blake?" Samuel exclaimed, his anger gone and replaced with a hint of excitement. "He's at the Watch House? Now?"

"Yes, sir," Manson continued. "Came in by the back door, not ten minutes ago."

"What is it, Sam?" Marie asked, her voice full of concern. "Is everything okay?"

"I'm sorry," Samuel replied, getting to his feet. "I'll make this up to you, I promise. It's just, this is something that can't wait."

"You're not in any danger are you?" Marie persisted.

"No, no, nothing like that," Samuel said, leaning down to kiss her. "No, this man Blake, he's on, well, special assignment. He'd only break cover if it was something important. I have to find out what."

"Okay," Marie said, smiling back up at him. A thousand thoughts were running through her head, about the assignment and the man's identity, but she did her best to make her face look relieved. She had never been the best at keeping secrets, always blushing and exposing herself when telling a lie, but fortunately for her, Samuel Larson was already running back towards the

Watch House.

VI

"I think we should make camp here," Carl suggested as the sun began to dip below the tree line. The long dark shadows it cast made it difficult to see, and he would rather have a fire going before night fell than scramble around to find dry wood afterwards.

The canopy above them was dense, blocking out all but the thinnest of setting sunbeams, but the fire he lit in the small clearing soon illuminated the dark. Carl removed food from each of the packs, as well as bottles of fresh water. The lighter everyone's pack became, the faster they could all travel, and they had passed so many sources of fresh water, so he wasn't worried about shortages.

"This is better than the skeet we were eating last time we travelled through here," Ben said with a grin as he tore a strip from some salted beef. The supplies that they had taken on in Mireford were tasty and so much better than the rations that were to be found in the galley beforehand.

"You're not wrong," Carl agreed between mouthfuls. "It may be edible, but it still tastes like chewing tree bark and leather."

"Can't say I've had the pleasure," Captain Reid commented. "I think this'll be the longest time I've spent on land in ten years or more."

They sat together and enjoyed their food in silence for a minute, until Ben asked, "Did you always want to be a sailor, Captain Reid?"

"Oh, it's just Reid, please, at least on dry land," Reid replied. "Did I always want to be a sailor though? No, not really, it was never something that I'd thought about."

"So what did you want to do?" Safran asked. She could relate a little to doing a job that he never wanted, and Captain Reid had already told them so many wonderful stories that she loved to listen to him speak.

"Honestly?" Reid asked, taking a swig of water to wash down his food. "I was always supposed to work in the bakery with my father."

"You don't look like any baker I've met," Carl remarked. Captain Reid had a tanned, leathery face with a thick, neatly trimmed black beard. He was tall, though not as tall as Carl, with large, powerful shoulders, used to hauling ropes in the high winds.

"No," Reid agreed, rubbing his chin. "Twenty years at sea will do that to a man."

"So what happened?" Safran prompted. "How did you end up here?"

"Life takes you along some unexpected paths," Reid mused, his voice a little distant. "I must've been eighteen or so when it happened. I'd been working with my father in the bakery for a while by then, learning the ropes as it were." He chuckled to himself at the unintended nautical joke.

"Never even been on a ship before then," Reid continued. "One morning, I find the bakery's been wrecked, my father beaten. Turns out he got into some debt with the wrong people, gambling as I recall. I never knew it, but they were making him smuggle Droca inside the bread he baked, to get it past the docks to Markay. The last shipment he sent, it was discovered and the gang blamed him. My father died the next day from his injuries and the Watch did nothing."

Reid paused, remembering the bloodied state that he had found his father in. He had carried him home and called for the nearest doctor, but there was nothing that they could do for him. His father had died, Reid at his side, holding his hand.

"I'm sorry," Safran said. "I never meant to-"

"No, no, it's fine," Reid said with a forced smile that never reached his eyes. "It was a long time ago."

They were all quiet for a minute, remembering those that they themselves had lost. All of them around the small campfire had experienced the loss and pain that Reid had felt, and it never really went away.

"Shall we get some rest?" Carl said after a short while, tossing his meat to the fire, his appetite gone.

"No, no need," Reid told him. "I'm just getting to the good bit.

"Turns out, I got the name of the local gang that had killed him. I arranged a meeting with one if their top men, offered to take over the bakery smuggling business. Greado, Grudo, something like that. I met him at one of the taverns in the Waterways."

"What happened next?" Safran asked, her voice bubbling over with excitement.

"I sat down opposite him, told him who I was. He started laying down the rules, about my cut and what would happen if I messed up like my father. Little did he know, I'd readied a pistol beneath the table. Over the years, the story got changed a bit, and some people say he shot first, but that's not how I remember it. I just shot him, dead, there and then. He never saw it coming.

"There was fight after, that's where I got this," Reid said, exposing his left shoulder to show them a ragged scar. "Then the watch burst in, dragged me before the Baron. I never denied killing him, so the Baron gave me a choice; join the military or end up in Balistae prison, and if you've ever heard any stories about that place, you'd know why I chose the military.

"And look at me know, captain of the fastest ship in the baron's fleet!"

"What's your timing on the Kessel run?" Ben asked, barley stifling a laugh.

"The what?" Reid asked, visible confused. Ben was lost to a fit of giggles as the others looked on, bewildered.

"Sorry," Ben tried to say. "It's just-" and he was laughing again, rolling around on the floor and holding his sides.

Reid looked on for a minute before announcing, "If I am to be mocked, I would know why!"

The tone of his voice shocked Ben into sudden silence. "I'm really sorry," Ben said. "Really, I am. I didn't mean to, it's just, it sounded like another story I heard."

"Then I pity them that have endured such loss as I," Reid said sombrely, looking towards the fire.

Ben looked at Carl, who shook his head slowly, then at Safran, who was glaring furiously in his direction. "Captain Reid," Ben said, his tone serious. "I'm really sorry about what I said. I didn't mean to insult you, or make fun of what happened. I heard a similar story a long time ago, that's all. I shouldn't have made fun of you."

"Good enough," Reid said, extending his hand. Ben shook it

briskly.

"If it's stories that amuse you, though," Reid continued, "then how about another? Let me tell you about the curious cabin boy who got more than he bargained for on a trip to the Kurn Empire."

Safran clapped her hands excitedly as Carl lay down beside the fire, content that, for a while at least, all was right with the world.

VII

"Thank you all for returning," Deacon announced to the much smaller crowd that had gathered in the warehouse. As he scrutinised his audience, he noted that only three of the larger city gangs were were represented, as well as a small number of independent thieves and specialists who hired out their skills to the highest bidder.

Deacon had hoped for more, a lot more, but he could work with them all the same. He had spent the last week debating and discussing his plans with Bran, Nathan and Catrina, and had grown to accept that they all needed numbers to have the slightest chance of success. In time, he hoped, as the others saw the outcomes of his actions, they would change their minds and choose to stand with him. If not, well, he had a very long memory, and they would grow to understand the consequences of disappointing him.

"I am pleased that you chose to stand with me," Deacon continued, "and I promise you now that you will be rewarded. Over the coming days and weeks, I will call on each of you to give you the opportunities to put your skills into practice. I may give you a task, or a target, and I will leave it to you to deal with it.

"There will be no opportunity for debate. If you agree to stand with me, you are agreeing to do as I ask, without question or hesitation. It may not at first make sense to you, but I will expect you to complete the task all the same. Are there any questions?"

The audience looked to each other, mumbling and muttering between themselves as they considered what he had said. For all of his rules, Deacon had always done right by them, and they had all made a profit before the Regent and his army arrived. True, many of them had argued that the profits from the Droca trade could be so much greater, but then, so were the risks.

More than one of them looked at the fading blood stains that discoloured the floor, a stark reminder of what would happen to those who tried to stand against the man who stood smiling before them. One by one, as Deacon looked to the gang leaders and their representatives, there were curt nods of acceptance.

"Thank you," Deacon said. "If it is any consolation, let me make you this promise. There will be blood, there will be fire, and there will be death."

As he spoke, he noticed many of the younger gang members smile at the thought of the carnage that would ensue. Deacon accepted that these were their talents; go there, hurt him, kill them. They weren't great thinkers or strategists, but they got the job done, and by the looks of things, they enjoyed it.

As the audience began to realise that the meeting was over, Bran followed them casually towards the rear door. He nodded and smiled at the comments the gang members and specialists made, but he always kept one eye on his target, placing his large hand upon the man's shoulder just as he was about to leave.

"I thought we were done?" the man said hurriedly, looking up into Bran's steely gaze.

"We are," Bran agreed. "Deacon has a task in mind for you already, that's all."

"Oh, okay," the man stammered, looking towards the exit as Bran escorted him back into the room.

"Thank you for staying behind," Deacon said, extending a hand. "Blake, is it?"

"What? No, no," the man replied, his eyes going wide with fear.

"Oh, I am sorry," Deacon replied with a grin. "Do you prefer sergeant?"

VIII

Marie kissed Samuel goodbye and made her way towards the Market District. More than once she passed a casual glance over her shoulder, checking that no one was paying particular attention to her activities.

Just as she had done the day before, when she had left the incriminating note, she took a slight detour from her usual path and slipped into one of the numerous alleyways surrounding the main market. The air instantly felt colder, denser, a weight that pressed down onto her shoulders as she took the seventeen steeps to the damp brick wall at its end. After one last look back towards the way she came, she pulled the loose brick from its housing and retrieved the paper from inside.

It was different, she noticed, to the note that she had placed there only the day before. The paper felt thicker, coarser, not as nice as the writing paper that she had grown accustomed to. With trembling hands, she hesitantly unfolded it, reading the single word printed upon its surface.

Agreed.

She looked at it again, turning the paper over, looking for more.

Agreed.

Deacon had agreed, to her request, to her plan, to her betrayal. She suddenly felt sick, the weight on her shoulders increasing as she looked desperately for a way out. The exit from the alleyway seemed to get further away as her vision tunnelled.

What had she done?It had all seemed so simple, meeting Deacon and proposing the terms. He'd told her that people would get hurt, but deep down she hadn't really accepted that. What had happened to Blake, the Watch Sergeant that she had told Deacon about? Blake, who was considered brave and honourable by his colleagues, Blake, who was always first through the door and always had your back. And what would Samuel say if he found out?

She staggered along the alleyway, holding onto the wall as she struggled to draw air into her lungs, gasping as her vision became darker and her heart beat loudly within her chest. She was only a step or two from the exit when she dropped to her knees and vomited.

IX

Samuel Larson kissed Marie goodbye and strolled confidently through the Palace District towards the Watch House. He was eager to get there, to find out what Blake had learned the night before.

The short meeting on the previous day had been very productive. He had learned that Safran was no longer in the city, and hadn't been for a while, and it wouldn't be long until they knew exactly who Deacon was working with and where they were located. It would be over within days, a week or two at most.

Upon entering the Watch House, it took him a moment to recognise the sombre looks his fellow Watchmen were wearing. As he approached the desk where the duty officer would be waiting for him, ready to detail the previous night's activities, a hand on his arm stopped him in his tracks.

"Commander," a quiet voice said, a voice tinged with fear and loss. "Don't look, sir."

"Don't look at what?" Samuel asked, taken aback. "What's going on?"

The small cluster of Watchmen parted, exposing a battered box lying atop the duty officer's desk. With each step Samuel took towards it, the surrounding officers took a step back.

"Really, Commander," the quiet voice persisted. "I wouldn't." Samuel brushed him off, pulling the box towards him and pulling apart the flaps.

Inside, staring back at him, was the severed head of Sergeant Blake, the mouth still open in a perpetual scream. Samuel stared at it for a full ten seconds, confused, disbelieving. He had been speaking to the man only the day before.

"There was a note," the duty officer said, drawing Samuel back to the present. He was still struggling to take his gaze away from the lifeless eyes, and took the note without realising.

Nice try. Better luck next time, it said.

Samuel felt his face flush as his heart beat faster and the adrenaline surged through his body. As he screwed the note into a ball, a red mist descended over his vision, clouding everything. "You lot, with me," he demanded, as he turned and left the Watch

House.

The officers did as they were instructed, following him on a swift march across the Penrock Bridge and into the Industrial District. They didn't know where they were going, but it didn't matter. The look on Samuel's face made it clear that he wasn't to be questioned, and the public on the streets could see that too. As the Watchmen pressed onwards, people gave them a wide berth, letting them pass without objection.

They'd gone too far, Samuel reasoned. Blake was a soldier, a warrior, and he didn't deserve to die that way. Deacon, the gangs, they really were just animals. Maybe Alexander was right about that, they really were all just miscreants south of the river, worse than a pack of wild skeets. Fine. If that was how they were going to behave, then so be it.

He may not know where Deacon was hiding, but the records in the Watch Houses detailed many of the other gangs who worked for him. He hadn't even realised where he was going until he looked up and saw the sign for the Belcher Brother's textile factory. They were well known to the former Watch, and Blake had mentioned seeing them at the meeting the week before.

"Commander?" one of the Watch Officers asked as Samuel began hammering upon the door.

"Break it down," Samuel replied, removing his pistol from its holster. The Watchmen stood uncomfortably around him, looking to each other. "Now!" Samuel screamed, turning his fury towards them.

After more furtive glances, two of the largest Watchmen began kicking at the door and then barging it with their shoulders. After several grunts of pain and frustration, the door finally splintered and then opened before them. Samuel was the first one through.

"I'm here for Borst and Kahler," he bellowed. The men and women who worked in the factory were trying to leave through another door as two burly looking men stood menacingly at the bottom of a flight of stairs. Their look of disinterest disappeared as soon as they saw the anger in Samuel's eyes.

"They're in a meeting," one of the men said, looking to the other for support.

"So go and tell them that the City Watch is here, and we want a word," Samuel replied menacingly.

"We just-" the second man began before Samuel stepped forward and struck him hard with the butt of his pistol. For just a moment, the first man looked as though he was going to put up a fight.

"Arrest them both," Samuel barked, stepping past them and onto the stairs. The Watchmen responded quickly, helping the fallen man back to his feet and binding their hands behind their backs.

Samuel continued up the stairs, pistol in hand. As he reached the small corridor at the top, he kicked open the only door, exposing a large office that overlooked the factory floor below. The two men inside, Borst and Kahler, stared at him with contempt as he entered.

"Downstairs, now," Samuel demanded, alternating the pistol between them.

"No," the man to the left, Kahler, replied. "You've got nothing on us, so we're not going anywhere."

Samuel scowled, his eyes going wide as he stepped forward and dragged Kahler from his seat, across the desk and threw him against the opposite wall. Borst stepped forward to defend his brother, until Samuel struck him sharply with his fist, breaking his nose. Borst dropped to his knees, hands at his face as his nose gushed.

As Kahler attempted to get back to his feet, Samuel kicked him sharply in the ribs, winding him. "Downstairs!" Samuel screamed, kicking Kahler again and again until he began to crawl painfully from the office.

Samuel walked behind them as Kahler and Borst helped each other down the stairs to the factory floor. "I'll get them back to the Watch House," one of the officers suggested, taking Kahler's arm.

"No," Samuel interrupted. "Not these two. Get them outside, this is for everyone to see." The Watchmen looked to each other, confused and concerned about the Commander's sudden change.

Reluctantly, the Watchmen escorted the brothers outside where Samuel forced them to their knees. "Kahler and Borst Belcher," he began. "You are hereby charged with aiding the criminal known as Deacon in the murder of Watch Sergeant Blake."

"No, wait," Kahler protested.

"You have both been found guilty," Samuel continued, ignoring him, "and the sentence for your crime is death."

"We didn't kill anybody!" Borst exclaimed, though with his broken nose it sounded more like *ge gign't gill genybogy*.

"I'm giving you one chance," Samuel said, facing them. "The first one to tell me where I can find Deacon, right now, gets to live."

Several of the factory workers had lingered outside and were watching in awe as Samuel gave the brothers his ultimatum. It was widely believed that the Belcher's were involved in counterfeiting and gambling, but none of them would have ever suspected them of murder.

"We don't know," Kahler pleaded. "We don't know where he is."

"You were both seen," Samuel reminded them, "at the meeting."

"No, no," Kahler persisted. "We didn't go back, not last night. We don't want to fight in any war."

Samuel rubbed at his temples as he fought to control the surging rage that was threatening to explode. "You know," he said, more to himself than anyone else, "I've been trying to change, to not be the man The Regent believes me to be. I've done terrible things, following his orders, and I don't want to be that man anymore.

"She's changed me, made me think about the future, made me see him for what he really is. I even started to believe that he was the monster, the real criminal here. But then, then, YOU DELIVER HIS HEAD IN A BOX!

"He was a good man, a soldier, following orders. You're right, this is a war, and soldiers die, but not, not like that. No one deserves to die like that."

"Please," Kahler begged, "we didn't kill anyone, we didn't know."

"No," Samuel continued, drawing the pistol from his belt and tapping it repeatedly against his forehead. "You're all the same, worthless skeets, lying and scheming, cheating and killing. You, the Regent, you deserve each other. I was stupid to think I didn't have to be a part of it."

"Please," Kahler said again. "We didn't do anything."

"Last chance," Samuel announced, levelling his pistol. "Only one of you gets to walk away. Three."

"You can't do this!" Borst cried.

"Two," Samuel counted.

"There has to be a trial," Kahler demanded. "Judgement by the Elders!"

"One," Samuel concluded.

"No, please," Borst begged, raising his hands in surrender.

With a faint shake of his head, Samuel fired, first at Borst and then at Kahler, killing them both. There were screams and cries from the crowd that had gathered, though Samuel barely noticed.

X

"General," Officer Hastings said as he slid stealthily into the tent. "There's word from the scouts."

Boshtok rubbed at his sleepy eyes and rose slowly from his bed, stretching before pulling on his uniform. The reports regarding the casualties had been disappointing, and sleep had eluded him for many nights since. Once suitably attired, he left his tent and joined Major Ellis and Major Alderman as the scout gave her report.

"Our count puts them somewhere between forty and forty five thousand troops," the scout was saying, "along with cannons and catapults. They look to be marching slowly and show little sign of fatigue."

"Any idea about who will be leading them?" Boshtok asked, prompting the scout to stand suddenly to attention and salute. "Please, relax," Boshtok added.

"Thank you, General," the scout replied. "Members of my unit were able to infiltrate the outskirts of their camp, but I can only report rumours at this time."

"Go on," Boshtok prompted.

"Many of the soldiers appear to be young and inexperienced, though they are engaged in daily training exercises," the scout informed them. "They speak in awe of a Lord Jonathan of

Ashford who is leading them."

"Jonathan you say?" Boshtok asked, a smile forming upon his lips.

"Is this cause for concern?" Major Ellis asked.

"No, quite the contrary," Boshtok replied. "From the reports I've read on him, he's an arrogant, self-important little man who favours overwhelming force over any form of strategic thinking. He'll send his forces at us in waves, one after another, hoping to grind us down, all the while bombarding us with his cannons and catapults. It should be easy enough to outsmart him."

"You're confident of this?" Major Alderman asked.

"Trust me, gentlemen," Boshtok told them. "Our forces will be breathing sea air by month's end."

XI

The sun was high in the sky, a searing heat through the trees as they glimpsed the small town in the distance. "Is that it?" Reid asked, shielding his eyes.

"Yes, that's it," Carl said. "I remember Victor's house up on the rise, that one over there." He pointed to a ramshackle looking building, part brick and part wood, with mismatched windows over two storeys. Like most of the buildings he remembered from Sanctuary, it looked to have been constructed from whatever they could find, and he was surprised that it was still standing.

"About time," Ben grumbled. "Hey, do you think we're in time for the big midday meal? Do you remember the last time when we were here, that big pot of stew on the town common?"

"I think that was probably a one-time thing," Carl suggested, "making the strangers feel welcome. We're not strangers anymore."

"Captain Reid is," Ben remarked sulkily.

Carl laughed and Safran poked Ben sharply in the stomach. "You're always thinking about food," she teased.

"I am not," Ben objected, poking her back. "Well, not always, anyway."

"Are they always like that?" Reid whispered to Carl.

"Pretty much," Carl replied.

"Oh, to be young and hormonal," Reid mused. "Better them than me."

"No argument here," Carl said grinning, watching as Ben and Safran fought playfully, poking at each other's midsection whilst trying to stop themselves from being poked in turn.

They left the shade of the trees and walked across one of the outlying farms, heading towards the town's main street. It was only when they got closer that they noticed the small crowd that had gathered.

"Carl, Safran, Benjamin," Victor's deep voice announced as he stepped forwards. "I know why you are here, and the answer is no."

CHAPTER 7

So, that didn't go according to plan. Victor doesn't want to listen to Carl's request. I suppose when you can read people's minds, you get all of their arguments at once. At least he gave us something to eat.

Captain Reid hasn't said much since we arrived. I think a part of him just wants to scream 'I told you so!', but deep down he was really hoping that this would all work out. We've told him about the Regent's army and the threat to his homeland, and he's of the same opinion as the rest of us. Without help, we don't have a chance.

Alexander wins.

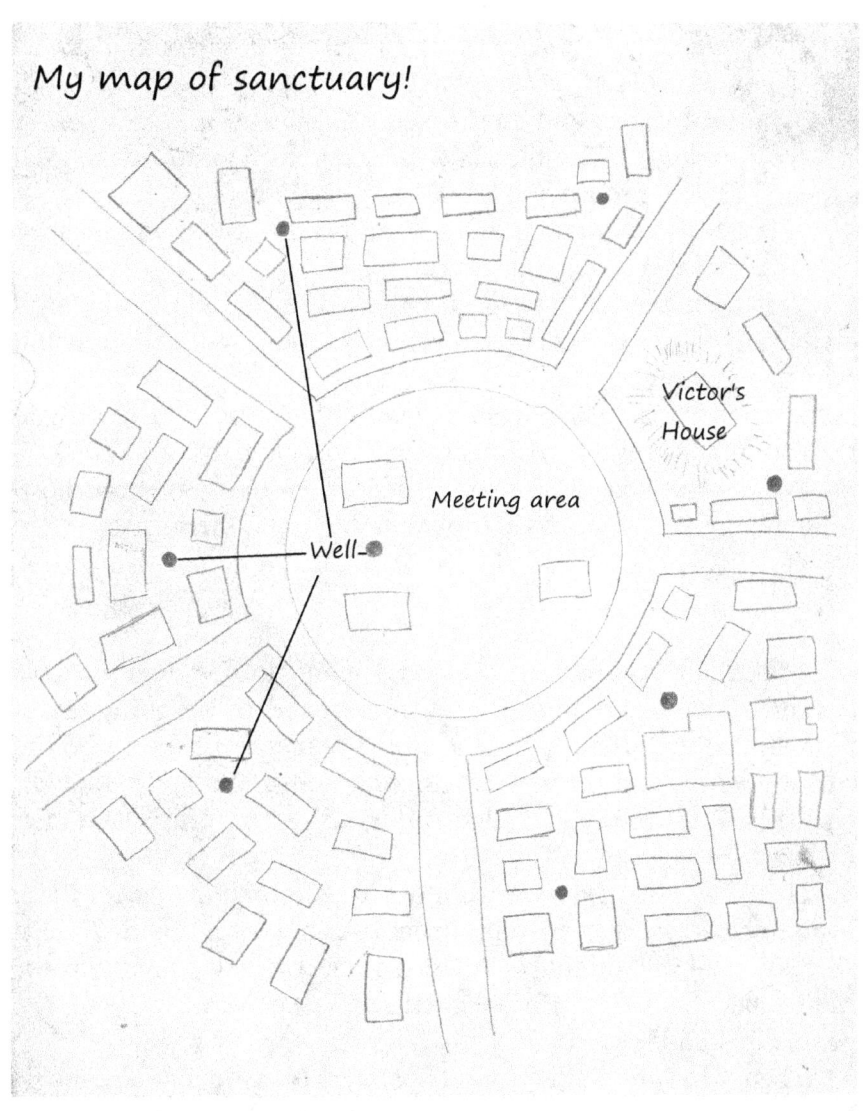

My map of sanctuary!

Victor's House

Meeting area

Well

I

"Just a minute," Carl protested. "You might think you know what we came to talk to you about, but you have to hear us out."

"I have already *heard* all that I need too," Victor told them, "as I know Catrina informed you."

"Wait," Captain Reid interrupted. "What's he talking about?"

"My apologies, Captain Reid of The Aero," Victor replied. "It appears that your journey has been a wasted one."

"Please," Ben added, his voice barely above a whisper. "Please, Victor. We've come all this way."

Victor scrutinised them, their tired eyes and their dirty clothes. They were weary, in more ways than one, and he could see that coming back to Sanctuary had been an act of desperation. "Come," he said at last. "I can offer you food and rest, but nothing more. My answer will not change."

With weary legs and heavy hearts, Ben and his companions followed Victor as the small crowd parted to let them pass.

II

Alexander stood wearily on the balcony, looking out over the city of Maleton, his city. Everything looked to be going on as normal. People busied about the streets, eager to get home before curfew. Stores and businesses secured their doors and windows. Officers of the Watch patrolled and investigated, diligent in their duties.

He'd been its ruler for almost five months, but for him, everything seemed to be going from bad to worse. It had all been so easy in the beginning, convincing the Elder Council and the Merchants Guild of Baron Stephen's treachery, rallying the people behind him.

Then it had all started to fall apart, with Safran and the rebels far more of a threat than he had anticipated. He'd stepped up his timetable, removing the Elders and the Merchants from power, cementing his rule under a cloud of fear, but still they fought back. After the theatre, he thought that they would have to succumb, to bend to his will, but they responded with the bomb beneath the palace, then the destruction of the Keye Bridge. Now the officer sent to infiltrate Deacon's meeting had been discovered and killed.

The dream had been plaguing him almost every night, disrupting his sleep, stealing away his energy. Even as he stood there, surveying his city, he felt the tiredness in his legs, the heaviness of his eyes. Every fibre of body screamed at him to stop, to lie down and rest, but he refused, confident that everything would settle once the rebels were defeated. He had the time, he had the resources, and more importantly, he had the will to succeed. There was nothing that he wouldn't consider to achieve victory.

"My Liege," a voice said from the doorway, interrupting his thoughts. "My apologies for the interruption, but Commander Larson is here, requesting an audience."

"Send him in," Alexander replied.

The Palace Guard bowed and left, retuning a moment later with Samuel Larson and closing the heavy throne doors behind him. "Larson," Alexander said without looking round. "Come join me on the balcony."

"Thank you, Regent," Samuel replied, stepping out into the evening sun.

"I assume you've come to tell me about the loss of your man?" Alexander continued, still looking down towards the city.

"In part," Samuel replied cryptically.

"Ah," Alexander said. "Interesting, but tell me first, Larson, what do you see?"

Samuel looked out over the city, following the Regent's gaze. To his left, the large Council Chambers stood taller than the smaller town houses that surrounded it. To the far right was the unusually shaped Merchant's Guild building, looking like the sail of a ship moving through the city. Below them, beyond the palace walls, people went about with their lives, scurrying from place to place or stood clustered in small groups, deep in conversation.

To Samuel, everything looked as it should do, just like any other day in Maleton. "I see the city and its people?" he said at last, unsure what the Regent was after.

"Exactly," Alexander replied brashly. "Just going about their lives as normal, oblivious to the decisions that we take, the battles we fight, and all for their well-being. We make sacrifices every day, Larson, and I suspect that even if they knew, they wouldn't understand. This is a thankless role, as I'm sure you'll agree."

"I do, Regent," Samuel replied, confused about the direction that the conversation was taking. He had expected to be berated, punished for his failure, but instead Alexander was speaking to him openly about his thoughts and fears. It felt almost like their early meetings, when they were still new to the city before them.

"Perhaps," Alexander said cynically, finally turning to look Samuel in the face. "Now, you wish to report the death of the Watchman you chose to infiltrate Deacon's meeting I assume?"

"No," Samuel said, meeting the Regent's gaze. "Blake's death isn't news to you, and if I may speak honestly-"Samuel paused as he waited for Alexander to nod, "It was to be expected. Whoever we sent in there, it was always going to end this way. Deacon and his followers, they're smart, too smart to fall for a ruse like that. No, Regent, I wish to speak on another matter."

Alexander took a subconscious step backwards, away from the man who was behaving so differently towards him. Without realising it, Alexander had placed his hand against the blade concealed along his belt. "Go on," he prompted.

"I don't think I've been quite myself lately," Samuel told him. "My work, my duties, they've become less important to me than they used to be, and for that I need to apologise. You've given me so much, the opportunity to make something of myself, taught me what it is to lead. I haven't always been as true to you and your goals as I should have been.

"You asked me some time ago if I was the right man for the job. This last month or two, I've had my doubts, but no longer. You're right, Regent, you were right about everything. These people, they're animals, and they deserve whatever they have coming to them."

Alexander relaxed slightly, smiling. "You aren't the only one with doubts, Larson," he said. "But it's how you resolve them that matters. Come, let's talk about what we do next."

Alexander placed a hand on Samuel's shoulder, directing him to one of the tables where they both took a seat. With new found energy, Alexander considered that perhaps the situation wasn't quite as bleak as he had feared.

III

The residents of Sanctuary were friendly, making polite conversation as Ben and his companions ate, though Victor was conspicuously absent throughout the meal. He returned just as the sun began to slide down towards the horizon.

"I have made space for you all in my home," he said. "Join me when you are ready."

"Are we really giving up?" Safran asked incredulously. Ben looked to Carl, who shrugged his shoulders in response and returned to finishing his meal.

"No," Ben said defiantly. "We're not giving up. Victor assumes that he knows everything about our intentions, but he should still hear us out."

"That's what I'm not clear on?" Reid interrupted between mouthfuls. "How could he know anything? He might suspect, but you all only decided to come here from Markay two weeks ago? There's no way he could have received word before we arrived."

Carl, Ben and Safran exchanged uneasy looks. Catrina had told them about Victor's power, but was it their secret to share? From what they understood, Victor even kept it from the other residents of Sanctuary. What would happen if they found out?

"Let's make our way up to the house," Carl said, looking at Reid intently. "If you'll join us, Reid, I'm sure everything will become clear. Just keep an open mind." Reid gave him a surprised look in return, but followed them without argument.

The villagers took their plates and glasses, thanking Carl and the others for their compliments and bid them goodnight as they climbed the small hill to Victor's home. To their surprise, the inside looked to be much more organised than the outside, with well-appointed rooms and amenities.

Stone stairs led from the hallway to upstairs rooms, while doors on the ground floor led to a large kitchen and a smaller sitting room where they found Victor adding logs to a growing fire. "It may be warm during the day," he said, "but come nightfall, the temperature can fall drastically. Have a seat."

"Don't we know it," Carl replied, remembering the nights that they had spent under blankets around a dwindling fire.

The chairs looked to be old and well worn, but they were comfortable. There were insufficient for everyone to sit, so Captain Reid agreed to stand, hovering near the door.

"Perhaps a drink before you retire?" Victor asked, walking towards a decanter surrounded by six chipped glasses. Carl and Reid were thankful for the offer, while Ben and Safran declined, Ben still wary after his previous encounters with the strong alcoholic beverage.

Once the drinks were poured, they sat in companionable silence, Victor's piercing green eyes scrutinising each of them in turn. Each time one of them looked as though they would speak, Victor turned to stare at them intently, smiling subtly to himself. Ultimately, it was Victor who spoke first.

"I have heard all of your arguments," he said, "and they will not sway me. Captain Reid, the answer is simply that I can read people, their faces and their thoughts." Victor paused as Reid frowned, eyeing him suspiciously.

"Yes, perhaps similar to the stories the Kurn's tell of the Storm Witches, though I do not claim to know the weather," Victor continued. Reid became wide eyed, staring at Victor with a mixture of fear and awe, as though Victor had plucked the very thought from his mind.

"You have suffered greatly since last we met," Victor went on, turning to look at Safran. "You have lost a great deal, but also found hope. I understand the stakes and your desperation, but I simply cannot do what you ask of me. Never again will I use my ability to force people to fight, no matter how noble the cause."

"You wouldn't have to convince Baron Eliza to fight," Safran interrupted, "only that the threat is real. Once she believes that Markay is in danger, she'll call upon the people to rise up and defend it. They'll want to fight to protect their homeland."

Victor smiled at her, shaking his head slowly. "Your father taught you a great deal about tactics, about diplomacy," he said. "You will make a fine Baron one day. You must see though, that if I compel someone to fight, or compel another to make them fight, the outcome is the same. Men and women will die, robbed of their ability to make their own decisions. I will not be a part of that, not again."

"But what about the threat to you and your people?" Carl asked. "What do you think will happen when Alexander has all of the Southern Baronies under his control? With Island City to the north, he'll want to unite all the lands under his rule, including the Wastelands in between."

"If his armies come," Victor replied, "we will fight and die to defend our homes, and it will be our choice to do so. If there are those who choose to back down, to surrender, so be it."

"You're right," Ben said, drawing the attention towards him. "We should never have come, asking you to use your ability like this. I understand, great power, great responsibility and all that. It's not your place, or ours, to force people to fight for what you believe in."

Carl and Safran looked at him with incredulity, unable to believe their ears. It had taken them two weeks to make the journey from Markay, and now Ben was agreeing with Victor, telling them all that it had been a waste of time. Without help, Alexander would succeed, they all knew it. Why was Ben being like that?

"Thank you, Benjamin," Victor said. "I am pleased that, you at least, understand."

"So let's ask you for something else," Ben continued, barely pausing for breath. "The tribes, Sanctuary-"

"They will not," Victor interrupted. "It is not possible."

"What's not possible?" Safran asked, more confused than ever. Victor opened his mouth to speak before closing it again, looking to Ben to explain.

"What Carl said," Ben told them, "about Alexander's plans. Once the Southern Baronies are under his control, he'll turn his attention north again. He won't risk leaving Island City undefended while his forces remain in Draxis. Matthew told me before about the Wasteland tribes and how they moved into Island City, making it their home. It wouldn't take much for one of the tribes to go and claim it all, with most of the people fighting Alexander's war in the south."

"So what are you thinking?" Carl asked.

"We went south, to the other Baronies," Ben continued, "looking for an army to fight Alexander's forces. What if we were looking in the wrong direction?"

"There are perhaps three hundred men and women living within Sanctuary," Victor reminded them. "Even if they wished to fight, their numbers would make little difference."

"But the other tribes?" Ben prompted.

"I say again," Victor insisted. "They will not. It is not possible."

"When people come to Sanctuary," Ben persisted, "you don't use your ability to convince them to stay, do you? No, you talk to them, show them a different way of living in the Wastelands, a better way. Some agree with you and some don't, but those that do, they live here by your rules. Matthew explained it all to us."

"That is true," Victor replied, eyeing Ben warily.

"So what if you could offer more tribes the chance to live like this," Ben went on. "The chance to live free from the constant fighting and struggles to survive? What if you could offer them a city to rival any in the Southern Baronies, better even than Maleton or Aldonis? What if you could offer them the power of electricity?"

"Ben, no!" Carl exclaimed.

"Electricity?" Reid stammered. "That's just a story, isn't it?"

"I see now it is not," Victor remarked.

"Would the tribes stand together, fight together, for something like that?" Ben asked.

"Ben, just think about this," Carl said. "Think about what you're saying."

"I have thought about it, Carl," Ben replied. "I'm tired of watching from the sidelines, watching as people get hurt. If you've got another idea, I'll listen, but I thought this was our last chance? I've been looking for something, waiting for something like this, a way to use what I know to help. What's the point of keeping this secret if we all die with it?

"I know it was important to keep it from Alexander. We all knew what he'd do with the power, how people would suffer, but this is different. We'd be in charge of it, we would control it. We'd only use it to help people."

"After you use it to fight a war?" Carl asked.

Ben was silent for a moment as he pondered what Carl had said. He was thinking on his feet, calculating the output from the fusion generator, designing a method of transferring the power to the substation in Garstang. From there, the electricity could supply the whole city and more besides, but was it worth the risk?

Carl was wrong; the secrets in the laboratory wouldn't be used to fight a war, but they'd be payment for helping them win one. Could he live with that? And once the secret was out, would he really be able to control it? Would it really bring people together, or would they just fight all the more to take it from him?

"You've always looked out for me, Carl," Ben said honestly, trying to make sense of the jumble of questions running through his mind. "I've been nothing but a burden since I arrived, and all you've done is take care of me when you could have so easily left me behind. It's my turn now, to give something back.

"If you think this is a bad idea, I'll listen to you, but I don't see anyone coming up with anything better. I know we've joked about it, but you really do remind me of my dad, and I respect what you think."

Carl blushed slightly as Ben spoke, clearing the lump that had formed in his throat. "You were never a burden," he said with a grin. "A pain in my ass, a son of a skeet, and an annoying know it all, but never a burden.

"You're right, I don't have any better ideas, and we're running out of time. You heard Matthew's voice on the radio. He didn't sound too confident about Morton's success against the northern army, and it may already be too late. Can you really make good on what you're offering?"

"I can," Ben said sincerely.

"Then I guess it's over to Victor," Carl acquiesced.

"This is, unexpected," Victor said thoughtfully. "I do not know what the other tribes would say to such an offer. They have lived their way for so long, but that should not stop us from asking the question.

"Let me think on it tonight, I will give you my answer in the morning."

Victor finished his drink in one gulp before going upstairs, deep in thought. He had vowed to never use his ability again in such a way. It had cost him his father and his brother, and so much more, but what if he didn't need to? What if he could bring his ideas to a larger audience, to build a New Sanctuary and bring peace to the Wastelands where it had never been? Surely that must be worth the risk?

Reid watched Victor leave before pouring himself another drink and taking a seat in the empty chair. "You people," he said, more to himself than anyone else. "What else haven't you told me?"

IV

"Hello?" Marie called out as she heard the front door open.

"It's only me," Samuel replied.

"Sam!" Marie exclaimed. "You're early, what a lovely surprise." She almost ran from the living room, straight into his arms. "Is everything okay?"

Samuel pondered the question for a minute, recapping the day's events in his mind. The day had been far from okay, but after his meeting with Alexander and coming home to the woman he loved, it had all been worth it. "It is now," he replied, kissing her again.

"I haven't even started dinner," Marie apologised, beginning to walk towards the kitchen.

"I'm not hungry," Samuel told her, pulling her back into his arms. "I want to talk to you, there's something I need to say."

Marie stopped dead, convinced in that moment that Samuel knew that it had been her who had passed information to the Rebels. The world suddenly felt far away as dread consumed her and a dead weight grew in the pit of her stomach. "What," she began, her voice a faint whisper as her mouth dried up. "What do you want to say?"

Sam looked at her quizzically as the colour drained from her face and her eyes went wide. "I love you," he said, kissing her forehead, "and I'm sorry for the way I've been these last few weeks. I've been a mess, full of uncertainty and doubt. I couldn't see straight, with the Regent and the rebels, and I brought you down with me. I'm sorry for all that but it's okay now, I'm okay. I know my place, my role. I know what I'm supposed to do.

"Thank you for being there, for sticking with me. I know it's been hard, but it's going to get better. I promise."

Marie looked up at him, finally hearing what he was saying. "Sam," she said, once she had found her voice. "There's nowhere else I want to be."

Samuel smiled and kissed her again, and she kissed him back, her fears fading as she cherished the moment. Everything was good, great even, and it was all going to work out for them in the end.

V

Ben woke early, his body having become unaccustomed to sleeping in a real bed. His stirrings woke Carl and Reid who were dozing on the narrow beds to his right.

"Morning," Carl said grumpily, sitting up slowly and stretching his weary muscles.

"Good morning," Reid added, rubbing at his temples. After Victor had left the previous night, he had taken it upon himself to finish the remainder of the whiskey, hoping that the alcohol's effect would help him to accept mind readers and electricity. "You know, sleeping in a cramped room with you two reminds me of why I love my ship so much."

"I'll bet," Ben agreed. "I don't know what was in that stew we ate, but come on, Carl, how much gas can one man produce?" Carl grinned and added an extra dose to the room for good measure, making Ben gag.

"Are you decent?" Safran asked through the door, knocking politely.

"Not even close," Ben remarked, "but we're all dressed if that's what you mean. Come on in, if you dare."

Saran opened the door cautiously, peeking through the crack. "Good mor-" she began before quickly holding her nose. "Oh, what died in here?"

"Whatever it is," Ben told her, "it's inside Carl. Let's get out of here and speak to Victor, see what his answer is."

"He went out," Safran informed them. "About a half hour ago, I heard him leave." Carl and Ben exchanged uneasy glances, each wondering what Victor's departure might mean.

"He'll be back," Carl said confidently. "He has to, it's his house. Let's go find the kitchen."

Safran led the way down the stairs and to the back of the house where a spacious farmhouse style kitchen was to be found. They sat around the large wooden table while Carl busied himself with the stove, starting a fire and heating a kettle of water.

"Where do you think he went?" Safran asked, breaking the silence.

"Hopefully to get some breakfast," Carl suggested, searching the cupboards for something to add to the hot water.

Their question was soon answered, as Victor returned in the company of an elderly lady who he introduced as Murphy. "She is the closest we have to a doctor in these parts," Victor informed them, "as well as my oldest friend. After our conversation last night, I thought it wise to seek her counsel."

"You can really make electricity?" Murphy asked Ben, surprised by the young man who sat before her. "What does it look like?"

"Sort of," Ben replied, "and it's one of those things that'd be easier to show you."

"In all our travels," Murphy said to herself. "So many stories."

"Murphy and I ventured far and wide in our younger days," Victor said. "We journeyed throughout the Wastelands and beyond before deciding to build this community. I have seen things you people would not believe."

Attack ships on fire off the shoulder of Orion, Ben thought to himself absent mindedly. Victor looked at him quizzically, receiving the strange image from Ben's mind. It was of two men, fighting on a rooftop in the rain. Victor was confident that he had never seen it before, but at the same time there was an overwhelming sense of familiarity to it, just beyond his reach.

"Like tears in the rain?" Victor asked, making Ben's skin crawl. "You are an unusual young man, Benjamin Knight."

"I suppose," Ben replied, the heavy feeling in the pit of his stomach finally receding. "Did you think about what we talked about?"

"I thought of nothing else," Victor remarked. "I will admit, this is something that I have long wished for, changing the way that the tribes of the Wastelands live. I have always chosen the path of caution, though, learning from my mistakes. Murphy, however, reminded me of our plans when we first built this community and she is, of course, right." He looked down at Murphy who smiled back at him affectionately.

"I have been cautious for too long," Victor continued, "speaking only to those who stumble across our town. We started our community with only five or six families, but soon that number grew, and look at us now. Life is no longer a torment out here in the Wastelands, it is a joy. If ever there was a time to show others what we have accomplished, this must be it.

"I will send word to the largest tribes that I know of and ask them to join us at Garstang. If they wish to pass through Sanctuary on their way, they may see first-hand what we have accomplished."

"And then I'll show them the lab," Ben said sombrely, the faintest hint of doubt creeping into his mind.

"We will show them how life could be if we worked together," Victor corrected, "and allow them to make their own decision."

"Live together or die alone," Ben continued, referencing one of his favourite television shows.

"In a manner of speaking," Victor agreed.

"So when do we leave?" Carl asked.

"I will be ready in an hour," Victor replied. "Murphy will organise some breakfast for you all."

VI

Lord Jonathan gave the order to advance as soon as his scouts brought word of General Boshtok's forces massing to the north. The cannons and catapults sent volley after volley in the direction of Boshtok's troops, appearing to drive them to disarray as line upon line of organised soldiers marched forwards. As his troops fell upon the scattered Island City forces, Lord Jonathan ordered the siege weapons to quiet, hoping to avoid any unnecessary casualties amongst his own men. It would be over in a matter of hours, he believed, the Island City forces no match for his numbers and discipline

General Boshtok looked on from his vantage point to the west. Lord Jonathan was behaving just as he had expected. Morton's forces were grouped together into tight formations, marching in a straight line towards the small number of soldiers stationed to the north. It was all going according to plan.

As Morton's cannons and catapults fired, Boshtok's forces appeared to scatter, fooling Lord Jonathan into believing that he had the advantage. As Morton's forces pressed forwards, Boshtok's men moved from their hiding places, attacking the siege weapons first. Morton's rear forces were not prepared for an attack, and the cannons and catapults were overwhelmed.

The combat was close and bloody, knives and daggers taking the place of pistols and rifles as Boshtok's men cut their way through the rear guard. Just as Lord Jonathan ordered the retreat, Boshtok's forces were already turning Morton's weapons against them, firing into the tight disciplined lines that Lord Jonathan prized so highly.

Morton's lines broke as the siege weapons cut through their ranks, the soldiers running in all directions as they struggled to avoid the onslaught. Lord Jonathan was cut down as he tried to organise a counter offensive, assembling his young and inexperienced troops into columns to push back against the enemy horde.

Lord Howard saw the futility of the tactics and instead called upon his men to retreat. They were surrounded and he had to choose a point for the remaining forces to push upon. He chose wisely, driving the remaining soldiers back through his own siege weapons where the lines of cannons and catapults prevented his troops from being truly overwhelmed.

They destroyed what they could as they retreated, setting light to the barrels of gunpowder as they passed. The smoke and devastation helped to cover their retreat, though their losses were substantial.

Lord Howard barely made it out alive, but the same could not be said for many others. As night fell and the Island City forces gave up their pursuit, there were less than two thousand men and women left under his command.

In the end, Lord Jonathan had been right. The battle was all over in a matter of hours, and Morton had lost.

VII

They were two days into their journey and making good time towards Garstang. Victor had dispatched messengers to several of the tribes that lived in the northern region of the Wastelands, including those who lived in the settlements of Cairns, Stark and Sovereign. The small towns were trade hubs for the Wastelands, allowing tribes to barter with each other for goods and supplies. Though they didn't live under the stricter rules of Sanctuary, Victor felt it was important to invite them along. If they were truly going to try and bring a degree of civilisation to the area, involving the already moderately civilised settlements was an important step.

Captain Reid had decided to stay with Carl and his companions, wishing to see the laboratory that Ben had described. He had heard stories about electricity since he was a boy, and just like most others as they grew up, came to believe that that was all they were, stories. Now he had the opportunity to see something truly wonderful, and he wasn't going to let it pass. Victor had been kind enough to send word to The Aero, passing on Captain Reid's orders to return to Ashford, and Reid began the journey to Garstang with them.

They made camp just as it was getting dark, gathering dry twigs and branches to make a fire. The night was far from cold, but the light made them all feel more comfortable sleeping beneath the trees. Ben was surprised at how easily both Victor and Murphy moved through the woodland, climbing and jumping with more grace and precision than Ben could muster. Victor looked to be in his fifties, and Murphy even older, but they moved with the agility of someone half their age.

"Do not be fooled," Victor said, snapping a branch in two. "I may look like I am able, but my aching joints beg to differ."

"I'm sorry," Ben said, blushing. "I didn't mean any offence."

"And none was taken," Victor replied. "Enjoy your youth while you can, Benjamin. It will leave you all too soon, believe me."

Before long, the fire was heating the pail of water and Carl set about dividing up the rations. They had brought plenty of food with them from Sanctuary, but his years on the Road Trains had instilled a sense of caution in Carl that he was unable to ignore. The meat was tender and the flat bread tasty, and once satisfied, the conversation became lighter and the mood more jovial.

"Do you have another tale of your adventures to share with us this evening, Captain Reid?" Victor asked, washing down his meal with a mouthful of warm tea.

"Reid on dry land, please," Reid reminded him, "and I'm always happy to share a story, but perhaps someone else should like a turn? Carl?"

"I'm afraid my stories rarely have a happy ending," Carl said sombrely, the look of acute sadness on his face dissuading anyone from pushing the issue.

"Hey, Ben," Safran said, trying to maintain the friendly atmosphere. "What about you? You must have stories from where you come from?"

Ben thought about it for a minute. Most of the stories he knew were from comics, films, and the occasional video game. Fortunately for him, they were unlikely to realise that. "Why not," he said with a grin, and proceeded to tell them about a city where he grew up, and the work of a hero known only as The Batman.

They ate it up, enjoying every minute of the adventure, marvelling at the twisted villains and electricity powered gadgets that saved the day. By the end of his tale, the fire was dimming and eyes were heavy, ready to sleep, but they all asked him to tell another.

"Maybe tomorrow," Ben promised, enjoying the spotlight.

"Let us get some more wood," Victor suggested, offering Ben his hand to help him stand.

"Okay, sure," Ben replied, the look on Victor's face suggesting that there was more than wood that he wanted to discuss.

Ben followed Victor a short distance to where the large branch of a tree had come down in high winds. Victor began breaking the smaller branches off, gathering them under his left arm. Ben followed suit, though found the task much more difficult.

"So, I suppose you know the story wasn't true," Ben offered, breaking the silence. "I didn't mean to trick anyone, honestly."

"A story does not need to be true to entertain," Victor replied. "Just ask Captain Reid."

"I knew it!" Ben exclaimed, snapping a branch in his excitement.

"No, it was another matter I wished to discuss with you," Victor continued.

Ben stopped what he was doing and looked Victor in the eye. He was reminded again of the intensity of Victor's green eyes that, even in the dim light, seemed to glow as they stared intently at him. "What is it?" Ben asked.

"During these last two days," Victor said, "your doubts have grown considerably. You worry that you have made a terrible mistake, that this is the wrong course of action, yet you are powerless to change your mind. I wanted to tell you that it is not too late, and we can return to sanctuary whenever you wish."

Ben dropped his gaze, twisting the branch in his grip as he considered the words. Victor was right, as soon as he made the offer, he began to think that he had made a mistake, but what else could he do?

"I've been remembering more about my time in the dungeons," Ben began. "Back in Island City. Alexander and the things, the things he did to me. He was prepared to do anything to learn about the laboratory and the secret to electricity, and I held out for as long as I could, but I know I told him everything. I couldn't help myself, I just wasn't strong enough.

"Matthew and Carl, they managed to stop the soldiers that had followed us, managed to keep the lab a secret from Alexander, and now I'm about to just give that secret away to someone else. I mean, I know what Alexander would have done with it, how he would have used it, but from what Matthew told me about the Wastelands tribes, are they going to be any different?

"I don't mean you, you know that, right? I've seen what you've done in Sanctuary, how the people there follow you. I know you wouldn't use the technology there to try and control people, to scare them into following you, but I just don't know what's going to happen when the other tribes come."

"If you knew of my past," Victor replied quietly, "you would think differently of me, but a man, men, can change. You are stronger than you think, Benjamin Knight, I have seen it within you. I cannot hope to understand where you come from, nor do I know if you can get back, but I know that you are capable of great things here, and your companions see it too. Carl believes in you, and so does Safran. You need only to begin to believe in yourself."

Ben was silent for a moment, thinking over what Victor had said. He hoped that Victor was right, that he could help them make a difference, but he still had his doubts. "Thank you," he said at last. "I'll think about it, about what you said. I really want to help, for everything to work out okay. Thanks, Victor, this has really helped."

"Then let me give you one more piece of advice," Victor said, gathering together the wood and turning back towards the camp.

"Please," Ben replied.

"I have seen the way you look at Safran," Victor told him, "and the way she looks at you. I do not need to know your thoughts to know how you feel about each other. Remember what I told you, Benjamin, to enjoy your youth while you can. Do not keep her waiting much longer."

Ben stopped dead in his tracks, face red and heart racing, utterly lost for words.

VIII

"Are you ready?" Catrina asked, checking the magazine in her pistol for the third time.

"Just say the word," Nathan replied, checking the road ahead of her. They were both crouched inside the doorway to a derelict building in the Industrial District, waiting for the patrol to come their way. Deacon's informant had done well, passing along updates on the changes in patrol routes and changeover times at the various Watch Houses.

The plan had been simple; use the information that they had been given to strike simultaneously across the city, letting the Watch and everyone else know that they were no longer so few in number. Even as Catrina and Nathan readied themselves, teams from members of the other city gangs were taking up similar positions in the Market and City Districts, waiting to strike.

"They're coming," Stan announced, dropping down through a hole in the roof where had had been keeping watch. "Four of them, and they haven't even got their weapons drawn."

Catrina smiled, eyes wide as she anticipated the impending violence, while Nathan and Stan closed their eyes and mentally readied themselves for the coming fight. "Safran Lives!" Catrina yelled as she kicked the door open and burst out onto the moonlit street, firing at the patrol. Nathan was only a step behind her, raising his rifle and adding to the assault.

Two of the Watchmen were cut down before they even realised what was happening, the remaining two diving for cover. Catrina began a cautious advance, pistol raised at the doorway where she knew the remaining soldiers must be hiding. She was just about to call out and taunt them when gunfire erupted from behind her, throwing sparks from the pavement at her feet and a sudden searing pain in her left thigh.

"Back," Nathan screamed, firing blindly towards the source of the gunfire as he dragged Catrina back into the building where they had only moments ago been hiding. Further gunfire peppered the doorframe as they fell inside, wooden splinters and stone dust cascading all around them.

"Who's shooting?" Stan asked, his apprehensive peek through the broken windows met with further gunfire.

"No idea," Catrina winced as the blue sparks danced around her leg, healing the wound in seconds. It never ceased to amaze any of them how Catrina was able to heal so quickly and completely, and they were thankful for it as a thud against the outside wall was followed quickly by an explosion.

"Just move, out the back," Catrina ordered, getting nimbly to her feet and sprinting towards the rear of the building. A second explosion behind her blew out the remainder of the building's windows, showering them all in glass shards. Both Nathan and Stan instinctively dropped into a crouch, hands over their heads, while Catrina ignored the glass splinters, instead searching for a way out.

The only other door was stuck tight, but was no match for

Nathan's bulk as he shouldered into it, almost tearing it fully from its hinges. It led out into a small gravelled courtyard with stone walls to all sides and the remains of a long dry well in its centre.

"I don't see a way out," Stan said hurriedly, the first hint of fear creeping into his voice. "Which way now?"

"Up and over," Nathan replied, already stepping towards the far wall. "Come on, I'll help you up."

The wall was a little over three metres high, and Nathan lifted Stan effortlessly up onto his shoulders, allowing him to pull himself up and over. "You next," Nathan said to Catrina, cupping his hands for her to place her foot. Catrina paused, looking up into Nathan's eyes as he urged her to do as he asked. "Come on," he said, "we're running out of time."

"No, wait," Catrina stammered. "What about you?"

"I'll be right behind you," Nathan lied, staring at her intently.

"What's wrong?" Stan called from the other side of the wall.

"Nothing," Nathan called back to him, still looking at Catrina. "Here she comes."

Catrina shook her head, her eyes filling with tears as she began to step backwards. Nathan grabbed her and pulled her towards him. "You've got to go," he said breathlessly. "You've got finish this."

"No," she cried. "No, no, no."

"Catrina," Nathan said, gripping her shoulders tightly. "Get over that wall and look out for the boy. Promise me."

"No," Catrina said again, tears running down her cheeks.

"Get him home," Nathan persisted. "Keep him safe, for me."

Catrina's objections were cut short as further gunfire tore through the damaged doorway, missing them by millimetres. Catrina dropped to one knee, returning fire, the satisfying scream of a wounded soldier her reward. "We can hold them off," she insisted, firing again.

"For how long?" Nathan demanded. "How many are there? How many more grenades do they have?"

Catrina didn't have an answer for him, knowing deep down that he was right. If she stayed, they both died, it was only a matter of time. "Get him home," Nathan said again. "Finish this."

Catrina nodded, allowing Nathan to lift her onto his shoulders. He pushed her feet as she pulled herself over the wall, dropping nimbly to Stan's side. "Run!" she cried at Stan, gripping his hand tightly.

"We've got to wait for Nathan," Stan objected.

"Run!" Catrina screamed again, dragging him along.

As gunfire sounded behind them, and Nathan let loose an agonised scream, Stan finally stopped struggling and ran.

IX

"General," Officer Hastings said quietly, rousing General Boshtok from where he was resting against the large map table.

"Hastings," Boshtok replied wearily, blinking his eyes into focus. "Do you have the preliminary numbers?"

"I do, General," Hastings informed him, rummaging through the collection of papers in his hands. "Major Ellis was keen to point out that these figures are estimates at best, but he counts the losses at somewhere between five and six thousand, wounded a little higher at eight thousand.

"Medical staff are working constantly, saving those that they can, but the number of deaths is likely to rise."

"Worse than I had hoped," Boshtok said to himself, "but not as high as I had feared. I presume the greatest losses were during the initial assault?"

"They were," Hastings replied. "The decoy units, positioned to draw fire from Morton's siege weapons."

"And the number of able bodied ready to advance?" Boshtok asked.

Hastings rummaged again, juggling the papers in his grasp. "Let's see," he muttered. "Ah, here we are. Somewhere in the region of twenty six thousand, give or take."

Boshtok stood and leant over the large map of the Southern Baronies, scrutinising it. His reports suggested that, though Morton's forces had been decimated in the attack, the large garrisons at Fort Solitude and Fort Danzig were not recalled to take part, and would no doubt be summoned to Ashford as a matter of urgency. The details were sketchy, but they numbered somewhere between twelve and fifteen thousand soldiers, those at Fort Danzig particularly hardened from their repeated skirmishes with the Kurns.

Boshtok was hesitant. Should even half of the injured survive, thirty thousand may not be enough, not to guarantee victory over Morton's forces and to then take and hold Ashford. Many of the siege weapons he had hoped to use against the city had been destroyed by the fleeing Ashford soldiers.

"Summon the messengers," Boshtok said at last, making his decision. "We'll send word to Maleton and call for reinforcements. You may give the Regent my assurances, Ashford will fall."

X

"Larson," Alexander said, looking up from his breakfast. "You bring me good news I hope?"

"I do, my Liege," Samuel replied. "The rebels attempted to strike against three of our patrols last night, just as you suspected."

Alexander's agents within the city had brought word of the plan, allowing Larson to position suitable reinforcements to turn the tables on the rebels. He wondered if he should feel bad for Sergeant Blake, the man he had ordered Larson to send into Deacon's meeting. He had never suspected for a minute that it would be successful, but by allowing Deacon and the rebels to find a traitor in their midst, it was easier for his other agents to continue to do their good work

"Survivors?" Alexander asked.

"Sadly not," Samuel said. "All of the rebels were killed attempting to flee. There was no sign of Deacon or Safran, but the smith from the Industrial District was amongst those killed."

"And the woman, from the Road Trains?" Alexander added.

"I'm afraid not, Regent," Samuel replied.

"Perhaps she did die beneath the palace after all," Alexander commented to himself. "Are you any closer to learning how the rebels learnt about the patrols in the first place?"

"No," Samuel said, thinking it over again in his mind. "I've spoken to the officers who knew about the changes, but I can't link it to any of them. They've all lost friends to Deacon and his people."

"There are many powerful motivators," Alexander reminded him, "as I'm sure you'll agree?"

"I'll look again, widen the net," Samuel assured him. "I'll find them."

"Be sure to bring them to me when you do," Alexander requested, his reptilian smile shining through. "It's been a while since I've had anyone to entertain me."

"Of course, Regent," Samuel replied, bowing slightly in an attempt to hide the look of revulsion that crossed his face.

XI

"Travelling like this," Victor mused, stepping over a fallen branch. "It reminds me of our first journey through the Wastelands."

"Me too," Murphy said, remembering better days. "I'll admit though, when I first found you I didn't think you'd survive."

"A testament to your skills," Victor complimented.

That made Murphy smile. "The things we saw," she continued. "The people we met."

"The nights beneath the stars," Victor said suggestively, making Murphy blush. "And yet, so many regrets."

Murphy was silent for a moment before asking, "Do you still think about your brother?"

"I do," Victor admitted. "I tell others to remember their past, to learn from it, yet I have wished so many times to forget mine. Darwin was, he was the best of us. What I did to him, I can never forgive myself."

"You're not the same man you once were," Murphy said honestly. "You've paid for your mistakes, many times over. Think of the lives you've changed, the lives you've saved."

"Perhaps," Victor replied sombrely. "I vowed never to use my ability again, yet how many times have I broken that vow? Whatever I do in the future, it will never be enough to make up for my past."

"I don't agree," Murphy said, kissing him on the cheek. "If you were as bad as you claim, I'd never have stayed with you all these years."

Victor smiled at that. "Thank you," he said. "You always know how to make me feel better. Come, we are lagging behind. We cannot allow these youngsters to think that we are tired."

XII

"But he might still be alive," Stan argued for the third time, wiping furiously at the tears that persisted in running down his face. They had gotten back to the brewery in the early hours of the morning, where Stan had collapsed onto his bunk and cried himself to sleep. Gavin had held him through the night, stroking his head and consoling him when he woke up screaming.

Catrina told the others what happened and had tried to rest herself, but sleep eluded her. She went over her final words with Nathan, again and again, torturing herself, looking for what she could have done that would have ended things differently. In the end she resigned herself to the truth. He was one more dead in her place, one more life she had taken just by being near them. He was doomed from the moment he met her.

"I am sorry, Stan," Deacon said, trying to console him, "but he would not have allowed himself to be captured, not again."

"What the Regent did to him," Catrina added, wiping away tears of her own. "He'd never have gone through that again. Deacon's right, we've got to let him go."

"He'd have gone back for you," Stan snapped angrily. "He loved you, Catrina, and all you ever did was hurt him. I can't believe you left him like that."

Deacon was about to object when Catrina placed a hand on his wrist, silencing him. "We all miss him, Stan," she said quietly. "We're all hurting, but Nathan made me promise to finish this. You and me, Stan, we'll end the Regent, we'll do that for him. Please?"

"Leave me alone," Stan cried, getting up from the table. Catrina let him go, not surprised by his outburst. Because he acted so grown up most of the time, it was easy for them to forget that, beneath it all, he was still so young.

"I'll go talk to him," Gavin offered, following Stan to one of the empty bunks on the other side of the room.

They were quiet for a minute, reflecting on how quickly their plans had fallen apart. They had lost eleven people in the ambush by the City Watch. The other gangs were already asking for answers.

"I know you did the right thing," Deacon said quietly, once Stan was out of earshot. "He will come to realise it too, in time."

"We'll see," Catrina said sombrely. "Nathan was like a second father to him. He feels like he's got no one left."

"He has us," Deacon objected.

"And what about the woman who set us up?" Catrina asked, her voice full of anger and hatred.

"Bran is already dealing with her," Deacon replied matter-of-factly.

XIII

"Do you have any oranges?" Bran asked, examining the sparse amount of fruit on the stall.

"They're rationed," Marie replied without looking round. "They're part of your allowance, at the warehouse. I have a few-"

Marie froze as she turned, her voice catching in her throat. She hadn't expected to see Bran again, not face to face. They had a system, an arrangement. She left the information at the drop, he left Samuel alone.

"Hello, Marie," Bran said, flashing his most intimidating smile. "Deacon suggested we have a chat."

"What about?" Marie hissed, her mouth dry and her hands sweating. The terror seemed to be crawling along her spine, paralysing her. The market was still relatively quiet, but there were enough people around who knew her, who knew Samuel. She couldn't be seen with Bran or Deacon or anyone associated with the rebels.

"Let's take a walk," Bran suggested, stepping around to the rear of the stall.

"Please, no," Marie begged.

"You'll only be away for a minute," Bran promised. "Unless you really want to do this here?"

Marie looked around, her eyes wide. She was already getting questioning looks from the neighbouring stalls, but they all knew Bran or knew of him, and there was no way that any of them would interfere.

Marie began walking, slowly, unsure of where she was going. Bran gripped her arm, gently, turning her towards the river. They walked in silence through the market square, finally sitting upon one of the wooden benches that overlooked the damaged remains of the Keye Bridge. Bran sat staring at the devastation, a relaxed smile upon his face.

"What do you want," Marie asked after a minute, the silence deafening.

"What do you think I want?" Bran asked cryptically.

"I haven't heard anything else," Marie whispered. "I told you about the new patrol routes. That's all I know."

"That's true," Bran agreed. "You did tell us about the new patrol routes."

He paused, letting the statement hang, waiting for Marie to jump into the gap, betray herself. Marie only stared at him, her face fearful but at the same time confused.

"Turns out," Bran continued, watching every reaction on Marie's face, "the watch were waiting for us. We lost some good people, some good friends."

"I didn't know," Marie said hurriedly. "Please, you have to believe me."

Bran stared at her, looking for any sign that she was lying, that she had played them all along. She was either the best actress he had ever seen, or she was telling him the truth.

"I didn't know that would happen," she pleaded. "I didn't know."

Bran relaxed a little, wondering what to do next. He had expected her to lie, to plead ignorance, but had hadn't expected to believe her. She had a face that seemed to betray every thought and emotion running through her mind, he had seen it at their first meeting.

"How did you find out about the meeting at Deacon's warehouse?" he asked, a spark of inspiration.

"Samuel told me," Marie replied, taken aback by the sudden shift in conversation.

"And how did he find out?" Bran pushed.

Marie thought it over, thinking back to the conversation that she had had with Sam. "The Regent, I think," she said, her voice uncertain. "He's got spies, informants. They're everywhere, Samuel said."

Bran considered what she said. Things had started to change when they had brought in the other gangs, started sharing their plans and information. He'd suspected some of them of passing information to the Watch before, so why should it be any different. Things were starting to make sense.

"Thank you, Marie," Bran said, getting up from the bench. "I'll let you get back to work."

"Wait, what?" Marie protested. "What about me? And Sam?"

"You keep up with the information," Bran informed her, "and we'll leave him alone, just like we agreed."

"You will?" Marie asked, disbelieving.

"We will," Bran replied. "Deacon always keeps his word."

Marie watched him leave, an overwhelming sense of relief washing over her, though she still had her doubts about how far she could trust them.

XIV

They stopped for lunch, allowing Murphy to rest her ankle. She had twisted it slipping on a wet log, and though she insisted that it was fine, the occasional grimaces of pain told a different story.

"Do you think she'll be okay?" Ben asked Safran as she ate.

"I hope so," Safran replied, looking towards Murphy sympathetically. "She seems really nice."

"Do you think Murphy and Victor are like, you know?" Ben thought out loud, watching as Victor helped bandage her ankle.

"Oh, can you imagine?" Safran exclaimed, almost choking on her food. "They're so *old*!"

Safran's comment caused them both to burst into hysterical laughter. They were both of an age where they believed that anyone over thirty was old, and people over forty were ancient.

They finished their food in silence, smiling awkwardly at each other as they struggled to think of something to say. Ben knew exactly what he wanted to say, but even after Victor's reassurance the fear that the thoughts elicited was overwhelming. Safran was getting ready to stand when the words burst out of him.

"I don't think it was a mistake," he said hurriedly, eyes fixed firmly at the ground at his feet.

"I'm sorry?" Safran asked, not sure what he had said.

"Back in Maleton, when you kissed me," Ben continued, the words pouring from him seemingly beyond his control. "I thought it was nice, really nice actually. It was great, and I think about it all the time, and I think I like you, Safran, like, really like you, and I know you like Stan, and he's so, you know, Stan the Man and everything, but I had to say something. I had to tell you, I've wanted to for ages, and I kept trying, and, well, it's been difficult, and everything, and, well, that's it, I think, isn't it?"

"Ben," Safran said quietly, reaching down to turn his face towards hers. "Just stop talking, you silly boy."

She leant down and kissed him, gently at first as he began to kiss her back, finding a rhythm. The world faded around them as they become lost in each other's lips, time ceasing to have meaning. It was perfect, everything that he remembered and so much more. Ben couldn't believe how breathless and alive he felt when the kiss finally stopped.

"Better?" Safran asked coyly.

Ben nodded, unable to find his voice amidst the thoughts and feelings that were coursing through him, before leaning in to kiss her again.

CHAPTER 8

Isn't life great? I mean, in a totally awesome, fantastic sort of way? I think so. Safran and I must have kissed about a million times by now, easy, and she keeps coming back for more! I hope I'm doing it right. I mean, I think I am, but I hope I am too. Would she say if I wasn't?

I know she's doing it right. Wow, so right, it's incredible. I wonder if she's had more practice? I thought I might ask her, but what if she says yes? What if they were better at kissing than me? I don't think I want to know, but then I sort of do. It's all so confusing, but great at the same time.

Maybe I should ask Carl?

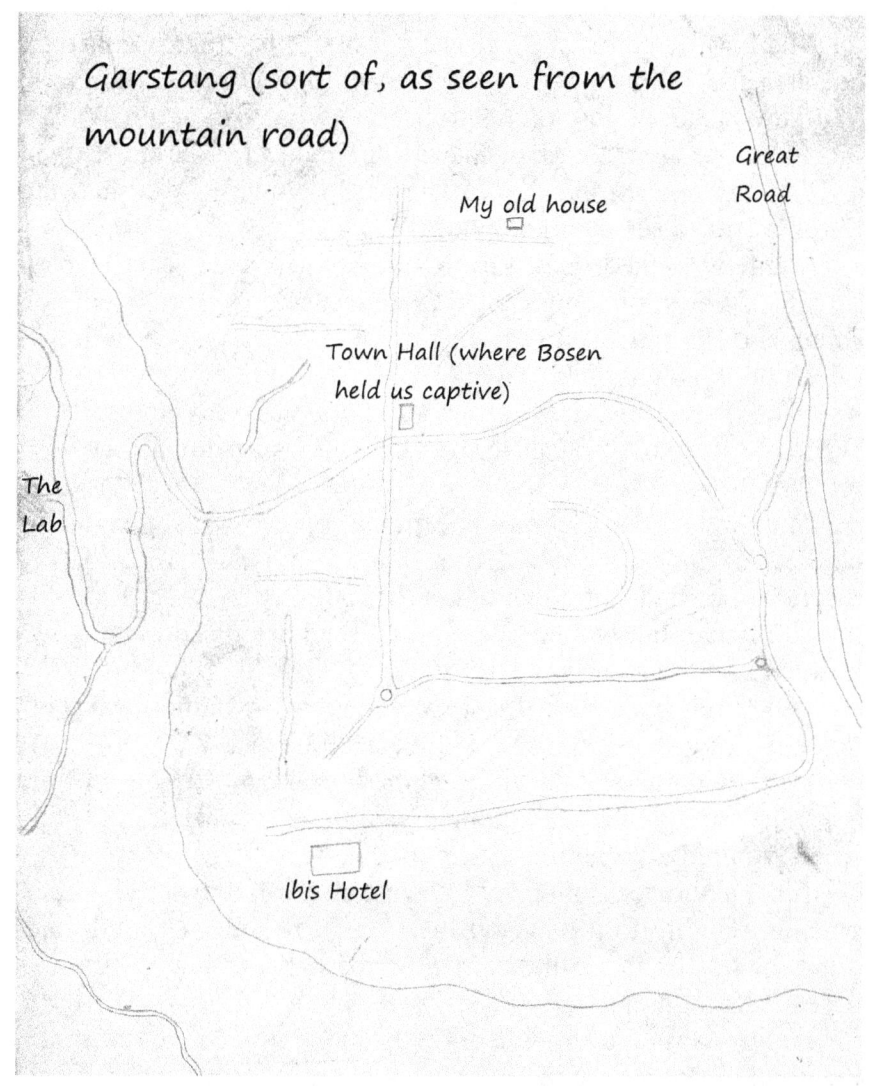

Garstang (sort of, as seen from the mountain road)

Great Road

My old house

Town Hall (where Bosen held us captive)

The Lab

Ibis Hotel

I

"Arian? Matthew?" Marcus called, banging loudly upon their bedroom door. "Please, open up. It's important."

Matthew got blearily to his feet, noting that it was still dark outside, the slim new moon offering little light. "Marcus?" Matthew asked, pulling on his trousers. "What's going on?"

"A messenger just arrived from the palace," Marcus replied as Matthew opened the door. "The battle didn't go well and the Baron wants to see us immediately."

Matthew looked back towards Arian who was still sleeping soundly. "She's still not well," Matthew said. "She's been sick again, and she's just so tired. This place, it doesn't agree with her. I don't think I should leave her."

"This isn't a meeting you can decline," Marcus pointed out. "I'll ask Juliet to sit with her and I'll meet you downstairs in a minute."

Matthew agreed sleepily and pulled on the remainder of his clothes, trying in vain to flatten his unruly hair. Arian barely reacted when he leant down to kiss her goodbye.

"I'll let her know where you are," Juliet promised, poking her head around the door.

"She's not been right for a week or two," Matthew said, his voice full of concern. "Do you think she'll be okay?"

"It should pass soon," Juliet replied reassuringly.

"The stress, the travelling," Matthew persisted. "Is that what's stopping her getting better do you think?"

Juliet chuckled to herself. "Trust me, Matthew," she said, placing a comforting hand on his. "She'll be fine. Go and meet with the Baron." Matthew nodded before turning reluctantly towards the door.

He was struck at how differently the tavern looked at night, the dark, narrow passages seeming to close in around him. There were no lanterns, and the minimal moonlight served only to emphasise the gloom. He found Marcus waiting for him at the bottom of the stairs, along with an impatient looking messenger.

"Matthew son-of-Astor?" the messenger asked, looking him up and down.

"That's me," Matthew said. "Can you tell us what this is about?"

"Follow me," the messenger replied, already walking towards the door. "Baron George has been kept waiting long enough." Matthew cast a questioning glance towards Marcus, who only shrugged his shoulders before both men followed the messenger out into the night.

The streets of Ashford were better lit than the tavern, oil filled lanterns illuminating their way. The messenger led them at a comfortable pace, through the winding Waterways and the exuberant Palace District. At the palace gates, the guards ushered them straight through and up the stone steps to the throne room. Baron George stood staring at a large unrolled map, listening intently as a younger man pointed to various locations.

"Baron George," Matthew and Marcus said in unison, dropping to one knee.

"Lord Marcus, Matthew," Baron George replied. "Thank you for coming at this late hour. This is Sergeant Tobias, he bears grave news of the conflict with Island City's forces."

"Lord Marcus," Tobias said, saluting. "Your reputation precedes you."

Marcus returned the salute without thinking, stepping forward to examine the map himself. It depicted the Barony of Morton in intricate detail, as well as the borders with Oster, Phalathlan and Gelders Ford. Small metal and wooden figurines depicted the site of the battle.

"Lord Jonathan marched us in this direction," Tobias began, moving the red metal figures, "towards what we believed were the main battalions of the Island City forces here. We proceeded into this valley here," he indicated on the map, "and before we knew it, we were surrounded. The enemy attacked our rear guard, here," he moved the black figures to the small wooden catapults, "and turned our own siege weapons against us. It was a massacre."

Marcus watched it all, shaking his head. "Lord Jonathan marched you all together like that?" he asked.

"He did," Tobias replied. "The lines never wavered, we were uniform until the first cannonballs struck." Tobias expressed the news with a sense of pride, that the organised structure to the regiments was important. Marcus looked on in stark disbelief.

"Lord Jonathan's methods and tactics were well known," Marcus informed them. "If Oster knew it, I'll wager the Island City forces knew it as well. He marched them straight into an ambush and didn't even consider the possibility."

"Lord Jonathan was an outstanding leader of men," Tobias fumed, pushing his chest out as he spoke. "I'll not have you sully his good name in these halls. What would Oster know of military strategy anyway? Skeet farmers and layabouts the lot of you!"

Marcus readied himself to retaliate until Matthew placed a calming hand on his shoulder. "The fight's out there," he reminded him, "not in here. What's done is done."

Marcus held his fighter's stance for a moment longer, staring intently at Tobias. "It was an obvious strategy," Marcus said, waving towards the map. "I'm surprised anyone survived."

"It was Lord Howard," Baron George said, changing the subject. He wasn't appreciative of Marcus' tone, but he could see the truth of his argument. Lord Jonathan had served Morton well for many years, but perhaps he had become set in his ways.

"How is he?" Matthew asked, latching onto the new topic. "Did he make it?"

"He was badly injured," Baron George informed him, "but my physicians believe that he'll pull through."

"He's a good man," Marcus commented, looking again at Tobias. "He'll be a useful asset when we strike back."

"Lord Marcus," Baron George said, raising his voice. "I did not invite you here to organise a counter offensive. You are here out of courtesy, nothing more. I have sent word to recall the forces from Fort Danzig and Fort Solitude, and I anticipate their arrival within the fortnight. Should Island City choose to march upon the city, they will pay most dearly for their folly!"

Marcus was momentarily lost for words. He had foolishly believed that the Baron would finally listen to him, mount a proper defence and end the threat that Island City posed. "You can't," Marcus replied, forgetting his place. "If you allow them to regroup, rearm, they'll-"

"Lord Marcus!" Baron George bellowed. "I will forgive your impertinence this time, but do not expect to speak to me in that manner again. The safety and security of this city, these people, is paramount. I will not send my remaining forces on another fool's errand!"

Marcus visibly calmed himself, holding back the arguments that demanded to spill forth from his lips. "Yes, Baron," he said through gritted teeth. "My most humblest apologies for my outburst."

"See that it doesn't happen again," Baron George remarked. "I think we're done here, I'll allow you to return to your rooms."

"Thank you, Baron," Matthew said, bowing slightly as he nudged Marcus towards the exit. "We'll find our own way back." Baron George nodded curtly and returned to scrutinising the map under Sergeant Tobias' instruction.

"Why did he drag us out of bed at this hour if her didn't want our input?" Marcus demanded once they were out of earshot of the palace.

"I guess if the Baron's up, everyone's up," Matthew remarked.

"The man's a fool," Marcus persisted.

"Maybe," Matthew agreed, "but he's still the Baron. Tomorrow, let's see if we can find Lord Howard and learn what really happened."

II

"My Liege," the guard said, taking a solitary step into the throne room. "I apologise for interrupting your breakfast, but a messenger has just arrived from General Boshtok."

Alexander was exhausted, another night's sleep denied him by violent dreams. "Boshtok?" he asked with surprise, forcing himself to concentrate. "Send him in, sergeant, I'll see him right away."

The guard bowed and left, returning a moment later in the company of a young man, his uniform muddy and rumpled from his time on the road.

"Thank you for granting me audience, Regent," the messenger said, dropping to one knee. "I bring word from General Boshtok."

"How goes the offensive?" Alexander asked, wiping his mouth with a napkin.

"Phalathlan and Oster are now under your rule," the messenger informed him, "and Morton should fall in a matter of weeks."

"Weeks?" Alexander asked, surprised. "What of the reinforcements from Oster?"

"Reinforcements, my Liege?" the messenger replied, confused. "Your forces suffered heavy losses during the Battle of Aldonis. I am not aware of any reinforcements."

"The Battle of Aldonis," Alexander said quietly to himself, rubbing at his temples. He had arranged for one of his best agents to infiltrate the Baron's Court in Aldonis, and the last time that he had heard from him, it was all going according to plan. Once Phalathlan had fallen, the Oster military should have joined with Boshtok's troops and marched on Ashford, securing the coastal Barony before advancing upon Gelders Ford.

"Regent?" the messenger said hesitantly into the silence.

"What is Boshtok's message," Alexander said angrily, rising from his seat.

The messenger remained kneeling as he spoke. "He requests a further ten thousand soldiers to support the cause," he said, aware of Alexander looming over him. "He assures you that ten thousand should be sufficient to rout Morton's reinforcements from Fort Danzig and Fort Solitude, leaving Ashford open to attack."

Alexander felt his rage grow within him, like a fire in his belly that spread outwards, consuming him. "Reinforcements!" he bellowed, screaming down at the messenger. "If he'd done as he was told, he wouldn't need reinforcements!" The messenger stayed quiet, his eyes fixed upon the floor of the throne room.

Alexander began to pace, fists opening and closing as his anger looked for an outlet. "Who ordered the attack on Aldonis?" he screamed at the messenger.

The messenger remained silent, unsure how to answer. "Answer me!" Alexander yelled, his face red.

"You did, my Liege?" the messenger replied, feeling utterly lost and alone.

Alexander crossed to him in three long strides, picking him up by his uniform. "I ordered no such thing," Alexander screamed into the messengers face, his hands closing around the messenger's neck. The messenger began to struggle but Alexander squeezed tighter, closing his grip around the man's throat and forcing him to the floor. The messenger tried to fight back, to push Alexander off, his fingers clawing at the Regents clothes. Alexander continued to squeeze, putting all of his strength into his arms, the muscles tense and the veins bulging.

Gradually the messenger stopped fighting and his legs stopped kicking. Moments later the messenger was completely still, but still Alexander squeezed, his breathing fast and erratic. It took a while for the red mist to fade, for him to see the purple face on the floor beneath him.

As he began to regain control, he slowly relaxed his grip, watching as the messenger's head lolled to one side, the tongue protruding from discoloured lips. Alexander rose to his feet, returning to the breakfast table and wiping his hands on the napkin before sitting to finish the remainder of his breakfast.

III

Unable to get back to sleep, Marcus quizzed the tavern keeper on the location of hospitals within the city. The main one, they learnt, was to be found in the Palace District, though there were other smaller hospitals and lone physicians to be found in the City District if Deniras were an issue. Marcus thanked the tavern keeper for his concern, but requested directions to the Palace District hospital anyway.

"This for the girl?" the tavern keeper asked.

"Girl?" Marcus asked, confused.

"With your friend," the tavern keeper clarified. "My wife cleans the rooms, said she'd been sick for days."

"She's getting better," Marcus assured him, reaching into his jacket pocket and removing twenty Deniras. "Pass this onto your wife for me, for the trouble."

"Thank you," the tavern keeper said, pocketing the money quickly.

Marcus directed Matthew to the Palace District hospital, a large, white stone building just a short walk from the Waterways. They walked from ward to ward, asking after Lord Howard. Each ward they entered seemed worse than the last, the sick and wounded crying out in pain, the smell of stale blood and faeces lingering on the air. They began to dread the condition that they would find him in.

Lord Howard was located in a room of his own, where a nurse was applying a soothing balm to his face. Matthew learned from one of the other nurses that Lord Howard had received burns to the right side of his face and chest, along with a broken left arm. He was lucky to be alive at all.

They knocked on the door to the room, the nurse opening it a crack. "Yes?" she asked, looking them both up and down.

"We're friends of Lord Howard," Marcus informed her. "We've come to visit him."

"He's too unwell for visitors," the nurse replied, moving to close the door.

"Please," Matthew pleaded. "It's important, we wouldn't be here if it weren't."

The nurse scrutinised them again, thinking it over. "Five minutes," she said at last, opening the door for them to enter.

Marcus entered first, closing his eyes and swallowing, trying to ignore the smell of burnt flesh that greeted them. "Lord Howard," he whispered, walking towards the bed.

Lord Howard turned to face them, his face and chest covered in a mixture of balm and bandages. They could see that every movement was agony.

"Please, stay still," Matthew offered, moving to the other side of the bed where Howard could see him. Marcus joined him, a tear in his eye at the sight of a fellow soldier in so much suffering.

"I'm so sorry," Matthew said, his voice full of emotion.

"Perhaps this was a mistake," Marcus suggested. "We should leave you to rest."

"No," Lord Howard mouthed, his voice barely above a whisper. "Droca. Helps. Pain. Better. News?"

Matthew and Marcus shared an uncomfortable look, unsure what they should do. "We met with the Baron," Matthew said, breaking the silence. "He's recalled the troops from Fort Danzig and Fort Solitude, they should be here within a fortnight."

"Survivors?" Lord Howard asked.

"We don't know for sure," Marcus informed him. "I think it

was somewhere in the region of two thousand."

"And that was thanks to you and your quick thinking," Matthew added. "You saved a lot of lives."

Lord Howard looked even more pained, if that was possible, the news weighing heavily upon his heart. "Need. Fight," he said, closing his eyes. "Save. City. Save. People."

"You fought bravely," Marcus told him. "This is our fight now, leave it to us."

"Go. North," Lord Howard continued. "Before. Regroup."

"That's enough," the nurse said, interrupting them. "Can't you see he's in pain?"

"We're sorry," Matthew said, starting towards the door. "We're done, anyway."

"Thank you," Marcus said, looking down at Lord Howard and saluting, the highest honour he could think to offer the man. "Rest now and heal."

"Save. Please," Lord Howard said as the nurse ushered them out of the door.

IV

"Bran," Sanjay said quietly, nervous about interrupting him.

"Yes, Sanjay," Bran replied, trying not to look as disinterested as he felt. He suspected that Sanjay was after more fighting or shooting lessons, or something else equally futile. Gavin was getting better, a lot better actually, and Dean could probably keep himself alive long enough to run from a fight, but Sanjay was a lost cause. If Deacon still had his network, Sanjay would have been found a role counting Deniras or adjusting shipping manifests.

"It's just, I came from the Markets," Sanjay continued. "I didn't know if Deacon had heard?"

That caught Bran's attention, and he sat up to look Sanjay in the eye. "Heard what?" Bran asked.

"The criers have been announcing it all morning," Sanjay said a little louder, his confidence growing. "Alexander, the Regent, he's going to announce something tonight. Everyone should attend the message said."

"What's he got to shout about?" Bran said to himself.

"Do you think he wants to brag about, you know," Sanjay suggested, tailing off as he turned to look at Stan. Stan had barely spoken to anyone for days, even pushing Gavin away. They were all increasingly worried about him, but he wouldn't let anyone get close enough to help.

"Maybe," Bran agreed. "I'll speak to Deacon, but perhaps we could keep this just between ourselves for now?"

"Yes, of course," Sanjay promised, nodding his head frantically.

"Good work," Bran said, making Sanjay feel over the moon.

V

By mid-afternoon they were within sight of Garstang. Carl had offered to scout ahead, and the sun was low in the sky by the time he returned to the small camp. As he crept between a thorny bush and a tall tree, he was suddenly faced with the barrels of two pistols.

"Hey, it's me," Carl said, raising his hands.

"Sorry," Reid said, lowering his pistol and tucking it back into his belt. Victor only nodded in Carl's direction as he too lowered his weapon.

"Well, how's it look?" Ben asked.

"All quiet," Carl said, taking a long swig from the water bottle that Reid handed to him.

"We thought that last time," Safran reminded him. "Do you remember how that turned out?"

"All too well," Carl replied, his mind flashing back to the capture by Bosen and his men and the subsequent rescue by Alexander's soldiers. "The building where they held us is nothing but rubble, same for most of the town as far as I can see. It doesn't look like anyone's been here for a long time."

Ben though back to his last two visits to Garstang, the first as he ran for his life in the snow, and the second as they tried and subsequently failed to evade capture by Bosen. The town was mostly derelict or fallen down buildings, the occasional wall or floor the only sign of a past home or place of work. The town hall, where Bosen had made his base, had been one of the few intact buildings left, and now that was nothing but rubble. His suggestion, to build a city powered by electricity, was looking to have been more than just a little optimistic.

"Straight through to the mountain road then?" Ben asked.

"Or we go around," Carl suggested. "Same options we had last time."

"That will not work," Victor said, shaking his head slowly. "Should the other tribes arrive and find the town hostile, we will have no hope of convincing them of our ideas. If there is still a threat, we must do what we can to discover it before that happens."

"Then I guess we go through," Carl said, removing the rifle from his shoulder and checking the magazine.

"We do not all need to go," Victor added. "I shall enter the town and announce my presence-"

"No," Ben interrupted. "We're not splitting up, not again. It's one thing to let Carl scout ahead, I get that, but if the plan is to go down there and try to pick a fight? No. I know I'm not a fighter but this was my plan, my idea, so we either do it together or not at all."

Carl stared at him, both impressed and surprised by his new found confidence. He didn't know for sure where it had come from, but he suspected that the new found closeness with Safran may have had something to do with it.

"That is a worthy sentiment," Victor began to say, but Ben cut him off again.

"I'm tired of being the damsel," Ben protested, not caring if anyone could understand his meaning. "I don't want to sit around anymore, waiting for the knight on his noble steed. It's about time I was that knight, that hero."

There was a pause, a hollow silence, a vacuum waiting for something to fill it.

"I agree," Carl said, speaking before anyone else had chance to object further. "Ben's right. This was all his idea, coming to Garstang, uniting the tribes. You're not that same scared lad anymore Ben, the one I found in the snow. You're one of us, and you've earned the right to make your own decisions."

Ben felt himself blush as Carl spoke, an overwhelming sense of pride and acceptance. He was tired of being the excess baggage, the burden, or any of the other terms that he had used to describe himself over the previous eight months. His doubt was finally gone and he was going to see his plan through to the end, no matter what.

"Thanks, Carl," Ben said, getting to his feet and offering Safran his hand. "Let's go."

VI

Sanjay mingled with the crowd as they gathered at the meeting area before the palace. The turnout was far fewer than the last time, when Alexander had promised to apprehend the rebels by any means necessary. The Palace Guard stood along the stone wall, eyeing everyone suspiciously, making the citizens of Maleton even more nervous. Many of them had been questioned by the Watch or knew of people who had, and then there were the rumours of disappearances, people taken who were never seen or heard from again.

Sanjay knew little of this, and neither did Deacon or Bran. Hiding beneath the brewery, making their plans, they had been out of the thick of it for weeks. So much more was happening in the city above their heads than they dared to imagine.

Alexander made his entrance and stood leaning on the balcony, looking down on the people below him. He took it all in, the anxious faces looking up at him, the hint of fear and suspicion that lingered over the crowd. He cast out his will, enveloping them, but it didn't seem to flow as easily as it had done before. His tiredness grew, exhausting him, his grip tightening on the rail as his legs became weak.

He'd never felt it before, a resistance to his power. His lack of sleep was doing more than draining his focus, it was draining his strength, his will. He closed his eyes to the crowd, breathing deeply as he drew it back in. He would have to try to convince them on the strength of his words alone.

"Good people of Maleton," he began, steadying himself. "I am pleased to see so many of you on this fine summer evening. There is much I must tell you, news I must impart.

"First, I bring word of the rebels and their defeat at the hands of the brave men and women of the City Watch. Four days ago, the rebels attempted another cowardly attack against those who want nothing more than to keep the people of this city safe. Fortunately, a fearless citizen from the City District came forward when he heard of their plan and, risking vile retribution from Safran and her supporters, he valiantly passed on the details."

It was all a lie, of course, but they couldn't know that. His informants in the city gangs had passed on the relevant details, allowing Samuel Larson to strike back.

"Bring out Safran," a member of the crowd shouted, loudly enough for all to hear. People started to mutter and mumble, waiting for her to be dragged from the palace or thrown from the balcony. An edge of excitement was beginning to build.

"Sadly," Alexander announced, raising his voice to be heard, "Safran was not one of those apprehended."

"Deacon, then," someone else cried out, eager for blood. The murmuring from the crowd grew louder, all eyes upon Alexander as they waited.

He hadn't realised how much he had begun to rely on his ability, how difficult it was to control the people without the strength to bend their will. He had rehearsed what he would say, over and over, but it was slipping away from him, just like the crowd.

"Deacon, too, evaded capture," Alexander told them, "though many of the most senior members of his organisation were not so lucky."

The crowd grew restless, agitated, those at the periphery beginning to wander away. Alexander made a gesture towards a guard, who promptly relayed the order, and soon twenty rifles were raised, firing in unison into the air. The crowd were stunned into silence, looking first at the guards who had fired and then back towards the balcony.

"I can assure you, good citizens," Alexander continued, his tone less caring and much more hostile, "that everything that can be done is being done, and that the terrorists who plague our city have suffered a significant blow."

Sanjay cast his gaze across the crowd, noticing how differently they were behaving to Alexander's previous announcements. As before, there were still those who looked upon Alexander with awe and reverence, held onto his words, but there were others, clustered in small groups, talking amongst themselves and eyeing Alexander with suspicion.

Alexander saw them too. They were easier to spot from his vantage point. There was doubt amongst the populace. No longer would they all believe a plausible lie. He tried to call forth his ability again, but just focussing on it drained him.

"People," he said, standing tall. "People. I promise you, all is well in your city this evening. These acts of terror will soon become a thing of the past. I say again, if any of you know of or suspect someone's involvement with the rebels, come forward. Speak to the City Watch or a member of the Palace Guard. You will be listened to, and you will be protected.

"It is with regret that I must also bring news of the war with Phalathlan. The brave men and women of our combined forces have successfully captured the city of Garet, but the Baronies of Morton and Oster have seized upon your soldier's fatigue and pressed against our borders. Even now they stand together, courageously battling the enemy forces, but more troops would ensure victory.

"I ask you again, good people, to look within yourselves, to stand for what is right. If you would stand shoulder to shoulder with your comrades, defend this great Barony, I will reward your family who remain behind. For every man or woman who joins the front lines, the remaining family members will receive one extra ration slip, that their bellies may be full as they think on their brave kin.

"Report to your nearest Watch House and join up, knowing that you do something great for yourself, for your family, and for your Barony."

There was further murmuring as the crowd discussed and debated the offer, considering who could go and who could stay behind. Alexander relaxed a little, smiling to himself. He had managed to turn it around, and once more he began to feel like their leader, their Baron.

"Return to your homes," Alexander suggested. "Speak to your husbands and wives, your fathers and mothers. Sign up tomorrow and embrace your future as a soldier of Draxis!"

VII

Ben led the way through Garstang's streets, Safran at his side. Carl kept a watchful eye over their shoulder as Reid and Victor took turns helping Murphy. Little had changed since their last visit; the streets remained dirty and rubble strewn, the foliage wild and overgrown, and the air, still and foreboding. They all felt it, the sense of tension that something could happen at any minute.

"You're sure that this is the fastest way to the mountain road?" Carl whispered to Ben for the third time.

"It's the fastest way I remember," Ben reassured him, slowing down as they approached a crossroads.

"It's just," Carl began, trying not to shatter the confidence that Ben had shown. "I, well, I don't recognise any of these roads from last time, that's all."

"We were running for our lives last time," Ben pointed out, a wry smile on his face. "We could go that way again, if it'd make you feel better?"

"I'll just keep my mouth shut, shall I?" Carl suggested with a grin, his humour hiding the nervousness that he felt.

"You won't last five minutes," Safran added, making both of them laugh a little louder.

The crossroads looked clear and they crossed it in a low sprint, Victor and Reid almost carrying Murphy as they crossed the open space. They stopped at the other side, breathing a little heavier than before.

"Perhaps a moment's rest," Victor suggested, leaning against a low wall.

"That's a good idea," Ben agreed, slipping the backpack from his shoulders. He removed a half-empty bottle of water and took a swig before passing it around.

"This is a large settlement," Victor pointed out, returning the bottle to Ben. "I wonder why no one has claimed it as their own."

"Bosen and his gang were here before," Ben replied. "Maybe they fought off anyone who tried?"

"Perhaps," Victor agreed, though his tone suggested he was not convinced. "This town, it feels different to the others that I have visited on my travels. It is though it is waiting for something, or someone. There is a sense of anticipation here, do you feel it?"

Ben thought about it, concentrating, searching for something out of the ordinary. His rational mind told him that a town couldn't make him feel anything, it was just a town. Victor was just a nice old man, who could do something impossible, true, but he was just imagining things. Deep down, though, a part of Ben did recognise that Garstang felt different to the other places that he had seen in the Wastelands and the Southern Baronies. He couldn't say how, but the feeling was there all the same.

"I think we're all just a bit nervous," Safran suggested before Ben could articulate his thoughts. "After last time, it's not surprising really. When that man touched me..." She shivered from head to foot at the memory of the revulsion that she had felt.

"Yes, that sounds right," Victor agreed, though he gave Ben a knowing look as he did so. "Murphy, are you ready to continue?"

"My stupid ankle," Murphy muttered. "I knew I should have brought some proper equipment. Yes, yes, I'm ready."

"There's a medical room in the habitat level," Ben told her. "Once we get to the lab, there should be something there that'll help."

"I'll be fine," Murphy protested, shuffling to her feet.

They continued through Garstang, growing more confident as they got closer and closer to the mountain road. There were no people, no skeets, no signs that anyone had been through since they left it months before. Ben thought again about what Victor had said, about the town feeling different to all the others that he had visited, that it was waiting. Waiting for what? Could it be waiting for them?

"Ben?" Carl said, interrupting his train of thought. "It's getting pretty late and it'll be getting dark soon. What's the plan?"

"We keep going, get to the lab as soon as we can," Ben said, pressing on.

"You remember how long it took for us to walk up that mountain road?" Carl reminded him. "In the dark, with Murphy's ankle? There are some nasty drops if we took a wrong turn."

Ben paused and thought about what Carl had said. His eagerness to get back to the laboratory was blinding him to the practicalities. "Sorry, Carl, you're right," he replied. "We should find somewhere to camp tonight, head up first light tomorrow."

"Good idea," Carl agreed. "Any ideas?"

Ben stood and turned around on the spot, looking at the various remains of buildings around him. As he looked to the south, he saw that the two storey hotel on the outskirts of Garstang looked to be relatively intact. "Let's try there," he said, pointing it out.

"You're sure?" Carl asked. "It looks pretty big, we only need somewhere dry, ideally with a roof."

"That's true for tonight," Ben agreed, "but what about when the other tribes start to arrive? Where are they going to stay?"

"I don't know," Carl replied. "I hadn't given it any thought."

"That used to be a hotel," Ben told him. "Kind of like a tavern, only bigger. If the rooms are intact, then the tribes could stay there, or some of them at least."

"Okay," Carl said. "Let's go check it out."

They turned onto one of the larger roads running south after cutting across the remains of several front gardens and a children's park. They crossed a dual carriageway and strolled across the large concrete car park towards the main door, the white lines of the parking spaces long since faded.

"Ibis," Carl read aloud, inspecting the faded letters above the main entrance. "Strange name for a tavern."

"They were a chain, I think," Ben informed him. "They had hotels like this all over the world."

"Incredible," Carl remarked. "How many? Three? Four?"

"Thousands," Ben continued. "Or so it said on their website."

"What, spiders told you?" Carl replied, waiting for the punchline of the joke. "I don't follow."

"It's," Ben began, thinking that he had probably already tried and failed to explain the internet to Carl. "Don't worry about it. Let's just have a look inside."

Ben allowed Carl to go first, his rifle ready in case of attack. He pushed open the cracked glass door and stood in the entrance, listening before waving for Ben and the other's to follow.

The lobby looked undisturbed, a fine layer of dust on everything. Ben went around behind the main desk looking for keys before realising that it would have likely had key cards and electronic locks. He hoped that the lack of electricity would mean the doors would open.

Ben took the lead then, through heavy wooden fire doors and into a long corridor. A door on the left led into one of the two large conference rooms whilst toilets were labelled to the right.

"The rooms would be upstairs," Ben said.

"I'd rather not separate," Carl suggested, the hairs on the back of his neck prickling. "I know we haven't seen anyone, but I still think we should stick together and post a watch."

"Okay," Ben agreed, a small part of him disappointed after secretly imagining spending a night in one of the rooms, alone with Safran. "That's probably for the best, until we know the town is clear."

"What's this room?" Carl asked, looking through the thin panel of glass in the conference room door.

"It's a meeting room, where people would get together and discuss things," Ben informed him.

"Hmm," Carl said, opening the door and inspecting the room. "Two exits, windows to the rear. Not ideal, but plenty of options if someone gets the drop on us. Victor? Reid?"

"It will suffice," Victor said, moving to the centre of the room.

"Yes, fine," Reid agreed. "You want me to take first watch?"

"No," Carl replied. "You've been helping Murphy, Victor too. I'll take first watch, you can take over at midnight. Victor, you happy with three o'clock?"

"Of course, Carl," Victor replied. "I shall wake you all at first light."

"Perfect," Carl agreed. "Let's eat, and then you guys should get some sleep. Tomorrow's a big day."

VIII

"They're ready for you, General," Officer Hastings announced, poking his head through the tent flap.

"Thank you, Hastings," Boshtok replied. "I'll be along shortly."

Boshtok rolled up his collection of maps and returned them to his strongbox before locking it securely. He had reviewed all of the details of Morton's forces and formulated tactics for the upcoming assault on Ashford, once the reinforcements had arrived. It wouldn't do for the enemy to learn of his plans.

The early morning air was warm and still, a stark contrast to the twelve men and women on their knees before his tent, quaking with fear and openly weeping. Boshtok stepped up to each of them, looking them in the eye before shaking his head slowly.

"You twelve," he began, "have been found guilty of desertion, and inciting other's to desert. There can be no leeway for such actions, and the sentence is death. Do any of you have any last words?"

One of the men began to sob, wailing at the news, while another raised his head, looking Boshtok in the eye. He was a very young man, perhaps no older than fourteen or fifteen, dirty and malnourished.

"Go on," Boshtok said, returning the stare.

"I just want to go home," the young man replied, holding back the tears that his glistening eyes promised. "We were only supposed to avenge Regent Cotran, not wage war on all the Baronies. I miss my mom. Please, let me go home."

Boshtok acknowledged the man's words with a swift nod of his head before asking, "Anyone else?" Apart from the man who was wailing, no one else made a sound.

"So be it," Boshtok continued, removing his ceremonial sword from its scabbard. He raised it high above his head before bringing it down in one swift motion. As he brought it down, the guards standing behind the deserters stepped forwards, placed their pistols against the back of the deserter's heads and fired.

The bodies jerked forwards, the bound hands trapped behind them, the faces making a soft thud as they hit the dirt. Boshtok raised his hand and saluted the executioners, taking a moment to look each one in the eye. Their role had not been pleasant, but it was necessary. To allow such actions to go unpunished, even from the conscripts, would lead to chaos.

"Hastings," Boshtok said, his voice quieter with a hint of remorse. "Be sure to display the bodies around the camp, and let their crimes be known. Any who would consider such actions shall meet the same fate."

"Yes, General," Officer Hastings replied.

General Boshtok saluted him and returned to his tent, thinking over the young man's last words. Missing his mother, what a pitiful excuse for his behaviour. They were at war and he was a soldier. His duties, his responsibilities, were clear.

If he truly cared for his mother, he would never have behaved in such a way. Now she would have to live on, knowing that she raised a traitor.

IX

The trek up the winding mountain road took them almost five hours, and everyone was breathless and exhausted as they turned off the main road and onto the dirt track that led to the hidden door. The boggy mud that had greeted them last time was gone, replaced with a dry, cracked red earth that blended well against the slowly rising rock walls that grew up around them. Ben was again impressed by the skill of whoever had constructed the hidden door. Even knowing where it was, he was hard pressed to make it out against the natural rockface that surrounded it.

As he slipped his backpack from his shoulders, reaching in for the pager that would allow them access, he was struck by a sudden realisation, a moment of enlightenment that had been lingering in the recesses of his mind and waiting for the correct trigger to awaken it.

"Why is it here?" he said to himself, pausing mid-motion.

"Pardon?" Safran said.

"Why is it here?" Ben said a little louder. "The lab? I mean, even the road, Garstang? Why?"

"It's where you come from?" Safran replied. "That's what you told us at least."

"No, you don't get it," Ben told her, beginning to pace. "When we were in Phalathlan, on the way to Ashford, I was tracking the stars. This isn't earth, not even the future, the stars are all wrong. This is somewhere else, somewhere different, so why is the lab here, my lab?"

"I don't understand," Safran said, dumbfounded, looking to Carl for help. He only looked between the two of them, shrugging his shoulders.

"Please, just give me a minute," Ben said, tossing his rucksack to the floor. Instead of the pager that he had been searching for, he instead held his tattered journal and was frantically flicking through the pages.

The laboratory, the experiment, drawing energy from the pocket universe.

The attack, the anti-gravity shield expanding and then collapsing, waking up in the lab. Where did all the bodies go?

Getting outside, snow and ice, Garstang in ruins and run by that psycho, Bosen.

The Road Trains, Carl, Matthew and everybody, finding me in the snow must have been a billion to one chance? So kind, so helpful. Technology, broken and disused, bits and pieces from the past.

The skeets, like dinosaurs. Not my past, certainly, but Earth's past?

Catrina's son, Daniel. Home again, home again, jiggity jig. That's from Blade Runner? Welcome home, J.F. Sebastian....

The big red bridge to Island City, like the Golden Gate Bridge in San Francisco?

Island City, so familiar and yet so strange, buildings like those at home in London?

Maleton, Ashford, buildings I've seen before but out of place, all mixed up. Ashford's Waterways, like Venice, but the roof tiles and the bricks. I see it now, it looked just like the Venice in the Assassin's Creed video game?

Victor, and Sanctuary. Victor's mental powers, like Professor Xavier from the X-Men. Now that I come to think about it, he even looks like Patrick Stewart? Who would that make Catrina?

Carl, reminding me of dad. It's not that he looks like him, just the way he says things sometimes, the odd little gesture.

The camp we made, beneath the electricity pylon. The stars, all out of place, not the sky I should be seeing if this was Earth, if this was home. Not even if it was the future.

Not dead, but not a dream? Why is everything made from my past if it's not in my head?

Maybe I've gone crazy? Maybe this is all a fantasy as I struggle against my restraints in a mental institution somewhere? So why aren't the drugs working by now?

No, if I can think I might be crazy, I'm probably not. What's the word for it? Insight? No, not crazy, not a dream, not dead. This is all real and happening to me.

The blue light in the lab, all around me, falling.

The pocket universe? Before it collapsed I was inside the sphere? Was I inside the pocket universe itself? The gravity well should have torn me apart, but what else is there?

Is this a world of my making?

"Impossible," Ben mumbled, the journal falling from his grasp as he swayed and sat forcibly on the ground.

"Ben!" Safran exclaimed, running over to him. "What happened? Talk to me, please."

Ben had gone deathly pale, his pupils pinpoint and unfocussed. "It's just not possible," he said again slowly, eyes staring off into the distance. "I brought the lab here, and Garstang. Or did I make it, piecing together the memories? Maybe that's why there weren't any bodies, I couldn't bring myself to face the people I'd killed with my experiment."

"Ben, please, you're scaring me," Safran cried out, looking to Carl to help. Carl crossed the distance at a sprint.

"Ben?" he asked, shaking the boy's shoulders. "Snap out of it, Ben, you hear me?"

"I think you're my dad," Ben said smiling, looking at Carl before looking past him, at the clear blue sky and the midday sun. It was the last thing Ben remembered before the world went dark and closed in around him.

X

"Hi, Sam," Marie said cheerfully as Samuel Larson returned home. "You're early again."

"Are you complaining?" Samuel asked. "I can go and find more rebels to arrest if you'd like?"

Marie punched him playfully before kissing him. "You know what I meant," she said. "Come and help me make dinner."

He followed her through to the kitchen, unhooking the pistol from his belt on the way and placing it on the table top. The food was almost ready and just needed a few finishing touches before being placed in the oven.

"Have you had many people come forward?" Marie asked, joining Samuel at the table as the food cooked. "To sign up?"

"Not many," Samuel replied distractedly. "Maybe the other Watch Houses have had better luck, but I think it's still in single figures."

"What will the Regent do?" Marie asked with a hint of concern. "He won't send you, will he?"

"No," Samuel promised her. "He needs me here. He needs the Watch. There's still so much to be done, with the rebels and the gangs."

"That's good then," Marie replied, relieved. "But I suppose that means you have to keep getting shouted at every day."

"You know," Samuel mused, "I think I'm finally beginning to understand him. I've been too hard on him at times, harsh even. I never understood the pressure he's under."

Marie was taken aback, disturbed by Samuel's new found respect for the Regent. The change was unexpected. She looked at him questioningly before getting up to remove the food from the oven.

"Oh, I stopped by the stall at lunchtime," Samuel said, looking up from his seat at the table. "You weren't around and no one seemed to know where you'd gone?"

"Oh, I, er," Marie stalled, trying to think of a reason to explain her absence when in reality she had gone to the drop point to leave some more information for Deacon. "I, I can't remember. Errands, probably."

Samuel watched her face get redder and redder as she lied, her breath quickening and her gaze everywhere but on him. "Okay," he said, a little confused. "A couple of the other stall holders were worried about you, said you were leaving your stall a couple of times a week or so and they didn't know where you'd gone?"

"They should keep their noses out," Marie hissed.

"Marie, if something's wrong," Samuel said earnestly, "you can tell me. I know Deacon used to shake down the markets, take his cut. If someone is after money, threatening you, you can tell me. I can deal with it, you know that."

"No, it's not money," Marie said, her hands shaking as she removed two plates from the cupboard. "It was just errands, I had to go and see about restocking the stall. That was it, that's all it was. Please, Sam, it's all okay, you don't need to worry."

Samuel sat back in his chair, watching as she busied herself in the kitchen, anything to avoid making eye contact with him. In his experience, when someone said not to worry that was the time to start.

"I'm sorry," he said. "You're right, I'm not at the Watch House anymore, and you're not a suspect. I sometimes forget to switch it off. Forgive me?"

"Of course I forgive you," Marie said quickly, smiling down at him. "It's really nothing, I promise you. It's fine, don't worry about me."

"I love you," Samuel said in return, smiling back at her. He knew she was deceiving him, but he didn't know why. As he watched her plate out the meal, he had already resigned himself to finding out what was really going on, one way or another.

XI

When Ben first woke, he imagined he must be dreaming as he looked up into Safran's face. She looked down at him, stroking his hair as he slowly came round. "There you are," she said, smiling sweetly.

"Hmm," Ben replied, smiling up at her. "I've had this dream before."

"Is he awake?" Carl demanded, stepping into Ben's field of vision and dragging him back to reality. "Ben? Are you with us?"

Ben sat up, his head pounding at the sudden movement. "What happened?" he asked groggily.

"You passed out," Carl informed him. "You've been asleep for hours, we couldn't rouse you."

"You were saying all sorts of strange things," Safran added. "About the laboratory being impossible or something? And that Carl is your father? We didn't know what to do."

"Oh, the laboratory," Ben groaned, rubbing his temples. "It sort of makes sense now, in a crazy, impossible kind of way. I think I finally know where I am."

"That's good then, isn't it?" Safran asked, though her face showed more disappointment than happiness. "You can get back, get home?"

"I think this is my home," Ben said, reaching out for her and gripping her hand. "It is now anyway, there's no way back. You're stuck with me."

Safran smiled and blushed a little, squeezing his hand in return. They got to their feet and dusted themselves off, the dry red soil clinging to their clothes.

"Hey, Carl," Ben added. "Do you remember when I asked you why the Wastelands were called the Wastelands, when they're all forest and woodland? I think I know the answer."

"Oh, yes?" Carl asked, confused.

"It's obvious, really," Ben said, more to himself than anyone else. "Half of the sci-fi films, books and games have a wasteland of some sort, so why wouldn't the world I created? I should have seen it months ago."

"A world you created?" Carl said, more confused than ever. "I don't get it."

"Join the club," Ben replied. "If I think about it anymore, my heads going to burst."

"I'm worried about you, Ben," Carl said, running his fingers over the boy's head. "Did you hit your head or something? I've seen this sort of thing before."

"I'm fine, Carl, honestly," Ben protested, squirming free of the bigger man's grip. "It's just, I've never believed in a God or anything, and now I might just be one. It's going to take me a bit of time to get used to it, that's all."

Carl and Safran exchanged a concerned look, but there was nothing that any of them could say. The concept of a God or creator was alien to them and they had no idea what he was talking about. True, they were used to Ben saying things that no one else understood, but this was different, even for him.

"I'm allowed to worry," Carl told him. "Apparently I might be your father or something, isn't that what you said?"

Carl smiled and Ben laughed. "I meant it more in a figurative sense," Ben said. "It's okay, I won't be asking you for child support."

That made Carl relax a little, seeing Ben smile and laugh. Carl was still worried, and he'd be keeping a close eye on him, no mistake, but at least Ben was starting to behave more like his old self.

"Come on," Ben said, placing the tattered journal back into his rucksack. "Let's get inside before it starts to get dark."

"Reid, Victor, Murphy," Carl called out. "Come over here, you're going to want to see this!"

Ben smiled to himself as he slipped the battery back into the pager, enjoying the familiar rumble as the enormous hidden door began to descend.

"Son of a skeet," Reid muttered to himself, his eyes wide and his mouth hanging open in awe.

CHAPTER 9

After a couple of days back in the lab, it's almost like I never left. Reid, Victor and Murphy were suitably impressed, but it's Safran who has surprised me the most. She has a million questions; about the experiment, the computers, the reactor, even the food and supplies. Everything is new and exciting to her and she wants to understand how it all works.

I don't remember her being this way last time, but things were different then. We were prisoners, and we didn't stay here long once we were freed. There was no time, we were always behind, rushing to get somewhere. Now we're just waiting, hoping the tribes that Victor invited will turn up and speak to us without trying to kill us first.

I still can't get my head around it, the laboratory and why I'm here. I've tried to apply Occam's Razor as best I can, but the only theory I have is impossible, so how does that work? I suppose that if I can't think of anything else, then the most ridiculous, far out, crazy hypothesis must be the truth. Either that, or I really have gone crazy.

At least there was some chocolate left. Safran promised to make it worth my while if I take her a bar later.

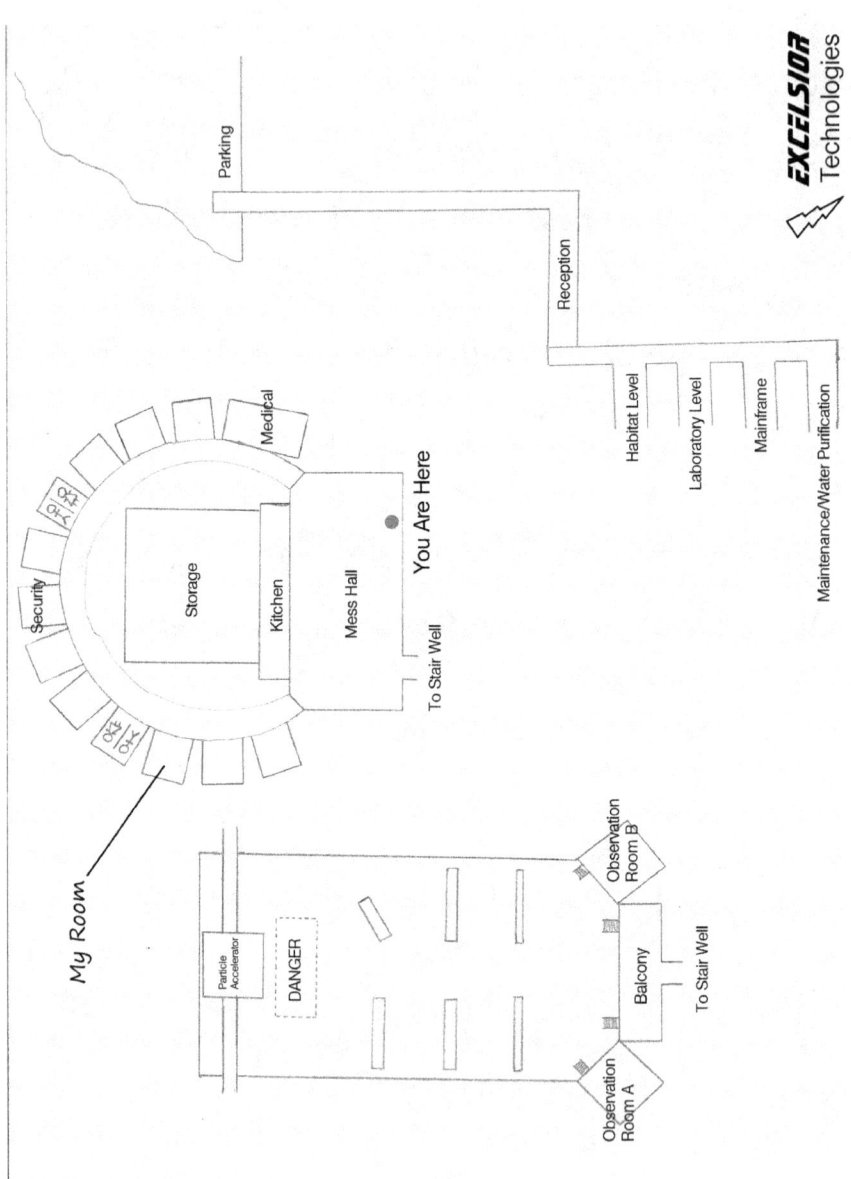

I

They had been at the laboratory for four days and had quickly made it theirs. Murphy had settled into the medical room and discovered the wonders of Ibuprofen, allowing her to treat her sprained ankle as nothing more than an inconvenience, even up and down the ladder in the lift shaft.

Ben had managed to link together a selection of emergency lights, allowing him to illuminate the lift shaft, whilst Carl and Victor were already discussing plans to build a stairwell from top to bottom.

Safran was excited about everything, wanting to know what everything was and how it worked. Ben enjoyed spending every minute with her, showing off the marvels that his laboratory contained, smiling every time her eyes went wide or she clapped appreciatively.

Reid was the only one to be anxious about the laboratory, choosing to stay in the large natural cavern after his first exploratory steps into the laboratory below. He put it down to being accustomed to a life at sea, the large open spaces surrounding him, and how tunnels and corridors below ground made him feel trapped. He was always the first to volunteer to watch for any signs of the Tribe's arriving.

"Oh, Ben," Carl said excitedly, stepping down from the back of the all-terrain vehicle. "Why didn't we take this to Maleton? It's incredible!"

"I wouldn't have the first idea how to make it work," Ben explained, shaking his head. "Besides, we were trying to stop a war, not start one. Do you really think turning up in a tank would have helped our... Actually, forget that, it probably would."

"There was a book inside," Carl said, waving it in front of Ben's face. "It's got pictures and lines that say what everything does. I don't think it's too different to the ground rover that I drove."

"Land Rover," Ben corrected.

"Yes, Land Rover," Carl agreed, thumbing through the manual. "This here is called a *Boxer Multi-Role Armoured Vehicle*," he read aloud, tracing the words with his fingers. "A type of ATV. Oh, look here! Bullets bounce off it! Actual bullets! And, and, it can withstand a *tactical nuclear explosion at medium distances*. What's that? Didn't you say that the laboratory was a nuclear something or other?"

"Sort of," Ben replied, taking the manual from Carl and flicking through it himself. Carl was right, the basics of driving were very similar to the Land Rover and it could probably get all the way to Maleton on it's tank of fuel. "If you think about the biggest explosive you can imagine, and then multiply it by a million., that's about what a nuclear bomb is."

"And you have one down in the laboratory?" Carl asked quietly, his face suddenly ashen. "Ben?"

"No, don't worry," Ben said, shaking his head. "It's different, it doesn't explode. It's just what generates the electricity."

"You're sure?" Carl questioned, staring at Ben intently. "Okay then, if you say so."

"It's fine, Carl, honestly," Ben informed him.

They were interrupted by a burst of static from the radio on Ben's belt, followed by Reid's voice. "Hello? Hello?" Reid said, his voice sounding a little hollow and distorted. He was stood half way down the mountain road with a pair of binoculars, overlooking the town and the surrounding woodland.

"Hi, Reid," Ben replied, unclipping the radio from his belt. "This is Ben and Carl."

"I can see movement, north of Garstang," Reid informed them. "Looks like a small group, possibly scouting ahead. If there's a larger group hidden in the forest, I can't see them."

Ben was impressed at how quickly Reid had taken to using the radio, unlike Carl who still insisted on holding the button down continuously. "We're on our way," Ben said, looking to Carl for agreement. "We'll bring Victor and go out to meet them, pick you up on the way."

"I'll keep an eye on them until you get here," Reid concluded.

They met Victor at the top of the ladder, Carl offering him an arm to help him up into the cavern. They all had radios tuned to the same frequency and therefore knew that their visitors had finally begun to arrive, which was why Ben was not surprised to see Safran and Murphy climb from the ladder behind Victor.

"I don't think I should have to stay here," Safran was saying before she had even cleared the lift shaft. "I know all about negotiations and diplomatic tactics, you should take me along."

"Next time," Ben promised, "we talked about this. When everyone's here, your help will be invaluable. We're just going to say hello, to show them where to stay."

"It's not right," Safran persisted, but her voice held none of its usual signs of protest. "Just be careful, please."

"Promise," Ben replied, kissing her on the cheek and handing her the pager, just in case.

Ben unhooked the power cable from the hybrid car and climbed into the passenger seat, letting Carl drive. The vehicle made almost no sound as they drove slowly from the cavern and down the winding mountain road.

II

"Excuse me, Lord Marcus," the tavern keeper said, interrupting their breakfast.

"Just Marcus, please," Marcus reminded him, wiping his mouth on a napkin. "Is something wrong?"

"No, no," the tavern keeper replied, smiling apologetically. "There's nothing wrong. I've just heard from the lad, that's all. The forces from Fort Solitude have been sighted and they're approaching the city as we speak."

Marcus looked to Matthew who nodded in silent agreement. "Thank you," Marcus said. "You've been most helpful."

"I don't mean to speak out of turn," the tavern keeper continued, his voice dropping to a conspiratorial whisper. "But I've heard some of what you've been talking about, and it makes a lot of sense. I hope you can convince the Baron and his Lords to agree with you."

"So do I," Marcus agreed, rising from the table.

Matthew kissed Arian goodbye as Marcus promised Juliet that they would return as soon as they could. The day outside was warm and bright, and they were soon sweating and a little breathless as they moved quickly through the Waterways and along the Great Road towards the north of the city.

As they cleared the city limits, the crowds seemed to grow instead of dissipate as many of the city's residents had gathered to witness the army's arrival. They lingered amongst the crowds for an hour or more, the sense of anticipation building, gauging the people's reactions to the possibility of war.

Opinions seemed to be mixed. Many of the older residents seemed content to agree with the Baron, holding the troops close to the city to defend its citizens. The younger citizens however were keen to send the forces north to destroy their enemy, many of them debating joining the fight themselves.

A murmuring spread across the crowd, that the army had been sighted. Matthew looked west, scanning the horizon, and was just about able to spot the haze of movement. Before long, the columns of marching soldiers were easier to make out, tightly grouped lines that moved with purpose and distinction. They were a sight to behold, but nothing like the number they would be facing from Island City.

As they watched, a small group broke away from the lines, moving towards the city. The bulk of the forces stopped where they were and began to make camp in the vast farms and fields that grew from the northern border of Ashford. As the small group moved closer, the crowds of residents began to cheer and applaud, offering welcoming smiles and hearty handshakes as the Lord and his senior officers moved through them.

Matthew and Marcus fought to wade through the sea of people, trying to get to the front and speak to the Lord themselves. The more they pushed forwards, the harder they were pushed back. They were getting nowhere, and already the small group had moved past them and was marching determinately towards the palace. Matthew pulled Marcus to one side, trying to cut through between the buildings surrounding the palace, but people were lingering there too, blocking their path. By the time that they had caught sight of the Lord and his officers again it was already too late. The palace gates were closing behind them.

The crowd slowly began to disperse, the excited citizens rejoicing that their safety was all but assured. Though they were divided on strategy, the mere possibility of failure was never considered. Ashford had never fallen to a foreign army, and it never would. The very idea seemed impossible to them. Marcus was struck by the image of Aldonis, the smoke rising into the sky, and wished, not for the first time, that he could erase it from his mind.

III

Carl slowed the car as he approached the scouts, the three men and two women staring at the vehicle with a mixture of fear and awe. They carried a selection of pistols and rifles and every barrel was aimed at the car as it drew to a stop.

"Arms raised," Carl said quietly as he reached for the door handle. "No sudden movements and we should be fine."

They got slowly from the car, arms held out to show that their hands were empty. Carl instinctively moved closer to Ben, ready to shield him if the bullets started firing, while Victor and Reid hung back, staying nearer the car.

"Hi," Ben said, stepping forward. "Welcome to Garstang."

"What's that?" one of the men said, waving the barrel of his rifle towards the car before pointing it back towards Ben.

"That's a car," Ben replied, "powered by electricity. It's why we invited you here."

"We'll take it," the scout said, stepping forward menacingly.

Ben hesitated, his mouth suddenly dry, but he and Carl had discussed it and knew that it might happen. He closed his eyes and collected himself, opening his mouth moments before Carl was about to step in. "And do what?" Ben asked. "Do you know how to drive it? How far will you get before the power runs out? Do you have a supply of unleaded fuel, because it won't take diesel?"Ben looked between the scouts, questioning them with his gaze.

"We want to talk about an alliance," he continued, "about building a community. Believe me, this car is nothing compared to what we have to show you."

The scouts looked at each other, a silent communication built from a lifetime of working together. After a moment's consideration, the lead scout lowered his rifle and stepped forward, offering Ben a hand. "I'm Silus, of the Corvin tribe," he said.

Ben shook his hand and smiled, his heart still racing in his chest. Silus was only an inch or two taller than Ben, but he had the thin, wiry body of a hunter, someone who could move as fast as a coiled snake. The strength in the grip brought tears to his eyes.

"Ben, Benjamin Knight," Ben said. "We're not a tribe, not really. You might know Victor though, from Sanctuary?"

Victor took that as his cue and stepped forwards. "Good morning," he said, extending his hand towards Silus. "I am Victor Freeman, of Sanctuary. You may not know of me, but I have traded with the Corvin tribe before. Does Alison still lead you?"

"She does," Silus replied, a hint of suspicion in his voice.

"She is a wise and honourable leader," Victor told him with sincerity. "I look forward to meeting her again."

"The rest of the tribe are camped about a half day's travel from here," the scout said, unsure where the words had come from.

"We can provide rooms for Alison and those closest to her," Victor continued. "The remainder of the tribe is welcome to camp within the remains of the city or in the outlying woodland while we wait for the other tribes to arrive."

"Other tribes?" Silus asked, surprised. "What other tribes?"

"The invitation was delivered to tribes throughout the Wastelands," Victor told him. "It is important that as many as possible hear what we have to say."

Silus considered what Victor had said, though it was clear from his face that he wasn't happy with it. "I'll have to report this to Alison," he said.

"I would expect nothing less," Victor said. "Return to your tribe, we shall be waiting for you here this evening. I hope you will return, but if not, we will understand."

Without another word, Silus turned and led his team north, moving quickly through the gardens and damaged buildings. Ben let out the breath that he hadn't realised he had been holding.

"Nice job," Carl said, his large hand slapping Ben on the back. "They'll be back, you wait and see." Ben beamed at the unexpected praise.

"They will," Victor agreed, "though whether they return in peace or in conflict remains to be seen."

"Perfect," Ben said sarcastically, returning to the car.

IV

Samuel Larson strolled slowly through the Market District towards Marie's stall. He was having a good day, having overseen the arrest and questioning of senior members of two of the city's gangs and was one step closer to finding Deacon and ending the terrorists once and for all.

As he approached the stall he saw that Marie was just closing up. Samuel was surprised, it was still early in the day and the market was busy. She hadn't seen him yet, so he hung back, ducking behind a large fabric stall, concealing himself behind a large curtain.

As Marie left he followed her, careful to avoid detection. He felt awful about it, sick and guilty about betraying her trust, but she had been so different of late. She had never been a very good liar, but the lies had become so frequent and strange. He loved her, he would do anything for her, but a part of him just needed to know what was really going on.

As she turned a corner he lost sight of her for a moment and he moved quickly to see which way she had gone. As he peered carefully around the corner, she was nowhere in sight, and he stepped forwards boldly, turning in circles to look for her.

The street was wider than the one he had exited, but she wasn't there. He moved off at a jog, peering through the windows into the stores he passed. He almost ran straight past the narrow alleyway, not even considering that she would be down there, but something drew him back. It could have been a sound, or a flicker of movement in the corner of his eye, but whatever it was, it made him stop.

He turned at the alleyway and looked towards the far end where Marie was working a brick out of the wall, a piece of paper in her hand. He crept up behind her, almost close enough to touch her before he spoke. "Marie?" he said questioningly, his voice barely audible, a mixture of surprise and confusion.

Marie turned around, eyes wide, the brick slipping from her grasp and thudding to the floor. "Sam!" she said, shocked. She could feel the pulse in her throat as her breathing quickened and her brain screamed at her to run.

"What are you doing?" Samuel asked, his gaze moving from

the hole in the wall, to the scrap of paper and then back to her face. There was only one way to describe the look on her face; guilty. He had seen it all too often in the preceding months, but he never imagined to see it on the face of the woman he loved.

"I, I, it's not," Marie stammered, looking left and right, searching for a way past him and back onto the open street. "I didn't. You weren't. Sam?"

Samuel reached down and removed the scrap of paper from her grasp. She resisted, gripping it as tightly as she could, but she was no match for him. He took it from her and opened it slowly, reading the contents. He had to read it twice, three times, to comprehend exactly what it all meant.

It was a list, similar to a shopping list, but so much more. A list of names and places, high ranking members of the City Watch and where they may be found alone and unguarded. The homes of the men and women that he worked with, day in and day out, that he realised Marie had spoken to him about casually over dinner. Enough details to find any one of them.

Marie began to cry, no longer looking for a way to escape. She reached for him, but he pushed her away, turning away from her. "You?" he said, still not believing that it could be possible. She had been the one that he could turn to, could confide in, the one he could be honest with. The Regent would have killed him for some of the things he had said to her, but he never had to worry about him finding out. They were a team, nothing could come between them.

"I did it for you," Marie began, the words barely audible between her racking sobs. "They would have killed you."

"Who, Deacon?" Samuel asked. "You went to him? You helped him, helped him kill all those people? The patrols?"

"I had to save you, Sam," Marie continued. "You can't see it. If Deacon doesn't kill you, the Regent will. This was all I could do to keep you safe. I won't lose you, I can't."

She reached for him again, but he stepped back from her, looking down, looking anywhere but at her face. "No," Samuel said, shaking his head. "You? It was you?"

Samuel turned and began to exit the alleyway, his head full of thoughts all fighting to be heard. It was Marie, she was the one, the one who had betrayed him, betrayed everything. How many men and women were dead, killed because of what she had done? Why hadn't he seen it? Why didn't he realise?

Alexander wouldn't forgive him, not for that. They were dead now, both of them. There was nothing that they could say to prevent it. He had to tell the Regent, didn't he? If he didn't, and the Regent found out? Their deaths then, they'd be so much worse. What should he do?

It came down to one question; Who was Samuel Larson, really? Was he Marie's lover, or Alexander's killer? What defined him?

Samuel stopped and turned. She looked so small, so childlike, perched on her knees in the filth of the alleyway, tears streaming down her face. She stared at him, pleadingly, begging for forgiveness, for understanding. "Us, me and you," he began, on the verge of tears himself, though tears full of anger and rage. "We're over, we're done. I won't tell him, I won't tell the Regent what you've done, but I can't see you again, not ever. I'll get my things from your house, but I won't be back. This is it, Marie, this is all I can do now."

"Please," she sobbed, reaching for him, but he had already turned around, walking out of her life forever.

V

The tension in the air of the conference room was palpable. In the end, five of the Wasteland's largest tribes had arrived at Garstang and agreed to hear what Ben and Victor had to say. Each of the leaders were sat around the large wooden table, sipping at fresh water while eyeing each other suspiciously.

They had been reluctant at first, demanding to speak to Victor or Ben individually, threatening to leave or attack if their demands were not met. Under Carl's instruction Ben had called their bluff, reminding them that the other tribes were just as likely to attack them, and in the end everyone would lose. If they wanted to be a part of what they had to offer, they had to start to work together. There was no other way.

Ben had suggested that they meet just as the sun was setting, allowing him to show off some of the technology from the laboratory. It had actually been Safran's idea, but she hadn't minded too much when Ben put it forward as his own. Victor and Carl had agreed and the meeting was set. All that was left was to make their grand entrance.

As Carl opened the far door, the occupants of the conference room turned around as one, some of them reaching for weapons tucked into their waistbands. Ben entered first, the electric lantern held before him, illuminating the room as he entered. Safran came next, followed by Victor and Carl. Reid and Murphy had agreed to stay behind at the lab and radio if there was any movement near the entrance.

Ben placed the lantern on the middle of the table, where the hundred tiny LED lights cast a swathe of light around the room. The tribal leaders stared at it intently, each of them trying to work out how such tiny candles could give out so much light.

"Leaders of the Wasteland tribes," Victor began, taking his seat. "Thank you for agreeing to meet with us and listen to our proposal."

"I've heard your proposal before," Alison interrupted. She was a broad woman with short dark hair and inquisitive eyes. "I agreed that the Corvin Tribe would leave you in peace, but that was all. What's changed?"

"Alison," Victor said. "So good to see you again, I remember our last meeting well. With regards to what has changed, well, I was sorry to hear of your hardships over the last two winters. So many of your people lost to hunger and illness-"

"How did you?" Alison demanded, rising from her chair.

Victor looked at her impassively, smiling until she returned to her seat. "Thank you," he continued. "Life in the Wastelands is hard. So many tribes come and go, often lost without trace or memory of their passing. The Corvin tribe has endured, but if you face another winter like those past, how long will you continue?

"It is true, another tribe may take on those who survive, perhaps even the Dubner or Patter tribes?" Victor nodded to each of the leaders of the respective tribes. "But then, the Corvin tribe is no more, their history lost to stories and rumours."

"Sanctuary is no different," Alison protested. "Your town isn't big enough to survive a significant attack, and you're just as susceptible to disease and hunger."

"We have endured much hardship," Victor said, "but I accept what you are saying. Sanctuary, as it is, will not last forever. We are too small, too vulnerable.

"Imagine, though, a city big enough to rival Island City or any in the Southern Baronies, doctors and medicines to help the sick, storage for food over the winter, farms overflowing with livestock and crops."

"Why build when we can take what we need?" Toby, of the Wilkin's Tribe, asked. To Ben, he looked like he should have just stepped off the beach, a surf board tucked under his arm. He had shoulder length blonde hair that framed his square jaw perfectly.

"People always fight to defend what they have," Safran said. "They might look weak, easy, but looks can be deceiving. Look at Victor, and Sanctuary? If any of you knew for certain that you would win, that you could take it, you would. You haven't though, have you? How many people would you lose in that fight? A hundred? Two hundred? More?

"What happens then, when you're weak, your fighters weary, or worse? How long until another tribe takes what you have, what you stole? Then another tribe fights them, it never ends."

"What would someone from Draxis know about life in the Wastelands?"Owen, of the Norton Tribe, spat. He was older than the others at the table and looked as though he had seen more than his fair share of combat. The three jagged scars that ran across his nose and right cheek gave him a permanent sneer as he spoke.

Safran paused, choosing her words carefully. "You're right," she said, slowly. "I haven't suffered as you have. I haven't fought for every meal, struggled to stay warm in the midst of winter, lost family and loved ones to disease. I haven't done any of those things, and I'm here to tell you that you don't have to either.

"We're not saying that you'll need to stay here indefinitely, far from it. You'll still be a tribe, you'll still be able to venture into the Wastelands whenever you choose. You'll just have a home to come back to, a place for your sick, your young and elderly. A community."

"That's all well and good," Lewis, of the Dubner Tribe, said. He was the only one of the Tribal leaders who seemed to be relaxed, sitting comfortably in his chair as he took in everything around him. His short dark hair exposed a thin and angular face with eyes that seemed to smile even when his mouth was not. "This idea isn't new. There are towns throughout the Wastelands, trading stops and the like."

"Feldinger, Thrall," Owen added.

"Exactly, and remember it was our ancestors who settled Island City," Lewis continued. "I don't care about any of that. I want to know about the electricity."

Ben was surprised that they had waited so long to mention it, they had been eyeing the lantern hungrily throughout the meeting. Ben leant forwards as he said, "What about it?"

"We've all heard the stories," Lewis said. "The electricity, the power to bring back the technology that litters the Wastelands, but they're only stories. This," he waved at the lantern, "it's a trick, you're trying to deceive us.

"You want something from us, something you haven't mentioned, at least not yet. I for one will not fall for your lies."

There was a murmuring of agreement around the table, as the tribal leaders looked to each other and nodded. Most of the time they were bitter enemies, but they were united behind their distrust for Ben and Victor.

"You're right," Ben said. "We do want something. We want your help, but we don't want it for free. What we're offering you, it's real, all of it. This," he picked up the lantern, "it's powered by electricity, I promise you. What can we do to prove it?"

Lewis held out his hand and Ben passed him the lantern, smiling as Lewis turned it over and over in his hands, sniffing at the LED's, touching one with the tip of his tongue. He passed it to Alison who did much the same.

"I may not know how you deceive us," Lewis said, though with less vigour than before, "but that doesn't make it any less of a trick."

Ben looked to Carl and Victor for support. Carl smiled and nodded. "Okay," Ben said, showing his palms in surrender. "The lantern, the car, they're not enough to convince you. I get that. We need to show you something bigger, something incredible, don't we? Something impossible that no one could fake, not in a million years.

"We need to show you the laboratory."

VI

Samuel Larson walked apprehensively along the long corridor towards the throne room. Alexander had requested to see him, to provide the numbers of people who had registered to join the war, but Samuel knew the truth. He was confident that the Regent knew what he had done, the secret that had kept him awake the previous three nights, and it was time for him to face up to it.

Samuel was ready, ready to die, ready to accept his fate. Part of him hoped that Marie hadn't suffered, but he realised how unlikely that was. The Regent hadn't had anyone in the medical room for weeks, and Samuel knew how much he enjoyed it. Perhaps if Samuel could convince the Regent that it was all on him, he might secure Marie a quick death.

"Larson, about time," Alexander said as Samuel was escorted through the large wooden doors. "What kept you?"

"I had to find the records, my Liege," Samuel replied, his voice monotone and his gaze fixed firmly on the floor at his feet.

"I see," Alexander said, scrutinising him. The Commander of the City Watch looked tired, pale and drawn, a shadow of his former self. "I'd heard that you'd spent the last few nights sleeping at the Watch House," Alexander continued, his voice displaying the barest hint of compassion. "Is it something we need to discuss?"

"No, no, Regent," Samuel said hurriedly, taken aback. "It, it's a personal matter but it won't interfere with my duties, I assure you."

"As you wish," Alexander replied. "Hand me the papers and take the rest of the day for yourself, I'm sure that the Watch can manage without you for one day."

"Thank you, Regent," Samuel remarked, handing the paperwork over quickly.

Alexander smiled and waved him off, taking his usual seat near the balcony. Unfortunately the papers didn't take long to digest. Sixty-seven, that was the final number. Sixty-seven people prepared to take up arms in the defence of their city. It was an insult, to him personally, that they would dare to treat him in such a way.

"Guard!" Alexander bellowed, tossing the papers onto to table and watching them scatter. "Send for a messenger immediately, these people need to be put in their place."

VII

As expected, the tribal leaders were in awe of the hidden door that led to the laboratory. "That, that was rock?" Owen said, stepping forwards and inspecting the door as it descended into the mountain. "How?"

"Titanium alloy," Ben corrected, stepping over the door once it was low enough. "You're right, though, it was made to look like a natural rock formation. It slides up and down on hydraulics I think."

"You built this?" Alison asked, convinced that she had somehow been drugged, that it was all a dream.

"Not me personally," Ben continued, "at least, not this bit. There were teams of engineers involved with converting the cavern and constructing the door. It was already in place before I started working here."

They joined him cautiously on the other side of the door, Toby and Lydia panicking as the door began to rise again. Within seconds they each had their weapons drawn.

"Relax," Carl said, hands up. "The door closes on its own. You're quite safe."

They were reluctant at first, until Ben stepped closer to the door with his pager, triggering it to descend again. The tribal leaders looked to each other before lowering their pistols, though Ben noted that they didn't return them to their holsters.

"Here you can see the girders and sheeting that make up the door," Ben said, trying to bring their attention back to the marvels of the laboratory. "The same alloys support the cavern roof, so it can withstand pretty much anything. Oh, and those lights are all electric, just like the lantern."

As the door closed shut behind them, the cavern remained brightly lit, the halogen bulbs reflecting off the shiny paintwork of the vehicles inside. The leaders wandered amongst the vehicles, opening doors and checking the interiors, running their hands along the smooth lines of the modern cars. They looked like children who had been let loose in a toy shop for the first time.

"I want this one," Lewis said, opening the door of a shiny red sports car and sitting behind the wheel. "Make it move."

Ben looked in through the passenger side, watching as Lewis pressed buttons and moved the gear stick, expecting a reaction. "That's petrol only," Ben said apologetically, "and there's not much left. Two of the cars are hybrids, though, and they can do short distances on electric power."

Lewis climbed slowly from the car, his face a mask of disappointment as his fingers lingered longingly on the glossy paintwork. "You led us to believe you had control over the electricity?" he said suspiciously. "Why not this one?"

Ben opened and closed his mouth, searching for the words that would make sense to him. In the end, he gave up and climbed into the passenger seat. "Get in," he said. "Let's see what I can do."

As Lewis climbed back into the car, Ben searched around for the keys. He eventually found them in a small compartment between the seats, remembering that most people who worked at the laboratory left their keys and belongings in their cars. There were no concerns about theft as everywhere was under constant observation, and most personal items weren't allowed past the security desk anyway.

As Ben reached over and turned the key in the ignition, the roar of the V8 engine made Lewis almost jump out of his seat. Within seconds, Carl and the other tribal leaders had rushed over to investigate the noise.

"You see that there," Ben said, pointing to the petrol gauge. "When it's on the red, it means the tank's almost empty. I don't know if there's any petrol out there, but I doubt it. Once it's gone, that's it."

Lewis didn't understand what Ben was saying, but the sound of the engine had been more than enough to put him off driving anyway. To him it sounded like an angry beast was inside the car, waiting to devour him. Ben turned the engine off, returning the keys to the small compartment.

They spent a further ten minutes exploring the rest of the cavern, asking questions about the other vehicles, refusing to believe that the two helicopters could actually fly. They were more relaxed and excited Ben noticed, their eyes wide with wonder. Everything seemed to be going to plan, until he attempted to show them the tablet computer and found that it was out of power. They were disappointed at first, until Ben promised to show them something better.

The corridor and stairwell were finally empty of rubble. Carl and Victor had been busy, dragging it to the lift and then pulling it up the shaft. There were several fluorescent tubes still out in the ceiling, but it was still bright enough to get by. Lydia insisted on touching every tube that they passed, unable to comprehend how it could give out light without heat.

Ben hurried them past the canteen level, which was to be the last stop on the tour. Reid and Murphy had been busy in the kitchen, preparing a meal with the various supplies. Reid had finally gotten over his claustrophobia and was in awe of the kitchen, his early teachings in the bakery coming back to him. The smells as they walked past were almost too difficult to ignore.

They carried on past the laboratory and into the mainframe below. There was so little to see in the laboratory since they had removed the broken computers and equipment, whereas the mainframe had the potential show them exactly what the laboratory could offer. They walked into the large, wide room, past the shelves full of replacement monitors, computers and electronic equipment. The mainframe was at the far end, attached to three large displays.

As Ben approached, he let out a sigh and shook his head, smiling to himself. Safran was sat on one of the three raised seats, doubled over in laughter as an episode of Friends played on the screen before her. He'd first showed her how to use the mainframe to help answer some of the hundreds of questions that she'd had about the laboratory, but she seemed to spend most of her time watching the numerous films and television shows that were stored in the mainframe's records.

"Ben, Ben," she managed between fits of giggles. "You'll never guess what Joey just said!"

"I've seen this one," Ben reminded her out, pausing the episode. "I thought you wanted to read about the reactor?"

"That was boring," she began, turning her chair around to find the tribal chiefs staring at her. "Oh, hello."

"Those people?" Alison asked. "Are they imprisoned? How do you make them stand so still?"

"There's no room behind there!" Owen exclaimed, stepping past the monitor.

"It's just a recording," Ben explained, resuming playback. "The people, they act out stories, like at a theatre. A machine records them and then we can watch it whenever we like." To demonstrate, he rewound the scene and played it again, making Safran laugh a second time.

Lewis smiled, though not at the jokes on the screen. He didn't understand how any of it worked, but he'd seen enough to know that it wasn't any trick or treachery on Ben's part. He wanted it, all of it, and he would do whatever it took to make it his. If that meant allying himself with the boy, so be it, but only until he knew how to work the machines for himself. However powerful their electricity was, they would all still bleed when the time came.

"I think it's time to discuss the terms of the agreement?" Lewis said, smiling from ear to ear.

VIII

"My Lords," the soldier said, poking his head into the tent. "Lord Howard's messenger has arrived."

"Ah, excellent," Lord Conner replied. "Send him in."

The forces from Fort Danzig had arrived the previous day and their camp had merged quickly with that of Fort Solitude. The troops numbered almost fourteen thousand, and they were all eager for battle, the news of their comrade's defeat spreading quickly throughout the camp. Lord Julian had brought word of the Baron's orders, to stand ready in defence of the city, much to the soldier's disappointment.

"How does he fare?" Lord Conner asked, inviting the men to sit before him. Lord Conner was a short but well built man in his sixties, his shoulders broad and his jaw square, hidden beneath a fine greying beard. Lord Julian was taller and much slimmer, bordering on skinny, with a narrow face and small dark eyes that darted around the room suspiciously.

"He weakens with each passing day," Matthew replied sombrely. "It may well be his final words I bring to you."

"You, you're not from Ashford," Lord Julian announced, standing quickly. "Guards! Arrest these men, immediately."

"Wait, hear us out," Matthew protested, raising his hands in surrender. "We've risked a lot to get this far, just to bring you a message. Lord Howard really did speak to us, I assure you."

The guards rushed in, weapons drawn, manhandling Matthew from his chair. "Hold that order," Lord Conner announced, stopping the guards in their tracks. "Let's hear what they have to say."

Lord Julian began to protest, but was silenced with a look from Lord Conner, who had become the highest ranking Military official by default. Matthew was allowed to return to his seat, though the guards remained inside the tent, just in case.

"From the Baron's description, you must be the trader, yes?" Lord Conner asked, making Matthew nod. "Then you must be Marcus, Lord Marcus of the Oster military? I've fought beside many of your brethren over the years. They speak most highly of you."

"Thank you," Marcus replied. "The Kurns are a constant threat to both our peoples."

"But nothing like the threat you face at present," Matthew interrupted, shaking himself free of the guard's grip.

"The Baron spoke of your concerns," Lord Conner acknowledged. "His advisors see things, differently."

"Which advisors?" Matthew argued.

"His military advisors," Lord Julian spat, his words full of anger and resentment.

"Lord Howard is all that's left of his military advisors," Matthew continued, his tone similarly tinged with aggression. "It's his advice that the Baron's so keen to ignore!"

"Enough," Marcus said, placing a hand on Matthew's and eyeing him warily. "The Baron's word is law. We aren't here to dispute that. We only wish to speak to like-minded soldiers, those who've seen battle and returned."

Matthew closed his eyes and visibly calmed himself, slowing his breathing. "I apologise," he said. "It wasn't my intention to insult the Baron, nor would it ever be."

Lord Conner nodded and waved the guards away, leaving the four of them alone in the tent. "I understand your concerns," he said quietly, "but we have our orders. Julian and I both spoke to the Baron on this matter, but his opinion will not be swayed. He views the protection of the city to be paramount, and won't consider leaving it unguarded."

"He said as much when we spoke to him," Marcus agreed, his voice similarly subdued. "When Island City's forces strike, which they will, you'll be caught between them and the city. Your tactics will be limited."

"We will prevail," Lord Julian insisted. "Ashford has never fallen to an enemy force, nor will it, and certainly not to those northern skeets."

"I do hope you're right," Marcus agreed, "but having faced those skeets, I think you're underestimating them. They may not have the numbers they once had, but their strategies and resilience are without equal in my experience.

"I have some ideas how best to counter them, but with the city at our back, it won't be easy."

"Our?" Lord Julian asked bitterly. "Baron George was most clear about that!"

"Oh, shut up, Julian," Lord Conner demanded, surprising them all. "Remind me how much action you've seen at Fort Solitude, will you? As I hear it, no one's seen anyone from Gelders Ford in years, let alone faced them in battle.

"Explain to me how ignoring information from someone who has actually faced our enemy is the wrong thing to do?" Lord Julian went red in the face, but managed to hold his tongue. Matthew couldn't help but smile surreptitiously.

"Our most effective tactic would be to advance, now, while they're weakened," Marcus continued. "Lord Howard felt the same way, and that was his message. The longer we, you, wait, the more likely they'll have received reinforcements. Phalathlan, Draxis, Oster, they're all under their control."

Lord Conner sat back in his chair, stroking his fine beard. "I agree with your assessment," he said, even more quietly than before. "I wish that the Baron would see it, but he won't be swayed. Even if we did order the armies to advance, too many of them know of the Baron's orders. They'd stay here regardless of what I said, dividing our forces and weakening us further."

"So how do we change the Baron's mind?" Matthew asked, casting a glance behind him before he spoke.

"We don't," Lord Conner accepted. "He's spoken, and the people accepted it. We do what we can with what we have."

"Perhaps," Matthew said, smiling wickedly, a plan already beginning to form in his mind.

IX

Alexander had ordered the majority of his personal guard, as well as most of the City Watch, to take up positions around the meeting area before the palace. He knew that what he was about to say wouldn't be popular, but he was done with the petty cries and complaints from the people below. Didn't they know how hard he worked for them? Didn't they know what he sacrificed to feed them, clothe them? They were behaving like ungrateful children, and it was time to tell them that.

He stepped forwards onto his balcony, looking down at them with disdain. "Citizens of Maleton," he began, casting his gaze over the crowd. He hadn't bothered casting out his will, he still felt weakened by the lack of sleep, but besides that, he didn't view them as worthy of it, not anymore.

"I stood here just a week ago," Alexander continued. "I spoke to you of a great need, of a service that you could provide to your city and its people. Every day, your brothers and sisters, daughters and sons are dying for the very freedoms that you take for granted. I asked that you might aid them, and be rewarded for that aid, but how did you respond?

"Sixty-seven, that's all. Sixty-seven of you prepared to make your families proud, to put food on their table and fight to defend your homes. Sixty-seven out of tens of thousands. You make me sick.

"No longer will this city care for you. No longer will this city support you if you will not support it in return. As of this moment, I have ordered the food warehouse be closed, your ration slips useless. As of this moment-"

The roar of anger from the crowd below drowned him out,

and he paused as he waited for order to be restored. The crowd pushed against the surrounding guards, who pushed back in kind, the butts of their rifles cracking skulls as they fought to get their message across.

"Enough!" Alexander bellowed, loud enough to be heard above the mayhem. As the guards aimed their rifles into the crowd, the people began to edge backwards, quieting as Alexander continued to speak.

"No longer will this city provide food to those who will not work for it," he continued, his voice carrying far and wide above the thousands of stunned faces. "As of this moment, only those who would stand up and fight for this city will find their families fed. There will be no exceptions. All food sales in the Market District will cease, their produce now the property of this city. Any who resist will be shot."

The crowd surged forwards, their angry cries a call to arms. The guards pushed back at first, struggling against the oncoming tide, but they began to lose their footing. As the crowd bore down on them, first one guard and then another lost their nerve, turning their rifle towards the crowd and opening fire.

The cries became screams as those at the front tried to back away, whilst those at the back continued to press onwards. Bullets flew and people fell, those still breathing trampled beneath the feet of those trying to get away. The meeting area was in chaos, parents trying to keep their children safe, friends turning upon neighbours in their fight to escape.

Alexander watched it all from his vantage point, a sneer upon his face. They were cattle, nothing more, so why had he expected anything different? He still looked for the best in people, he accepted, the idea that those below were like him. He would do anything, everything, in the pursuit of his goals. It had been his mistake to assume that the people below would behave in the same way.

They'd learn, he reasoned, they would have to. Those who didn't learn, who didn't follow his example, would starve, and the city would be better for it. Maleton, Draxis, the entire Southern Baronies would be better without the weak-willed, demanding people who scurried below him. He would better them, elevate them into the hard working, obedient citizens that a ruler like him deserved.

He would be the greatest ruler that the world had ever seen, and he would make his father proud.

X

"I think that went well," Carl suggested, savouring the taste of a single malt whiskey that he had found in the store room.

"It did," Ben agreed. "And Reid, wow, that food was amazing."

"If only my father were alive to see that kitchen," Reid said wistfully, taking the bottle from Carl and pouring himself a drink.

The tribal leaders had returned to their camps throughout the town of Garstang, though many of them were already beginning to refer to it as 'New Sanctuary'. Victor was the only one who wasn't smiling.

"Victor?" Ben asked, looking at him quizzically. "What's up?"

Victor smiled, though it failed to reach his eyes. "Lewis, of the Dubner tribe," he began, a worrisome look upon his face. "He lies about his intentions."

"We all knew this wouldn't be easy," Carl reminded him, offering him a drink.

"He is already making plans," Victor continued.

"And what about the others?" Ben asked.

"Alison, Lydia and Owen are eager to side with us," Victor informed them. "Alison had already reconsidered my offer some months ago, but her seniors persuaded her against it. Toby is unsure, but his intentions are true. If he sides with us, it will be for the right reasons."

"Making deals with the Wasteland tribes," Carl muttered to himself. "If only Astor were around to see it."

"So what do you think we should do?" Ben said.

"The Dubner are the largest tribe to have met with us," Victor reminded them. "If we ask them to leave, the other tribes may take offence, especially as you will not be able to explain why. They may turn away too, or worse, join the Dubner when they turn on us."

"Carl?" Ben said, looking to the older man for answers.

"I can't make this decision for you," Carl said. "This is your plan, your idea. It's up to you to see it through."

"Reid?" Ben said desperately, but the sailor only smiled and sipped at his drink.

Ben began to walk around the mess hall, considering all of the scenarios that he could think of. They were all safe inside the laboratory, but what good would that do them? If they just hid away, their friends would all die and Alexander would win. If what Victor said was right, though, it was only a matter of time before Lewis and his tribe turned on them, and hiding inside the lab may be their only option. Ben couldn't imagine being able to change Lewis' mind, so where did that leave them?

"Lewis will want to learn all about the lab and how it works?" Ben asked Victor. "Is that right?"

"It is," Victor agreed.

"So that's going to take time," Ben reasoned aloud. "Time during which he'll agree to our terms, send his soldiers south to defeat Alexander and his armies."

"So we use him?" Carl said, happy that Ben had made the right decision. The men had all realised what had to be done, but telling the boy wouldn't help him in the long term.

"Exactly!" Ben said grinning. "Then, once everything is sorted, well, we'll think of something. You never know, he might come around to our way of thinking on his own."

"Yes, maybe," Carl agreed, but deep down he knew otherwise. He already had plans for Lewis, but telling Ben about them would only upset the boy. No, better to let them take the victory and keep the blood from their hands.

As Carl knew all too well, it wouldn't be the first time.

XI

The remaining members of the Elder Council and the Merchant's Guild were bloodied and bound before him. They had been so eager to speak to him, or so he'd been told, so Alexander had them brought forcibly to one of the smaller state rooms in the palace.

"You're insane," Elder Paul said again, spitting a clot of

congealed blood at the floor near Alexander's feet.

"You're not the first to say so," Alexander remarked dismissively, "but which amongst us in in chains?"

"You fired on the very people you promised to protect!" Elder Paul continued, no longer concerned about his own safety. He had seen the look on Alexander's face as the guards had systematically beaten them; no one was making it out of there alive. "How many dead? How many more wounded? Do you even know?"

"The numbers will be here somewhere," Alexander replied with a casual wave of his hand. "Does it matter though, really? I spent months offering them kindness and compassion, and this is how they repay me. It's time the people learned their place, and that place is wherever I deem fit to send them."

"Please," the head of the Merchant's Guild begged. "Please, let us go. We'll leave, I promise, you'll never see us again. We have Deniras, they're yours, all of them. Please?"

Alexander laughed, a chuckle that grew in intensity until it could be heard from one end of the palace to the other. It overwhelmed him and he held his hand to his stomach as he lost his breath. "You think," he stammered between outbursts of laughter. "You think you can buy your way out of the mess you've made? Can't you see that's what brought you here in the first place?"

Alexander calmed himself, slowly wiping the tears from his eyes. "It's your greed, your arrogance, that have infected the people out there. They no longer care for their neighbours, their friends, their family. They care only about themselves, about stuffing their bellies and growing fat on the suffering of others.

"I offered them a chance, a chance to stand up for their city and their Regent. I even offered to reward them for their sacrifice, but it wasn't enough. It would never be enough. You, you and your guild, giving everything a price. You told them that everything was for sale, even their loyalty, and now, now they'd be happy to stand by and watch this city burn.

"No, I won't let that happen. I'll make them fight, make them stand up for what's right, or they'll starve, every last one of them."

"Are you listening to what he's saying?" Elder Paul tried,

looking pleadingly towards the guards as he spoke. "Can't you see how crazy he's become? How many more people have to die before you realise how wrong this is?"

"You're wasting your breath," Alexander said quietly. "Guards, take them outside and execute them, throw their bodies to the fire."

"My Liege," the guards said as one and without hesitation dragged the Elders and Merchants from the room. There were cries and tears and feeble resistance, but their fate had been sealed before they'd entered. Alexander closed his eyes and massaged his temples as he waited for the sounds of distant gunshots.

He jerked himself awake an unknown time later, unaware that he had even fallen asleep. The sun was perhaps a little higher in the sky, but he hadn't been out for long, a half hour at most. He rose to his feet and stumbled, his weary legs giving way, making him sit back down with a thud.

The dreams had been getting worse, robbing him of even the briefest minutes of refreshing sleep. He had finally given in and accepted the sleeping draught from the physician, but so far it had only served to make him drowsy in the day. He knew all too well the effects of sleep deprivation, he had employed it more than once during his interrogations, but it was more difficult to see the signs when he himself was the victim.

His thoughts were so muddled, so confused at times, but he had to stay true to himself. Everything had to proceed as planned; the rebels crushed and the Baronies defeated. He understood that, knew it to be true, but in moments like those, when he had to concentrate so hard to string words into a sentence, it would have been all too easy to give in, to quit and return to Island City.

Alexander realised that those thoughts were due to the lack of sleep. He had never doubted his convictions, never thought to abandon his plans and tread the easy path, accepting whatever life threw at him without question or complaint. His mother had trodden that path and she had died alone and unknown, abandoned by Alexander's father and the safety and security that was due to her. He had tried to forge his own path, but time and again he had been beaten down, prevented from realising his true potential. They'd given him no choice, and so he had devoted his life to reclaiming his birthright. He would not be swayed, not when true victory was within his grasp.

Just a little longer, just a little more, and he would finally be able to sleep.

XII

"I'm still not sure I believe it," Alison said, "even now I've seen it with my own eyes. You really can make the ancient technology work again?"

By mid-afternoon they had gathered together in the hotel meeting room to discuss the proposal. The tribal leaders had spent the morning gauging the opinions of their seniors and high ranking members of the tribes and were finally ready to make a decision.

"Well, sort of," Ben admitted. "The laboratory, it's powered by electricity, and I intend to extend that to all of Garstang. Any technology that still works will run off the electricity in the buildings, and I'm more than happy to try and repair anything that you find.

"Outside of the city, though, it's just not possible. Anything with batteries, like the lanterns, okay, but they'll run out of power pretty quickly. Maybe a day or two at most."

"I believe what Benjamin is trying to say," Victor interrupted upon sight of the confused looks the tribal leaders wore, "is that we are offering you a place in this city, a city to be powered by electricity. This is not something that will happen overnight, but with your assistance, we will build something unique, here, in the middle of the Wastelands."

"But we live by your rules?" Alison asked.

"I do not intend to dictate how you must live your life," Victor replied.

"But some rules won't be up for debate," Ben interrupted. "We're trying to build a community here, so we have to start with an element of trust. Everyone needs to try to get along, and if people can't get along, it will be up to the council to deal with it."

"Council?" Lydia asked.

Ben looked to Victor and Carl before answering. He hadn't

discussed his idea of a council with them, but it was the only way he could see the new city working. "We'll establish a ruling council," he began nervously. "I'll be on it, and so will Victor as well as a representative from the Road Trains if they wish. We'll also have a member from each of the tribes that sign on with us, yourselves or someone you nominate. We'll work together and make decisions together, you see?" Victor smiled subtly to himself, though Ben was facing the wrong direction to see it.

"And in return, we abandon our ways, our traditions?" Toby asked suspiciously.

"Not at all," Victor answered. "We ask only that you respect those who share this community with you. There will have to be rules, laws, but you will have a hand in shaping them, and they will only determine how to treat others who live in the city with us."

"I think we're getting a bit ahead of ourselves," Ben said. "The details, they'll take time to establish, but the basics are already in place. Work and live together, try to get along, don't take from those around you and help out where you can. It's going to take a lot of work to rebuild this town, but can we at least agree on those as a start?"

The tribal leaders were silent for a moment, but nothing that Ben had said was unreasonable. "I'm about ready to agree," Owen said, breaking the silence, "but we still haven't heard what you want from us, not all of it."

"No, you're right," Ben admitted. "We haven't told you everything, not yet. I think it's best if Carl explains."

Carl leant forwards, resting his large forearms on the table. "You don't know me," he said, "but you'll know of the Road Trains, yes?" The tribal leaders nodded. "On our last trip to Island City, the Regent there used our arrival to start a war between them and the entire Southern Baronies."

"Several of my scouts saw the armies of Island City earlier this year, travelling along the Great Road," Toby said.

"Exactly," Carl replied. "They've already taken control of Draxis, Phalathlan and Oster, and last we heard, Morton didn't favour their chances. If they fall, it'll only be a matter of time before they turn their attention north and bring everywhere from Island City to Ashford under their rule."

"You have this on good authority?" Lewis asked.

"We do," Carl lied. "We were able to speak to Baron George of Morton himself."

"So this is it," Lewis remarked. "This is what you ask, for our tribes to fight against the forces of Island City in the name of the Southern Baronies?"

"No," Ben said quickly. "You fight for yourself, not anyone else. The Regent managed to pit the Baronies against each other, divide them so he could defeat them more easily. The only way to defeat him is to unite and make a stand, but you do it for your own sake, not anyone else's."

"Your tale is convincing," Lewis admitted. "You know where this stand is to take place?"

"Not yet," Carl replied, "but we do have a way of speaking to Ashford without being there."

"Another marvel of your electricity?" Lydia asked.

"It is," Ben said. "I'll be happy to show you, but we need to know what we're going to tell them first."

The tribal leaders were quiet as they each thought over what had been said. "We will give you some time to consider and discuss," Victor suggested, rising from his chair.

They walked down the corridor and out to the lobby where Reid was speaking to several of the tribal seniors. "How's it going?" Reid asked as he joined them.

"We're close," Carl replied. "I can feel it, they all want to say yes."

"That's the impression the seniors were giving too," Reid suggested.

"What's the deal with the seniors?" Ben asked.

"Tribal rule varies between tribes," Victor explained. "The more warlike tribes often have a single leader, someone young and strong who leads them into battle. Others have a council or union of leaders, often made up from seniors, members of the tribe who have lived long enough to offer wisdom and experience. A younger, strong leader may be chosen to be the face of the tribe, though they will only make decisions with the support of the seniors."

"Like the ones we just left?" Ben asked.

"Exactly," Victor replied. "And you are right, Carl, in your assessment. They are all ready to join us, they just need someone else to be first."

"And what about Lewis?" Ben whispered, checking first that he couldn't be overheard. Both Carl and Reid leant in to hear what Victor had to say.

"His plans have not changed," Victor replied. "It appears that he does not have the support of his seniors, but he will act as he wishes regardless."

"Do we need to change our plans?" Ben asked, concerned.

"Not yet," Victor said, casting a momentary glance in Carl's direction. "He will fight with us as he waits for an opportunity to strike."

"Okay, cool," Ben mumbled. "So what now, we just have to wait?"

"Relax," Carl suggested. "We're nearly there."

They mingled amongst the seniors and made small talk as the afternoon passed into evening. Members of the Norton Tribe brought them bowls of hot stew, satisfying the hunger that they all felt, but as the shadows grew long in the lobby, they had already run out of conversation. As the sun began to set, Alison finally poked her head through the door and called them back into the meeting room.

"We're prepared to agree to your terms," she announced.

"But with some conditions," Lewis added.

"Like what?" Ben asked.

"Between us, we can raise almost ten thousand seasoned fighters," Lewis continued. "Those who don't join your fight will remain behind in the city, to begin to construct the homes that you promised."

"Yes, I mean, of course," Ben agreed. "I kind of expected that anyway."

Lewis nodded. "Secondly," he continued, "our people will not die needlessly for your war. If the enemy is as powerful as you state, and the odds look overwhelming, we'll retreat without engaging. You'll be left on your own."

Ben looked to Carl, who shrugged in acceptance. "Okay, yes," Ben said. "I suppose that sounds fair, anything else?"

"The food and supplies you have hidden in your laboratory," Lewis said. "You'll provide half to those who stay behind, and half to forces who march south to battle. The people here will still hunt and gather, but the farms will take time to cultivate, the livestock to mature. They'll need to be well provided for in the absence of our strongest fighters."

Ben thought it over. He was reluctant to give it up, but Lewis was right. He couldn't allow the people to go hungry, and if they didn't make it back, the food would just sit there until it rotted away anyway.

"Yes," Ben said eventually. "The food, that's fine, but nothing else. The vehicles, any technology, it all stays inside the laboratory until we return. Oh, and just so we're clear, no one gets inside the lab while we're away. They couldn't anyway, only I can open the door."

Lewis filed that scrap of information away and looked to the other leaders for their agreement. They nodded and smiled and gave him their support.

"Then it looks as though you have your army," Lewis said, extending his hand. Ben cast one last glance towards Victor and Carl before accepting Lewis' hand and shaking it vigorously.

CHAPTER 10

The Boxer is surprisingly comfortable, and we even found a few cd's in the other cars to have some music on our journey! I suppose I shouldn't be surprised that Safran is already humming along to whichever generic Boy Band is playing at the moment, but really, how can she say that it's better than Biffy Clyro? Just wait until we get back to the lab, I'll play her some tracks from the mainframe that'll make her change her mind!

Carl managed to siphon off every drop of fuel from the other cars, so added to the full tank in the Boxer we should have enough to get all the way to Maleton. I'm not convinced that we'll have enough to get back, but I guess we'll deal with that when the time comes. I mean, if we're still alive, of course.

There I go again, cheering myself up!

I

"The rumours were right," Bran said, wiping the rain from his face. "The Regent ordered the food warehouse closed, fired on the crowd, and now the Elder Council are dead. Their heads are on spikes beside the palace gates."

"And the riots?" Deacon asked.

"There's been some trouble in the City District," Bran continued. "I don't know if I'd call them riots though, at least not yet. The Watch came down on them pretty hard by all accounts."

"This is our chance," Catrina interrupted. "This is what we've been waiting for!"

"She's right, Deacon," Bran added.

"The Regent's lies have been exposed," Catrina continued. "We can finally show the people whose side they should be on."

"The people arc scared," Deacon reminded them. "At present, they fear both us and the Regent. We need to make them realise our intentions."

"It's decided then," Catrina stated. "We liberate the food warehouse, leave the doors wide open."

II

It was early morning as the ATV rolled up the slip road and onto the Great Road, heading south. Carl was driving and the armies of the Wastelands were following behind them, moving at a fast walk to keep up. To Ben it looked like footage from the London marathon.

"So then, Carl," Ben said. "How does this compare to a Road Train?"

Carl was grinning as he looked over the dials and readouts. "What's that word you're so fond of?" he asked. "Oh yes, awesome!"

Ben chuckled. "How's everyone doing back there?" he asked, turning towards the large back compartment that had lines of chairs to either side. Safran was sat closest to him, with Reid, Victor and Murphy opposite. The Tribal leaders were closest to the door, and more than one of them didn't look to be handling the journey too well.

"Does it shake like this all the time?" Alison asked, her face beginning to take on a greenish hue.

"I think so, probably," Ben said sympathetically. "I can put the air conditioner onto cold, that might help?"

"I, I think I'll walk," Alison said, placing her hand over her mouth and stumbling for the door. Carl brought the vehicle to a stop and lowered the back door to make a ramp.

"I should stay with my people, too," Toby said, stepping out and sucking in deep breaths of cool air.

Safran was giggling. "They look like you, those first few days on the Aero," she suggested.

"I remember," Reid agreed, laughing. "I've never known anyone take so long to get their sea legs!"

"That's not fair," Ben protested. "I think I had the flu or something." Soon, everyone else was laughing, making Ben blush.

"We all have our weaknesses," Carl said.

The door closed and they were soon on their way, enjoying the music that Ben played from a selection of compact discs. When a loud hammering sounded against the side of the vehicle, they were surprised to see that four hours had passed.

"Time for a break," Victor suggested, getting to his feet. He was too tall to stand at full height, and stooped over as he watched Carl bring the vehicle to a stop.

The Wastelanders barely looked out of breath, but they were happy to accept the rest and relaxed across the Great Road and the grasses beyond, enjoying the sunshine. Only Ben chose to stay behind inside the ATV, examining the console as he ate.

"It's lovely outside," Safran said, startling him. "What are you doing in here?"

"I'm trying to tune the radio so we can speak to Matthew," Ben replied. "I don't know the exact frequency, but I know how many turns I did on the wire so I should be able to work it out."

"Do you think I can talk to my mother, too?" Safran asked, her eyes lighting up at the prospect. "And Justin?"

"Of course," Ben told her, smiling. "I just needed a bit of quiet to think straight."

Safran sat and hummed quietly to herself, managing almost

three minutes before interrupting his train of thought. "What's that?" she asked, pointing towards the console.

"What's what?" Ben replied, a little perturbed.

"That, on the screen," Safran continued, leaning over him to show him exactly what she was pointing at. Ben got a face full of her hair, mixed with her sweet scent that made his heart race and palms sweat.

"That's the GPS system," he said, leaning closer. He had completely lost his train of thought with respect to his calculations.

"And?" Safran persisted.

"It works out where we are, but it's not working right," Ben informed her. "The maps relate to earth, my home, so the numbers don't match up."

"How can the numbers tell you where you are?" Safran said, her face showing her confusion.

"They work out longitude and latitude," Ben said, realising too late that the terms wouldn't mean anything to her. "There shouldn't even be any numbers, unless, unless there's satellites up there somewhere for the Boxer to talk to?"

Safran waited for Ben to continue, but he was already lost in his own little world, trying to piece together the idea of working satellites. If he'd made everything else, he reasoned, then why not satellites too, there were thousands of them orbiting the earth.

"I think I'm going to go back outside," Safran said at last, a little disappointed.

"Sorry," Ben said, smiling up at her. "I'll think about it another time, maybe use the computers back at the lab to try and contact the satellites. I'll work out the frequency for the radio so you can speak to your mom when we get moving again, okay? You should probably speak to Reid about maps and longitude and latitude, he'll be able to explain it better than me. Ask him about a sextant."

"I will not!" Safran exclaimed, blushing. "Benjamin!"

"It's, it's not what you think," Ben stammered, blushing himself. "It helps sailors navigate, with the sun and the stars."

"Hmm," Safran replied, giving Ben a disbelieving look before leaving the Boxer.

They returned a short while later full of laughter and good

spirits. Carl set off again at a slow pace as Ben tuned the radio into the frequency that he had calculated. He passed the handset to Safran who was still giving him dirty looks.

"Hello," Safran said, pressing and releasing the button. "Hello, can anyone hear me?"

The background static was quickly replaced with a male voice. "I have sent for Baron George," it said.

"This is Safran," Safran replied. "Please, I'd like to speak to my mother, and also Matthew or Lord Marcus." There was no response that time and so they sat in silence, waiting.

"Safran," Baron George's deep, booming voice announced. "So good to hear from you, it's been a while."

"Good day, Baron," Safran replied, using her most formal tone. "I was hoping to speak to my mother and then Matthew or Lord Marcus?"

"Your mother is on her way," Baron George informed her. "Though I thought you would have contacted us sooner? How was your journey into the Wastelands?"

"Very productive," Safran said, though her face bore a look of suspicion. "We bring additional forces to engage with the armies of Island City."

"That's excellent news!" Baron George replied. "Though I suspect that by the time you get here, they'll no longer be needed."

"Why, what's changed?" Safran asked. "When we last spoke you were awaiting the return of your forces from Fort Solitude and Fort Danzig? Have there been further developments?"

"As we speak, my forces are preparing for the defence of the city," Baron George assured her.

"And the rest of your Barony?" Safran persisted. "How long until you march and engage the enemy?"

"You mother is here now, Safran," Baron George said, changing the subject. "She is most eager to speak to you."

The radio went quiet for a moment as the microphone was handed to Karan. "Safran, how are you?" Karan asked. "We've missed you so much."

"Mom," Safran said, a tear in her eye. "I've missed you too, and Justin. I'm good, we're all good. Please, I'm sorry, but I need to speak to Baron George some more."

"Safran?" Karan asked, the upset plain to hear.

"I'm sorry, mom, please," Safran said quietly, fighting to hold back the tears.

"Safran?" Baron George said with surprise.

"George," Safran said, louder and more forcefully than before. "I don't believe I'd finished."

"No, of course you don't," Baron George said sarcastically. "What did you want to say?"

"I am waiting for you to tell me how you intend to protect the rest of your Barony by waiting for the enemy to come to you?" Safran said, matching the Baron's sarcasm.

"How I choose to govern is no concern of yours," Baron George insisted.

"Then I demand to speak to Matthew and Lord Marcus," Safran continued.

"They are not available," Baron George replied.

"Then make them available," Safran demanded.

"Lady Safran," Baron George began.

"Baron Safran," Safran interrupted. "It seems you have forgotten my title, George. This is not a matter for debate. I demand to speak to both Matthew and Lord Marcus, and I would consider it a personal insult to both myself and the Barony of Draxis if you refuse."

Safran looked around the ATV to see a mixture of stunned and impressed faces turned in her direction. She smiled nervously as she waited for Baron George to respond.

"I shall send for them," Baron George replied, though the tone of his voice betrayed exactly how he felt about.

"Wow," Ben said once the radio had gone dead. "That was, well, awesome!"

"Awesome," Carl agreed with a chuckle.

"Yes, well," Safran said, clearly flustered. "We need to find out what's really going on and George wasn't going to tell us anything."

"Awesome," Ben said again, which this time earned him a punch on the arm.

III

It took a little over two hours for the messenger to bring Matthew and Marcus to the palace. Baron George was sat beside the radio, eyeing them with disdain as they entered.

"Let me be clear," he said. "If you say anything that threatens the security of this Barony, or this city, I shall have you executed."

"Of course, Baron," Matthew replied, bowing slightly as he spoke. Once satisfied, Baron George instructed the guard to hand over the microphone.

"Ben? Carl?" Matthew said.

There was a burst of static before Safran answered. "Matthew!" she said excitedly. "It's so good to hear from you."

"Baron Safran," Matthew replied, remembering the title at the last second. "It's so good to hear your voice. I'm here with Baron George and Marcus, is Carl still with you?"

"Hey, boss," Carl said. "Ben's here too, as well as a few other people that I think Safran's getting to."

"We've secured almost ten thousand troops from the Wasteland tribes," Safran said. "We set off from Garstang this morning."

"Wasteland tribes?" Matthew asked, confused. He had only ever fought against them, never beside them.

"Victor helped," Carl added, hoping that it would clear up any doubts in Matthew's mind.

"Enemy of my enemy," Matthew muttered to himself.

"We're approximately," Safran began, looking to Carl.

"Two weeks," Carl whispered.

"Two weeks north of Maleton," Safran continued. "If you can force the Island City forces in that direction, we can attack them from behind and trap them between us."

"Baron George's advisors have suggested that the surviving Morton forces remain south, in defence of the city," Matthew said, watching the Baron's reactions as he spoke.

"That could add another two weeks to our journey," Safran protested. "The Island City forces will have attacked by then."

"Baron George has been very clear about his orders," Matthew said, choosing his words carefully. "It's our duty to support him."

Safran was about to object when Carl placed a cautioning hand on her arm. "Of course, Matthew," Carl said. "You're right, we'll join you at Ashford."

"Thank you, Carl," Matthew replied. "We'll see you in a month. Oh, and thank Catrina and Deacon from me too, I'm looking forward to working with them again soon."

"Will do, boss," Carl said. "We'll speak again soon."

"Looking forward to it," Matthew said, before the radio was switched off.

"What was that about?" Ben asked into the silence that followed. "Catrina and Deacon are in Maleton?"

"Exactly," Carl said with a grin. "It means Matthew's got a plan."

IV

Even at that time of night the area around the food warehouse was busy, the local people choosing to ignore the curfew and voice their frustration at the Watch officers on guard. So far it had been peaceful, nothing more than insults traded between them, but that was about to change.

They mingled with the crowd for a few minutes, gauging the mood. The people were clearly unhappy with what had happened, and there was talk of fighting back, but they all appeared to be unarmed and hungry. They were scared, Deacon realised, after the guards had wounded and killed so many at the palace. They weren't quite ready to rise up against the Regent and his soldiers, at least, not yet.

Deacon caught Bran's eye and joined him in the middle of the group, Stan and Catrina following close behind. Stan was still angry at the world, but when given a chance to take out his frustrations on the City Watch, he jumped at the chance.

Deacon and the others looked to each other and nodded or smiled, declaring that they were ready. They didn't have much of plan, they didn't really know what they were up against, but the intent was simple; retake the food warehouse by any means necessary.

Bran and Catrina pulled the pins on their explosives and

tossed them towards the cluster of soldiers that stood between the crowd and the warehouse. At first the soldiers thought that they were missiles, bricks or stones that the crowd had thrown their way, and raised their guns in a threatening manner. It was only when one of the soldiers looked and yelled, "Grenade!" that they dived and ran for cover.

As the grenades exploded, driving both the crowd and the soldiers into panic, Deacon and his people pushed forwards, picking out the Watchmen one by one. Deacon had his blades, driving them deep into chests or slitting throats, while the others had silenced pistols, killing the soldiers with well-placed head shots or bullets to the chest. By the time the remaining Watchmen realised what was happening, seven of their comrades were already dead.

"Take cover," Bran yelled, as the remaining soldiers began to fire indiscriminately into the fleeing civilians.

Catrina saw two people fall, blood oozing from wounds on their back, before the crowd was lost to the dark of the alleyways of the Market District. Stan and Deacon returned fire, though it was impossible to tell if they hit their mark.

"Hold your fire," Deacon hissed, re-sheathing his blades and removing the pistol from its holster. "Conserve your bullets. We do not know how many remain."

"Sorry, Deacon," Stan said sheepishly, while Bran only nodded and removed his magazine to check how many bullets remained.

"I saw at least four run back inside," Catrina said, poking her head around the low wall as she spied the entrance.

"There'll have been another four or six inside at least," Bran added, "on hand for exactly this type of thing."

"Four against ten," Deacon said, smiling gleefully. "Exactly my kind of odds. Give me some covering fire, and when you hear gunfire or screams from within, press on the main door."

The others nodded and fired towards the front of the warehouse, watching as Deacon slipped into the darkness beside the western wall. Gunfire was returned, the bullets striking the brickwork that they hid behind, but then it was quiet as both sides waited for the other to make a move.

Deacon crept along the wall, listening intently with each step.

The warehouse was a huge, square building, made of brick at the bottom and steel sheeting at the top with windows high up in the construction. There were no doors or windows that Deacon could see on the ground level, but he hoped that that would change as he progressed. If there was only one entrance in or out, they would have to rethink their plan.

As he neared the rear of the building, a single lamp hung above a closed door illuminating a small cone of the darkness. The door was closed and Deacon aimed carefully with his pistol, shooting the lantern. It shattered and glass fell, though there was no flame left to ignite the oil that splattered the ground and wall.

He waited, listening, letting his eyes readjust to the darkness. A full minute passed, and then two before he was happy that no one was coming to investigate. He edged forwards and crouched beside the door, testing the handle delicately.

There was a burst of noise from the front of the building, the snap of rifle fire followed by the quieter sound of bullets from an pistol. The others were running out of ammunition, and Deacon was running out of time.

The door opened noiselessly on well oiled hinges and Deacon eased inside, pulling it closed behind him. He found himself inside a small office, with a further door opposite that led into the main warehouse. That door was bolted on his side, so her slid the bolt open and edged into the warehouse proper.

The warehouse looked even bigger on the inside than the outside. Deacon was surrounded by shelving and tables, some of it reaching so high they were near the ceiling. Boxes, crates and sacks were arranged on the various shelves, obscuring his view of the rest of the warehouse.

"Can you see anything?" a voice whispered to his right, making him freeze in mid-motion.

"It's too dark out there," a second voice replied. "I think they're still crouched behind the wall."

"Fire another warning shot, see if you can draw them out," the first voice ordered.

As the second voice fired two shots through the open doorway, Deacon moved towards where he believed the voices came from, crawling beneath a table and around a stack of wooden boxes. At the end of a narrow corridor between the lines of shelves, he finally saw the two soldiers, crouched behind a large wooden chest. Taking aim, he shot one and then the other in the back of the head before they could even react.

"They're inside!" another voice yelled from somewhere to his left, and suddenly the narrow corridor was lit by gunfire. Deacon scrambled over a crate and beneath a shelf as he struggled to get away.

The others saw that as their cue and sprinted towards the large door, taking up positions to either side of it. Bran poked his head around the door, spotting a lone Watchman leaning over a wooden crate and shot him twice in the back.

The soldiers began to panic, calling out enemies from all sides, shouting to each other to regroup or fall back. Deacon followed the voices and killed two others before a third managed to catch him with a lucky shot, shooting him in the shoulder. Deacon scrambled backwards, rolling beneath a tall shelf as further bullets peppered the space where he would have been.

Bran, Catrina and Stan moved quickly between the rows of boxes and shelves, killing without mercy, the remaining soldiers falling before them. Within minutes, the warehouse was quiet, still and seemingly empty.

"Deacon," Bran shouted, moving cautiously forwards.

"Here," Deacon whispered, reaching out and grabbing a familiar foot. Catrina looked down, startled, almost shooting him before recognising who it was.

"Deacon!" she exclaimed, shocked and concerned by the amount of blood that had pooled around him.

"A hand, please," Deacon asked, his voice weak and his face pale. Catrina reached down and pulled him from beneath the shelf, the pain of the movement evident upon his face.

As Catrina placed a hand on the wound and closed her eyes, calling forth her ability, Deacon pushed her away. "Wait," he said. "Do not exhaust yourself. Save your strength."

"I'll just stop the bleeding," Catrina promised. "You'll die if I don't."

Deacon looked at her and nodded, lying back and closing his eyes. He felt the pain as Catrina laid her hand back over his shoulder, calling forth her power and directing it into the wound. The blue light cast eerie shadows in the darkness as the sparks danced across the torn flesh, stopping the bleeding as the wound began to close.

She caught her breath and removed her hand, falling slightly as she moved away from Deacon. "It's done," she said wearily, resting back against a crate.

"Thank you," Deacon replied, climbing painfully to his feet. His shoulder was uncomfortable but he would manage. "Where are the others?"

"Over here," Bran told him. He was walking towards them with a single watchman before him, hands bound behind his back. "This one surrendered. What do you want me to do with him?"

"Execute him," Deacon suggested without thinking.

"No, wait," Stan pleaded, running up behind Bran. "He surrendered."

Deacon saw the look of fear and revulsion on Stan's face, rethinking his decision. "You are right, Stan," Deacon said. "He surrendered, it is not up to us to decide his fate."

Stan helped Catrina to her feet and they followed Deacon as he left the warehouse, cradling his injured arm to his chest. A small number of the crowd had returned, gathered around the two fallen civilians. Beside one unmoving woman a man was openly weeping. However, the other person looked to be still alive.

"Can you help her?" Stan asked, looking towards the fallen woman.

"I can try," Catrina replied, though her voice was weary.

Stan helped her over to the fallen woman, where the people moved aside for Catrina to get close. There was one wound, low in her back, and Catrina placed both her hands over it, calling forth her ability.

The crowd stepped back as blue light spilled into the fallen woman, watching with surprise and awe as the wounded woman cried out in pain and then settled, her eyes opening. As Catrina collapsed to the ground, the woman sat up, her voice both fearful and thankful. "You saved me?" she said. "How?"

Catrina was barely conscious, breathing heavily as she fought against her body's desire to close her eyes and sleep. She leant heavily on Stan as he helped her to her feet. "Safran lives," she said quietly, unsure where the words had come from.

"Sorry?" the woman replied, confused.

"Safran lives!" Stan said louder, a wry smile on his face. "Safran lives!"

The woman smiled, then laughed as she turned towards the slowly growing crowd. "Safran lives!" she cried, raising her fist into the air. "Safran lives!"

The crowd begin to join her, chanting the phrase as the woman hugged her husband tightly, both of them weeping tears of joy as others inspected the wound that was almost healed on her back.

Deacon raised his hands, inviting the crowd to quiet. They slowly did, all eyes on him. "People," he said. "Fellow citizens of this great city. Some of you may know me, but to those who do not, I say only that my name is not important. It is the message that you must hear.

"We have been fighting to free this city from the Regent and his soldiers for many months, and we are not the monsters that those in power would have you believe. Today we have struck a decisive blow against his tyranny, and have liberated the food warehouse for you, the people.

"Do not fight for another man's war, fight for yourself! Fight to be free of oppression. Fight to end the curfew and the rationing. Fight to be free!"

The crowd were hanging onto his every word, but what they didn't realise was that it was very similar to the speech that he had given when he took over control of the gangs and rose to power as leader of the criminal element of the city. It didn't matter though, the message was still the same.

"Now," Deacon continued, taking the bound soldier from Bran and pushing him towards the crowd. "This is one of the soldiers who fired upon you. We will leave him for you to decide his fate, and to spread word of our actions this night.

"The time of your liberation is at hand!"

The crowd cheered, chanting 'Safran lives' over and over. A few at the front dragged the bound soldier towards them, while others kicked and punched him as he was driven to the ground. Deacon didn't believe that they would let him live, but Stan had been right. It was for the people to decide.

Sadly, Deacon hadn't really understood Stan's hesitation. If he could see the look of disappointment on Stan's face, as the crowd beat at and kicked at the fallen guard, he may have realised the anxiety that Stan was feeling with every life they took in the name of freedom.

V

Alexander was surprised to be woken in the early hours of the morning, as a guard hesitantly knocked at his door. "My Liege," the guard said quietly as though he didn't really want to be heard.

"What is it?" Alexander demanded, rubbing the sleep from his eyes. He had only just managed to fall back to sleep, after being woken twice already by dreams of his enemies.

"Commander Larson, he's here to see you," the guard replied before hurrying from the door.

Alexander dragged on his clothes and made his way to the throne room, where Samuel Larson stood on the balcony, overlooking the city.

"Larson?" Alexander asked as he approached. "What can't wait until the morning?"

"It's the rebels, sir," Samuel replied, looking down towards his feet. "They've taken control of the food warehouse."

"What happened to doubling the guard?" Alexander retorted.

"I did, Regent," Samuel apologised. "I don't have all of the details, but a sizeable crowd is already inside, helping themselves to the food and supplies."

Alexander shook his head mournfully before massaging his temples. "Take it back," he said. "By any means necessary, take it back or burn it to the ground. I don't care which."

"Of course, Regent," Samuel replied, mentally formulating his plan as he hurried from the throne room.

VI

Baron George stepped out onto the platform overlooking the large meeting area before the palace, Lord Conner at his side. Lord Julian had chosen to remain with the forces garrisoned outside the city, or at least that was what Baron George had been told. Lord Conner couldn't risk him interfering, so had arranged for him to remain behind whether he liked it or not.

A large crowd had gathered and were talking excitedly as the Baron stepped forwards, raising his hands and enjoying the jubilation that greeted him. "Good people of Ashford," Baron George began. "I stand before you with Lord Conner, leader of Morton's forces currently garrisoned outside of the city. I'm sure you've heard a great many of the rumours currently circulating, and I'm here to reassure you that they're not true.

"Within this city you are safe and under my protection. The soldiers have been recalled as a matter of routine, there to reassure you good people of your security. This city has never fallen to an enemy force, nor will it. Should the northern army dare to strike at our heart, they'll find twelve thousand of Morton's greatest soldiers standing in their way!

"I say, let them come!"

The crowd cheered at the news that their safety was assured, applauding the Baron as he stood before them, smiling from ear to ear. He didn't notice Matthew's entrance, stood atop a cart, until it was too late.

"Thank you, Baron, for those fine words," Matthew said loudly, turning and bowing towards Baron George as he spoke. The Baron's eyes widened in surprise, though as he waved his guard towards the cart, they suddenly found themselves accosted by members of Lord Conner's forces.

The idea had come quickly to Matthew, a make or break proposal that would save them all or condemn them to the worst death imaginable. He was a salesman at heart, just like his father and his grandfather before him, and it had been said that he could sell anybody anything. In the past that may have meant a broken piece of old tech, or a herd of cattle that were way past their best. What he had grown to realise though, what he had also sold so many times in his life were ideas. Promises that what he had, what he was prepared to part with, albeit for a price, could make life, could make everything, better.

"I don't wish to speak out of turn," Matthew began, "but on behalf of these people before you, I wish to thank you for what you do for us and this great city!"

The crowd cheered again, agreeing with Matthew, thanking

the Baron for everything that he did.

"I ask you though, Baron," Matthew continued. "What can we, the people, do for you? You promise us safety and security, and we are eternally grateful, but if I may ask the good people of this city; are we but children that need our Baron's protection? Are we too weak to stand up for ourselves, to stand side by side with the men and women of our brave military? Are we too scared to stand up and face this feeble army from the north?

"Tell us, Baron, please. What may we do for you?"

Baron George was red faced and fuming, glaring at Matthew with eyes full of hatred. He composed himself before speaking, forcibly removing the anger from his voice. "It is my duty to serve," he said at last, loud enough to be heard across the meeting area. "I ask nought from you good people, only that you allow me to continue to act in your best interests."

Matthew applauded and soon the crowd had joined him, celebrating the brave Baron for all of his good deeds and his humility. "You are wise and noble," Matthew continued. "If only we might face this enemy head on, show them the might and ferocity of our military, with Baron George at the head. They would flee before facing such a formidable opponent.

"What say you, Lord Conner?"

Lord Conner looked towards the Baron and smiled, slyly, before stepping forwards. "As always," he said, "the soldiers of Morton serve you, the people. If you tell us to stand, we stand, and if you tell us to fight, we fight!"

This was met with further cheers and shouts from the crowd, which Matthew encouraged. "Then why do we wait?" he shouted, the crowd quieting that they might hear him. "Why are we waiting for these foreign invaders to come to us, when we might show them the strength and conviction of our military? Why not make them fall before us or flee in terror?

"We thank you again, Baron, for your kind words and protection, but the time to wait has passed. In Baron George's name, I say we stand up and fight! Fight! FIGHT!"

By the third fight, those standing around Matthew were chanting along with him, and soon the entire crowd was calling for the soldiers to march north and fight. Baron George's knuckles were white as he squeezed his hands into fists, his face bright red with anger. He turned towards Lord Conner, pulling him close so that he could be heard above the crowd. "I'll see you hang for this," Baron George hissed. "And the trader, his friends. All of them."

"If we make it back," Lord Conner said, his determination visible, "you're welcome to try."

Baron George reluctantly stepped forwards, raising his hands to quiet the people before him. "If this is the will of the people," he said, a fake smile on his lips, "then so be it. Tomorrow, at dawn, the forces of Morton will march forth and show this northern army the error of their ways!"

The cheers and applause went on and on, back and forth across the crowd, as Matthew was taken upon the shoulders of those around him. Baron George made the best of it, smiling and accepting the praise of his subjects, all the time planning on how he was going to make Matthew and his companions pay.

VII

"Matthew," Arian sad sweetly, waking him. "Sun's almost up."

"Arian?" Matthew replied blearily. She was sat on the edge of the bed, smiling sweetly at him. She looked better than she had done in weeks, positively glowing.

"Father's already downstairs," Arian continued. "The streets are full of people looking to march north with you and show Island City their folly."

Matthew sat up slowly, trying hard to ignore the pounding that was going on inside his skull. After the meeting outside the palace on the previous day, he had been carried on the shoulders of excited revellers and found himself taken to several taverns on his way back to his rooms. The ale had flowed freely, and Matthew had been reluctant to refuse the generosity of those around him.

"How are you feeling?" he asked, his tongue dry and foul tasting. "You look good, great even."

"I'd wager better than you," Arian remarked with a wry smile. "Do you even remember getting in last night?"

"I remember The Crown, and The Duck's Beak was it?"

Matthew tried. "Then something about Black Marsh Brew or, something, I don't know. No I guess, not really."

"Then I'll forgive you," Arian laughed. "Come on, hurry up. Mum wants us to set off early. We should be in Hopewell late tomorrow."

"Hopewell?" Matthew asked, confused.

"You really don't remember do you?" Arian replied. "Last night, when you got in, Mum and I were talking? Father suggested it and you agreed it was best to be as far away from the fighting as possible, in my condition."

"Condition?" Matthew asked, looking at her for the first time, his tired, blood shot eyes struggling to focus. "I thought you were better?"

"For the smartest man I know," Arian said, leaning down to kiss him delicately on the forehead. "You can be pretty dumb at times. The sickness, the tiredness, you really didn't put it all together?

"I'm pregnant, Matthew."

Matthew suddenly found himself sober and steady. He jumped to his feet and stood looking down at his wife to be. "Pregnant?" he asked, struggling to get the words past the enormous smile that was spread across his face.

"I am," Arian said, looking up with a tear in her eye.

Matthew pulled her to her feet, wrapping his arms around her. "No, sorry," he said suddenly, releasing her. "I didn't mean to, are you okay? Did I hurt you?"

"Matthew!" Arian exclaimed. "I'm pregnant, not fragile! Now come here."

She wrapped her arms around him, kissing him passionately. "I love you," he said as their lips parted, the truth of his words showing plainly across his face.

"I love you too," Arian agreed. "Now, hurry up or you'll have my father to answer to."

"Grandpa," Matthew said before chuckling loudly. "That's going to be fun."

"Oh, and Matthew," Arian said, her voice taking on a more serious tone. "Don't you dare think about not coming back to me. You and my father, you make it back alive, okay? No matter what."

"I promise," Matthew said, gazing at her intently. "No matter what."

VIII

"The last time we met," Deacon said to the packed warehouse, "I made you certain promises. I made it clear that there would be blood, fire and death, and the time has almost come to make good on that commitment.

"By now you will have heard of our liberation of the food warehouse in the Market District, a significant blow to the Regent and his hold over this city. The people are finally ready to stand up for themselves, and all they need is one last push. Over the coming week I will call on each of you, giving you tasks and targets that will-"

"Deacon!" a breathless voice called from the back of the room. "Deacon!"

The room turned as one, many of the gang members readying their weapons. "Jimmy?" Deacon asked. "Is that you?"

"It's the food warehouse," Jimmy continued, pausing to catch his breath. "The Watch, they're attacking it, now!"

Deacon drew his own weapon as he got to his feet, checking that it was loaded. "It would appear that our timetable is to be stepped up," Deacon announced. "The Watch must not be allowed to succeed."

Deacon started towards the exit, Bran close behind him. The gang members followed, smiling, readying their weapons as they enthusiastically discussed fighting the City Watch. It took them almost half an hour, moving at a fast jog through the streets and alleyways of the Industrial and Market Districts. By the time that they arrived, a large group of civilians were already engaged in a fierce battle with the men and women of the City Watch.

The Watch numbered forty or fifty by Deacon's estimation, striking remorselessly through the large group of civilians that attempted to prevent their access to the warehouse. They carried a variety of knives, clubs and firearms, and seemed happy to maim or kill anyone who stood in their path. As he watched, those at the back of the group were already losing their resolve and trying to flee as those at the front bled and died for their freedom.

Men and women were cut down without hesitation, the soldiers firing indiscriminately into the crowd as they trampled on the dead and dying at their feet. No one was off limits, and Deacon even spied a small cluster of children, hiding behind their parents as they tried to get to the relative safety of the warehouse.

"Protect the people," Deacon commanded as he slid the pistol back into its holster and unsheathed his two curved blades. "Select your targets carefully."

The message was passed between the thirty or so gang members as Deacon and Bran ran head first into the battle, slicing and stabbing at the Watchmen in their path. The people saw what was happening and began to push back, rejoining the fight with renewed vigour. Once the rest of the gangs joined the conflict, the Watch were sandwiched between the two and their attack became a desperate struggle for survival.

Deacon lost count of how many he killed. He was grateful that Catrina had healed his shoulder as he moved gracefully from one soldier to the next, his blades slitting throats and burying themselves hilt-deep in chests. In a matter of minutes it was over, his face splattered with blood as his he searched for his next target. It was only when Bran placed a cautious hand on his shoulder that he began to relax.

"That's the last of them," Bran said, wiping his dagger on his jeans.

"Make sure that there are no survivors," Deacon instructed. Bran called several of the gang members to his side, and one by one they systematically checked that each of the Watchmen were dead before casting the body into the River Brachen.

The dead civilians were treated with respect, many of the gang members offering up their jackets or shirts to cover their faces, while the injured were taken into the warehouse where members of the public were already trying to help them.

"People," Deacon called, drawing their attention. "You see now what this Regent would do to maintain his hold over you and this city. This time he sent fifty soldiers to take what is yours, next time it may be a hundred, two hundred, more. I say to you, do not wait for him strike again.

"Your time is at hand! Return to your homes and wake you brethren. Tonight we take back this city! Tonight we destroy the soldiers at his command, and then we march on the palace itself!"

The crowd cheered, raising aloft the weapons taken from the fallen Watchmen. "Safran Lives," they cried as one, a battle cry as they went street to street, knocking on doors and calling those around them to action. As Deacon and Bran made their way back to the hidden room beneath the brewery, the streets were already filling with citizens, fired up and angry, a mob with a single demand.

No more.

IX

Samuel Larson sat at his desk, trying to concentrate on the papers before him. It had been hours since his men had left, ordered to retake or destroy the food warehouse. There should have been news, word of their success, something.

"Commander," the officer said, bursting into the room without knocking. "They're burning, sir, the Watch Houses."

"Say again?" Samuel said.

"In the City and Market District," the officer continued, fear in his eyes. "Watch Houses are on fire and there are people on the streets. They're armed and they're coming this way."

"How many?" Samuel asked, collecting his pistol from the desk.

"I don't know, sir," the officer replied. "A lot. What do we do?"

Samuel considered his options, hesitating before giving the order. "Sound the alarm," he said at last, "and make for the palace. Stick together and don't engage unless you have to, we won't have the numbers to hold them back. I'll meet you there as soon as I can."

"Sir?" the officer asked, questioningly.

"There's something I have to do first," Samuel explained, grabbing his rifle from the stand near the door. "If the palace is under threat, you close the gates, okay? Whether I'm there or not."

Samuel didn't give the officer time to answer, running down the stairs and from the building at full speed, a single thought in his mind. As he wove through the streets of the Palace District, he realised that he could see light across the river as the flames reached up into the sky.

As he reached the familiar door, his heart was pounding, his lungs burning. He no longer had his key but that didn't stop him. On his fourth kick, the lock splintered and the door caved in. "Marie!" he screamed, running up the stairs. "Marie!"

As Samuel burst through the bedroom door, Marie screamed, reaching for the pistol that Samuel had given her for protection. "Sam," she said confused, her hands shaking as she lowered the weapon.

"Get dressed, now," he demanded, dragging clothes from the wardrobe and throwing them towards her. "We've got to go and we're running out of time." His face was a mask of fear and anger, conflicting emotions that distorted his features. To Marie, he looked wild, savage, on the verge of unspeakable violence.

"Sam, please, what is it?" Marie cried, the tears beginning to flow.

"Get dressed!" Samuel screamed at her.

Marie stood quickly, wiping away the tears as anger overtook the fear that she had been feeling. "No!" she yelled, silencing him. "Not when you speak to me like that. I demand to know what's going on?"

Samuel stopped, consciously slowing his breathing. He felt so conflicted, his love for the woman before him clouded by the anger and hatred that he felt for her actions. So much of him wanted to hold her, to protect her and keep her safe from harm, but a piece of him still couldn't forgive her for what she had done.

"It's the rebels," he said quietly, looking down towards the carpet. "They're rioting, south of the river, and it's only a matter of time before they head this way. I need, we, we have to get to safety.

"Please, just get dressed, and come with me."

Marie tossed the gun towards the bed before reaching down and finding suitable clothes from the pile that Samuel had made. She said nothing as she dressed and he avoided looking at her, both of them feeling uncomfortable as she removed her nightclothes in front of him.

Once dressed, Samuel led the way, running from her house and past the Council Chambers towards the palace. The streets were getting louder, a dull cacophony of noise behind them as they ran beside the white stone palace wall towards the gate.

"Hurry, inside," the Palace Guard said as they rejoined the road and caught sight of the palace gates. There were two lines of Palace Guards, one behind the other, weapons ready and aiming in all directions. As Samuel and Marie crossed into the palace courtyard, the first of the rioters were spotted, moving past the walls of the Merchant's Guild and towards the palace.

The Palace Guard opened fire on the rioters without mercy or hesitation, falling back as bullets struck the tarmac at their feet. "Close the gates!" came the order as guards took cover within the courtyard, firing indiscriminately as the rioters attempted to storm the palace. The large gates were heavy and slow to move, but the Palace Guards managed to hold the rioters back, resting only when the gates were closed and the heavy wooden beams were in place.

"Larson!" Alexander yelled from the top of the stairs. "I demand to know what's happening. Immediately!"

CHAPTER 11

It's amazing how quickly the ATV began to smell of stale sweat, even with the air conditioning. It's better than the alternative, though. I don't know how the tribes do it, walking as far as they do in this heat. It must be 300C out there, easy.

At least there's plenty of water. I suppose it must have been the Road Trains, diverting rivers and streams so that they'd flow near the Great Road. Carl said it may have been, but he's not really sure. It could have been before his time.

He thinks we're about half way to Maleton, so another week or so I guess. Everyone's in good spirits, and I don't think there's been too much trouble between the various tribes, at least not that we've been told. The nights are full of song and merriment, and without the need for fires and shelter, we're making good time.

This might actually work out after all.

I

"Hey, boss," Carl said into the radio. It was a little after dawn and the tribes were gathering their belongings for another day of travel along the Great Road.

"Carl!" Matthew said. "I wasn't sure this thing still worked."

"I'm surprised to hear from you too," Carl continued, banging against the side of the ATV to draw someone's attention. As a surprised face looked in through the large back door, Carl mouthed the words *get the others*.

"When I told Lord Conner about the radio and what it could do," Matthew replied, "he insisted on taking it from the Baron. Suffice to say there was, well, a bit of an argument and I was worried that it had been damaged."

"Well you're coming through loud and clear," Carl said. As he spoke, Ben, Safran and Victor clambered into the back of the ATV, eager to hear what what going on.

"So you managed to convince Baron George to change his mind?" Carl asked once everyone was seated.

"Not entirely," Matthew told them. "If we make it through this alive, I don't think I'll be showing my face in Ashford any time soon. I suspect the Baron might hold a grudge."

"When he's taking credit for your victory, he'll change his mind?" Carl suggested.

"We'll see," Matthew replied. "How's the journey?"

"Going well," Carl told him. "I'd say we're four, maybe five days from Maleton. You?"

"Half a day from Oster's border," Matthew said. "Lord Conner's scouts report the Island City forces are just over the other side, west of the Great Road."

"What's the plan?" Carl asked.

"Same as before," Matthew told them. "We've acquired a large contingent of civilians to bolster our ranks, so we're hoping to drive the Island City forces north and trap them between us."

"Good luck," Carl said, edging the ATV forwards as the Wasteland tribes began to march. "Update us when you've sight of the enemy."

"Will do," Matthew replied. "We'll speak later."

The radio cut to static and then silenced, leaving the interior of the ATV unnaturally quiet. Carl focussed on the road ahead, avoiding eye contact or conversation with the others.

"I guess someone's got to say it," Ben said once the silence had become unbearable. "This is really happening isn't it? This is it."

II

It had been four days since the palace gates had been closed and Alexander was struggling to think of a scenario where they would open again. The rebels on the meeting area in front of the palace had been celebrating constantly, calling for Alexander to surrender. He had no intention of showing his face, let alone submitting to their demands, but it was only a matter of time. He knew that the walls of Maleton Palace had never been breached, but how long could they survive on what they had behind the walls?

"My Liege," Samuel Larson said, bowing slightly before the Regent.

"Finally," Alexander replied aggressively. "It's about time."

"My apologies," Samuel replied, standing to his full height. "The kitchens are still unstable after the explosion. I thought it wise to move as much of the food supplies from there as possible."

"Just give me the report," Alexander snapped.

Samuel took a deep breath before speaking. "Counting the current number of guards and staff within the palace," he began, "there's sufficient food to last for approximately three months. With rationing, that could be extended to four, perhaps a little longer. I've ordered the guards to begin to stockpile water, just in case the Rebels discover how to cut off the supply."

"Three months," Alexander muttered to himself. "Continue."

"The gate has been reinforced," Samuel continued. "And the guards report that they've shot twenty-seven individuals attempting to climb the palace walls, with no further breaches attempted for the last two days. It would appear that they've learnt their lesson."

"So how do they intend to enter?" Alexander asked pointedly.

"My Liege?" Samuel replied, confused.

"Do you think that they're going to stand around outside until they get tired and go back to their homes?" Alexander yelled. "They're out there, day and night, planning on how to get in here and kill us all. What are our weaknesses? What do they intend to do?"

"I, I don't know," Samuel said. "The walls are sound, the gate secured. The tunnels beneath the palace are still blocked. I've not been able to identify any weaknesses, my Liege."

"Then what will they do?" Alexander demanded, the barest hint of fear in his voice. Though he had barely left the palace before the siege began, he was beginning to feel like a caged animal, trapped and alone, pacing in circles around his throne.

"I really don't know," Samuel told him honestly. "As I see it, we either wait inside the walls until we run out of food, or we surrender to those outside and accept our fate."

"No," Alexander said defiantly. "I won't accept that. It doesn't end this way. I've seen it, Larson, the dream, it told me. We only have to crush the rebels and everything else falls into place. You're still with me, aren't you?"

"To the end, Regent," Samuel replied, though he struggled to put the conviction in his words. He had seen the Regent slipping, losing control of the city and his mind, but now he was putting his faith in dreams. It was only a matter of time, Samuel believed, before Alexander lost it completely.

"Then we only have to wait," Alexander said earnestly. "Once Boshtok realises his reinforcements aren't coming, he'll return to find out what happened. He'll quash the Rebels and retake the city. Then the Southern Baronies will have no choice but to fall.

"It's not over, Larson, you hear me? It's not over until I say it's over!"

Samuel turned and left as the Regent's statement descended into maniacal laughter, the eerie sound echoing along the long corridor behind him.

III

"General," Officer Hastings announced. "The scouts have

returned."

"Good, good," Boshtok said. "Send them in."

Officer Hastings saluted and stepped back out onto the field, calling the scouts forward. The two young women were red faced and breathless but stepped into General Boshtok's tent without hesitation.

"Report," General Boshtok said, waving away their salutes.

"Ashford's forces are approximately a half day's march from here," the first scout said. "They number somewhere between twenty and twenty-two thousand, with the forces from Fort Danzig at the fore."

"Twenty-two thousand?" General Boshtok asked, a little confused. "Do you concur?" he asked the second scout.

"I do, General," the second scout replied. "There is a large contingent of civilian conscripts marching with them."

"Weapons, supplies?" General Boshtok prompted.

"I spied only a small number of cannons, less than fifty," the first scout informed him.

"And wagons to the rear only contain basic rations," the second scout added. "They're moving quickly without the burden of siege weapons and extensive supplies."

"Thank you," General Boshtok said, his mind already beginning to consider the strategic possibilities. "Get yourselves some water and report to Major Ellis for further assignments." The scouts saluted before leaving the tent, their footsteps barely making a sound.

General Boshtok unfurled the map before him and began to scrutinise it. The map showed their current position in high detail, as well as the surrounding settlements and important landmarks. He'd picked the spot to make his stand on the basis of twelve to fifteen enemy troops, the large open expanses of grassland giving his men ample view of their approach and the opportunity to surround them by sheer numbers alone. An additional ten thousand enemy soldiers would make that much more difficult.

He stood, trying to get a different view on the map before him, but however he looked at it, he didn't like what he was seeing. He pulled alternative maps from the chest, scouring them for ideas or strategies that he missed. However he looked at it though, the answer came back the same. His soldiers were vulnerable and he could no longer guarantee victory in his own mind. If only he had the reinforcements from Maleton or Garet, they would make all the difference.

"Hastings," General Boshtok shouted, making his decision.

"Yes, General," Officer Hastings said, stepping back into the tent.

"Begin to pack my things immediately," General Boshtok said. "And send for Major Ellis and his officers, we're moving north."

"Of course," Officer Hastings replied, hiding his confusion.

"We'll regroup once we meet up with the reinforcements," General Boshtok continued. "They can't be more than a few days away by now. Let's see how well the Ashford forces fair when an additional ten thousand troops fill out our ranks."

"They won't have a chance," Officer Hastings said, returning the maps to the chest.

IV

The meeting area in front of the palace in Maleton was full of people celebrating their freedom. Deacon stood near the palace gate, looking for any sign of weakness. Several of the gang members and civilians had tried to scale the walls, but all had suffered the same fate. The guards inside were alert to any such breaches, and the only way that Deacon could see to taking the palace was a combined assault.

"Deacon?" Bran said, bringing him back to the present.

"Bran," Deacon replied wearily. "Did you say something? My mind was elsewhere."

"I've been down into the tunnels like you asked," Bran continued. "There's no way through, the rubble's too thick."

"It is as we thought," Deacon said. "Unless we can breach the gate or walls, we will have to wait for him to come out."

"I've been around the wall more times than I can count," Bran said. "It's solid, through and through. The gate's the only weak spot."

"And yet it failed to succumb to the explosives," Deacon reminded him. "This will not be as simple as we imagined."

"What's the plan?" Bran asked.

"Come, let us meet with Stan and Catrina," Deacon said. "Perhaps they have had better luck."

Bran followed Deacon through the appreciative crowds. There were cheers and shouts of support as he passed, from the very same people who, only months before, had stood on the meeting area calling for his head. Deacon tried to ignore them as best he could, the constant attention they sought from him was exhausting.

They found Stan and Gavin building a fire, light and warmth for the summer evening that quickly approached, while Catrina looked on. Deacon sat next to her and Bran took up his usual position behind Deacon's shoulder. They sat in silence as they watched the young men work.

"What did you find?" Deacon asked once the flames began to take hold of the dry branches.

"The food warehouse is a mess," Catrina said quietly. "They damaged as much as they took, so there's spoilt fruit and broken crates all over."

"Was it the Watch?" Bran asked.

"If only it were," Deacon replied. "Sadly it was ignorance that destroyed half of the city's food, not malice. Was anything worth saving?"

"Not much," Catrina told him. "We added it to the stores over there, but that's not going to last more than a week or so. After that..."

"After that," Deacon finished for her, "we begin to lose our support. The people will rally behind whoever promises to feed their children, even if that turns out to be the Regent."

"I won't let that happen," Catrina assured him. "One way or another, the Regent dies or I die trying. That's the only way this ends."

"At the moment, our only option seems to be convincing the Regent to come to us," Deacon said sombrely. "I do not like our chances, but what other choice do we have?"

They sat together in silence some more, watching as Stan and Gavin took to battling each other with sticks, the boy's laughter insufficient to lift their mood. They were so close, mere metres from ending the occupation of their city, but it was a distance that they couldn't cross.

Deacon racked his mind for a solution but nothing was forthcoming. The plans and schemes that he was known for were just beyond his grasp, fleeting and elusive. He only had one thing left to bargain with, but he didn't believe that Alexander cared enough about the men and women under his command. He had to do something though, he had to try.

"Bring out the prisoners," Deacon said at last. "Let us see if we can convince this Regent to do the right thing by his people."

V

"Was it really that easy?" Matthew asked, surprised.

"They're certainly in retreat," Lord Conner replied.

The four men stood surrounded by their troops, a pair of binoculars passing between them as they scoured the horizon ahead. The scouts had informed them an hour before that General Boshtok's forces were marching north, away from the border. They were able to see a blur within the heat haze at the horizon but nothing more.

That had been the plan, of course, to drive the Island City army back towards Maleton where the Wasteland reinforcements would be waiting, but none of them had expected it to happen so easily. Their soldiers were waiting for orders, and no one seemed sure exactly what to tell them.

"Remember," Marcus reminded them. "Boshtok's clever, he wouldn't have ordered a retreat if he didn't already have a plan of his own. I wouldn't underestimate him, or his forces."

"He's scared," Lord Julian scoffed. "He got word of our advance and turned and ran like the skeet he is. I say we chase him down and put him out of his misery."

Lord Conner and Marcus exchanged an annoyed glance. Lord Julian had been making similar statements for days, each one more frustrating than the last. If it wasn't for the fact that they needed the forces under his command, he would have already been dismissed back to Ashford or Fort Solitude.

"I don't agree," Lord Conner remarked, holding his tongue. "Lord Marcus here is right, we need to be cautious. This apparent retreat could be nothing more than a ruse, a trap to catch us off guard. We need to know what we're getting ourselves into."

"After all the stories they tell about you," Lord Julian mocked, "I'd never have taken you for a coward."

Lord Conner turned on him, poised to strike before thinking better of it. He would be playing right into Julian's hands, he realised, striking a fellow Lord. He could be placed under arrest and removed from duty for such a crime, leaving Lord Julian in charge. He consciously calmed himself, slowing his breathing as he chose his next words carefully.

"Julian," Lord Conner said, his tone sufficiently biting. "The fact that you believe caution to be cowardice says more about you than even your posting at Fort Solitude. I pity the men and women under your command and the nonsense you must instil in them."

"How dare-" Lord Julian interrupted.

"I'm not finished!" Lord Conner barked. "You are here solely because we cannot win this war without the forces under your command. You might believe that you're in with the Baron, poised to replace me when this conflict is over, but a lot can change on the battlefield, a fact you'd well know if you'd ever been on one.

"Heroes can be made and killed, history written with a single bullet. I wouldn't be so eager to question my future when yours is by no means certain."

Lord Julian was red faced and fuming, his mouth opening and closing as he struggled to find the words to express his outrage. The thinly veiled threat wasn't lost on him and it would all be going into his report. He was Lord Protector of Fort Solitude, not some lackey that could be spoken to like that. Once Baron George knew of the depths to which Lord Conner would steep, his rank, his position, would be over.

"Do you have anything you wish to say?" Lord Conner asked pointedly.

Lord Julian closed his mouth and shook his head, staring daggers at all three of them. With an effort he turned and left, heading towards his troops where he could begin to compile his report.

Matthew and Marcus stayed silent, waiting for Lord Conner to speak. The soldiers within earshot were doing a good job of ignoring what they had heard, but within hours the story would have passed from one end of the company to the other. Lord Conner realised that he had overstepped his mark, but as far as he was concerned, he had much bigger things to worry about.

"My apologies, gentlemen," he said, straightening his uniform. "Where were we? Ah, yes. General Boshtok. Let's examine the maps before we press on, see if we can work out where he might be setting his trap."

VI

Deacon walked slowly in front on the seventeen members of the City Watch. The men and women were on their knees, hands bound behind their backs, their faces a testament to the brutality of the gangs and civilians that had apprehended them.

Though they wore the uniform of the City Watch, Deacon understood who they really were. Not one of them were members of what he referred to as the Old Watch, citizens of Maleton who stood up for the laws of the Barony and the rights of its people. He understood the Old Watch, knew what they did and why they did it, respected them in their choices though they rarely fought for the same side.

Those before him though were nothing but soldiers of a foreign invader, following the orders of the Regent without question, no care for the people who looked to them for help. He had always made a point of not harming members of the City Watch, not unless he had to. It was far better to buy their silence than to silence them permanently, to make friends of an enemy so that everyone could profit. He had similar rules regarding the civilians of the city, and was even stricter in their adherence.

Not the people before him though. They deserved their fate. He had heard the stories of abductions and disappearances, men and women taken from their homes and never returned. Those before him cared nothing for the city and its people, so the people should not care for them.

The crowd around him hushed as Deacon stopped and turned towards the palace, raising his hands to his mouth to amplify his voice. "Regent of Island City!" he shouted, loud enough so that everyone could hear. "Show yourself!

"I speak for this city and its people. I have here seventeen members of your City Watch. You are ordered to surrender yourself and stand trial for your crimes. In return, your people will be allowed to walk free from this city. If you fail to heed these demands, I will execute one of them every hour until you do.

"You have one minute to show yourself and declare your intentions."

The crowd was silent as they stared longingly at the balcony, hoping that Alexander would step forth and surrender. Deacon knew that his demands were pointless, the Regent cared only about himself, but he had to maintain his role of leader or risk everything falling apart. Sadly he knew of only one way to command the kind of respect that he was used to; fear.

He looked at his watch, counting the seconds as the minute wore away, the balcony still as empty as it had been for days. He closed his eyes in regret as the minute passed and removed the pistol from his belt.

"So be it," he called out as he took aim. He selected one of the soldiers at random and fired, the bullet snapping their head back as he fell to the ground, dead. The crowd watched and cheered as the man died, calling for Deacon to continue, to kill them all.

Deacon ignored them as best he could, tucking the pistol back into his waistband as he returned his attention to the balcony. "You have one hour," he announced.

VII

"Yes, I understand," Samuel said with disappointment. "But, they're my people out there, they're my responsibility."

"This isn't open for discussion," Alexander replied sternly. "The gates remain closed. Do not make me rethink my decision of allowing you protection behind them."

"My apologies, Regent," Samuel replied. "I didn't mean to question you. You're right, of course. I won't mention it again."

Samuel hated having to agree with Alexander. It was their fifth day trapped inside the palace, or at least that was how Samuel saw it. Every day behind the walls, he had witnessed more and more of The Regent's fear and paranoia, his ability to see spies and traitors at every turn. He believed that Alexander would do exactly as he threatened, cast him out for daring to disagree with him. To make matters worse, he had to listen to seven of his people being executed, just beyond the wall, and the clock was already counting down on an eighth.

He left the throne room and began to pace along the winding corridors that led to the kitchens and bedrooms. It was with a heavy heart that he found Marie in the room that she had taken, sleeping fitfully. They had hardly spoken since he dragged her to safety inside the palace, but he had nowhere else to turn.

"Sam?" Marie said sleepily as he stroked her hair. "Am I dreaming?"

"I can leave if you'd like?" Samuel replied.

"No, please," Marie pleaded, blinking as she forced herself to wake. "Don't go."

Samuel smiled down at her, though it failed to meet his eyes. Marie knew him well enough to see through his charade. She pulled herself up to a sitting position and wrapped her arms around him, holding him tight. "Talk to me," she said.

Samuel hesitated, searching for the words that would make it all better, but nothing was forthcoming. "I," he began. "I shouldn't be here. This was a mistake."

"No," Marie protested. "It's not a mistake. We need to talk, Sam, you and me. I need to make you understand."

"What is there to understand?" Samuel said. "You betrayed me, you betrayed us. You got my people killed."

"Don't you dare, Sam," Marie said, angrier than before. "Don't you dare. How many lies have you told me? How many secrets? I know who you are and I know what you do.

"How many people have died because of you, because of what you did for the Regent? I saw a chance to keep you alive and I took it. What would you have done if my life was in danger?"

Samuel didn't want to say. He knew the answer, knew it before she had even asked the question, but he couldn't bring himself to speak it aloud.

"You brought me here," Marie continued more quietly. "You left your people behind to bring me here, to the palace. You did it to keep me safe. Why is that any different?"

"It's just," Samuel replied. "I, I don't know. I don't know anymore. Everything's falling apart. I just knew I had to protect you."

"You see?" Marie asked. "I'd do anything to protect you, no matter the cost. I'm not going to apologise for that. I knew the risks when I made the choice. If you can't forgive me, if we can't be together, I'll understand, but I'd do it all again if it meant keeping you alive.

"I love you Sam, nothing will ever change that."

They were both on the verge of tears, arms wrapped around each other as Samuel struggled to deal with the conflicting emotions. "I love you too," he said at last, barely more than a whisper. "I need time, time to think, that's all."

"I understand," Marie said soothingly, squeezing him tight. "And I wish we had the time, but we can't stay here Sam, we can't. How long until Deacon and his people get into the palace? Days? Hours? We need to get out of here."

"I don't know that we can," Samuel said honestly. "I've searched, but there's no way out, not without being seen. If the rebels don't kill us, Alexander will. For now, we're safest here, behind the walls."

Marie pulled him down towards the bed and they lay there, arms wrapped around each other. "When this is all over," she said optimistically, "let's get away from here, start again somewhere new. We could go to Island City and you could show me where you grew up? Will you do that for me Sam, please?"

"I will," Samuel said sweetly. "I promise."

VIII

"When I pull the trigger," Deacon whispered, "you will fall to the floor as though dead. If you do not make it look convincing, I will make sure it looks better the second time. Are we clear?"

The terrified eyes of the Watch Officer turned to look up at him in surprise. Deacon had been reluctant to allow the captured members of the City Watch to live, but in the end Stan had managed to convince him.

The young man had been upset when Deacon killed the random prisoner, which soon turned to anger. Deacon was unaccustomed to allowing members of his gang speak to him in such a way, but Catrina had convinced him to listen. Stan was struggling to understand the killing of a bound prisoner, someone who had willingly surrendered, and when put on the spot, Deacon had found it difficult to explain.

He tried the reasons that came instantly to mind, that the Island City soldiers would have done it to them, that leaving an enemy alive allows them to kill you later, but they failed to ring true. He was changing, he realised, though for the better or worse he didn't yet know.

Catrina had suggested faking the executions, taking them out one at a time before dragging them back to a separate cell, and Deacon had reluctantly agreed. As long as the message was consistent, that the Regent had to surrender, there was no loss in not killing the Watchmen as long the Alexander believed that he had. If it looked to the surrounding citizens that they had died, Alexander would see the same, and so the trick was done. If they tried to run, to get away, Deacon had no qualms about killing them for real.

He settled the barrel of the pistol against the back of the Watchman's head, then checked his watch. At exactly one hour, he looked up towards the balcony, which was just as empty as the last seven times. The crowd were unable to see him move the pistol very slightly to the right, the barrel aiming just past the man's head. As he pulled the trigger, the bullet cut along the side of the man's scalp, a spray of blood in its wake as the man fell forwards into the dirt, the cheer from the crowd letting him know that the illusion had succeeded.

With one last look up towards the balcony, Deacon grasped the back of the man's shirt and dragged him along the grass towards the Merchant's Guild where Bran awaited with a canvas covered wagon. There, they placed the scared but very much alive Watchman beneath the sheet and returned to the celebrations in front of the palace.

IX

"Just a little further," General Boshtok said to himself as he tapped his foot impatiently. He had led his forces back through Phalathlan and towards Maleton, though the soldiers of Morton were never far behind. They were only a day or so's travel from the city, and the reinforcements that he had expected were nowhere to be seen.

After consulting his maps, he selected the best position to lay in wait for his pursuers and try to catch them off guard. He still had the greater numbers, and with the high ground and the element of surprise, he should have no difficulty in dispatching Morton's army once and for all.

The enemy was marching in columns, long lines of dark green and grey, outlined by the civilians in their regular clothes towards the rear. They would be easy pickings once the main force was dealt with, and then he would be able to return to Maleton and find out what had happened to his reinforcements.

"That's it," Boshtok muttered, smiling to himself. "Almost there."

"General?" Officer Hastings asked.

"In one more minute," Boshtok ordered, "call the attack."

X

Lord Conner and his forces had lost sight of the Island City army shortly before nightfall, and the scouts were yet to report back on what they had discovered. "You're confident that this is where he'll hit?" Lord Conner asked for the third time.

"I would," Marcus replied. "He's a day from Maleton, easy enough to retreat but not close enough to endanger the city. My guess is he's somewhere over here," he pointed to the map. "The high ground would give him the advantage and the tree density almost guarantees we won't see his troops until they're right on top of us."

"Exactly my point," Lord Conner remarked. "If we weren't following them, I would never have considered passing so closely to the forest."

"Remember," Matthew said. "He's fought against Morton's

forces before and he thinks he knows how they'll act. If we can make him believe that you'll march your troops in tight lines, just like Lord Jonathan did, he'll be overconfident and that's when we'll have him."

"I don't like it," Lord Conner muttered. "Not one bit."

"Please, if you've another idea?" Marcus suggested.

"I only wish I did," Lord Conner replied. "No, it's either follow your plan or return to Ashford, and I'd rather die in battle than at the end of a rope. I assume by the way you're talking that you have a suggestion of how best to counter his trap?"

"I do," Marcus said with a smile. "Though I'm not sure you're going to like it."

XI

Morton's forces marched in tight lines, regimented and structured. The deep blue waters shimmered far to their left, the lake beneath the waterfall for which Marston Falls was named. The remains of the town were still visible upon the higher ground, though fortunately it was no longer smoking.

The ground rose steadily as they marched, a dense canopy of forest ahead of them. Matthew had visited Marston Falls many times and knew of the dense woodland east of the town. As a boy his father had named it the Dark Forest and told him stories of the monsters that hid within its depths. He had realised as he got older that they were nothing more than a ploy to keep him from wandering off, but the sight of it still filled him with a sense of dread.

A horn sounded deep within the forest, followed by hundreds of men and women surging forwards and firing upon Morton's left flank. Boshtok had expected the soldiers to be taken off guard, to turn and try to return fire or run for cover as his troops cut them down from behind. Instead, as one the forward soldiers dropped to their bellies, exposing Marcus' secret.

As most of the soldiers lay flat on the ground, carefully selected troops swivelled the forty eight cannons that had been concealed within the tight lines and aimed them at the advancing forces. They fired in almost perfect unison, decimating Boshtok's attack and sending the survivors into panic.

Lord Conner's soldiers returned to their feet and split into smaller teams, some diving for cover and returning fire while others sprinted in different directions, finding narrow animal paths into the woodland. Matthew and Marcus each led their own small team, creeping through the dense underbrush as the canopy of leaves cut out most of the light. It was just as dark as Matthew remembered, even on that sunny summer morning.

The small teams spread far and wide, locating the large number of Boshtok's troops that were spread out within the forest. Boshtok's soldiers were in disarray, their orders to advance upon Morton's forces no longer valid since the cannons had driven the advancing forces back. Boshtok was trying to distribute his orders but it was proving more difficult that he expected.

"Hasting's" he yelled. "Where are those runners?"

"Here, General," Officer Hastings replied, escorting the young men and women towards the General.

"Send word to the commanders," Boshtok ordered. "Fall back and regroup, rally where the siege weapons are located. We'll flatten this forest if we need to."

Matthew and the men under his command used stealth to surprise clusters of Boshtok's soldiers, slitting throats or subduing them with brute force. When necessary they used the rifles and pistols that they carried, though never when grouped together where the enemy could return fire.

It was chaos, soldiers spread throughout the woodland trying to pick friend from foe, and Marcus realised that Boshtok's forces killed as many of their own troops as the enemy. They were spooked. It wasn't going according to plan at all, something that Boshtok was unfamiliar with.

The sound of cannons reminded Matthew that he was still in danger. He'd been following the retreating soldiers, picking off the stragglers where he could. He was knocked back as a cannonball splintered a thick oak tree before him, almost felling it. He took a moment to clear his head before climbing groggily to his feet. There were cries and screams all around him as further artillery rained down.

Marcus whistled and waved his arms, directing his soldiers to clear out and move towards the northern and southern borders of the forest. His message was passed along and soon the surviving Morton forces were positioned at either end of the forest as Boshtok continued to fire towards its centre. Trees were burning and smoke lingered beneath the canopy, making breathing hard and eyes water.

A horn sounded at the northern end, followed by a similar sound from the south. The Morton forces emerged, moving yet again in smaller groups towards the enemy siege weapons, trying to move on their flanks. The Island City Soldiers returned fire as the Morton forces concentrated on the operators of the siege weapons. Up close the catapults were useless, and the cannons difficult to reload under a barrage of bullets.

A bloody conflict ensued, Boshtok's troops caught between the two halves of the surviving Morton forces. Rifles were cast aside as ammunition ran out, knives and swords becoming the weapon of choice. Blood sprayed and limbs flew, scenes of barbarity and carnage visible in every direction. By mid-afternoon it seemed that Morton may have the upper hand, making Boshtok rethink his plans.

"Retreat!" he ordered. "Retreat to the town!" His soldiers obeyed, falling back towards the ruins. Marcus pressed on, striking where he could, but as more of Boshtok's surviving forces disappeared into the remains of Marston Falls, he called his soldiers to a halt, shouting for the order to be passed along. Following them into the town would be suicide, especially once night fell.

As afternoon became evening, the battlefield quietened. Boshtok's forces were entrenched within the remains of the town, while Morton's had fallen back and regrouped on the edge of the forest. The only sounds were the screams of the dying, men and women caught in a blood soaked no man's land that separated the two armies.

"Lord Conner?" Marcus asked, wincing as the wound in his left arm was bandaged.

"I don't know," Matthew replied. "No one saw him fall, but he's not with the survivors. If he's out there..."

"I know," Marcus said sombrely. "And Lord Julian?"

"He was killed in the attack on the siege weapons," Matthew informed him. "I saw it. He died bravely and saved a lot of people."

"So much death," Marcus sighed. "How many men and women?"

"Somewhere around two thousand still able to fight," Matthew replied.

Marcus shook his head in disbelief. "Boshtok didn't fare any better," he said. "If we try to rout them from the town, it'll be a massacre on both sides."

"He won't surrender," Matthew said. "From what you've told me about him, it's not in his nature."

"No," Marcus agreed. "He'll see this through to the bloody end, no matter the cost."

"Get some rest," Matthew suggested. "I need to see if Ben's radio still works, try and speak to Carl. If Boshtok won't come out, we'll soon have ten thousand Wastelanders to go in."

XII

Carl caught sight of Maleton's outlying buildings and the wispy plumes of smoke that rose from various quarters of the city. He feared that perhaps Boshtok had made it all the way back to the city and the battle was raging between the buildings.

"The smoke," Safran said, leaning over Carl's shoulder to get a better view.

"Do you think Matthew and his soldiers are fighting in the city?" Ben asked.

"Maybe," Carl replied. He was worried, more worried than he had been in a long time. Matthew was supposed to wait for reinforcements. If they had been forced into fighting in the streets and buildings of Maleton, something had gone terribly wrong.

They sat together in silence for almost ten minutes, watching the smoke, willing the tribes to move faster. Carl knew how fast the ATV could go but he didn't want to risk leaving the others behind, at least not with two of the leaders in the back. He needed to know what was happening though, he needed to know that the people he cared for were okay.

Carl nearly jumped out of his skin when the radio began to crackle. Matthew's voice was difficult to make out from the background static, prompting Ben to adjust the radio frequency. It wasn't perfect, but they were just about able to determine what each other was saying.

"Matthew?" Carl said. "Matthew, are you okay? We're having trouble hearing you?"

"The radio's been....battle....bullet holes," Matthew replied.

"We're close," Carl said, fear in his voice. "Where are you? Are you injured?"

"Not injured," Matthew said. "Boshtok....Marston....Can't get."

"Matthew," Carl continued. "We're on the outskirts of Maleton. Did you get that?"

"Maleton, yes," Matthew replied. "Survivors....East of Marston Falls."

"Marston Falls," Carl acknowledged, but the radio was only receiving static. Ben cycled through the frequencies but if Matthew was still speaking, the radio at his end was no longer transmitting.

"It'll be the radio," Ben said reassuringly. "I'm sure Matthew's fine, the radio just gave out."

"East of Marston Falls," Carl muttered. "That's what? Twelve, maybe fourteen hours?"

"Perhaps a little longer," Safran suggested.

Carl brought the ATV to a halt and turned to face the others in the back. Only Lewis and Lydia had managed to grow accustomed to the erratic movements of the ATV, the other tribal leaders choosing to walk alongside with their tribes.

"You look like you have a plan?" Lewis remarked.

"Not really," Carl replied. "Matthew's south of here, near Marston Falls from what he said, along with survivors. I hope that means the soldiers from Morton.

"Looking at the city though, we need to know what's going on in there. I know it's not ideal, but I think we need to split up."

"I agree," Ben said. "We need to know what's happening but we can't leave Matthew."

"What do you suggest?" Lydia asked suspiciously.

"We take a small force into the city," Carl said. "Small enough to fit in here, that way we can make it in and out more easily if we're in trouble. Lewis, do you have someone that you can delegate to, a number two or whatever?"

"Of course," Lewis replied.

"That's good," Carl continued. "I'd like you to pick five of your best and have them join us, you too." Carl was wary of letting Lewis out of his sight after what Victor had told them, just in case he chose to use the time to enact his scheme.

"And me?" Lydia prompted.

"You and the other tribal leaders," Carl replied. "We need you to head straight for Marston Falls, just follow the road beside the river. Victor, Reid, will you join them please? We'll need the space in the back, just in case."

"Of course," Victor smiled, reading Carl's thoughts. Lydia was very suspicious about what was happening, but by asking for two Carl's people to go with her, it would help to alleviate some of her fears.

"I'll go too," Murphy suggested. "Your friend might need my help."

"You'll need to walk through the night, as fast as you can," Carl told them. "I hope Ben's right, I hope it is the radio, but I've just got a bad feeling about it."

"It's fine, really," Reid acknowledged. "We won't stop for anything until we get there."

"And once we know what's happening, we'll come join you," Carl promised.

Lewis and Lydia stepped from the back of the ATV, followed closely by Reid, Murphy and Victor. Victor turned and gave Carl a brief nod, acknowledging his thought to *be careful.*

It only took Lewis a few minutes to locate the five tribal members that he had selected, and shortly after that Carl was driving much faster along the Great Road towards Maleton, while the rest of the Wastelanders cut south across the farmlands on their journey to Marston Falls.

XIII

The strange rumbling sound caught Alexander off guard. It was like nothing that he had ever heard before, even when he travelled on the strange Road Trains from Island City to Maleton. The sound was deeper, heavier somehow, making his chest vibrate as it got louder and louder.

He peered instead from the anonymity of the throne room, managing to lean forwards until he could just make out of the source of the sound. Moving slowly onto the grass of the meeting area was a large, eight wheeled vehicle like nothing he had ever imagined. The small slits at the front prevented him from seeing the occupants, but he didn't need to see them to work out who it must be.

"Benjamin Knight," Alexander muttered to himself, a sense of dread growing within him. "I should have killed you when I had the chance."

"My Liege," Samuel said breathlessly as he ran into the room. "The men on watch, they-"

"I've seen it," Alexander remarked curtly. "Tell the men to make ready, the rebels will be attacking soon."

CHAPTER 12

It was great to see Catrina and Stan again, even Deacon I guess in a strange kind of way. They told us about Nathan. This war, it's taken so many lives, I wonder if Alexander will ever be held accountable?

They explained how the palace is sealed up tighter than, well, the reference was crude but they can't see a way of getting in. Carl said he had an idea but he wants to check it out tomorrow when the sun comes up. If it doesn't work, we'll just have to wait them out, but it looks like they've got a lot more food inside the palace than the people have out here.

Maybe when the tribes get back from Marston Falls, the sight of them might make Alexander change his mind.

I

As Carl drove the ATV along the Great Road, he was surprised to see the streets filled with large groups of people. It was the opposite of what he had expected. The roads were full of revellers, a stark contrast to the thin plumes of smoke still rising from the various districts of the city.

Upon sight of the strange vehicle the groups scattered, most running towards the palace. Carl followed them slowly and was surprised when he first caught sight of the camps that occupied the large meeting area. As he drew the vehicle to a stop on the muddy grass the crowd hung back, waiting to see who, or what, would emerge.

"Do you think we should open the door?" Carl asked, looking at the guns suddenly aimed at the vehicle.

"Do we have much choice?" Ben said.

"I guess not," Carl replied with a nervous smile. "Stay behind me until we know that they're not going to kill us."

As the door of the ATV opened downwards on its hydraulics, the crowd collectively held their breaths. Carl stepped hesitantly from the vehicle, arms raised as he looked left and right for a familiar face. It wasn't until Safran stepped down that the mood of the crowd changed. Though many of them eyed her with suspicion, the scattered cries of 'Safran Lives' were enough to make the crowd relax a little. Ben placed a hand on her shoulder and pulled her towards him as she looked towards the ground, shaking a little at the attention.

A narrow channel opened, funnelling them towards the remains of a fire where Deacon stood waiting for them. Even from that distance they could see the smile upon his face.

"Deacon," Carl said as they met. "I never thought I'd say this, but it's good to see you."

"You too, Carl," Deacon agreed, extending his hand. Carl smiled as he shook it, letting everyone see that he was friendly.

"We came to help, but it looks like you don't need it," Carl continued, looking out towards the throngs of excited people.

"Much has changed since you left," Deacon told them. "The Regent has hidden himself inside the palace, but the rest of the city is free of his control."

"And his army?" Carl asked, but Catrina interrupted them before his question was answered.

"Carl!" she exclaimed, wrapping her arms around him. "I thought....we were so worried!"

"We're good," Carl said with a grin. "We're all good. Tell me about Matthew though and the armies of Island City?"

"I do not know about Matthew," Deacon said. "But the last we heard of the armies, they were fighting the forces of Oster and Morton."

"A lot's changed there too," Carl said. "The Regent's forces took Aldonis and all of Oster as far as we can tell. Matthew was leading the forces of Morton to try and defeat them. When we saw the smoke, we thought the fighting had spread as far as here."

"You've spoken to Matthew?" Catrina asked. "Where is he, is he with you?"

"We spoke to him an hour ago," Carl said, his voice full of concern. "He said he was near Marston Falls. The rest of our forces have gone to join him."

"He has a radio," Ben interrupted, though the word did nothing to enlighten them.

"And you have acquired an army?" Deacon surmised. "Come, Carl, and let us catch up on current events. Perhaps we will be able to help each other."

II

"Marcus, wake up," Matthew whispered, shaking the older man's shoulders. The surviving men and women had spread themselves out along the western border of the forest, taking it in turns to get some rest as the scouts kept a close eye for any movement in the ruins of the town.

"What is it?" Marcus asked, instantly alert.

"The scouts are reporting a lot of movement to the north," Matthew told him. "The road alongside the river."

Matthew helped Marcus to his feet and passed him the binoculars. In the dim light of dawn it was difficult to make out details but there was definitely movement along the road.

"There's a lot of them," Marcus acknowledged. "Friend or foe do you think?"

"Carl did promise us support," Matthew suggested. "I think we've had enough bad luck, isn't it about time we had some of the good stuff?"

Marcus chuckled in spite of the anxiety that he was feeling. "You're right," he agreed. "Let's go say hello."

The two men moved stealthily across the no man's land and towards the river. As they got closer to the advancing forces, it became clear that they weren't wearing uniforms and were instead dressed in the irregular attire that Matthew had seen on his many travels through the Wastelands. He pulled Marcus to a stop and they stood in the middle of the road, arms above their heads as they waited for the troops to arrive. As the Wastelanders drew near, those at the front raised their weapons in readiness.

"Matthew," Victor said, steeping from behind the line of guns that were pointed at the two men.

"Victor!" Matthew exclaimed, wrapping his arms around the older man. "You've no idea how good it is to see you again."

"You as well," Victor said with a smile. "After we heard you on the radio, we feared the worst."

"It doesn't matter now," Matthew said. "You're here, and you brought friends."

"Almost ten thousand of the finest warriors the Wastelands has to offer," Victor said with pride.

Matthew led them towards the remains of his army, the rising sun casting long shadows behind them. He was sure that the Island City forces hidden within the ruins of the town would have seen them, but from everything that Marcus had told him he didn't think even that would be enough to make Boshtok surrender.

"How many remain inside?" Toby, leader of the Wilkins tribe, asked.

"Somewhere in the region of two thousand," Marcus answered. "Give or take."

"If only they'd surrender," Matthew said sombrely.

"Boshtok doesn't know the meaning of the word," Marcus remarked. "Let's give them an hour. If they haven't sent forth messengers by then, we have to attack."

Matthew looked out over the no man's land at the remains of the town, wishing more than anything that the enemy would emerge under a white flag.

III

"You really think this is going to work?" Ben asked worriedly.

"No idea," Carl said with a smile.

Ben secured his seatbelt and checked it repeatedly as Carl drove the ATV back towards the Great Road. Once there, he turned the vehicle slowly around and pointed it towards the palace gate.

"Last chance to get out?" Carl said as he fastened his own seatbelt. He had an odd look on his face, a mixture of fear and excitement. Ben was mesmerised by the wild glint in Carl's eyes and shook his head. "Then hold on tight!"

Carl manoeuvred the ATV into gear and began to accelerate towards the gate. As they built up speed, Ben wondered if one of the compact discs had Ride of the Valkyries on it. It seemed appropriate to the situation.

The ATV was travelling at eighty-eight kilometres per hour as it struck the gate. Ben and Carl were thrown against their four point seat belts and if the gate had been a little stronger they would have both suffered more serious injuries. However, the force of the collision was sufficient to splinter the lower portion of the gate, allowing the vehicle to continue forwards for several metres. As the Palace Guards began to open fire, they both instinctively covered their heads and ducked.

It took Carl a few seconds to remember that the ATV was bullet proof, but as the shots hammered against the walls of the vehicle, he slowly sat up, massaging his bruised chest muscles. "Awesome," he said with a grin.

"Ow," Ben grumbled, unfastening the seatbelt so he could move. "That was, ow, I mean, I can't be dead because it hurts too much."

IV

Deacon watched as the ATV struck the gate and ploughed straight through it, the wood splintering and the steel bending as the vehicle continued into the palace courtyard. As soon as the opening appeared, he ordered the people forwards to commence the attack.

Bran, Catrina and Stan kept pace with him, the assault rifle's tight against their shoulders as they took cover around the ATV and picked out their targets. The people of Maleton were mostly unaccustomed to combat, and more than one ran headlong towards the Palace Guards where they were cut down mercilessly. Deacon barked orders in every direction but for the most part they were ignored.

Lewis and his tribal members fared better, holding back nearer the gate as they advanced slowly, working as an organised group. The courtyard was huge, much bigger than Deacon imagined, and the guards had done a good job of erecting barricades of wood and stone between the gate and the marble stairs that led to the palace entrance.

Deacon struck the butt of his rifle against the back door of the ATV, signalling for Carl to move. The front left wheel squealed as the vehicle advanced, the metal of its frame twisted by the impact with the gate. Carl drove it onwards, ignoring the sound, every metre closer to the stairs one more closer to victory.

The vehicle moved slowly, a mobile wall that allowed Deacon to take control of the closest barricades. As soon as they were liberated, Lewis ordered his men forwards to hold them, followed by small groups of civilians who clamoured behind their relative safety.

The battle was slow and bloody. Bullets struck the ATV and tore holes through the numerous barricades. Grenades bounced left and right, throwing clouds of dust and dirt as they exploded. Bran watched as two of Lewis' men were killed as they made a dash from one wall to another, their heads exploding like overripe fruit. Civilians and Palace Guards fought for territory, stepping over the bodies of friends as they desperately tried to make it to the next defensive position. Everywhere he looked he saw death, allies and enemies in equal number.

Catrina was desperate to move on, to charge up the stairs and into the palace. She could sense how close she was to Alexander, the cause of all her misery and torment. As the guards fell back, covering each other as they retreated into the palace itself, she tried to dash forwards. It was Deacon's hands that held her back and stopped her running into a barrage of bullets.

"Let me go!" she screamed, turning her rage against him as she fought to get free. Deacon gripped her tight, staring her down as she clawed at his faced and punched his chest.

"We will get him," Deacon promised. "You have my word."

V

Samuel awoke, startled as the first explosion echoed around the palace. "Sam, what's happening?" Marie exclaimed.

"It's started," Samuel replied, jumping to his feet and beginning to pull on his trousers.

"No, please don't go," Marie pleaded, reaching for him. Samuel turned to look at her, at the tears on her face as she begged him to stay. The idea of avoiding the fight, of hiding away seemed alien to him, but the look on her face made him think again.

"If you go out there," Marie continued, "they'll kill you. You promised, Sam, you promised me."

"Those are my people out there," Samuel argued.

"And I'm in here," Marie reminded him. "What can you do, one man against the entire city? It's over Sam, we both know it. Don't die for the Regent. Live, with me."

Samuel was torn, caught between honour and love. He was duty bound to join the fight, but Marie was right. If the rebels had entered the palace, it was over. His heart thudded as he searched for the right answer.

"Please," Marie said again, and he gave in. He sat on the edge of the bed and hugged her as she cried into his shoulder. "Thank you," she said, over and over. "Thank you."

VI

In the end, Marcus waited two hours before finally giving the order to attack. He had tried to send a messenger of his own, but as they neared the city an unknown gunman opened fire. It was only because the messenger had the sun to his back that the shooter missed his target.

The Wasteland tribes roared a ferocious battle cry as the order was given, running at full sprint across the no man's land, weapons ready. The remains of Morton's forces ran with them, screaming a cry of their own as they poured into the remains of the town.

Boshtok's forces had occupied the homes and businesses, firing from burnt out windows and behind collapsed walls. They were well secured and the going was slow, but Matthew's forces moved like a relentless tide, going from building to building and killing any who stood in their path.

Marcus lunged for Matthew, pulling him out of the way as an Island City soldier opened fire from a second floor window. "Thanks," Matthew said breathlessly as he ducked behind the remains of a garden wall.

"No problem," Marcus replied. "I'm far more scared of my daughter than any of this lot."

"Very sensible," Matthew said with a smile as further bullets struck the brick work before them.

Matthew readied his pistol and signalled for Marcus to move right. Marcus did, drawing the gunman's fire as Matthew raised the pistol above the wall and shot the gunman dead.

As they advanced on the centre of town the resistance grew stronger, pockets of armed men and women secured in the sturdier stone buildings. As Lydia led a group of her tribal members across the open ground towards the Town Hall, powerful automatic fire opened up from several of the windows, almost cutting Lydia in half.

"Fall back!" Marcus ordered. He directed his forces to surround the Town Hall, occupying the very building that they had so recently cleared of Boshtok's troops. As everyone took a moment's respite, Marcus considered his options.

"We've got to take that building," he said. "If Boshtok and his officers are alive, they'll be holed up in there."

"They'll cut most of us down before we get close," Alison pointed out. "I'm not going to send my people to be slaughtered."

"No need," Marcus promised. "We've got the numbers and we've got the fire power. Here's what we're going to do."

VII

Deacon stood beside the palace door, inspecting the explosives that Bran and Catrina had placed. The oak door may have been sturdy, but it was nothing like the gate and the explosives would reduce it to splinters.

"Last chance!" he shouted. "Send out the Regent and surrender your weapons. I promise you will be treated fairly."

He stepped back from the door and down the marble stairs, expecting no response. Alexander had made his intentions clear. There would be no surrender.

"Give them five minutes," Deacon said, squatting behind a wooden barricade. "If they do not emerge, light the fuse."

Bran nodded, checking his watch. It felt like the longest five minutes of his life.

VIII

"Lewis," Carl whispered, crouching down beside him. "I was sorry to hear about your men, they fought bravely."

"Thank you, Carl," Lewis replied. "I have hope that Ethan may yet live."

"Here's hoping," Carl agreed. "Here, that pistol's not going to do you much good inside the palace. Come back to the ATV with me, there's spare weapons from the laboratory in there."

Lewis smiled and followed Carl away from the stairs and towards the back of the ATV. Everyone was transfixed on Deacon as he inspected the explosives and made his final demands. The courtyard was a mess, small craters and rubble strewn everywhere. With the slowly settling dust clouds, it was difficult to see the palace door as they turned past the rear of the vehicle.

"Where are they?" Lewis asked as he stepped inside. "I don't remember seeing them during the journey."

"You really shouldn't have threatened Ben," Carl said quietly, wrapping his large left arm tightly around Lewis' throat. "He might be naive, but his intentions were true."

"No, wait," Lewis tried to say, but Carl was already choking the life out of him.

"Victor told us what you were planning," Carl continued. "You should have just played nice."

Lewis struggled, trying to break free. His arms reached behind him, scratching at Carl's face, searching for his eyes. Carl increased the pressure, twisting his arm as he did so, and with one last push, he heard the neck snap as Lewis went limp.

Carl dragged the body out of the vehicle and around the side, out of sight of anyone in the courtyard. He waited, pistol settled over Lewis' heart, and as the door to the palace exploded Carl pulled the trigger. The sound of the gunshot was lost amongst the much louder explosion, and in the absence of witnesses Lewis' death was nothing but a tragic consequence of the battle.

One more name to add to the others. One more brave soldier who gave his life for the greater good.

IX

"That's five minutes," Bran said, double checking his watch. He looked to Deacon who only nodded in response.

All eyes seemed on them as Bran struck the match and put it to the fuse, the familiar hiss running quickly along the ground and up the marble stairs. Deacon placed his fingers in his ears as he waited for the bang, counting to himself. Bran and he had set a great many explosives in their time together, and Bran was the best at calculating burn times on the fuses.

At almost exactly ten seconds the flame met the bomb, tearing the door from its hinges and reducing it to splinters. The blast was angled towards the long corridor and more than one guard was killed as they were pelted with shards and shrapnel.

Deacon was already on his feet, Bran and Catrina at his heels as he sprinted to the left of the doorway. Stan met Carl as they ran around to the right, staying out of the line of fire from the open door.

"Are you ready?" Deacon asked, a manic glint in his eyes.

"Let's do this," Carl said, smiling back at him. Together they each removed a grenade from their belts and tossed them into the corridor. The combined explosion blew dust and blood back into the courtyard and shook the ground at their feet.

They stepped through the opening, crouched low, looking for targets in the gloom. Deacon caught movement ahead and opened fire, a pained cry his reward. The unseen guards and Watchmen fired blindly towards them, making them duck into one of the many alcoves.

"Keep pushing forwards," Carl shouted, firing his assault rifle back along the corridor.

They moved as a unit, pushing forwards step by step. The guards had occupied the numerous staterooms and offices, but with the support of the citizens of Maleton, they were more than a match. One by one the rooms were cleared, the dead left where they lay as the people took back what was rightfully theirs.

They were a little over half way along when Catrina cried out. "I see him!" she said, beginning to run and leaving the others behind. Carl reached for her, shouted for her to stop, but he was already too late. Catrina was running for the throne room and there was nothing he could do to stop her.

X

Catrina saw him, saw Alexander, pushing the throne room door closed. "I see him!" she cried, running before she realised, her only thought to get to him before he could escape.

A bullet tore through her left thigh, making her stumble, but she refused to stop. Her leg burned as blue light danced around the injury, repairing the damage as another bullet struck her right shoulder. Her arm went numb and then screamed in pain as the light seemed to cover her entire body, wavering in her vision.

She barely registered the door as she barged through it shoulder first, finally losing her footing. As she tried to climb to her feet, a foot kicked her squarely in the stomach, forcing her back to the floor.

"You stupid, stupid, skeet," Alexander screamed down at her, emphasising each word with harder and harder kicks to her midsection. "You think this is over? You think you've won?"

As the blue light enveloped her, Alexander drove the heel of his boot against the side of her head, making her vision fuzzy and the throne room move in and out of focus. Her brain wanted desperately to power down, to turn itself off and allow her body to heal. Catrina resisted with every fibre of her being, willing herself to stay awake, to keep going, just a little longer.

That's it Mommy, keep going.

Catrina managed to get one knee to the floor before Alexander kicked her again, another blow to the side of her head. The throne room seemed to be spinning, moving in circles around her.

It's not bedtime Mommy, you can't go to sleep now!

Catrina kicked out as Alexander came near, the heel of her left foot connecting with his knee. Alexander screamed, a mixture of agony and rage as he stumbled. She tried to kick him again, but this time Alexander saw the movement. He moved to the side and stamped down hard on her outstretched leg, smiling as he heard the bone snap.

"Come here," Alexander bellowed, dragging Catrina towards him by her hair. She tried to resist but her strength was fading, her vision darkening as every inch of her body screamed in pain. "You're my ticket out of this mess."

XI

"Hold until I give the order," Marcus said, checking that his pistol was loaded and ready to fire.

"Be careful," Alison replied.

Marcus smiled in response. "Me?" he said. "I'm going to be a grandfather. There's no better reason I can think of."

"Let's get to it then Grandpa," Matthew remarked, though the bravado was nothing but a smokescreen to hide their fear.

Marcus led his forces between the two buildings, the thick stone walls of the Town Hall one hundred metres ahead of them. There was no cover, no defence, but if everything went according to plan they wouldn't need it. He had ordered the tribes to take up positions in the buildings opposite, weapons aimed at the windows. Once he gave the order, they'd fire on every opening that they could see, a continuous barrage to keep the Island City forces in hiding or kill any who dared show their face.

"Go! Marcus yelled, beginning his sprint towards the heavy

wooden doors of the Town Hall. Matthew was to his right and over two hundred of Morton's finest were at their heels, running for all they were worth.

The sound of gunfire behind them was deafening, but it did what it was supposed to. An occasional head popped up above the window sills, but they didn't look out for long. Though legs were aching and lungs were burning, they kept up their pace, kicking down the door without stopping and barraging through.

Once inside they fanned out, finding cover as further gunfire erupted from the various rooms. Marcus ordered the larger force to secure the ground floor, while he and Matthew led the smaller group upstairs.

The wide staircase led to a dimly lit corridor with door on each side. Marcus kicked the first door open, and when no gunfire greeted him, he poked his head inside carefully, weapon ready. A large machine gun had been erected at the window, but two of the operators were dead beside it, blood oozing slowly from their heads. A third man, no more than a boy really, sat weeping beside them, his head in his hands.

"Secure him," Marcus instructed, "but don't hurt him unless you have to." Reid nodded curtly and entered the room.

The remaining rooms were similarly occupied, the Island City soldiers either dead or surrendering to the Marcus and his troops. It didn't take them long to clear, and soon the only door left was the large double door at the end of the corridor.

The door opened without resistance, the four soldiers stood against the opposite wall, hands on their heads. Before them stood a short, stocky man in full dress uniform, almost black in colour with a line of medals pinned to his chest. He stood to attention, hands behind his back.

"I am General Boshtok," he said. "Commander of the Regent's armies and protector of Island City. My forces are prepared to surrender, but I will only submit to your commanding officer."

"I'm Lord Marcus, of Aldonis," Marcus announced. "I lead these forces."

"Then I submit," Boshtok said, bowing his head slightly.

Marcus advanced, ready to take the General into custody. It was Matthew who saw the flash of the blade as Boshtok drew it from behind his back. "No!" Matthew screamed, but it was already too late. General Boshtok had driven the knife hilt deep into Marcus' stomach.

Matthew dashed forwards, knocking the General backwards. Boshtok still had the knife and came back at Matthew, slashing wildly. Matthew gripped Boshtok's wrist and twisted until he dropped the blade, snapping the bone in the process. Boshtok screamed as Matthew swept his legs from under him and drove him to the floor.

"Kill me!" Boshtok demanded, trying to get up as Matthew knelt heavily against his chest. "I slaughtered your brethren, I killed them all. Kill me!"

Matthew looked down at him, the pitiful face and tear filled eyes. "No," he said, shaking his head slowly.

"Kill me," Boshtok pleaded. "Kill me."

"No," Matthew said again. "There's been enough death, too much. You'll stand trial for your crimes, you'll answer for them. You don't get away with what you've done that easily."

The other soldiers bound Boshtok's hands as Matthew crawled over to where Marcus lay. Marcus was awake but in pain, his hand pressed tightly against the wound that continued to ooze between his fingers.

"You'll be okay," Matthew reassured him, taking over the application of pressure.

"You bet I will," Marcus said with a pained sneer. "I'm going to be a grandfather."

XII

Alexander wrapped his arm tightly around Catrina's throat, shielding his body with hers. As the door to the throne room burst open he pressed the barrel of the pistol he was holding tightly against her head.

"That's close enough," Alexander barked.

"Let her go!" Carl demanded, aiming the barrel of his assault rifle straight at them.

"Lower your weapons and we'll talk," Alexander said with a mocking smile.

"It is over, Regent," Deacon replied.

"It's not over!" Alexander screamed. "I say when it's over!"

Catrina squirmed in his grip, trying to break free. Alexander squeezed tighter and pressed the barrel of his pistol harder until she stopped.

"I know about her healing," Alexander continued. Stan was trying to ease around to the side, but a glare from Alexander made him stop.

Catrina closed her eyes, focussing all of her energy on staying conscious. She couldn't let Alexander escape, let him get free. He had to die. He had to pay for what he had done, no matter what.

You're so brave Mommy.

Her left hand found the grenade attached to her belt and she barely had to move to pull the pin. It slid from her fingers and dropped to the floor, barely audible against the sound of Alexander's voice.

"But do you really think she'll survive a bullet through the head?" Alexander asked.

She opened her eyes, her vision clouded by tears. For the briefest of seconds she imagined that she could see them standing before her. Edward, Daniel, Adam. They were smiling.

We love you.

"I'm going to walk out of here," Alexander insisted, "and she's-"

The explosion was deafening within the confines of the throne room. Stan was knocked off his feet and hit the wall hard, making him see stars. Carl was screaming, calling Catrina's name. Deacon was trying to move forwards as Bran held him back, the crack in the throne room widening as a portion of the outside wall dropped down into the gardens below.

"Catrina!" Carl called again, tossing his rifle aside as he scurried forwards into the dust and debris. The floor was slick and slippery and, as the dust began to settle, they all caught sight of what she had done.

Neither Catrina or Alexander were recognisable. Chunks of flesh and bone littered the space, but as to who they belonged to it was impossible to tell.

Carl dropped to his knees and wept.

XIII

Almost an hour had passed since the explosion and the remaining Palace Guards and Watchmen had surrendered. Carl was in a daze as he sat in the rear of the ATV, fearing that if he had to deal with the prisoners he would take out his anger on them. Gavin held Stan as Safran held Ben, their tears finally slowing but the pain they all felt growing as time passed.

"She finally got her revenge," Deacon said as he entered the rear of the ATV.

"It didn't have to end this way," Carl replied, his eyes still puffy and his cheeks red, the scar almost purple.

"No," Deacon agreed. "It did not, but she made her choice. It is our duty to honour that choice, to honour her."

Carl looked at Deacon, the man who had until recently been the bitterest of enemy, and nodded once. In a way, Deacon was right. Catrina had wanted nothing more than to kill the Regent, and with her final act she had done just that.

"Deacon?" Bran said, showing his head through the back of the vehicle. "You're needed."

Deacon offered Carl a questioning glance. "Go," Carl said. "I'll be okay."

Deacon followed Bran back towards the palace. The courtyard was in ruins, the marble stairs cracked and pitted with bullet holes, the grounds scorched and potted with craters. "What is it?" Deacon asked once they were out of earshot of the others.

"The Watch Commander," Bran replied.

Bran led Deacon to one of the small staterooms where Samuel Larson was bound to a chair, his left eye half closed as a purple bruise developed. Marie was screaming at the two guards to let them go, that she had a deal.

"You," she said as Deacon entered. "We had an agreement. We did what you asked. Now you have to let us go."

"Yes," Deacon said matter-of-factly. "You are right." The two gang members looked surprised, but knew better than to object.

"Bran," Deacon continued. "Please untie him and escort them both to the city limits. They are not to be harmed."

"Of course," Bran replied before beginning to unravel the knots that held Samuel to the chair.

"But know this," Deacon said, looking directly at Marie. "If you value your lives, do not return to this city under any circumstances. Are we in agreement?"

"Yes, yes," Marie said as she helped Samuel to his feet. "You'll never see us again."

Deacon met Larson's gaze, a momentary look of understanding, perhaps even respect, passing between them. Deacon nodded and stepped aside, allowing Bran to lead them through the door and out of Maleton forever.

XIV

The Wasteland tribes arrived late that night, making camp to the south of the city. Matthew led Victor and Reid through the city district, where the mood was surprisingly jubilant. Murphy had stayed behind to keep a close on Marcus, whose wound fortunately wasn't too severe.

"What's happened?" Matthew asked of a particularly drunk reveller.

"The Regent's dead," he slurred in response. "We're free!"

Matthew's heart lifted and he hugged the man tightly before setting off at a sprint towards the Industrial District. He checked his warehouse first, and then the Road Train yards, but they looked as though they hadn't been occupied in months. His next thought was the palace and he led the way excitedly.

"It's over," he said to Victor as they walked. "The Regent, Boshtok, it's all over. We did it!"

Victor laughed as they picked up the pace, crossing the Forworn Bridge and past the Council Chambers. The celebrations were even louder than in the other regions of the city and it took Matthew almost twenty minutes to find someone he recognised.

"Bran," he said, shouting to be heard above the noise of the crowd. "It's me, Matthew. Where's Carl and Ben? Where's Catrina?"

"Matthew," Bran said, a sympathetic smile on his face. "Last I saw, they were in the palace courtyard."

"What is it?" Matthew asked, a sense of dread spreading from the pit of his stomach. "What's wrong?"

"Go, speak to them," Bran replied, placing a comforting hand on Matthew's shoulder. "I'm sorry."

Matthew wanted to say more, demand to know what was going on, but Bran wasn't talking. Instead he set off at a sprint, pushing his way through the crowds of people as he fought his way to the palace gates and into the remains of the courtyard. It wasn't hard to find his friends. They were sat around the ATV, their faces in stark contrast to the happy revellers outside.

"Oh, Matthew," Safran said upon seeing him, rushing forwards to hug him tightly. "I'm so sorry."

"What is it?" Matthew asked, his sense of dread growing stronger. "What happened?"

"It's Catrina," Carl said, looking up from his spot beside the fire. "She didn't make it."

Matthew didn't understand at first, didn't want to understand. It was over. They'd done it. They'd freed the city and ended the war. "What do you mean?" he asked. "Where is she?"

"She died," Ben said sombrely. "She died killing the Regent."

"No. Where is she?" Matthew demanded, his voice getting louder.

"I'm sorry, boss," Carl said, his own tears flowing again. "There was nothing we could do."

Matthew dropped to his knees, his hands in front of his face as he began to sob.

XV

Victor suggested to Reid that they leave Matthew to his friends. They returned to the party outside the palace but neither of them felt much like celebrating.

"Anwin?" a surprised voice said from behind them. "It cannot be you."

Victor turned around in surprise. "Darwin?" he said.

"Who is he?" Reid asked, confused.

"He is my brother," Victor replied.

"Anwin," Deacon said again. "Why are you here?"

"I am sorry, Darwin," Victor replied. "I do not believe I have ever told you that, but I am truly sorry for what happened."

Both men stared at each other, the tension growing between them. Reid flinched as Deacon suddenly ran forwards, wrapping his arms around Victor.

"My brother," Deacon said. "I have missed you."

XVI

Ben stood, taking it all in. Alexander was dead. The war was over. Outside the palace walls the people were rejoicing, singing songs and drinking heavily as they celebrated their freedom.

As Ben gazed through the remains of the palace gate, he saw Deacon and Victor hugging. Reid looked on, a confused smile upon his face.

Matthew hadn't stopped crying. Carl comforted him as best he could, but there was nothing that anyone could say or do that would make it better.

"This is it," Safran said as she joined him. "This is what we've been waiting for."

"Is it?" Ben asked, eyeing the destruction that surrounded him. "If this is winning, I'd hate to see what losing looks like."

Safran kissed him gently on the cheek as they stared out together over the remains of the courtyard.

CHAPTER 13

We won, that's what I keep telling myself. We won and it's over. So why don't I feel good about it?

Carl's slowly coming to terms with Catrina's death, but Matthew's a different story, blaming himself for what happened. I'm glad I didn't have to see it. So much death, so many people gone forever.

Edward. Peter. Conrad. Simon. Donald. Tom. Joe. Mike. Daniel. Nathan. Lydia. Lewis. Catrina.

I'm sure there's more, people I've forgotten, lives lost in payment for this victory. I hope it's worth it.

We won. That's what I have to keep telling myself.

I

Three days after the Battle of Maleton, as the people were calling it, Ben sat waiting for Safran to finish one of her many meetings. Though most of the people still viewed her with scorn and mistrust, there was no one else to take her place and the responsibility of rule had been thrust upon her.

"Ben!" Safran said with a smile as she emerged from one of the few surviving staterooms. The throne room was off limits, the crack having grown bigger as more of the outside wall had crumbled. Stone masons were desperately trying to repair what they could, but much of the palace was out of bounds.

"How did it go?" Ben asked.

"Everyone they suggest for the Elder Council has an agenda of their own," Safran replied. "I don't know how my father did it."

"You'll get the hang of it," Ben said with a smile.

"I hope not," Safran said cryptically.

Ben looked at her, a confused look upon his face. "Why?" he asked.

Safran laughed as she hugged him, squeezing him tight. "I'm not staying," she said whimsically. "This place, it's not my home anymore. The people here don't want me. I'll never be Baron in their eyes, too many lies have been told about me. My mother, Justin, they'll do a much better job of ruling Draxis than I ever could."

"I don't understand?" Ben said, dumbfounded.

"I'm coming with you, silly," Safran told him, leaning in to kiss him as realisation struck.

II

Matthew traced his fingers along the lettering that had been carved into the stone. There were still so many more names to be added, but he had insisted on Catrina's being the first. He could never forgive himself for what had happened, for not being there in her final moments, but at least no one would ever forget.

A little over a week had passed since the battle, and though most of the stone masons were busy attending to the palace, Matthew had handed over a sizeable sum of Deniras to have the monument in place before he left. It stood in the middle of the meeting area, a pale stone monolith almost twice as tall as Matthew.

"Boss?" Carl said quietly behind him.

"She deserves so much more than this," Matthew said.

"We'll remember," Carl said, placing a hand on Matthew's shoulder. Matthew flinched at first but slowly relaxed, turning to face his oldest friend.

"We will," he said. "Always."

"Reid and Marcus are waiting for you," Carl continued. "I can come with you too, if you'd like?"

"No, Carl," Matthew said with a forced smile. "Victor's already left with the Wasteland tribes and I'm trusting you to get Ben and Safran back to the laboratory safely."

"With my life," Carl replied, adding his own forced smile. "We'll see you soon though, won't we?"

"You will," Matthew promised. "I'll return with Arian as soon as I can."

At the thought of his wife and his unborn child, Matthew smiled for real, a warm sensation in his heart where only pain and emptiness had been. He looked Carl in the eye, ignoring the tears that began to flow. "You're a good friend," he said. "The best."

"You too, boss," Carl replied, pulling Matthew in for a hug. "You too."

III

Marie and Samuel made camp just two hundred metres from the Great Road. They were approximately half way to Island City, and the going had been tough. They had no food, and though there was plentiful water, they were exhausted and hungry all of the time.

"I managed to scavenge this from an old camp," Samuel said, handing Marie a piece of dried meat. It was well past its best, but it was more than she'd eaten in days.

"Thank you," Marie said, devouring it quickly. "We can't

keep on like this."

"We can and we will," Samuel said sternly. "Look at what we survived. This is nothing in comparison."

"What will you do?" Marie asked. "When we get there?"

"I don't know what state Island City's in," Samuel replied. "I might be able to return to the palace. I don't know."

"Whatever state the city's in," Marie said, "they'll need someone to take charge, a strong leader."

"I don't think Alexander really cared what happened to the people he left behind," Samuel remarked.

"But you do," Marie continued. "You care about me, the people under your command. You're a good man, Sam, with a good heart."

"What are you saying?" Samuel asked.

"Why return to the palace as a soldier?" Marie said. "You know what Alexander saw in you, what he wanted for you. You don't have to follow anymore, you should lead. Alexander saw that and I do too."

"You think I could be Regent?" Samuel said, laughing at the absurdity.

"No," Marie replied sternly. "I believe you should be Regent and I'm going to make sure it happens."

IV

After two months, the city of Maleton was slowly getting back to normal. Autumn had been gentle and a good harvest had belied the fears over food shortages. Karan was ruling in Justin's name and the people were returning to their normal lives.

"The word on the street," Bran said, "is that Brosnan and his gang were behind the theft."

"He did not clear it with me," Deacon remarked. They were sat in the Skeever's Claw in one of the upstairs rooms, enjoying one of Jimmy's finest beef stews.

"No, and now they're nowhere to be found," Bran continued.

"These people," Deacon said to himself. "How soon they forget. Put the word out that I would like to speak to Brosnan in person, and any who aid me will earn my gratitude."

"Will do," Bran said. "And when you find him?"

"I am going to cut off his thumbs," Deacon replied with a chuckle. "I run the gangs in this city, and any who forget will be reminded most convincingly." Bran laughed with him, happy to see the old Deacon back in charge.

"Stan and Gavin are having some success with the new boys," Bran said. "And I put Sanjay to work in the counting room. I hope you don't mind."

"I imagine he will be running it this time next year," Deacon remarked. "How is Stan, I have not seen him recently?"

"He's doing better," Bran told him. "He visits the monument every week, but he's doing okay. I think the work helps, gives him something to focus on."

"He is an asset to our business," Deacon said. "If he is in need of anything, let me know."

"I heard him and Gavin talking about finding somewhere to live," Bran suggested. "They're still bunking down in the brewery, but it's getting a little crowded."

"Then make it happen," Deacon said, smiling. "Somewhere nice, with a view of the river."

V

Matthew walked slowly down the slip road towards Garstang, or New Sanctuary as it was now called. The journey from Hopewell had been long, especially as Arian's stomach grew. She was exhausted most days by lunch, and they took several breaks to make it through the day. Marcus and Juliet had been supportive, and though Matthew was loathe to admit it, at times the trip had been fun.

"So this is finally it?" Marcus asked, looking across the town towards the mountain beyond.

"Yes," Matthew replied. "Ben's grand idea, a city powered by electricity." Arian and Juliet joined them, taking it in.

The town had changed since Matthew had last seen it. Though the buildings on the outskirts were still mostly rubble, those nearer the centre had begun to be patched up, new walls built to replace the old. The streets had been cleared of debris and there was an overall sense of peace wherever they looked.

"This way," Matthew said, leading them down the slip road

and towards the main street into town.

The walk was leisurely without the fear of attack at every turn. The people they passed were friendly, waving hello as they went about their business. There were no looks of suspicion, no animosity. As far as they could see, the town seemed to be working.

"I'm glad they tore that down," Arian said as they passed the remains of the town hall.

"It probably fell down," Matthew suggested.

"Either way," Arian continued, "I'm glad I don't have to look at it. That man, Bosen. It still makes my skin crawl to think about it."

Matthew was about to comment when Carl came running up to them, waving his arms. "Matthew!" he shouted. "Arian! You're finally here!"

"Carl," Matthew said, embracing his friend. "Blame the lady here. Apparently being pregnant makes you lazy."

"Hey," Arian exclaimed, punching Matthew hard in the arm.

"It doesn't make her any weaker though," Matthew grumbled, rubbing his shoulder.

"You look wonderful," Carl said to Arian. "And Marcus, Juliet. So glad you decided to come."

"We visited Aldonis on the way here," Marcus began, struggling to find the words.

"It's just not our home anymore," Juliet finished for him, squeezing her husband's hand sympathetically.

Carl removed the radio from his belt and pressed the button. "Ben, Ben," he said. "You there?"

"Hey, Carl," Ben replied. "What's up?"

"We've got guests," Carl said cryptically. "Can you bring the car?"

"Is it Matthew?" Ben asked excitedly. "I'll be right there!"

While they waited, Carl pointed out some of the changes that they'd made to the town. "Ben was able to connect the electricity from the laboratory to the town," he began, pointing out the electricity substation at the base of the mountain. "A few of the houses have it up and running already."

"He really made it work?" Matthew asked, surprised.

"Turns out all that stuff he used to talk about isn't nonsense,"

Carl remarked. Matthew shook his head, chuckling to himself.

They strolled towards the mountain road, meeting Ben along the way. He drew the car to a halt and almost fell in his urgency to get out of the door. Safran stepped from the passenger side with her usual grace, the smile on her face beaming.

"Matthew, Arian, you made it," she squealed, running up to them. She looked to have grown up a lot Matthew noticed, no longer the impetuous, headstrong girl that he had taken to Island City only a year before.

"Safran," Arian said, smiling. "You look beautiful."

"Thank you," Safran replied. "And you, you're positively glowing. How long now?"

"Another four months," Arian complained. "I can't imagine getting any bigger."

"I can't wait to meet them," Safran continued.

"Me either," Matthew remarked. "He's going to be great."

"Or she," Arian corrected.

"Or she," Matthew agreed.

"I'm so glad you're finally here," Ben said, shaking Matthews hand enthusiastically. "I don't know if anyone's said this to you yet, so I will.

"Welcome to New Sanctuary."

VI

As the first of the winter's snow began to fall, twenty-two men and women gathered on the open ground before the laboratory. They carried with them two makeshift goals and a ball. After some discussion, they split into two teams with a goalkeeper at each end.

Ben had explained the rules of football to them several times, but after a lot of confusion he resigned himself to just showing them. They were all excited to get out and play, despite the sudden change in the weather.

With a blow of the whistle, Ben kicked the ball to Matthew who kicked it towards the opposing goal. It was all going too well Ben realised, and was unsurprised when Carl came running over to him, waving his arms.

"Hey Ben," Carl shouted, ignoring the ball as it landed at his feet. "Can you explain this off-side rule to me again, one last time?"

EPILOGUE

"Captain Reid," the sailor shouted, banging loudly against the captain's door. "Come quickly."

"What is it?" Captain Reid barked. "It's the middle of the night." The Aero was docked at Ashford and most of the crew were on some much needed shore leave.

"It's the, the thing," the sailor replied. "In the hold. It's started making some strange noises."

Reid pulled on his trousers and followed the sailor into the belly of the ship. "What's going on?" he asked.

"It started about twenty minutes ago," the radio operator said. "A series of tones and beeps and then it stops for a few minutes before starting again."

Reid listened. It was certainly strange, almost musical but without any noticeable beat or rhythm. "Has it ever done anything like this before?" he asked

"No," the radio operator said. "It crackles or it talks, that's all."

"Make a note of it as best you can," Captain Reid said. "And you," turning to the sailor. "Recall the crew and make ready to sail for the Wastelands."

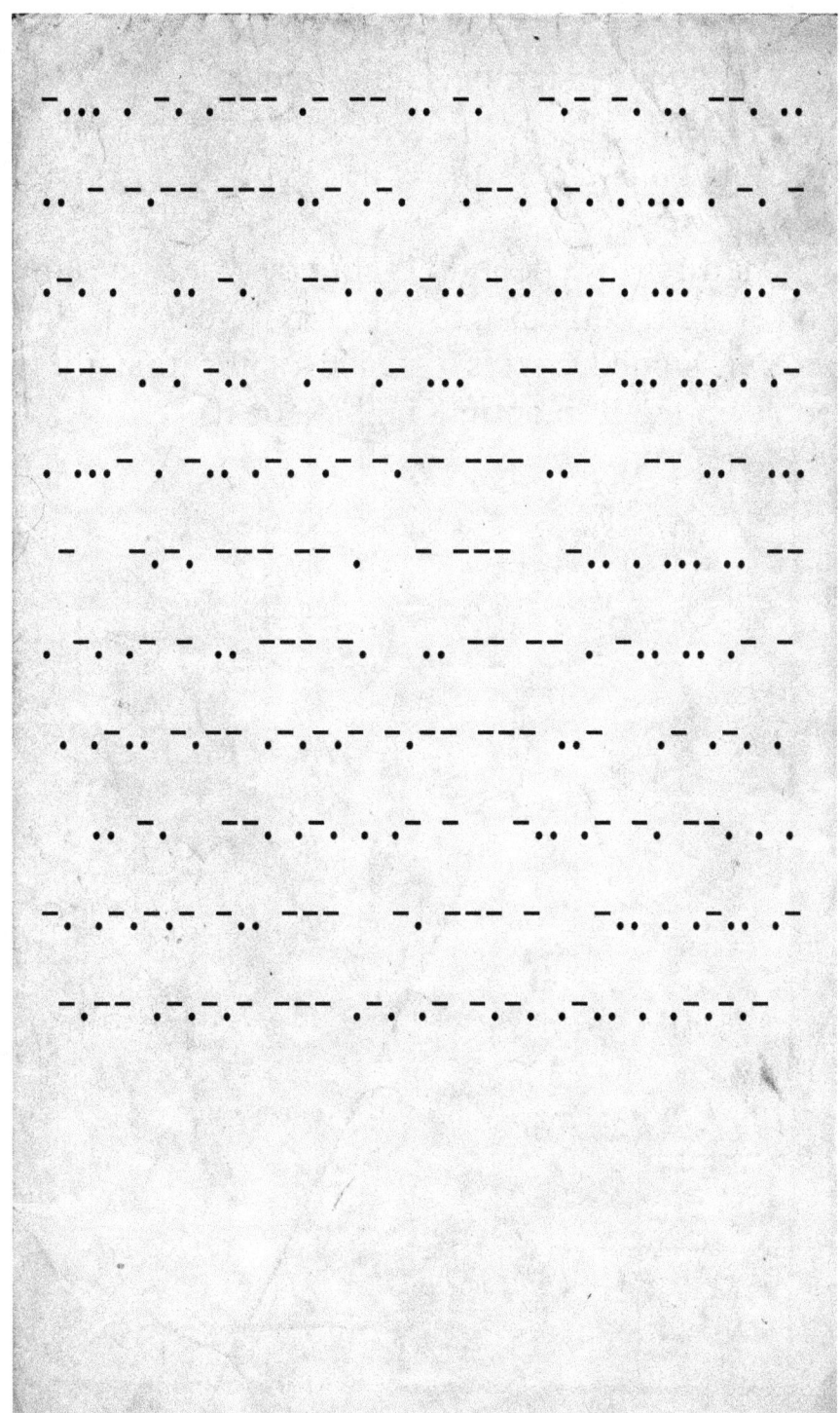

What do the strange sounds mean?

Can you decipher the code?

The first five people to correctly decipher the code (and contact me via my website) will receive signed copies of each of the first three books in the Benjamin Knight series!

THE CHRONICLE OF BENJAMIN KNIGHT

BOOK 4

ORACLE

COMING SOON

WHATEVER YOU THINK MAY HAVE HAPPENED IN GELDERS FORD, IT WAS WORSE.

VISIT

WWW.JACKSON-LAWRENCE.COM

FOR MORE DETAILS